THE RED DRIFTER OF THE SEA

PIRATES OF THE ISLES

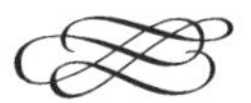

CELESTE BARCLAY

HAWK & DOVE STRATEGIES

Published by Celeste Barclay and Hawk & Dove Strategies

❀ Created with Vellum

To all who sail away on this adventure with me, I wish you fair winds and following seas.

Happy reading, y'all,
Celeste

SUBSCRIBE TO CELESTE'S NEWSLETTER

Subscribe to Celeste's bimonthly newsletter to receive exclusive insider perks.

Have you read *The Highland Ladies Guide*? This FREE first in series is available to all new subscribers to Celeste's monthly newsletter. Subscribe on her website.
Subscribe Now

PIRATES OF THE ISLES

The Blond Devil of the Sea **BOOK 1**

The Dark Heart of the Sea **BOOK 2**

The Red Drifter of the Sea **BOOK3**

The Scarlet Blade of the Sea **BOOK 4**

CHAPTER 1

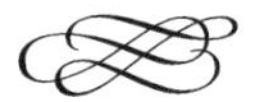

Moira MacDonnell peered around the narrow staircase leading from the family chambers into the Great Hall. Her gritted teeth felt as if they would surely crack, and she suspected deep grooves were forming around her lips from pursing them in disgust so often. She observed her brother Dónal, the MacDonnell chieftain, dribbling grease onto his sleeve before taking a healthy draught of Scottish whisky. Her gaze shifted to her sister Lizzie.

"Shameless trollop," Moira muttered as Lizzie slid her hand between her body and Aidan O'Flaherty's to cup his groin. In turn, Aidan pinched Lizzie's nipple, eliciting a deep moan from the willowy blonde. Moira swept her gaze across the diners in the Great Hall, but as usual, no one paid attention to the antics of those seated on the dais. Moira's nephew Sean darted across the hall, followed by his friends and his ever-loyal Irish wolfhound. She snapped her gaze back to Lizzie and Aidan, Sean's parents, but they were oblivious to their son as he ran wild. Aidan was in port for a few days and spent more time dropping anchor in Lizzie than being a father to Sean. Lizzie was little better as a parent, having ignored Sean for most of his life, except for when Ruairí MacNeil had visited.

A smug smile pulled at Moira's lips as she recalled the last time the Dark Heart appeared at Dunluce. Despite being a year ago, the memory of his visit burned bright in Moira's mind. Ruairí arrived with his wife Senga on his arm, and Lizzie made the dreadful mistake of trying to—as before—pass Sean off as Ruairí's son. She compounded her error by trying to seduce him in front of Senga. The pirate queen nearly gutted Lizzie before the entire clan, yet not one person flinched. Manipulative as the serpent in the Garden of Eden, Lizzie had sworn since before Sean was born that Ruairí was the boy's father. Everyone who could count to nine knew it wasn't possible, since Ruairí had been nowhere near Ireland, let alone Dunluce, when Lizzie conceived Sean.

She must think we're a right daft lot. As though none of us knew the moment the lad was born that he's Aidan's. The lad has his father's black hair, not Ruairí's blond.

It was Senga who forced Lizzie to finally admit that Aidan was the then-five-year-old Sean's father. Since then, neither Lizzie nor Aidan—who had never been discreet—made any attempt to hide their liaison. But neither did they intend to wed. With no heirs of his own, it forced Dónal to acknowledge Sean as the next MacDonnell chieftain, despite the boy's bastardry.

I will bear no man a bastard. I'd have to be coupling to do that, and since that isn't in my future, I suppose I have nothing to worry about. Selfish pile of shite. Pay a bluidy decent dowry if you want me off your hands, Dónal. But then who would run this pile of cracked bricks and rotting mortar? Sure as bluidy hell won't be Lizzie.

"Moira!" Dónal bellowed before belching. "Where the devil are you, you worthless wench?" Dónal may have muttered the last words, but Moira knew plenty of people heard. She doubted any of them cared. They were far too used to Dónal's domineering attitude toward her. Dónal didn't care what Lizzie did, as long as the men she bedded brought more trade to clan MacDonnell. That had been the entire point of trying to lay a trap for Ruairí.

Moira slipped from behind the staircase and entered the Great Hall. She wasn't certain if Dónal's grimace was from indigestion or disgust at seeing her. She assumed it was both. They had never gotten along, even as young children. Lizzie and Dónal were cut from the same jib: their father's. Moira didn't resemble either of her siblings; she was the spitting image of their mother. She was diminutive in stature and looked years younger than twenty-two. Her light brown hair felt dull and dreary when she looked at her siblings' thick flaxen locks. Despite being unwed, she wore her hair up since she spent most of her days toiling alongside the servants.

Preparing herself for her brother, she blew a puff of air before plastering a shy smile she didn't feel at all. She clasped her hands before her as she came to stand in front of the dais.

"Where is the rest of the meal?" Dónal demanded as he belched again.

I think you've eaten most of the meal already. I'm surprised no one's lost a finger from you snatching the food away.

"The last dish was already served, Chieftain," Moira forced herself to address her brother by his title, even though no one who sat at the dais did. He insisted upon it. She twisted away as a bone flew in her direction.

"This slop was barely edible, and now you tell me there is nothing more?" Dónal roared.

If it's such slop, then why would you want more?

Moira forced herself to keep her expression neutral. Years of practice taught her that any reaction would end poorly for her.

"I will see what I can find, Chieftain." Moira kept her answer succinct, dipping her head before turning toward the kitchen. She would never understand how a corpulent man like her brother could move so quickly. His chair flew backwards, and he met her at the bottom of the dais steps as she passed by. He grabbed Moira's upper arm, his stubby fingers biting into the flesh. Moira darted a quick glance over Dónal's shoulder and found Aidan watching, but she knew the man would never speak on her behalf. He never had. Instead, he reached for his mug and drank, keeping his eye on the chieftain and sister until Lizzie's roaming hand once more found his rod.

"See what you can find? See what you can find?" Dónal spluttered. "I expect three more courses served, back to back."

"The servants already served five, Dónal," Moira hissed, her voice low so only her brother would hear. She would appease him when others could hear, but she wouldn't when they spoke in private. "There is nothing else prepared. You've eaten it all."

Dónal shook her, but Moira stood firm. She'd learned to steel herself against Dónal's fits of temper. He often attempted to intimidate her with his substantial height and girth. The clan council had drawn the line two years ago when Dónal threatened to drive his fist into Moira's cheek for spilling wine on him while she trembled with fever. She recognized she lacked the size or the training to fight back physically, but she found inconspicuous ways to retaliate. Small things like pulling out chairs in his solar that she knew he would stumble over in his drunken stupors. She placed ants on his pillow and mused that it was the leftover mead at his bedside that must have drawn them. She'd even gone so far as to dip the hems of his breeks in beef fat, leading the keep's hounds to knock him over and bite his ankles.

"You stupid sow. No wonder no man will take you off my hands. You haven't the sense of a gnat and can't run a keep to save your life," Dónal snarled before shoving Moira. Despite her tiny size, especially when compared to Dónal, she had the sea legs of an old sailor. After years of Dónal's tyranny, she no longer swayed and was able to stand her ground. She didn't bother to hide her mutinous glare as she notched up her chin before staring at the clan council members who sat at the table Dónal abandoned. Her silent defiance dared him to lash out further, even in front of the men who could strip him of his seat as chieftain.

"Get out of my sight," Dónal spat. Moira was only too happy to comply. Without a second look, Moira glided toward the staircase. She might not have the lithe figure that Lizzie had even after bearing a child, but their mother drilled the same grace in Moira's movements as she had Lizzie's.

"Moira," Lizzie called. "Don't forget to take Sean."

Moira adored her nephew, but Lizzie knew it was salt in an open wound: of the two of them, Moira was the one who wanted children. But it was unlikely that she would ever have them, since Dónal was too stingy to pay an adequate dowry. Lizzie had flown into a rage to rival an angry sea god's when baby Sean called Moira "mama." The aching pain had come with a sense of satisfaction as Moira bounced Sean on her hip. She'd shrugged at Lizzie and taken Sean to lie down for a nap. Just as she had done nearly every night of his life, Moira helped Sean prepare for bed, then laid on the trundle bed in his chamber. He'd had night terrors for years, and Moira didn't remember the last time she'd slept a full night in her own chamber. She now went to the trundle bed by habit.

One day. One day when I'm certain Sean is cared for, I will be done. I will leave and not look back. Well, mayhap one glance if I can see Sean. But then, never again. Moira's eyes drifted closed as she drifted off.

CHAPTER 2

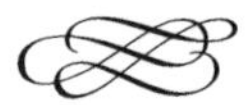

"I don't understand why you're making such a fuss," Lizzie whined the next evening as she ran her hand over Aidan's chest, pressing her breasts to his body.

"I'm making a fuss because the agreement is that you bed no one but me when I'm here," Aidan pushed Lizzie away. "I don't try to control you when I'm gone, but our arrangement will end faster than you can drop your skirts if you tup another man while I'm in port, Lizzie."

"But I had to," Lizzie pleaded, as Aidan scoffed. "Dónal wants to know O'Malley's secrets, so he can better negotiate. What other woman is going to get that information? Moira? She could stand naked, coated in honey, and no man would offer her information in exchange for a roll."

"So you came to your brother's aid by rolling around with the messenger," Aidan snapped.

"What do you care? You abandon me here as easy as you please," Lizzie whined.

"Mayhap I picked the wrong—" Aidan's voice came out smothered as Lizzie covered his mouth with hers. "—after all."

Moira watched in disgust as the couple reconciled with a

kiss, Aidan's groping hands settling on Lizzie's backside. She wondered why, after all these years, anything the couple did or said surprised her. It was as if she watched a stranger's horrible accident. She didn't care for the people, but she couldn't tear her eyes away. Turning to the serving women, she nodded and walked toward the dais while the others brought food to the lower tables. The platter she herself carried threatened to slosh over the sides as the roasted duck bathed in cream sauce slid back and forth.

As she rounded the table closest to the dais, she watched in horror as Dónal glanced at the hounds begging below the raised table, then threw a leg of pork at her. The three massive wolfhounds stood above her waist when they were on all fours; standing on their hind legs they were nearly a foot taller than her. The animals plowed into her, vying for the meat laying at her feet. But unlike when Dónal tried to push her over, she couldn't withstand the impact of the three dogs. The sauce from the platter poured down her front as her feet came out from under her. She tried to keep her balance, but her heel landed on a dog's paw, making him headbutt her in the back. She pitched forward, and the roast skidded across the floor and with it the dogs' attention. She landed hard, bashing her chin on the floor and knocking the wind from her lungs.

"Aunty Moira!" Sean yelled as he rushed forward. Moira pushed herself onto her hands before manly palms grasped her around her ribs. She looked over her shoulder as Aidan settled her on her feet.

"Are you hurt?" Aidan whispered.

"No more than in the past," Moira muttered as she pulled away from him and brushed rushes and crumbs from her kirtle. She sighed before looking back at Aidan. "Thank you."

"Clumsy wench," Dónal mocked.

"Aunty Moira," Sean slipped his hand into hers and looked up at her. She tried to smile at the child, but she'd bitten her tongue hard, and her chin burned. She wanted to rub it, but she wouldn't give Dónal the satisfaction. She sensed more than saw Aidan step away before he returned to his seat beneath Lizzie. "Your chin is bleeding," Sean whispered.

Moira looked down at Sean and felt a drop of blood land on her chest. She glanced at it and sighed. She was filthy and had a gash on her chin to match her humiliation. Until it healed, it would remind everyone of her ungainly performance before them and, worse, the clan's guest.

"No wonder the O'Malley demands such a high dowry," Lizzie chortled. "He knows he'll be replacing everything in sight once you plow through it."

Moira froze as the blood leached from her face. She doubted her heart still beat in her chest, and it was only Sean's hand in hers that let her know she hadn't gone numb. She turned to look at Dónal, then cast her gaze at the O'Malley messenger who shifted in his seat, attempting not to look at her. She'd wondered why the man ate at their table, since the O'Malleys and MacDonnells were on hostile terms. Now she understood. Dónal intended to fob her off on Dermot O'Malley, a man old enough to be her father. The last sliver of hope that she might one day make a love match like Ruairí and Senga's vanished in a breath.

"Perhaps he knows I'm worth more than my used-up older sister," Moira spat. "You should wed first, but no one's beating down our doors for your hand, either. You can't even get the man who sired your son to stay with you for more than a sennight at a time. You're no more than a free whore to any man Dónal sends you to."

Moira clamped her mouth shut, remembering far too late that Sean stood beside her. She squeezed his hand, but his fingers flexed. She released him, expecting him to run away, but he remained at her side. Lizzie darted from the dais and yanked Sean behind her before she lashed out and slapped Moira.

"I'm still the one getting married," Moira taunted.

"You bluidy little bitch. Say what you want, but we all know you can't keep a man in your bed," Lizzie crossed her arms and gloated.

"Aye, and I'd rather sleep alone than having to ask for tonics to cure the pox," Moira crossed her arms to match her sister.

"Enough," Dónal roared as his fist pounded the table. "Remove yourself, Moira. You belong in the sty with the other sows."

Moira cast a challenging glare at the O'Malley man before turning her withering stare on Dónal. Despite being shorter, she looked down her nose at Lizzie as she walked away. Standing behind his mother, Lizzie had no chance to stop Sean before he ran to Moira's side. Moira cocked her eyebrow at her sister as she went. Moira MacDonnell had drawn the line in the sand, and her family would now have to accept that she had a voice and would use it. After all, if she was forced to marry Dermot O'Malley, she was likely headed to her death anyway. He'd already strangled his first wife in her bed after she bore him a stillborn son. Moira didn't hope for anything better.

CHAPTER 3

Moira opened her eyes but remained still, trying to determine why she'd woken from the deepest sleep she'd likely had in years. When she heard a soft knock at the door, she glanced over at Sean, who slumbered in his bed beside her trundle. She looked back at the door as another knock sounded.

"Moira," a soft voice called to her. "Moira, it's Beagan."

Moira's brow furrowed as she rose, once more checking on Sean. The head of their clan council had never visited her at night; in fact, he'd barely spoken to her since she was a child. She opened the door a crack and peered out to find Beagan standing with other members of the council. Behind him were Curran and Cormac, brothers who'd been on the council since her father was chieftain. Devlin, Finnian, Grady, and Hogan stood behind their fathers Curran and Cormac. Loman and Malone stood on either side of Beagan. The only two members missing were her brother and his second, Orran.

"What's this about?" Moira leaned her head into the passageway and looked both ways. Her astonishment at finding the group of men outside her door had led to her stomach churning with fear. She prayed they wouldn't attack her with Sean sleeping behind her, but she had no way to know.

"Your brother has gone against the council once more. None of us voted for you to marry the O'Malley. Just the opposite, in fact. He is not an ally we wish to make," Beagan explained. "He will rob us blind. Your brother has always been a wee slow on the uptake, but since his injuries on Lewis when we fought the MacLeods, he is even more of a tyrant."

Moira listened with surprise that she struggled to keep from her expression. She never dreamed any of the council members would speak against her brother, at least not outside her brother's solar or to someone not on the council.

"Lass, the O'Malley will take your dowry, kill you, then attack us," Devlin spoke up. "You don't deserve the mistreatment you receive here, and you certainly don't deserve to die for your brother's greed."

"Has he already signed the contracts?" Moira whispered, listening for any movement behind her.

"Aye. After the meal. The messenger leaves in the morn," Grady spoke in low tones. "We will get you away, but you must come now."

"Away?" Moira repeated and shook her head. She tilted her head toward the bed within the chamber. "I can't."

"Your time to raise the lad is over. You've done more than any of us could have expected. But once you're shipped off to the O'Malleys, you won't have the lad with you. This way, you'll live."

"But until it's time, I have a duty to stay with him," Moira argued.

"Aunty Moira," a soft whisper came from beside her. She'd never heard him stir, let alone walk across the chamber. "Is Beagan here to rescue you?"

"Rescue me? Why do you say that, lovie?" Moira stroked back the mop of black curls from Sean's sleepy face.

"Because Uncle Dónal is going to hurt you before I'm big enough to defend you," Sean stated, with a tremble in his voice. Moira pulled her nephew into her embrace, her heart breaking to know that the boy understood more than she realized. Guilt sank its teeth into her; as duty bound as she felt toward Sean, the little tyke felt the same for her. "I don't want you sent off to the fucking O'Malleys."

"Sean!" Moira gasped. "Where did you learn that? I'll wash your mouth out with soap."

"Uncle Dónal. All the men. We all talk like that," Sean said with a shrug.

"You aren't a man till you have hair on your chin," Moira asserted. "So that filth will not come out of your mouth. Promise me that, Sean. Don't do what Uncle Dónal does." She gripped both of the boy's shoulders before bending over to embrace him.

"I'm sorry, Aunty Moira." Sean stretched to kiss her cheek. The light flickering in the passageway shone on his upturned face, and it stunned Moira to see how mature he looked. It was a glimpse at the man he would one day become. With a stoicism she didn't know he possessed, he continued. "If Beagan is here to rescue you, you must go. I won't say a word to anyone. I'll pretend that I have no idea where you've gone."

"Moira, we have to hurry," Beagan pressed. "We must get you away while the tide is with us."

"We're sailing?" Moira looked at the faces of the hardened warriors, who were also among the best sailors in Ireland. Or at least that was what her clan boasted.

"We'll take you to Fionn first. We can make it look like we did a trade run," Grady explained. "From there, either he and his men or we will take you to Ruairí and Senga."

"Ruairí and Senga," Moira breathed. She couldn't think of a better place to make her home. She'd met Senga during her only visit the year before, but she'd taken to her immediately. She'd always liked Ruairí, and while he was usually indifferent to her, he was never unkind. She'd marveled at the changes she'd seen in Ruairí since he met Senga, and she wondered if going to the Isle of Barra would offer her the opportunity to find love, too. If nothing else, it would gain her a reprieve from her brother and sister.

"Let me dress and slip into my chamber for a few things," Moira whispered as she picked Sean up and clung to the boy. He smelled of soap, the scent clean and fresh. She suspected she would never see the boy again, and that caused her a moment of doubt.

"You must go, Aunty Moira," Sean murmured against her ear, seeming to sense her upheaval. She kissed each of his cheeks, his forehead, and the tip of his nose, just as she had every night since he was born. She lowered him to the floor and watched him scamper back into bed. Looking down the passageway once more, she eased the door shut behind her.

"Grady and I will sail with you," Malone explained as they walked to her chamber, the other men seeming to vanish into the darkness as they padded away. "Pack only what you must."

Moira was in and out of her chamber in less than five minutes. She pulled a sack from her chest, swiping a bar of soap and her comb from the washstand. She grabbed two chemises and two kirtles before donning a fresh chemise and gown. She looked in the corner, where her ruined gown from earlier that night lay. She turned her back on it as easily as she turned her back on her life at Dunluce. With stockings and boots on, she swept her gaze around the chamber, not with a longing last glance but a practical mental checklist. When the door closed behind her, she only considered what was ahead of her.

Moira gritted her teeth as she stood at the prow of the MacDonnell ship as it eased through the waves, drawing them closer to where Moira knew the O'Malleys trolled the waters. Grady and Malone already explained that they would drop anchor in a cove a day's sail north of the O'Malley stronghold, then wait to sail past in the dead of night. The last thing Moira needed was for the O'Malleys to attack them. She would be served to Dermot like a stuffed Christmas goose. Despite her trepidation, she eased her grip on the railing and watched as the western horizon softened into hues of reds and oranges. She'd been at sea for three days, and the wind was not in their favor. She'd stayed below deck the first day, fearful that any passing ship would wonder why there was a woman aboard. But once they were well out of the popular shipping lanes, she ventured into the fresh air and spent hours watching the churning surf against the hull.

With the sun setting, the air grew chill, so Moira abandoned her post for the cabin Grady had given her. There was only a skeleton crew aboard the ship; only men Grady and Malone trusted never to tell Dónal of her escape. The men said little to her, and the pity in their eyes rankled, but she was grateful for their willingness to risk their lives to aid in her flight from Dunluce. Unused to the bracing air and brisk spray that coated the deck, Moira fell asleep easily and slept through the nights. She'd never considered how exhausted she was from years of waking with Sean's night terrors. But the uninterrupted sleep was more restorative than manna from Heaven. It felt like only moments after shutting her eyes that they snapped open to pounding on her door and voices bellowing orders above deck.

"Moira, open the door!" Malone's voices pierced through the wood. "We're under attack."

Moira sprang from the bunk and yanked the door open. "O'Malleys?"

"Pirates."

Moira sucked in a whistling breath before she nodded. She knew Aidan wouldn't raid them, and both Ruairí and Rowan MacNeil had retired. There were no pirates sailing along the Irish coast that she could count on as more friend than foe. Malone said no more before dashing back toward the ladder well. She shed her chemise and pulled on the oversized leine and leggings that one of the men had given her when she boarded in case this very situation arose. She stuffed her meager belongings into her sack before easing the door open. She could hear metal clashing against metal, and the stench of blood flooded her nostrils. Breathing through her mouth, she raced to the hatch that led to the hold. She slid more than stepped down the ladder until her feet hit the damp floor. She glanced around and spied the outline of a stack of crates and barrels that she could hide behind before tugging the rope that closed the door.

As the battle waged above her, Moira said all the prayers she knew and made up as many as she could conjure. She couldn't tell from the muffled voices which side would be victorious. When she bounced against the bulkhead, she wondered if the jarring impact that sent her sailing was from a cannon or the pirate ship ramming them. She waited for water to rush in and engulf her, but when not even a sliver of light entered the blackness, she knew they hadn't been rammed. That only left a cannonball. Few ships were equipped with the new weapon, but Moira suspected pirates would be among the first to arm themselves. She feared the deck would be alight and that she would still go to a watery grave when the ship burned around her. But she had no alternatives. If the MacDonnells were defeated, and she expected their tiny crew would be, she would die whether she entered the fray on deck or waited to sink with the ship.

As suddenly as the noise and turbulence began, everything fell silent. Moira didn't dare move. Grady and Malone had been very clear with their instructions. In case of attack, she was to remain hidden unless one of them came for her. She wasn't to trust anyone but them. If anyone found her, she was to appear and act like an adolescent boy rather than a woman. She'd fretted about appearing scrawny for years, but she prayed it would come in handy if the pirates discovered her. She wondered if she should try to climb into a barrel or crate, but that would mean discarding the container's contents, and that would appear suspicious. She opted to remain crouched, curled up as tiny as she could make herself.

"Check the hold," an order sounded from above. Moira frowned. Something about the voice was familiar. It was clearly Scottish, even if there was only a slight burr. "We have room in ours, so take everything. The MacDonnells always have goods worth a pretty penny."

Bluidy hell. If they're to take everything, they'll find me. I should have hidden in something while I had the chance.

Moira had no time for further recriminations as the hatch swung open. The sound of men descending the ladder echoed. Remaining in the shadows, Moira blinked as light from several torches swept the cargo area.

"Ye heard the Capt'n. Nothing remains," came the clipped words of a man Moira could only imagine would look as rough as his voice. She fought to keep her breathing quiet, praying that the pirate captain would be too impatient to wait for them to load everything. Perhaps the cargo she hid behind would be abandoned.

But do I actually have a better chance with them? I can't sail this ship alone. Even if I swam to shore, what would I find? O'Malleys? Would I prefer pirates to Dermot O'Malley?

Moira had no chance for further wondering when the crate in front of her face was pulled away and a light shone in her face.

"Ay-up. What have we here?" A burly pirate with several missing teeth glared down at her. Moira refused to cower, choosing to make a show of bravado she didn't feel. She stood and raised her chin, daring the man to say more. "A stowaway."

"More like a rat," another man snorted. "Scrawny runt. Even Braedon had more meat on his bones when Ruairí took him in."

Moira struggled not to react when she heard the former pirate's name. Were these men from the *Lady Charity*? Would that help? She stumbled when an enormous paw wrapped around her arm and pulled her from her hiding place. She tried to dig her heels in as the man attempted to maneuver her in front of him, but his growl was enough warning for Moira to know that this wasn't the time or place to stand her ground.

"Up you go."

Moira's grazed chin banged against a rung of the ladder when the pirate shoved her forward. She scaled it with ease, grateful to be in leggings and not her skirts. As she turned to face the ladder well that led to the top deck, she came face-to-face with a man whose flame-red hair and freckles made her stomach clench. She had most certainly been found by the crew of the *Lady Charity*.

"Who's this?" The redheaded man barked.

"Stowaway, Capt'n."

"Toss her, Snake Eye." Moira realized she was standing before the pirate captain.

"Does she get a plank?" The man named Snake Eye asked, to which the captain shrugged one shoulder.

"You're going to drown me?" Moira gulped. The captain reached out and gripped her jaw between his thumb and fingers, pulling her toward him.

"That might be your fate. I'm setting you adrift."

"Why?" Moira struggled to say. When the gathered men chuckled, she glanced around.

"Because that's what I do," the captain responded with another nonchalant shrug.

"Seems the lad hasn't heard of you," Snake Eye grunted.

"He has now," the captain looked down at Moira. "The Red Drifter gives you his regards, whelp."

Moira tried to pull the man's thumb from her jaw, but he squeezed harder. She grabbed his pinky with both hands and pried it as far back as she could. His hand squeezed once again, but Moira saw the flash of pain in his eyes. The dim light didn't disguise her pleasure either, because the red-haired man shoved her away from him.

"I have no need for stowaways. Set him adrift like the others."

Moira had only a second to decide. She knew her choices were between likely death and certain death. She preferred to delay the inevitable as long as she could.

"You might want to keep me, Kyle MacLean." The air stilled as the men's eyes widened, and the captain took a predatory step toward her. "Ruairí might not care if you ransom me, but Senga will have your cods if you kill me."

Moira banked on the crew still seeing the retired pirate and his wife. She banked on either of them caring about her. She banked on the captain believing even a smidge of her bluff. She saw the flash of recognition. With a jerky nod, Kyle spoke to Snake Eye but never looked away from Moira.

"Take the captive to my cabin. String 'em up. I have better things to tend to," Kyle sneered, but he blinked twice when Moira didn't flinch. He narrowed his eyes before turning away and barking orders for the ship to burn once the cargo transfer was complete. Moira didn't look back as Snake Eye pushed her toward the rail, so she missed Kyle's speculative look.

CHAPTER 4

The early morning rays offered just enough light for her to make out bodies scattered across the deck. Moira struggled not to collapse on the deck as she recognized one fallen man after another. The sparse crew were all accounted for, and all dead. Moira said a prayer of thanks that Kyle had set none adrift to drown, become shark food, or to die of thirst. It was no longer a matter of them risking their lives for her; they'd given their lives for her. She knew all the men had wives and children who would never know what became of them. Their bodies would settle in the deep, but she wondered if their souls would ever be at peace. She wasn't certain if hers ever could be as guilt, a seemingly constant companion throughout her life, tugged once more at her heart.

"Best you do not look, lad," Snake Eye whispered. "They put up a valiant fight, but they were no match." Moira nodded, wondering why the outlaw offered the words of solace. She wondered if it might have been a point of honor.

As she crossed the plank onto the *Lady Charity,* none of it seemed to matter. She was now the captive of a pirate captain who couldn't have appeared less thrilled to recognize her. Once upon a time, she'd fancied Kyle MacLean. The fiery mane and the piercing green eyes were a powerful draw. She remembered meeting him when she met Senga. She usually stayed out of site whenever the men from the *Lady Charity* came into the keep. She did that when any pirates visited. But she'd emerged to be a hostess for Senga, and she'd even asked who he was. At the time, he'd been Ruairí's first mate. Now he was the captain of his own ship. Gone was the jovial smile and wink he'd once offered her. She'd never underestimated that he was lethal, but he hadn't been as hardened as the man she met aboard her clan's ship. Obviously responsibility and power had changed him.

"In you scoot," Snake Eye ordered as he pushed a door open. Moira looked around the cabin, spacious compared to the one she'd occupied for three days. The room was clean, and the bunk crisply made. Books were stacked on a table and a map was unfurled beside them. She noticed a chest at the foot of the bed and one against a wall. While the table took up most of the center of the cabin, there was a washstand tucked away and another, smaller table that held more scrolls and what Moira assumed were ledgers. There was a porthole through which filtered light poured.

Snake Eye nudged Moira across the cabin, producing rope Moira hadn't noticed before. When he stooped to bind her ankles, she considered fighting him, jamming her knee into his face, kicking him backwards. But even if she escaped the cabin, she wouldn't escape the ship. And even if she could escape the ship, where would she go? Jump into the sea? Being set adrift was what she'd attempted to avoid by speaking up. Moira knew her only current choice was to bide her time until she could speak to Kyle.

Her eyes flew to the ceiling when Snake Eye tossed the rope he'd finished binding her hands with over a hook. He'd left enough slack for her arms to be pulled over her head, and now she was stretched onto her toes. She watched him tie it off to another hook on the wall behind her. It only took her a moment to realize the rope was intended for someone far taller than her. To make it reach the wall hook, she practically dangled from the hook in the ceiling. Her arms burned with pain before Snake Eye slipped from the cabin. She did what she could to twist until she had a view of the porthole. Her intuition told her Kyle would leave her down there for as long as he could, so she settled for gazing out at the desolate expanse of water. The freedom it had offered the night before now seemed like an endless cage.

Kyle forced himself to remain focused on the new cargo being stored in his hold. He did a quick inventory and estimated the value, pleased that they'd commandeered the MacDonnell vessel. His mind floated back to Moira over and over. He'd recognized her the moment he'd seen her, but he assumed she didn't recognize him. He'd been relieved when she spoke up because he hadn't been sure he could throw her overboard, even though he'd given the order. She was still the delicately boned woman he remembered from a year ago, but there was spunk in her eyes he hadn't witnessed before. She'd been meek and servile in front of her brother and sister. He remembered Senga's suspicion that Dónal MacDonnell beat Moira, but he hadn't imagined he'd send her on a voyage with a less-than-adequate crew. He'd been suspicious when he discovered how few men there were on the Irish ship as he and his men attacked in the dark. Now he questioned why Moira was on board, and why she dressed as a lad.

"Capt'n," Tomas, his first mate approached. "Found a sack near where the stowaway hid. It has women's clothes in it."

Kyle drew him out of earshot from the men working around them. “Aye. We’ve captured Moira MacDonnell.”

Tomas looked aghast as he shook his head in disbelief. “That bastard Dónal’s sister?”

“The very one.”

“Too bad it’s not Lizzie. At least we could have a good rut before doing away with her.” Tomas paused and cast an assessing look over Kyle. “You’re not planning on getting rid of her.”

“I’m not sure yet. There are too many questions to be answered before I can decide how best to use this unexpected boon,” Kyle said speculatively.

“Boon? She sounded ready to piss vinegar earlier. I don’t think you’ll be counting it a boon for long. She’s not like she was a year ago.”

“So I noticed,” Kyle responded flippantly.

“How long are you going to keep her down there wondering if you’ll swing her from the yardarm?”

“I have work to do up here. I’ll get to her when I can,” Kyle tried to sound nonchalant, but Tomas’s snort signaled he’d failed.

“Afraid of the wee lass, are you? I would be. Vinegar, I tell you. Vinegar,” Tomas warned with a chuckle as he walked away shaking his head. Kyle remained above deck and at the helm until late afternoon, when he knew he couldn’t avoid Moira any longer. He needed to decide what to do with her; if it was a ransom, he needed to send a messenger overland immediately. Kyle swung down the ladder well, not bothering with the steps, then paused to take a deep breath before opening the door to his cabin.

“Fuck,” Kyle hissed as he lurched across his cabin. It had only taken a second to see Moira was unconscious, her head lolling against her arm. As he rushed toward her, he noticed the sleeves of her tunic had slipped down. Her arms had bruises, but the unmarred skin was deathly white. He realized she stood on her toes and could only imagine the agony she'd experienced for hours, surely feeling like her arms were being ripped from her body. He nearly counted it a blessing that she'd passed out. He tugged the rope free from the wall hook and lunged to catch her as she sagged forward. She felt like little more than a rag doll as she hung over his arm.

Bracing her with one arm, he pushed her hair from her face and tapped her cheeks. After seeing the bruises mottling her arms, he was hesitant to slap her cheeks. Between the injuries she had before she came aboard and what she suffered from Snake Eye's carelessness and his own neglect, the shred of conscience he still had barked at him not to hurt her any further.

"Moira. Lass, can you hear me?" Kyle looked around before looping his foot around the leg of a chair and dragging it toward him. He eased Moira into the seat, but she was so deeply unconscious that her body keeled sideways. "Moira."

Still trying to hold her up, he strained for the flask of whisky on the small table beside the wall. He pulled the stopper free with his teeth before setting the potent alcohol beneath her nose. She twitched as she inhaled the aroma, and when she lifted her head on her own accord, Kyle placed the flask to her lips. With her bound hands, she held the container and drew three large gulps before pushing it away. Kyle expected her to cough and splutter, but instead, she turned bloodshot eyes to him.

"You knew it was me," Moira observed. Kyle wasn't sure that he should admit that he'd known it was her. "You would have let me die even though you knew from the beginning."

"Aye," Kyle forced the word. But as he looked at Moira, he knew it for the lie he wanted her to believe. He wouldn't have been able to do it. But he wouldn't confide that to anyone, least of all his prisoner. Moira gazed up at him and nodded. He wasn't sure what to make of her acceptance.

"How far have we sailed?" Moira asked as she rubbed the pins and needles from her right arm.

Kyle was unprepared for the question. He expected her to plead and whine, but he supposed he should have known that wasn't like Moira. That would have been Lizzie, not her sister.

"A few hours," Kyle hedged. He watched as Moira pushed herself to her feet. He reached out to support her, but her scathing glare had him snatching back his hands.

"We head south. So you aren't taking me to my brother," Moira stated as she worked on her left arm.

"Not yet."

"Not ever," Moira countered while she flexed her fingers.

"But the ransom," Kyle said as he cocked a patronizing eyebrow.

"That he won't pay," Moira raised a matching eyebrow.

"What were you doing on that ship, Moira?" Kyle stepped closer when she shrugged and returned to looking out the porthole. He watched her lips press together and noticed her body tensed when she moved her arms. "Moira, answer me."

While dangling for hours, Moira had realized that even if Kyle threw her into the water, she wasn't yet near the stretch of sea the O'Malleys frequented. It was unlikely that they would find her, as they might have if Kyle had gone through with his earlier threat. She'd rather be eaten by a shark than die at Dermot's hands. It would likely be far less painful. She also understood that Kyle left her alone for hours on purpose to break her spirit, but she suspected he hadn't anticipated her dangling like she'd gone to the gallows. The remorse she saw as she opened her eyes felt like vindication.

"Ignoring me doesn't bode well for your lovely arse," Kyle warned. Moira slowly angled her head toward him and swept her eyes over him from head to toe and back up again. Without a word, she turned back to the window. Kyle couldn't fail to recognize the spark of interest that flared in Moira's eyes at his threat, and his already hardening cock stood at attention. The feel of her in his arms had aroused him in an instant. He'd blamed it on not being with a woman for several months, but as Moira cast her assessing gaze over him, heat shot to his groin. He stepped closer, wondering if she would react to him crowding her. The Moira he'd met a year ago would have cowered, or at least he'd assumed she would. But the woman before him didn't spare him a glance. Bemused, he whispered, "Who are you?"

"You know who I am, Kyle." Moira's voice came out raspier than she expected, but Kyle's closeness disconcerted her despite how she fought not to show it.

"You're not the woman I met last year," Kyle murmured.

"I am. She's always been there," Moira corrected.

"You still haven't answered my question, Moira. I expect an answer," Kyle gave himself a mental shake, pulling himself out from the peculiar haze that had settled over his mind.

"You'd beat a woman you've had strung up like a flank of beef?" Moira asked with disgust.

"I'm not your brother, Moira. I don't beat women. I—"

"Leave them to die," Moira countered. "After all, you're the Red Drifter now. Had I not spoken up, I would likely be in some fish's gut by now, or washing up on the O'Malleys' shore."

"Something has loosened your tongue these days," Kyle grumbled.

"Gag me if you wish to shut me up," Moira rejoined.

"I can think of something to shove in there," Kyle muttered as he brought the whisky flask to his mouth.

"Torturing me wasn't enough? Now you intend to rape me?" Moira seethed. Kyle froze before he took his first sip.

"I've committed many sins in my life, few of which I regret. But I have never forced a woman, Moira." Kyle's penetrating green eyes bore into her until they eventually crinkled at the sides with his grin. "I don't have to."

"But you think to shut my mouth with your cock inside it," Moira pointed out. When Kyle's eyes widened, she chuckled. "You assumed I didn't understand what you implied. How could I not if I asked if you'd force me?"

"What does a maiden know of that, even if your sister is Lizzie?" Kyle snapped.

Moira looked at him with a furrowed brow and a smirk. "Perhaps you shouldn't keep assuming that you know me so well."

"Are you saying you're not a virgin?" Kyle's voice rasped.

"I'm saying you shouldn't make so many assumptions," Moira said smugly. She squeaked when Kyle pounced. He pulled her against his body, her hands trapped between them as his mouth descended to hers. Rather than panic and pull away, Moira pressed herself closer and opened to him. He stepped Moira backwards until her back pressed against the bulkhead. He didn't need to make any more assumptions: he was kissing a woman with experience. With her hands caught between them, she fisted his leine as he pressed his rod against her mons. Frustrated by not being able to feel her breasts pressed to him, he raised her arms and pinned them against the wall, but her whimper of pain made him jump back. He'd forgotten that she'd suffered his neglect all day. She had been tortured, just as she accused.

"I'm sorry. That was thoughtless of me," Kyle murmured as he kissed her cheek near the corner of her eye, tasting a trace of salt that he knew didn't come from the sea air. She had been crying earlier. "I've wanted to do that since the first time I saw you. At Dunluce, not your ship."

Moira bit her bottom lip, pulling the puffy flesh between her teeth. "I wanted the same thing."

"Is that all you wanted?" Kyle whispered. Moira looked at

him for a long moment before she shook her head. His large hand slipped between her arms and palmed her small breast. He watched as her eyes drifted closed and her lips parted. It was one of the most sensual sights he'd ever beheld. He massaged the pert mound, brushing his thumb over her nipple. The loose leine had hidden her breasts well, so she hadn't bound them. Now Kyle could feel every contour. "Why were you on the ship?"

The trance ended as abruptly as it started. Moira pushed Kyle's hands away and moved to cover her breasts with her upper arms. Her hands shielded her mons. She might enjoy Kyle's kisses and his touch, but she didn't trust him with the truth.

"Back to being recalcitrant," Kyle tsked. "I warned you it wouldn't serve your proud little bottom well." Kyle didn't expect Moira to turn around and press her hips back at him in offering, the challenge written clearly in her eyes as she looked back over her shoulder. He hooked his fingers into her waistband and tugged her backward until she landed over his lap once he was seated. With her hands and feet still restrained, she was powerless to stop Kyle from pulling the laces free from her leggings and pushing them down over her hips. The first spank echoed in the cabin, but Moira made no sound. The second and third elicited sighs that Kyle felt rather than heard. The fourth and fifth made her shift restlessly.

"Who have you been with, Moira?" Kyle demanded. "Who spanked you? Taught you to enjoy this?"

This truth she would give him. "No one. I would have fought off any other man."

Kyle rained down another sharp slap along the crease where her buttocks met her thighs. He gazed at the reddening skin and wanted to groan. He was certain Moira could feel his arousal. How could she not, when his cock pressed against her ribs? He angled his hand for the next slap so his fingers dipped between

Moira's thighs. He did groan when he found what he suspected. She was dripping for him.

"I already know you like this, Moira," Kyle whispered as he pulled a dirk from his belt and leaned over, cutting the bindings from her ankles. He slipped his fingers between her thighs, caressing her folds once then resting them against her heated skin. "And I know you're familiar with what I can offer you next. Answer my questions, and I'll give you what you want."

Moira struggled not to concede. It had been years since a man had touched her, but her body hadn't forgotten the neediness, the longing for more. No man had spanked her as Kyle was, but she'd received one or two in the heat of passion and reveled in it. As Kyle's cock twitched against her, she had the strongest urge to slip from his lap and free his sword until her mouth could become its sheath, just as Kyle had implied earlier. She kept her eyes closed and tried to calm her breathing, but she fought and failed to stifle her moan when Kyle's fingers dipped within.

"Lusty, are you?" Kyle mused. He worked his fingers within her, and Moira was certain there had been nothing more divine. Then his thumb pressed against her nub. She shifted again, trying to create the friction she knew would bring her release. "Answer any of my questions, Moira, and I will give you what you crave. Why were you on the ship? Who was he?"

Moira shook her head, but her breath caught. She struggled to show no signs that her release washed over her, but the stinging spanking that followed made her back arch. It pressed her mound against Kyle's hard thigh, triggering yet another torrent of feeling from her core into her belly and out through her limbs. She'd gone so long without that her body had taken little prodding. She squeezed her eyes shut as she felt her heart pounding in her throat.

"I didn't give you permission to climax, sweet one."

Moira twisted to see Kyle bring his fingers coated with her

dew to his tongue. His gaze was purely predatory, gloating, as he licked them clean, knowing he'd satisfied her. Moira shuddered and shut her eyes, but the defiance that she'd smothered for too many years reared its head. Her mind was at war with itself, warning her that she didn't know him well enough to be certain he wouldn't beat her. But the louder voice urged her to challenge him, to test what she could get away with. She slipped from his lap and pressed her shoulders between his knees. Kyle did nothing to stop her as her still-bound hands pulled at the laces to his leggings.

Kyle feared he'd climax without Moira so much as touching him when she licked her lips as his cock sprung free. Her hands wrapped around him, stroking him thrice before her lips brushed against the tip of his rod. She looked up at him as her tongue circled the bulbous head, and air hissed from between Kyle's teeth as she lowered her mouth onto him. He scooped her hair back as her eyes drifted closed. Kyle almost believed she reveled in the task, but reminded himself that few women enjoyed the act as much as they claimed. But Moira's moans made him wonder if she was one of those rarities.

Kyle felt his bollocks tighten as she took his full length, allowing the tip to slide down her throat. Releasing her hair, he pulled the neckline of her leine apart, tugging until he exposed the tops of her breasts. He tried to press her away as he felt his release surging forward. But Moira batted his hands. Grasping her hair and tugging enough to sting, he barked, "Stroke me."

They both watched as Kyle's seed splashed against her lips and chin before coating her breasts. Moira ran her tongue over her lips and chin as she awkwardly swiped her fingers across her chest before bringing them to her mouth. Kyle sat panting as he watched Moira cast him a look of smug satisfaction before dropping her gaze to the floor. She kneeled before him, her hands resting in her lap, her head bowed, and her gaze averted. Kyle's cock twitched, struggling to come back to life so soon after such a draining release. The picture of submission Moira made as she rested between his knees tempted him to toss her onto his bunk and sink into her. But as demure as she looked now, she had still defied him more than once. He would discover what Moira hid from him and learn if she was the type of woman he'd sought, but accepted that he would never find.

CHAPTER 5

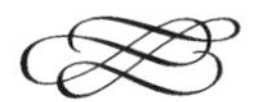

Moira felt Kyle's gaze upon her, but she kept her head bowed. She didn't want him to see her gloating, and she sensed that the longer she remained kneeling, the more he approved. She'd given up seeking anyone's approval once her mother died. She'd failed each time she tried, but something about Kyle suddenly brought the need back. She longed for it, craved it. Squeezing her eyes shut, she chided herself for being ridiculous. She was physically attracted to the man, and he was satisfied with having her in his cabin. They'd both gotten something from their time together. Moira reminded herself that only hours earlier, he had been set to kill her. Now she was bowing before him.

But if he can make my body feel like that again, I might sell my soul to the devil.

Moira's head jerked up when Kyle pulled her to her feet. With her feet no longer tethered, he commanded her to step out of the leggings. He adjusted the bindings around her wrists, and Moira thought she was getting a reprieve from how the coarse material bit into her skin. She balked when Kyle pulled her back to where she'd stood before. She flinched when he pulled the rope over the hook in the ceiling, but he didn't pull her arms over her head as she feared. Since her hands were no longer connected to her ankles, the rope was slacker. Her wrists hovered in front of her face, but her arms didn't strain.

"You don't trust me, Moira, so I would be a fool to trust you. Until you tell me the truth, you will remain here. Your choice," Kyle warned.

"I didn't survive my brother by giving up," Moira muttered. Kyle tipped her head back and gazed into her blue eyes, which were the color of cornflowers.

"But you never desired your brother and what his cock can do for you." Kyle pressed a brief harsh kiss on her mouth, intending to pull back and leave her wanting. But Moira opened to him, flicking her tongue against his lips. Lust gathered in his groin and made his cock swell yet again. Frustrated with himself as much as he was with Moira, his fingers bit into her sore backside until she yelped and pulled back. "I can give you pain, and I can give you pleasure."

He stalked to the door, but Moira's soft voice made him freeze. "And if I want both?"

He glanced back at her, uncertain what to make of her expression. He forced himself out of the cabin before he turned back and ravaged her with a savagery he'd never felt toward a woman. With the door closed behind him, he slid against the wall and leaned his head back. If she wouldn't have heard, he would have banged it.

What is she doing to me? What is it about her that goads me, entices me, satisfies me? How can one look, one sound, one touch or taste make me want her so damn badly that I'm ready to burst again? Again! No woman has sucked me like that, and yet, I want to march back in there and thrust into her. I almost don't care if I hurt her. Not if I can be inside her. Not if I can feel her.

Kyle clenched his fists and his jaws. There were few things he and his twin brother Keith weren't willing to do, but they'd never intentionally attacked ships with women aboard. They'd agreed upon that when they each became captain of the MacNeil cousins' ships. They avoided any boats they thought might carry female passengers, only raiding slavers and freeing men and women.

But if I'd known a woman was aboard, I wouldn't have Moira in my cabin. I wouldn't have felt her cunny squeeze my fingers as she climaxed. I wouldn't know what it feels like for her to swallow my entire bluidy cock. But she won't tell me the answer to such a simple question as why she left Dunluce. I don't even care who she's bedded. I need to know why she left home. How can I protect her if I don't know?

Protect her? Daft sod. You should put her off at the first port you find. Give her some coin to get to wherever she headed, then wash your hands of her. Women aboard ships bring nothing but foul luck. Even Senga brought her fair share of trouble, and she was like no other woman I ken. Kyle turned his head toward his door and opened his eyes for a moment before shutting them again. *She's like no other woman I ken. I never desired Senga, but Moira. Ha, ha. Moira will get into my blood if I don't watch myself. I need air.*

Moira knew Kyle stopped outside his door. The walls were thin, and she'd heard booted footsteps earlier in the day. She strained to hear any voices, but there was nothing there for so long that she wondered if she imagined him waiting outside the cabin. Then she heard one thump against the wall, as if someone hit it, then the clomp of boots headed toward the ladder well. She twisted once again, so she could look out the porthole. Her arms ached, but the scorching pain from earlier had abated. With her hands before her face, she studied the rope and knots. She tried to picture how she could uncoil the bindings, and she even considered trying to use her teeth. But what would she do once she was free? She could sit in the chair Kyle had occupied earlier, perhaps throw her feet up onto the table and wait for his return. Mayhap she would strip off the leine and recline on his bed, the invitation clear.

As much as those ideas appealed to her, she felt a deeper need to remain where she was when Kyle returned dominated her thoughts. She wanted him to be pleased that she'd obeyed at least one command. She'd challenged him on the others, but she didn't want to push too far. And the kiss. The power she'd felt when she enticed him into the kiss with only her lips at her disposal. The restrained power in Kyle's body that could have easily crushed her with no way to defend herself. For whatever reason, to some degree—at least with her body—she trusted him. And she wanted to repay that trust by at least offering some submission to his demands.

She'd touched herself plenty of times over the years. It was the only way to find the release she'd discovered by being with a man. When Kyle touched her, the need intensified even as he soothed it. Her body reacted to him on an elemental level she'd never imagined. She'd thought she'd been in love before, and yet, it had held none of the same compelling need that she felt with Kyle. She had no way to apply reason to the situation because it defied it. She only gave herself a headache while she tried. She resigned herself to waiting until their next round of cat and mouse.

As the hours ticked by and the sun moved closer to the western horizon, Moira wondered if Kyle intended to starve her into compliance. She questioned whether he would return to the cabin that night or find reasons to avoid her, to torment her with loneliness and uncertainty. She wanted to believe that his desire for her equaled what she felt for him, and that need would drive him back. But she'd already learned once that men did always reciprocate her desires.

Moira's eyes were dropping shut when she heard the door open. She didn't turn around, instead waiting to find out would come next. She heard something set on the table before hands slid beneath her leine and around her waist. One hand traveled up to her breast while the other cupped her mons. She pressed her hips back, knowing it was Kyle without looking. She recognized his touch, his scent. She recognized the bulge that pressed back against her.

"Are you hungry, sweet one?" Kyle murmured as he nibbled along her neck, which strained as she granted him more access. She recognized the seduction, the manipulation, but she cared not while he continued to touch her. "I didn't hear you, Moira."

"Yes," she rasped.

"And what would you like to feast upon now?" Kyle asked as he pinched her nipple.

"You know I would do it again," Moira confessed.

"Do you ken what my favorite food is, Moira?" Kyle whispered as he rubbed her tiny bundle of nerves that lay hidden in the thatch of dark curls his hand covered. She shook her head then turned her neck, trying to press the skin to his lips. "A very special kind of honey. A kind that has only one source."

Kyle twirled Moira to face him before sinking to his knees. His shoulders pushed her legs apart as his tongue flicked out to brush against her nether lips. Moira bucked her hips when Kyle slung one of her legs over his shoulder, then wrapped his arms under her thighs and over her hips, pinning her opening to his mouth. He laved her swollen lips before sucking her nub into his mouth, grazing his teeth along it. He reveled in her taste as he listened to her short, shallow pants.

When Moira couldn't stifle a moan, Kyle slid three fingers into her, pulling his mouth away, which earned him a whimper from Moira. He worked her core, sensing that she was drawing closer to release. He flicked his tongue over her bud and felt her body tense. Releasing her, he stepped back. Moira looked at him in shock as she struggled against her bindings. He knew her body ached with unspent lust. Just as he wanted.

"You found your release without my permission earlier, Moira. Then you refused to admit you had," Kyle pointed out.

"But I tried to make it up to you," Moira gasped.

"And you did," Kyle kissed the tip of her nose. "But in nearly the same breath, you refused to answer my simple questions. Give me the answers I seek, and I will give you the pleasure you crave."

Kyle watched as Moira fumed. Her nostrils flared with each inhale, and her chest rose and fell as she struggled to maintain control. She narrowed her eyes at Kyle but remained silent. Kyle shook his head and turned to the table where he sat and lifted a bowl of soup to his mouth. He sighed as the warm broth slipped down his throat, chasing the chill of the early evening air from his bones. He watched Moira as he lowered his bowl and picked up the other. He stepped to her side and brought the soup to her mouth. She looked at him with such distrust that he nearly reconsidered his plan. He nodded, and she slipped her lips around the edge. He held it to her mouth until he sensed she needed a moment.

When she finished her soup, he brought a heel of bread and a sizeable chunk of cheese back to her. He broke off pieces and fed them to her. She licked his fingers with each bite, sucking them into her mouth. Lust reflected in their gazes as Moira ate each item he brought to her. When she could eat no more, she watched as Kyle ate. Despite his taunting at the beginning, he'd fed her each bite and forewent his meal until she was full.

"I don't understand you," Moira blurted as Kyle chewed the last bite of bread.

"What is there to understand? I am captain of this ship and in command of all who are on board. Obey me, and you shall be content," Kyle explained with a diffident shrug.

"No." Moira shook her head. When she didn't elaborate, Kyle

came to stand beside her. She gazed into his eyes, and for the first time in years, she felt tears threatening. She saw the doubt flicker in Kyle's eyes when he realized she was close to crying. "That."

"What?" Kyle asked in confusion.

"That. That moment where you want to be kind, but you won't let yourself. I don't understand you. You insist upon trying to intimidate and manipulate me as the dreaded Captain Red Drifter, but then you let me see Kyle MacLean. And it's confusing because I think you're both men. I just wish I knew how to prepare when your mood shifts," Moira whispered.

"You can believe Kyle MacLean still exists, but you will only be disappointed," Kyle warned, disconcerted by Moira's perceptiveness.

"I may not have confessed my secrets, but I haven't lied to you either. Don't lie to me," Moira countered.

"What lie have I told?" Kyle challenged her.

"The one you just spoke. Kyle, Drifter, whoever the bluidy hell you want to be called. Perhaps you are the coldest, most calculating man I've met. Perhaps you use gentleness and kindness as your weapon against me, silently coercing me. I don't know because I don't understand. But Kyle MacLean, the man I met last year, still exists." Moira closed her eyes and turned her head into her arm, suddenly too drained to argue, to even think. She didn't open her eyes when she felt the rope slacken, but they flew open when she felt a blade slip under the binding. She watched Kyle free her; just as she had earlier that day, she sagged against him. "I can't any more tonight. I'm just too damn tired to fight, to keep up with you. Please, just let me sleep."

Kyle looked around, realizing he hadn't thought about where Moira would sleep. He'd held other captives in his cabin before, and he'd kept them bound and standing throughout the night. But Moira wasn't a hardened sailor or another pirate. She was a woman who had left home with an inadequate guard. He remembered the bruises he'd seen earlier, and in the dim candlelight, he lifted Moira into his arms and sat at the table. He pushed her sleeves up and sucked in a breath, noticing the extent of the bruises. Fingers digging into her petal-soft skin clearly made each set. He feared looking elsewhere in case it was worse, but he forced himself to lift the back of her leine.

"He doesn't hit me. Just squeezes my arms," Moira muttered. "I'm fine. Just tired."

Kyle leaned around Moira to see her eyes were open, but her lids drooped.

"Dónal?" Kyle whispered.

"Who else? I have no father, and I have no husband."

"But you have a lover," Kyle pointed out.

"Had. Not have." Moira looked at Kyle and sighed. She closed her eyes, inhaled deeply, and shook her head. "Had until he left my bed and went to my sister's only to sire her child, who I've raised."

"Aidan O'Flaherty was your lover?" Kyle was incredulous.

"Hard to believe he was, isn't it? But not so hard to believe he chose Lizzie instead."

"Why would you ever lie with a man like that?" Kyle snapped.

"You've seen him. He's handsome as the devil, dark hair and all. I thought we loved each other, but it was one-sided. And now I realize it wasn't anything but twisted infatuation. When he realized he could get all the information he wanted from me without marriage, he left my bed and went to Lizzie's. He can barely stand her, but obviously her talents exceed mine."

Kyle sat mute, too stunned to know what to say. He closed his eyes and tried to grasp the one fuzzy thought he could latch on to. "Why would any man choose Lizzie over you?"

"What man wouldn't, given the choice?"

"I sure as hell wouldn't. The woman may be your sister, but she's vile."

"Maybe. But that doesn't mean you haven't bedded her," Moira said as she turned to look at Kyle, surprised by the shock and revulsion on his face.

"Those were Ruairí's fields to plow. Not mine. I never bedded your sister and never will. I'd rather stand naked before the British navy than touch her."

"But surely..."

"Never, Moira. Never. She made the offer more than once when Ruairí and Aidan were too deep in their cups, but never did I accept it."

"But," Moira countered. "I know she went to your chamber the time before last."

"Aye. When she slipped into my bed, I thought she was the serving wench I'd flirted with. But even in a whisper, I recognized her voice. I grabbed my breeks in one hand and my boots and sword in the other. I spent the night in the stall with my horse." Kyle saw the uncertainty, the disbelief in Moira's eyes. He pressed her against his chest, and her head rested against his shoulder. "Moira, I swear to you, I never bedded Lizzie. I've never even wanted to. And given the choice, I hope you've already realized the MacDonnell sister I want is you."

When Moira nodded, Kyle thought she accepted what he said. But he realized that she was nestling closer to him and was already asleep. With a sigh, Kyle carried Moira to his bunk and tucked her under the covers. He lifted the plaid from the foot of the bed and sat beside the head of the bed. He leaned against the wall, allowing his head to rest on the side of the mattress. He hadn't realized how exhausted he was until he sat down with a sleeping Moira next to him. He tilted his head back to watch her sleep, reassured by her steady breathing. The only time he'd ever watched someone sleep was when Ruairí or his twin Keith was ill or injured. He found it soothing to listen to Moira's rhythmic breathing and to watch her peaceful slumber. He drifted off without realizing it.

CHAPTER 6

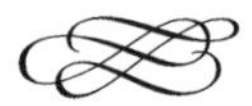

Moira came awake to the sound of soft snores near her ears. She recognized they weren't Sean's, but it took her a moment to recall that she wasn't in the child's chamber at home. She was in Kyle's cabin aboard the *Lady Charity*. Despite lying still, she knew within a breath that she'd woken Kyle.

"I didn't mean to disturb you," Moira whispered.

"Is anything wrong?" Kyle sat up and looked at Moira. He brushed back the hair from her face. She pushed up onto her elbow and started to shake her head until she realized the positions they were in.

"Have you been sleeping on the floor?" She asked aghast.

"I wasn't going to string you up or leave you on the floor. And I don't have the right to share the bed with you," Kyle explained.

Moira huffed and frowned before slipping from the bed and padding across the floor to the table. She felt around until she found the flint and the candle. Once lit, she turned back to Kyle and sighed. She shooed him off the floor and onto the bed. Careful not to reveal too much, she climbed onto the bed and sat cross-legged near the foot while Kyle lay on his side, watching her.

"I still don't understand you, Kyle," Moira admitted. "Why are you so thoughtful one moment and domineering the next?"

Before Kyle could answer, she held up her hand and shook her head. He waited for her to speak, wanting to reach out and smooth the furrows between her brows. "Kyle, I don't understand why I trust you with my body as I do. Maybe it's just desire. Maybe it's knowing I'm not a virgin and have no reason to fear anyone finding out. Lizzie took care of that by announcing Aidan had left my bed to go to hers. But I'm just not ready to trust you with everything. The more you manipulate me, the more I fear telling you."

"I don't know how to take care of a woman, Moira." At her skeptical look, Kyle laughed. "I know how to pleasure a woman, but I don't know how to take care of one. The last time I tried, I was seven and my mother died anyway." Kyle expected to see pity in Moira's eyes, but instead, he recognized something he hadn't seen since Senga was on board: sympathy.

"I was ten when my mother died," Moira responded. "I tried to care for her too, but she wasted away despite my efforts."

"You did? Where was your sister or the healer?"

"Lizzie was already being Lizzie. She's three years my senior, but she's been turning boys' and men's heads since very early on. My mother held a tight rein on us until she fell ill. Then Lizzie turned wild, and I became the responsible one. I'd been the one my mother fretted about. I learned the lessons she taught me about comportment and grace. I learned what I could about being a chatelaine from her. But the moment my lessons were through, I fled. I'd go riding or fishing or for walks along the cliffs. I'd come back filthy, with rips in my stockings and twigs in my hair. When my mother fell ill and it was obvious no one in my family would tend her, there was no choice but to leave my childhood behind."

"You became chatelaine when you were ten?" Kyle was incredulous.

"Not really. I mean, our cook and our head of house continued my lessons about keeping home and hearth in one piece. Our seneschal continued my lessons in reading and maths, so I learned to mind the ledgers. At fifteen I was still naïve, even though I had taken on all the duties as lady of the keep. When Aidan started paying attention to me, I was awestruck. His visits allowed me chances to leave the keep, the walls, and do the things I missed. He'd take me for walks and out on his dinghy to fish. We'd go riding for hours. It seemed natural when he pressed for more. I thought he loved me. I thought it meant he wanted to marry me. I didn't notice that he never actually talked about love, and he never mentioned marriage. Ever."

Moira paused, unsure if Kyle wanted to hear her tale of woe. But his encouraging nod had her drawing a breath before she continued.

"Once Lizzie discovered what we were doing, she decided she wanted Aidan for herself. She announced to everyone in the Great Hall how I was hopelessly besotted with Aidan and thought he would propose soon. She was right, of course. Aidan laughed harder than anyone until he saw my face. He tried to explain that he'd made no promises, and I agreed. Before I finished speaking, Lizzie slid into Aidan's lap and reassured him they could continue on as they had, and that she would never be so foolish as to expect him to marry her. I learned he was already bedding her. Within a year, Sean was born. I had Aidan's son to care for just as I'd daydreamed, except he wasn't mine."

"Was learning that you were no longer a maiden what made Dónal mistreat you?"

"Sort of. He's been a bully all my life. I've always been small, so he took advantage of it. He'd do little things to intimidate me while our father was alive. But once he was chieftain, and there was no one to stop him, he began to pinch my arms or push me. Lizzie revealing what started as a secret and became my greatest shame let Dónal think he could forever berate me about everything. Fighting back wasn't worth the fear of a more severe beatings, so I remained quiet, did what I was told and what I had to, and kept out of sight most of the time. That's why I didn't meet you until last year. Once things went sour with Aidan, I avoided being around him. I avoided being around any of my brother's associates. Once bitten, twice shy."

"Did you run away? Is that why you were a stowaway?" Kyle pressed, but he regretted it as soon as he did. He watched Moira withdraw, and he wanted to kick himself for pushing when she'd already told him she didn't trust him. But she'd confided so much already, he assumed she was willing to tell him more. "Did you know I have a twin?"

Moira frowned as she tried to follow the abrupt change of topic. She shook her head but tried to imagine what it would look like to have two men standing side-by-side with the same appearance. She knew Ruairí and his cousin Rowan were so close in appearance that many mistook them for twins.

"Keith. We don't know which one of us is the elder. Our mother said she could never tell us apart. To this day, we're not sure whether either of us has the correct name." Kyle attempted to laugh, but he feared it sounded brittle. He wasn't sure why he was sharing things no one but Keith knew. He'd never even told Ruairí that. But he felt he owed Moira something secret since she'd shared hers. "Our father abandoned us when we were bairns. Mother said he couldn't stand the sound of two squalling bairns when they'd only married because he got her with child."

Kyle paused, lost in a memory. Moira watched him until he turned a soft smile toward her. She nodded, encouraging him to tell more of his story.

"Mother was sickly for as long as I can remember," Kyle

continued. "One village woman or another was always shooing Keith and me out of the cottage to let her rest. We played with some other children, but most parents didn't want us near their weans. They feared we'd give them bugs or the ague, since we always seemed to have a runny nose. When our mother died, a neighbor took us in but soon decided that two seven-year-old lads ate too much but couldn't do enough work. She turned us out."

"Merciful saints," Moira breathed. She suddenly felt shallow, complaining about thwarted love that never was and obnoxious siblings when Kyle grew up with nothing. He reached out and covered her hands with his.

"Don't feel guilty because your life wasn't what mine was. You've had more burdens on your shoulders than you should have, too." Kyle squeezed her hand and was prepared to pull his back when she turned her hand over. Their palms rested together as Kyle continued. "There was no poorhouse in our tiny village, but we did odd jobs for scraps of food and cast-off clothing. Keith and I stole when we had to, and I'm certain people turned more than one blind eye because we were always polite. We learned early that minding our Ps and Qs let us get away with mischief. But Laird MacLean learned of the twin urchins when he visited the spring after Mother died. He refused to allow us to remain homeless and penniless. He sold us into indenture instead. We would run away every time someone would threaten to separate us until Laird MacLean finally grew too fed up. He dumped us on the coast and said we would sink or swim, but we were no longer his problem. That night we were pulled from the crates we hid behind and brought on our first ship."

"You were only eight?"

"As best we ken. We might be a year older or a year younger," Kyle said with a shrug. "Just as with our indenture, we fought and ran away any time a captain threatened to separate us. We even fooled a captain for three moons into thinking there was only one of us." Kyle grinned, and Moira couldn't help but return it.

"How did you come to be on the *Lady Charity*?"

"Actually, we were on the *Lady Grace*. That's Keith's ship now. We joined the crew the autumn before Rowan and Ruairí joined in the spring. We were about five-and-ten, so Keith and I are close in age to Ruairí and Rowan. Rowan had barely healed from being deathly ill, and while both were experienced sailors, neither had been on our type of ship."

"Pirates, you mean."

"Aye. Keith and I kenned from the start what type of men took us. Rowan and Ruairí were duped into thinking they were joining a merchant ship. After a few years, the captain had to trade Ruairí to another ship when he killed a man in a tavern brawl. It was the other captain's right to replace his fallen man. The son of a bitch was worse than any man we'd ever sailed for. Rowan inherited the *Lady Grace* from the previous captain, and his crew voted to keep him on as captain. Ruairí led a mutiny on his. Once he had command, he reunited with Rowan, and the captains gave Keith and me the choice of becoming first mates. I came aboard with Ruairí, and Keith stayed with Rowan."

"You must have missed your brother terribly once you were on separate ships. After all that time fighting to stay together." Moira snapped her mouth shut when he realized what her comment implied. Kyle tugged at her hand until she crawled toward him. He settled her beside him with his arm beneath her neck.

"I did. But Rowan and Ruairí had fought hard to stay together, too. They were only apart for a few months before Ruairí became captain. Most of the time the *Grace* and the *Charity* sailed together. And when we didn't, we were rarely apart for more than a moon or two."

"But what about Keith now?"

When Kyle didn't answer immediately, she rolled over to look up at him. She didn't understand his bright smile. "Lass, the *Lady Grace* is to the starboard side. That's why you can't see her. I spotted your ship first, so Keith had to let me have it. My brother and I always sail together. We're strong alone, but we're invincible together." Kyle watched a cloud pass over Moira's face as she nodded before looking away. "What is it, sweet one?"

"No one is invincible, Kyle. My father thought so, and he died for his arrogance. Dónal thought so, and nearly didn't return home from Lewis."

"Dinna fash, lassie," Kyle said with an exaggerated brogue. "Ye Irish think ye can spin a yarn, but ye dinna ken what a Hebridean or a Highlander can do. Ye have naught but bedtime stories compared to us."

"Prone to exaggeration. Is that what you're trying to tell me?" Moira rolled back onto her side and cupped Kyle's cheek. "You are who you are. I think I'd like you to stay alive long enough to remain that way."

Gazes locked for several long moments, then their lips brushed one another's before fusing together. Kyle pressed Moira onto her back, and she pulled at his shoulder to urge him to follow. Finding her hand, their fingers entwined before Kyle raised her arm, allowing him to rest on his forearms. He kept his weight off her, partially afraid he would crush her much smaller frame, and to ensure she knew he wouldn't force her. He slid his thigh between hers, and she clamped her legs around it. Moira's back arched as she writhed beneath Kyle, the feel of his thigh against her mound reigniting the unspent lust from earlier that night. Releasing her hand, he pulled the leine down her shoulder until he could free one of her breasts. His tongue flicked her nipple over and over until it puckered, then he suckled as she pressed his head to her chest.

"Kyle," Moira rasped in desperation.

"I ken, sweet one. I'll bring you what I denied you earlier."

With a moan, Moira captured Kyle's head before he returned to her breast. She guided him to look at her. "Do I have your permission to find my release?"

Kyle stilled for a moment before he launched an assault on all of her senses. Each moan that escaped Moira's throat drove him to bring forth another. When her fingers bit into his upper arms and her back bowed off the bed, he pulled back to watch her climax.

"Kyle, more," Moira begged.

"Wheest, Moira. Soon, but not tonight."

"What? Why?" Moira pleaded.

"Because you've been through too much today, and I've pushed you too hard. When we come together, it will be solely your choice."

"And if I choose now?" Moira demanded.

"You said you trust me with your body. Trust me with this. Trust that I want to care for more than just your body."

Moira stared at Kyle in the flickering candlelight. Just before the candle burned out, she nodded. Kyle wrapped Moira in his embrace and pulled her against his side. It was the first time either of them slept through the night with someone else beside them.

CHAPTER 7

Moira came awake once more, but she knew she was alone in the bed, in the cabin. As she sat up, her eyes swept the cabin. Someone, assumedly Kyle, laid a tray on the table with more bread and cheese. But as she looked around, she couldn't spy the leggings he'd stripped off her the night prior. She suspected someone found her sack of clothes while they raided the MacDonnells' ship. As she climbed out of bed, a groan escaped. She'd slept on her side and stomach all night, so she hadn't realized how sore her backside was from Kyle's punishment. Heat flooded her as she recalled the feeling of his hands on her—in her. She felt the blush creep into her cheeks, and she was relieved she was alone. She'd given in the night before and been more wanton that she ever was with Aidan.

As she moved around the cabin, still in search of her leggings, Moira was forced to accept that they were missing. She gazed at her calves that showed below the leine's hem. She glanced around, wondering where her boots were.

Bluidy bastard. He gives me more than bread and watered ale, but not by much. Then, rather than stringing me up like a butcher does a heifer, he's taken my clothes. He knows I won't dare leave the cabin without being properly covered up.

Moira squinted her eyes as she glanced at the door. She would give Kyle the time it took for her to eat before she tried the door. She sat down and gobbled the food before her, not aware of how famished she'd been. She shifted her gaze to the door several times, wondering when Kyle might return. When she didn't look at the door, she looked out of the porthole. She estimated it was midmorning. She never slept that late, but then again, she'd never hidden from pirates, feared for her life, or been tortured by a man she was ready to couple with only hours earlier. She figured she was entitled to being a little tired.

I wasn't exactly tortured. The pain might have felt like it, but it was more neglect than anything else. I doubt that man Snake Eye realized what he was doing; he was only doing what he's undoubtedly done many times before. Kyle didn't know until he finally decided to give me his presence. Arrogant bastard that he is. But a handsome, arrogant bastard at that. I blame my willingness to give in so easily on being distraught. But were you really all that distraught? Not once you realized he wouldn't kill you immediately. Not once he touched you. But damn it, I didn't have to give in that easily. Aidan wooed me for months before I gave in. Kyle didn't woo me at all, and it was a matter of minutes.

Not again. Not unless it's on my terms.

Moira searched and found a small comb on the washstand that she ran through her hair. She'd had it pinned up and under a cap while she was in the hold. Her hair had fallen out of its braid sometime while she waited for Kyle to return to the cabin the first time. She attempted to make herself as presentable as possible before she crossed the cabin and tried the door.

Idiot. He really does believe I won't leave this cabin without being properly covered. I spent the night in a pirate captain's cabin. I shred any reputation I might have had the moment I stepped aboard this floating prison. And what do I care about these men and what they think of me?

Taking a deep breath and firming the resolve she pretended to possess, she stepped into the passageway and looked around. She could hear men above her, but she saw no one in the corridor. Seizing the opportunity to orient herself on the ship, she moved away from the ladder well that would take her to the top deck. She tried doors as she slipped along, finding the galley and another cabin. She assumed that was for Kyle's first mate. When she came to the hatch leading to the hold, she debated whether she should try to slip inside. She opted against it, fearful that she might lock herself below. Instead, she retraced her steps, took another fortifying breath, and ascended the ladder well. She paused for a moment while still out of sight and let her eyes adjust to the dazzling sunlight reflected off the water. Blinking against their watering, she glanced around at what she could see. Furrowing her brow, she gazed at a cloud for several moments before she realized it remained in the same position. They weren't moving, or rather the boat's movement was from bobbing in the tide, not from sailing.

Have we sailed at all? He said a few hours when I asked him, but maybe we haven't gone anywhere. Why are we stopped? Whatever the reason, at least we're not any closer to the O'Malleys.

Moira continued to observe the crew on the deck. Men swabbed the deck, worked the riggings, and a few slept. She caught sight of Kyle at the helm, but she knew he hadn't seen her. Why would he? He wouldn't expect her to appear before him. She took the first step onto the deck, careful not to get a splinter in her foot from an uneven plank. When no shouts went up, she set her shoulders and lifted her chin.

With all the grace she possessed, Moira glided across the deck toward Kyle. His fury was obvious the moment he noticed her. He barked an order to someone she didn't know and left the wheel. Moira watched a man of a similar build to Kyle, but a little shorter, dash to take control of the ship. Kyle's stride was purposeful but unhurried. Moira understood he meant to intimidate her by making her wait, but after years of Dónal's tantrums, it took more than an angry stride and glaring looks to sway her. She continued forward until they met in the middle.

"Good morning, Capt'n," Moira crooned.

"Get back in my cabin now," Kyle hissed.

"But I was lonely," Moira said innocently. She gave him an expression to match her tone.

"You will go back over my knee," Kyle warned.

"Promise?"

"Moira."

"Kyle," Moira whispered.

Kyle's arm shot out and wrapped around her waist and hefted her off her feet. He clomped over to the rail and lifted her to sit on it but held her securely with his brawny arm as they both looked at the water. He pressed his chest to her back, his strength more of a reassurance than a threat to Moira.

"I can swim. Besides, you have a woman to bed aboard your ship. You won't toss me when you have me captive to do with as you like," Moira reasoned.

"You may be more trouble than you're worth," Kyle snarled.

"You won't know until you try me." Moira couldn't believe the words she was uttering. It was as though she'd turned into a stranger. Or worse: she'd turned into Lizzie.

"Painting yourself as a whore?" Kyle slid his free hand along her thigh and under the leine until his fingers brushed the curls on her mons. "Is this what you want? Is this why you're parading yourself around half-dressed? Or are you offering yourself to my men? Because I'm certain they will accept."

"If you don't want me to appear like this before your crew, you should've left me my leggings or my kirtles."

"Or I can be sure never to leave without locking the door," Kyle retorted. Moira said nothing, but opened her legs wide in further invitation. He slipped a finger inside her sheath and felt, rather than heard, her sharp inhale. With her hands gripping the rail, she forced herself not to let her head drop back against Kyle's chest. She suspected the men couldn't see what Kyle was doing with his hand, but they could see if she leaned against him. "Do you like people to watch, sweet one?"

Moira had an answer, but she couldn't force the words out between her lips. Her breasts ached, and her nipples stung from both the crisp Irish air and from the need for Kyle's attention. They remained silent as Kyle continued to work Moira's channel until she could no longer fight the response.

"May I climax, Drifter?" Moira whispered. With a growl, Kyle increased the pressure and speed of his ministrations until he felt Moira's inner muscles clench around him. Her fingers now wrapped around the forearm that kept her from slipping over the rail.

"And what shall you do for me now, sweet one, that you've given me a rampant cockstand?" Kyle whispered against her ear before pressing a brief kiss behind it.

"What do you want from me, Drifter?"

"Don't call me that. Not like this," Kyle muttered.

"What do you want from me, Kyle?"

"To be inside you. To let my men watch as I plow you, so none are in doubt that you're mine."

"You'd want them to see me like that? If not naked, with my arse to the breeze?" Moira asked with feigned incredulity. "You brought me aboard your ship. I slept in your cabin. Your hand is up my leine and in my cunny. I'm pretty certain there isn't a man on this ship who doesn't know I'm your captive."

"And if I want you as my mistress instead?"

"In this case, are they not one and the same?"

"If I refuse to return your clothes and shoes, if I lock you in my cabin, will you still call yourself my mistress?"

"Will you be tupping me?" Kyle's only response to Moira's

question was a growl as his fingers pinched her nipples until he was certain it was painful.

"Do you still want me to?" Kyle wondered.

"What else will there be to entertain me?" Moira shrugged. "So captive or mistress. Captive and mistress. One and the same at this point, wouldn't you say?"

"But you decide how you're treated when I'm not between your creamy thighs, sweet one." Kyle trailed his fingers along the inside of her thigh, and Moira couldn't fight the shiver of arousal it created.

A particularly rough wave slammed into the ship's boards, and icy water from the Irish Sea splashed up Moira's legs, soaking the ends of her leine. Another wave, even larger than the first, drenched the front of Moira. With a shiver, Moira accepted that she had to admit defeat.

"Kyle, this leine will be sheer now and is going to stick to me. It was one thing when I knew your men could see the bottom of my legs and my feet. I didn't intend for them to see my nipples," Moira confessed. "They'll see everything."

"And you wish for me to save you the embarrassment, the shame?" Kyle scoffed.

"I'd like to keep how I look private for just you," Moira spat. "But if you're set on humiliating me..."

Kyle lifted Moira down from the rail, setting her on her feet, and using his larger body to shield her, he grasped her buttocks and squeezed. "I will take you to my cabin, where you will strip off the shirt and give it to me. And you will await me there, kneeling in the corner just as a naughty wean would, until I return to dole out your spanking."

"And if I don't agree?" Moira argued.

"You already did. Each time you let me touch you without a fight. Each time you come apart with my hands. When you took me in your mouth and hummed. You like this as much as I do, Moira."

"I do, and I don't understand why," Moira whispered, tears threatening once again. She didn't know if it was being cold or another wave of exhaustion, but she was confused and had no will to fight Kyle or the truth. Kyle's emerald eyes met her sapphire ones, locked in a gaze that communicated physical need. He could see the truth in her gaze, and he understood that while Moira might know the acts that went on between a man and a woman, might even enjoy them, she was out of her depth to understand the power exchange they shared. She didn't understand why she wanted to submit. Even so, he was certain that she did want to submit. He lifted Moira over his shoulder, her hair tumbling down his back and swishing against his thighs as he carried her to the ladder well. He swatted her bottom with one stinging slap that echoed even on the open sea. "Was that for your men's sake?"

"Aye. And yours. You will remain silent until we reach my cabin, and I'm done talking." Kyle felt the fight go out of Moira as her body relaxed against his shoulder. Once they were inside, Kyle lowered her to her feet once again, and motioned for her to raise her arms. Still sore from the day before, she groaned as Kyle pulled the sodden leine over her head and tossed it onto the back of a chair tucked under the table. He looked over Moira's shivering body, and just as it always seemed to do when she was within reach, his cock took notice.

Kyle watched Moira as her eyes settled on the bulge within his breeks. She glanced up at him, and he could read the question in her eyes. It nearly killed him to shake his head. He might not have any qualms about denying Moira her pleasure, but it was agony to deny his own. He pulled the MacLean plaid from the foot of his bed and wrapped it around Moira, rubbing her arms and back. She'd spoken the truth that only her arms were bruised. He'd noticed her grazed chin, but there weren't any other noticeable injuries. At least, there were none on the surface.

"Moira, you knew what you were doing by coming above deck in nothing but a man's leine. You did it to instigate trouble and to gain my attention. You disregarded the common sense I'm certain you possess by traipsing around half naked in front of not only men, but pirates!" Kyle took a calming breath as he felt his blood pounding in his neck. "While I may not have explicitly ordered you to remain here, you knew that's what I wanted because I removed your boots and leggings. You defied me, Moira, and I will not tolerate any defiance aboard my ship. I don't allow it from my men, and I won't allow you to inspire mutiny because they suddenly think I'm weak. If you were a man, your defiance would earn you the lash before the rest of the crew. Instead, you shall receive your punishment in the privacy of this room. But do not doubt that I will mete out justice, Moira."

As Moira listened, she only half-heard what Kyle said. Each time he used her name, she wanted to cringe. In the space of a day, she'd grown accustomed to him calling her "sweet one," and it was jarring to hear him address her any other way.

"Are you listening to me?" Kyle demanded.

Moira looked at him blankly before hesitantly shaking her head. "How do I earn back being called 'sweet one?'"

"What?" Kyle expected her to beg for forgiveness, to blurt out an apology, to even sulk. He was unprepared for her question.

"I don't like you using my name," Moira confessed.

"I'm displeased with you," Kyle stated flatly.

"I know. And I want to know what I can do to earn back your—" Moira didn't know if it was his trust, his affection, or his lust that she wanted to earn back. Whatever it was, it was a need that threatened to swallow her just as the waves crashing against the hull would.

"Kneel in the corner until I return, Moira." Kyle waited until she was positioned in the nook, with her nose inches from the corner. He crossed the room and bent over her, tugging back on her hair. He pressed his lips to hers, plunging his tongue into her mouth as she immediately surrendered. His other hand pulled the plaid apart and cupped her breast, squeezing gently as his thumb ran over her nipple. Just as Moira made to reach out for him, he once again pinched her nipple until he knew it was painful. He pulled away and stalked back to the door. "And don't you dare touch yourself."

Moira watched the door swing closed and heard the key in the lock. She turned back to face the wall and contemplated what she'd gotten herself into.

CHAPTER 8

Kyle shaded the candle with his palm as he turned in the direction of the goods they'd stolen from Moira's ship. Looking between containers, he finally found what he sought. He reached for Moira's sack, then placed the candle on top of a barrel. He opened the bag and rummaged through it, finding only a few changes of clothes. There were no coins, nothing personal.

Where could she have been going that she didn't need more clothes or any money? Who would take her in with just the clothes on her back and nothing to offer in return? Maybe she intended to work wherever she went. Would she find a village and claim to be a widow? As far as I know she doesn't know anything about running a farm or livestock. At least, I don't think she does. But how the hell would I know? Maybe she was going to a town where she could hire herself out to be a seamstress or a servant. Can she cook? I'm certain she sews. What lady doesn't? She's better suited for giving orders than taking them.

That's not true. She's already told me that Dónal treats her like a servant. Did that bastard give her the cut on her chin? Maybe she could be a servant. I would wager she's a hard worker and asks for very little. Her defiance is based in fear. She fears me, and why wouldn't she? She'd be daft not to fear the man who threatened to set her adrift.

Kyle looked inside the sack and considered whether he wanted to return the clothing to Moira. He pictured her as she'd been when she walked on deck. Her trim legs emerging from the bottom of the leine. He'd truly believed taking her leggings and boots would be enough to keep her inside. He even thought to test her by leaving the door unlocked, giving her just enough freedom to feel trapped. He'd meant to control her, and instead she'd taken control. Kyle felt equal parts annoyance and intrigue. The Moira who boarded his ship was not the woman he'd spied at Dunluce, not the woman he'd heard about in passing.

Scowling, Kyle closed the bag and dropped it back where he found it. He would indulge himself in having a half-naked woman in his cabin, and he would ensure Moira understood who captained this ship. If she refused, then he would put her ashore somewhere. He'd give her enough coin to find her way back to Dunluce or to start fresh somewhere. What she did once she was out of sight wasn't his problem.

Do you really believe that?

The same mix of conscience and desire that forced him to bring her onboard the *Lady Charity* rather than have her thrown overboard reared its head. He admitted to himself that he wanted Moira to be his problem. He wanted to see if she was the woman he sensed: a woman who wanted to submit to him. A woman who needed a teacher, a mentor of sorts, to show her what lay dormant within her. A man who would shoulder the burden of the outside world while freeing her inhibitions.

Kyle's cock hardened as he pictured several scenes that he longed to enact. Some were ones he'd held for years and never been able to fulfill while others were specific to Moira herself. The sounds she'd made while his fingers worked her core had nearly pushed him over the edge. As he remembered them, his cock ached so badly that he adjusted himself to ease the discomfort. His eyes swept the hold, and he was tempted to stroke himself until the need to dominate eased, until he could be inside her.

Kyle scowled at the sky as the gale hurled icy drops of rain against his face. He'd emerged from the hold to discover the sky had turned gray, and heavy clouds threatened to release their torrent. An hour later, Kyle was soaked and freezing. He longed for nothing more than to slip into his cabin and rub himself dry before donning fresh clothes and wrapping himself in his plaid. He considered where his plaid had been last: wrapped around Moira.

Wrapping myself around Moira would be a more pleasurable way to get warm. I should check on her. The seas have been rough, and she's unaccustomed to the jarring feel. She might be ill and suffering. She's been kneeling for more than an hour. That punishment should suffice.

But Kyle had no choice. He had to remain on deck while the storm battered the ship and crew. He prayed Moira had enough sense to give up kneeling and at least sit on the floor, if not a chair or the bed. As the ship rocked and the wood creaked, Kyle wondered if this was the storm that would rip the *Lady Charity* apart. He'd survived worse, but he wasn't sure if the ship would. He wiped the water from his eyes as he craned his neck to see the crew of the *Lady Grace,* which bobbed in the water alongside him but a safe distance to prevent the waves from crashing them together. He could make out the matching waves of red hair standing at the helm. As though he sensed his twin, Keith looked over at Kyle. The brothers waved to one another as they braced themselves against the wheel.

"Tomas!" Kyle called out to his first mate. Bent against the wind, Tomas fought his way to Kyle's side. "We can't go anywhere now. We must anchor and furl the sails before we're blown into the cliffs or the *Lady Grace*. Go to the rail and call over to the *Grace*." He'd been prepared to signal to his brother that they should be underway once more as he left the hold, but the brewing storm made him wary. There'd been no wind and the seas had been calm, so the *Lady Charity* and the *Lady Grace* had remained near where Kyle attacked the MacDonnell ship.

While Tomas struggled to the side of the ship to call out to the nearest crewman on the *Lady Grace,* Kyle called out orders for the men to drop the anchor. All the other hands worked to bring down the sails. He glanced up to ensure that Braedon wasn't in the crow's nest. Looking down, he found the boy instead lashed to the mainmast. Without the weight of the adult men, Braedon would have been blown hither and yon, more likely to wind up overboard. Ruairí had ordered the boy to tie himself to the mast during any rough seas, and Kyle kept the same mandate. Braedon sat with his knees drawn to his chest and his head tucked. Kyle breathed easier.

The boat shuddered as it jerked in place as the anchor bit into the sea bottom. He noticed the *Lady Grace*'s crew lowered their sails, and the ship remained alongside his. Calling Snake Eye over to keep watch at the helm, Kyle pushed against the gusts to stand on the starboard side. Keith met him when their ships drew close enough for them to yell over the storm's noise.

"We have to wait it out," Keith called.

"I know. Look," Kyle pointed to the sky in all directions. "This isn't going to blow over any time soon. We're stuck here for at least the next day."

"Then we'll have to assess the damages. I don't like the sounds coming from my yardarm."

"Is it going to give?" Kyle worried.

"It might. I don't want to risk it, so when this stops, my crew will have to repair it."

"I must give the hull a look while you work on that. Nothing I can do about damage below the water for now, but I can sure up any boards that we can reach," Kyle thought aloud.

"This isn't an ideal place to remain," Keith pointed out. "The O'Malleys sail these waters, and they won't hesitate to attack."

"I ken. Why can't they stick to their own bluidy side of the island?" Kyle grumbled.

"Because no one sails that strip of the Atlantic?" Keith mused. "Anyway, I'm headed back to the helm. I suggest you and your men tie yourselves down. I shall do the same."

"I love you," the brothers mouthed, knowing this might become the storm that could separate them.

Kyle called out the order that the men tie themselves to the rigging, and he used rope to bind himself to the wheel. He wondered how Moira fared below deck. He wished more than ever to check on her, but the wind and rain had only intensified while he talked to Keith. He'd barely made it to the helm without sliding and falling. As the boat continued to pitch and heel, Kyle was relieved that he'd ordered the men to tie themselves down, or several would have likely slipped overboard. Moira was surely being tossed about the cabin. He was going to his cabin the first chance he had.

CHAPTER 9

Moira gripped the headboard as the ship rocked from side to side. She watched as books and maps flew from the table, the bowl on the washstand crashed to the floor, and Kyle's trunks slid across the cabin. She'd remained kneeling until a particularly powerful swell made her lose her balance and knock her head against the wall. She abandoned her punishment, reasoning that Kyle would want her safe; if he didn't, then she cared not. She'd scrambled onto the bed, waiting out the storm that seemed intent upon tearing the boards apart. She listened to the creaks and groans, fearing the boat would splinter at any moment. She could hear the wind above, but the sounds of the ship rattled around her.

As the storm carried on, the air in the cabin grew colder. Moira shivered as she pulled Kyle's plaid more snuggly around her and burrowed under the meager covers. Never would she admit it, but she longed for the warmth of Kyle's body beside her. She even wished for her draughty chamber back at Dunluce. If such a storm had pounded her home at night, she would have crawled into bed beside Sean to calm his fears. She would have stroked his soft inky curls as she sang him lullabies.

When he tired of those, she would tell him stories of the ancient kings of Ireland, or the monsters that roamed the sea around Rathlin Island and Ballycastle.

Moira's stomach roiled as the boat tilted precariously to port. She squeezed her eyes shut, praying she could sleep through the rest of the storm. As the hours passed, she wondered how Kyle was surviving above. She had waves of panic that he'd been washed overboard, drowning in the churning abyss. A headache throbbed behind her eyes, and she wasn't certain if it came from the noise and movement or her concern for Kyle.

Why do I care? Is it because I don't want to be left aboard this bleeding ship without his protection? No. You know that's not the truth. I'm worried about him. I'm worried that he won't return to challenge me, to—what? Pleasure me? Is that my priority? No. I just wish to see his face, touch him and know that he's well. I'm so bluidy scared. I wish he could come below. I wish he could climb into bed beside me and hold me. I just wish he could make this all go away.

Eventually, fatigue drained Moira of her strength. She rolled as close to the wall as she could, using the pillows as a barrier to the edge. She hoped they would be enough to keep her from falling off the bunk. She let her eyes drift closed. Without realizing it, she was asleep.

The howling rain let up long enough for Kyle to inspect the hull. He breathed easier when he found only small dribbles of water rather than pools. He could have his men reinforce the spots that seemed weak, but there was no reason to fear that the boat would capsize or swamp. With Moira onboard, he felt even more compelled to ensure the ship's condition. He'd never once considered a sole person's well-being when he made decisions about his ship, but knowing Moira was with him created an urgency he hadn't felt before.

When he finished touring the hold, he made his way to his cabin. Unprepared for what he might find, he steeled himself for the mess and an irate woman. He eased the door open, first taking in the mess, then catching sight of Moira sleeping on his bunk. He smiled to himself as he wondered how long she'd slumbered and how she was even able to sleep through the storm. But worry took hold when he feared she wasn't sleeping, but unconscious. He crossed the cabin and peered down at Moira. Her eyes fluttered open, and she screamed, unprepared to find a face hovering over hers.

"Bluidy bleeding hell, Kyle," Moira snapped. "You leave me down here to rattle around like teeth in an old woman's head, then terrify me when you wake me."

Kyle reeled back from the biting words, reminding himself that he had startled her, and she likely spent the entire storm petrified. But her murderous glare tested his already frayed patience. Gritting his teeth, he stepped away from the bunk, noticing the puddle he'd created. With a scowl, he stomped across the cabin to where one of his chests landed and ripped open the lid before pulling out drying linens. He slammed the lid shut and moved to the other chest that held his clothes. Kyle tossed a fresh leine and leggings on the table before pulling his sodden boots from his feet. Peeling off the clothes that stuck to him like a second skin, he ignored the watching Moira.

Unwilling to let her witness his arousal, which stirred despite his annoyance at both her and his own body, he remained turned away from her. When Moira gasped, he looked back over his shoulder to find her staring at his legs.

"What?" Kyle growled.

"The bruises," Moira hissed as she pointed to the back of his thighs. He knew what she meant. He'd tied the ropes around his ribs and thighs to keep him upright.

"Wishing I'd been cast overboard?" Kyle snarled as he pulled leggings on but left them unlaced. He walked past the table, not bothering with the leine despite being chilled. "While you slept away the day, I tried to keep us afloat."

Moira's eyes widened as she realized her sour mood when she awoke only provoked Kyle's frazzled nerves. She kneeled at the edge of the bed and beckoned him to sit on the bed beside her. Despite narrowing his eyes, he relented and sat down. Moira shuffled to kneel behind him as she massaged his hunched shoulders. She'd grown cold earlier, but Kyle's skin was like ice. She dropped the plaid from her bare shoulders.

"You'll catch your death. Come lie with me, so I can warm you."

"Lie with you?" Kyle smirked, purposely misinterpreting her meaning. "Is that all you think about, you lusty little wench?"

Moira's lips pursed before she returned his smirk. "At least the only important part of you would be warm." Her eyes widened when his eyes turned thunderous. "I jest," she whispered.

"I came to ensure you were safe, and you've hissed and snarled like a harpy. Then you tell me the only thing you care about is my cock. Fear not, sweet one, I shall give you just what you want." Kyle pressed Moira onto her back before he rose and stripped off his fresh leggings. He crawled onto the bed, waiting for Moira to cower, to shun him. Instead she opened her arms to him and made space for him between her legs.

Kyle drove into her with a single thrust, the feeling as close to heaven as he could imagine. He gazed down at Moira to ensure he hadn't hurt her. Her welcoming smile urged him to capture her mouth in a punishing kiss as he surged into her with abandon. He used his body to pin her to the mattress as he plundered her mouth and her sheath. Unable to move with him, Moira tried to writhe, but Kyle captured her wrists and lifted her arms over her head.

"My cock is all you wanted, so it is all you shall get," Kyle growled. He watched Moira's pupils dilate until they nearly flooded her sapphire irises. He knew she must be in pain from how he relentlessly pounded into her, but she said nothing, giving no indication that she wanted him to stop. She looked aroused. All too soon for his taste, he felt his bollocks tightening. He intended to punish Moira, but he hadn't intended to punish himself. He wanted to draw out the sensations of being within her body, the bliss that came from joining with Moira for the first time. But what his mind—and his heart—wanted didn't coincide with his body's need for release. Unable to hold back, he withdrew, with his essence spreading across Moira's belly. He moved off the bed, not looking at Moira as he put his leggings back on and donned his leine. He retrieved dry stockings from his chest and found his spare pair of boots scrunched between the chest and wall.

Kyle knew she would ache with the unspent lust. He knew she'd be uncomfortable until he deigned to remedy her predicament. If his rod was all she wanted, then that was all she would get. She wouldn't get his sentiments, his need to ensure her pleasure. She would get the one part she wanted, but he wouldn't let her have what she desired. He crossed back to the bunk to stand beside a shivering Moira, who watched him as though he were an unpredictable wild animal. He supposed he was.

"Touch yourself, and I shall know. Ease the ache in your quim, and you will earn yourself a thrashing, Moira. We shall see if my cock is the only thing you want from me. I gave you what you said you wanted. You never asked for release."

"Would you have given it to me if I asked?" Moira wondered.

"No." Kyle turned his back on her yet again and stormed out of the cabin, leaving Moira distressed and unsatisfied.

Kyle felt unsettled after leaving Moira. He assumed it was the need to set his crew to work since the rain had slowed, and the wind was manageable. But he couldn't push Moira from the forefront of his mind. It was one thing to deny her pleasure while they were engaged in their foreplay, but it was the second time he'd done it as a punishment. He hadn't thought twice about it the first time, and he didn't feel guilty the second time. But he missed seeing the rapture on her face, hearing her moans as he made her climax. He felt hollow.

With tasks aplenty to keep him busy, he ordered men into the hold to repair the weakened spots along the hull. He sent a handful of men to the *Lady Grace* to assist Keith's repairs to his yardarm. Several of the sails on the *Lady Charity* had been tattered by the wind before they had been lowered. He ordered them down and mended. The rain kept him chilled just as his heart felt. He wished he could offer his men respite in the galley and passageways, but with the weather still unpredictable, they had to work while they could. It wasn't the first storm they'd pushed through.

"Braedon, how do you fare?" Kyle asked as he stood beside the adolescent. "Not too battered?"

"No, Capt'n. A wee banged about, but no worse for wear."

"Good. I don't want you in the nest until this wind ceases altogether. The last thing I need is for a gust to carry you off," Kyle warned with a grin. He was fond of the lad, seeing much of himself in the youth. He and Keith had been barrel men at different points in their piratical lives. He knew the freedom that came from spending his days in the crow's nest, the feeling of soaring above the world. But he also knew the perils of a captain who didn't care, who ordered the scouts up the mast in inclement weather. He was harsh with his crew, but he didn't purposely endanger their lives, and he drew the line at risking a mere boy.

With some time to prepare before the next onslaught, men

pitched tarps that would provide them some protection for when the storm inevitably returned. They worked until the grim cloud cover made it impossible to see. Ordering his men once more to batten down the hatches and lash themselves to the gunwales, he tied the wheel in place before tying himself to it. The minutes felt like an eternity as the crew of both ships waited for the new deluge. When it came, it made the previous storm appear like a spring shower. Water washed onto the decks as swells crashed over the sides. The only blessing Kyle saw was that the boat keeled away from the waves, sending the water off the opposite side rather than accumulating on the wood planking. He kept his eyes on the water, trying to predict each surge and how it would hit.

Despite more than two decades at sea, Kyle had never experienced a storm as intense as the one that battered them. It was impossible to tell if it was day or night because the sun or moon was blocked. The sea was slate colored, and he expected Neptune to rise from the depths and skewer the *Lady Charity* and *Lady Grace* with his trident. Not as superstitious as most sailors, Kyle still wondered if a sea creature would emerge to wrap its tentacles around the ships and draw the men to their deaths. When he dared look away, his eyes traveled to the hatch leading to where his cabin lay. He may have watched the water, but his mind returned to Moira over and over.

A bolt of lightning struck the water not far off the *Lady Grace*'s starboard side, creating a phenomenon Kyle had never seen. The epicenter of the strike sucked water into a sinking whirlpool while the water surrounding the site pulsated, driving waves in all directions. The enormous ripples slammed into the *Lady Grace* first, then the *Lady Charity*. The ships trembled as though a giant swung them between his fingers. Both ships keeled so far to port that the gunwales nearly touched the surf. Then just as suddenly as the water roared toward the ships, it was drawn back toward the whirlpool. In the next blink, the sea returned to its regular churning brew.

With the next monstrous clap of thunder and gust of wind, two of the shrouds–the lines that supported and kept the main-mast upright–snapped. A loud crack warned Kyle only moments before the foot of the mainsail tore from the mast. It crashed to the desk, the weight of the rolled sail adding to its force. The front of the beam pierced the deck and disappeared under the planks.

Moira!

The beam would have entered the cabin across from the bunk, but he had no way to know where Moira was at the time of impact. He fought the soaked rope with fingers so cold they felt as though they would snap. Once free, he fought against the rolling waves and wind as he descended the steps from the helm. Grabbing the rope that was tied between the helm and mast, he pulled himself hand over hand. He heard Tomas's voice, but he didn't try to make out the words. His only concern was getting to his cabin.

When he reached the mast, Kyle paused to catch his breath, his heart pounding behind his ribs. He could only hear the howl of the wind, the rain making it impossible to see. The crew tied ropes in a cross from the mast, connecting the bow and stern and each side in case they needed to move around the deck just as Kyle was. Taking a deep breath, Kyle pushed on, trying to calm his fears and his breathing.

Kyle fell more than jumped past the ladder well and stumbled as he slammed against the bulkhead. Crashing from side to side, he made his way to his cabin. He tried to push the door open, but something obstructed the doorway. He pounded on the door.

"Moira!" Bang, bang, bang. "Moira!" He knocked another loud trio, but he heard nothing from the cabin. For all he knew, she was screaming and he couldn't hear her. Or perhaps she couldn't hear him. He leaned his shoulder against the door and pushed, but the ship tilted away from the cabin's side. His feet slid on the floor as he tried to gain purchase. Just as quickly as it listed to one side, it pitched to the other. The force allowed Kyle to drive the door open.

"Kyle!" Moira clung to the headboard as she had during the first round of the storm. The table had slid against the door and remained unmovable as the ship pitched back and forth. Unable to push it out of his way, Kyle scrambled over the tabletop and rolled onto the bed. He swept Moira into his arms as she trembled. The jagged point of the foot beam that stuck inches into the cabin drew his gaze. It hadn't breached the cabin as badly as he expected, and the post was nowhere near Moira.

"I'm here, sweet one. I'm not letting you go," Kyle promised as he buried his face in Moira's hair, relieved to find her unharmed.

"I thought the—" She waved a hand in the sail's direction without turning her head away from Kyle's chest. "Whatever that thing is, was going to skewer me when it burst through the wall. I tried to get above deck, but I couldn't move the table. It was wedged between the door and bunk. I was so scared that thing was going to slide further into the cabin."

"I know, sweet one. That's why I came to you. I feared the same," Kyle confessed. Moira clung to Kyle as she recited every prayer she knew at least twice. He couldn't keep his lips from twitching when he heard his name more than once. He suspected God had forgotten about him long ago, so "redemption" and "savior" didn't sound like achievable requests for his fate. But he felt Moira's body release some of its tension as she prayed. He would support anything that eased her fears.

"The wind sounds so horrible. And from the way the water slapped against the porthole, I knew it was washing onto the deck. I was so scared you would be washed away. All I could picture was the ropes around you fraying and the wind carrying you off before it dropped you into the depths," Moira said around the lump in her throat.

"I told you, I'm not letting you go," Kyle murmured. Moira tilted her head back, and their lips brushed against one another. It was light and quick before Moira tucked her head back under Kyle's chin, but it was reassuring to them both.

As the minutes turned into hours, Kyle remained with Moira. He thought about returning to the helm, obligation and duty clawing at him, but he knew he wouldn't be able to make it. The ship kept pitching to the bow and forcing the stern, where the cabin was located, higher than the other end. It would have been an uphill struggle to even reach the ladder well, let alone climb it and drag himself back to the helm. He hoped his crew survived and that if needed, Tomas could get to the wheel.

Moira and Kyle sat in silence throughout the night in the pitch-black cabin. Moira wondered if not being able to see the porthole was a blessing or an omen. With no way to tell the time by the stars or to see the water level, neither Kyle nor Moira could guess what had happened outside.

Sometime near dawn, the boat stopped heeling from side to side. It swayed on calm seas, and the water no longer pounded against the porthole. The skies were lighter, and the wind no longer howled. The sound of rainfall continued, but it was more a gentle pitter-patter than the driving nails that had pounded the wood during the gales.

"I'm sorry," Moira blurted as Kyle loosened his hold. "You startled me when I woke up earlier, and I spoke without thinking. I offended you without intention, but then you taunted me. I'd been terrified during the first storm, and instead of finding comfort with you after my first typhoon at sea, you ignored me. I lashed out. I'm sorry."

"I know, sweet one. I, too, lashed out. I was cold and tired, hoping for a warm welcome from you. When I didn't get it, I let my disappointment get the better of me," Kyle confessed.

"Even before the second storm hit, I swear to you, I didn't disobey you," Moira promised. She had no idea why she felt that was the moment she should declare her innocence. But Kyle had said she'd disappointed him, and she wanted redemption. She wanted to offer him some piece of news that didn't bring more frustration or fear.

Kyle cupped her jaw as he gazed into the blue depths that reminded him of the sea on the calmest of days, when its gentle tide lasted to lull him to sleep at night. He saw the honesty in Moira's gaze, and her need for him to believe her. The notion that she'd been pleasuring herself while the ship nearly blew apart hadn't occurred to him, but he saw how badly she needed him to accept her pledge. He sensed her need for something familiar that would set her at ease. He knew she needed some predictability that she could rely on after being alone and afraid.

"I'm glad to hear that, Moira," Kyle chided. "I would be very disappointed if I touched you and found you no longer yearned for me to pleasure you. I would have known if you were sated rather than aching for me."

"I know," Moira whispered. Kyle watched Moira and noticed her hands still trembled. His acceptance had soothed some of her nerves, but she was still dithery.

"You may not have intended to speak out of turn when you woke, but you spoke without thinking. Your words were unwarranted and unkind, Moira. All of them."

"I know," Moira repeated.

"You received your punishment already, yet you don't seem to be at ease. All is forgiven, sweet one," Kyle reassured. Moira nodded, but she looked no more convinced than she had when they started talking. "Have you not forgiven yourself?"

Moira shook her head, her eyes lowered. She came to her knees and rested her hands in her lap. The need to rub her thumb over her knuckles to soothe herself was tempting, but she remained still. She waited for Kyle to speak again, and while it was only a few seconds later, it felt like an eternity before she heard his voice.

"What do you need, Moira?" Kyle nudged her chin up, but she kept her gaze averted. "Look at me, *mo ghràidh*."

Moira sucked in air, the Gaelic term feeling like an anchor in her emotional storm. It might not be the Irish Gaelic she spoke, but she understood its sentiment . Swallowing, she lifted the hem of the leine to her waist. Kyle had found one during the storm, realizing Moira was still naked beneath the plaid.

"Are you asking for a spanking, Moira?" Kyle watched the color rise in Moira's cheeks. "You must say it aloud. Make your request and explain why you think you deserve it."

The command in Kyle's voice excited Moira. She wanted to lie across his lap and let Kyle decide what happened next. She wanted to feel his command as much as hear it, knowing she would feel just as safe and protected as she did when he held her, but her conscience would be cleared.

"I still feel guilty about how I spoke to you, and I would like a spanking. Please. Capt'n," Moira said.

"And why do you still feel guilty if I've already punished and forgiven you?" Kyle pressed. He suspected guilt was only a sliver of why Moira wanted the spanking. He watched her swallow as she worked through what she wanted to say before she started.

"I—I like the feel of the sting and burn, and I like to know it's you touching me," Moira began. "But that's not all of it. When you're spanking me, you're in control. I don't have to fear what will happen next because I know. I don't have to try to be in control because I know you are. I don't have to think about duty or responsibility, or fear or uncertainty, when you're spanking me. I don't know why I feel like that. Surely anyone—even you—hearing me must think I'm a fool."

"And if I said I want you to surrender that control and

submit to me, so I can ease that burden? What if I told you that I understand why you enjoy the punishment, why you feel unsettled and unresolved right now?"

"I'd say I think you're the only one who could possibly understand."

"Come here, Moira," Kyle said as he leaned back, allowing Moira to lie across his thighs. Pushing the leine up to the middle of her back, his hand kneaded her supple globes before he landed two light spanks on each side. "I will administer ten slaps, and you will count them. Do you understand?"

"Yes, Capt'n," Moira's muffled voice carried to him. Kyle brought his hand down over and over, Moira counting in between. She squirmed as her body reacted to the stinging pain, feeling her body slipping toward pleasure.

"You will not climax from rubbing your quim against my thigh, sweet one, or I will deny you again," Kyle warned.

"Yes, Capt'n," Moira mumbled. When the spanking was through, Kyle righted Moira and eased her onto the bed. She brushed the hair from her face, and Kyle witnessed the anxiety disappear from Moira's visage. He cocked an eyebrow, and Moira offered him a half-smile. "I feel better now, Kyle."

CHAPTER 10

Moira remained below deck for the next three days, impatient for fresh air and a change of scenery. But Kyle refused to allow her to leave the cabin, nor did he return her clothes. He warned her that the deck was in no condition for her to go traipsing around. Frustrated by his orders, which seemed more like an overreaction, Moira sulked in the cabin. When Kyle checked on her throughout the day and brought her meals, she alternated between shooting him glares and sullen pouts. She earned herself several trips over Kyle's knees, but that was the only time she felt cared for. Left alone with little to do but sleep, eat, look out at the water, and read books that didn't interest her, Moira wanted to climb the walls.

She grew withdrawn, answering Kyle's questions with the barest minimum of words. She knew she was testing his patience when he was already preoccupied with repairs to the *Lady Charity*, but she resented being locked away when it was never her wish to come aboard in the first place. He continued his attempts to coerce information from Moira, but she only stared mutinously at him, earning those spankings each time. She had moments of contrition after each spanking when she noticed the haggard expression Kyle wore. She was remorseful and eager to make amends after each run-in, and Kyle forgave her each time, easing her need just as she did his. His adept fingers and tongue pushed her toward ecstasy over and over. But it wasn't enough to keep her from repeating her sins when she was left alone for long stretches.

Kyle accused her of tormenting him as her revenge because she disagreed with him about remaining in the cabin. She disagreed only with his order. She knew she was being petulant, but it felt like the most surefire way to garner Kyle's attention for the ten or fifteen minutes at a time that he spent with her. She understood the work and strain he was under, but she wished each visit didn't start with him asking questions she was unwilling to answer. The only time they were at peace with one another was at night, when Kyle finally retired for a few hours of rest. They lay together in silence, Kyle's larger frame wrapped around her back, his heavy arm holding her in place. There was nowhere she would have rather been.

It came to a head on the third day when Kyle brought Moira the midday meal. She refused to look up from the book she feigned reading. She exaggerated each turn of the page, running her finger below each line of words as though it fascinated her. When Kyle spoke to her, she only made sounds of agreement or disagreement, refusing to look at him or speak to him properly.

"Moira, put the book down now," Kyle ordered. "I have put up with your insolent attitude for three days, accepting that this is a frightening and overwhelming experience for you. But you are worse than a spoiled wean. You are being willfully disrespectful and defiant. I don't tolerate such nonsense from my crew, and I won't tolerate it from my mistress."

Moira turned a disinterested mien toward him and sniffed before she returned to her book. Inside, she quivered as she sensed Kyle's growing anger. Part of her wanted to leave the ship and leave him. She'd escaped Dunluce expecting to make her way eventually to Barra, where she could live in peace and security. Instead, she found herself aboard a pirate ship with a man who desired her body but cared little for her person. She was certain there was a crate somewhere on deck where she could sit unobtrusively. But Kyle refused the suggestion each time she made it.

"And you are too controlling. I never actually agreed to be your mistress, Kyle. You brought me on your ship and stuffed me in your cabin. You assumed I would want to bed you. You assumed I would want to stay. You assumed I wouldn't mind being ordered around when I ran away to escape that very thing. At least I had the freedom to move around Dunluce as I chose. You have me caged like a mongrel."

"Then don't snap and whine like one," Kyle snarled.

"Are you calling me a dog?" Moira hissed.

"You're acting like a bitch," Kyle pointed out. He barely missed the book Moira hurled at him. Her wide eyes, pulled-in chin, and shaking head told him she'd reacted without thought or intention, but he cared not. He stalked over to her and pulled her from the bunk. He nearly shook her, but she already trembled. "Throw something at me again, and I won't bother giving you a plank before I toss you into the drink. You're not so talented that I can't find another woman to suck me."

Moira gasped as tears sprang to her eyes. Kyle had intended to be hurtful, and he had hit the mark. He'd come to the cabin to tell her that he might be able to take her to the top deck that evening, but she'd vented her spleen at him before he had the opportunity. Now he didn't even want to lay eyes on her.

"Go to the corner, Moira. You're not worth the effort to spank. Kneel there until I'm calm enough to return. Only then will I decide what to do with you," Kyle said before slamming the cabin door. Moira looked around the cabin, her appetite for the midday meal gone. She swallowed as she considered what Kyle had said, and also what had been left unsaid. She knew he'd been intentionally mean out of spite, but she couldn't wholly disagree with him. Feeling dejected, Moira went to the corner willingly. She knew it would likely be hours before Kyle returned. She could have stayed on the bed and run to the corner when she heard the key in the lock. But she'd let him down enough times already.

The least I can do is have a little honor and take the punishment I earned. What was I thinking? I've never thrown anything at anyone out of anger. Why would I test him like that?

Moira sighed as she lowered herself to the deck and inched closer to the corner. She closed her eyes and wondered what had become of her life. She was too tired to fight Kyle. It was getting her nowhere, and it was only widening the chasm between them. He'd told her that he wanted to care for her, and she realized this was the only way he knew how. He ordered her to remain out of the way to protect her, not punish her. The consequences she received were from her actions, not his intentions.

Bluidy bleeding hell. Shut your gob, Moira. You've got the brass balls of a Lombard. Why are you being so uncooperative and unreasonable? I'm not even negotiating like a bluidy pawner. I'm just digging my heels in. And a load of good it's doing me. You can't have it both ways, Moira. Either you're willing to accept Kyle's rules and submit, or you need him to drop you ashore. I'd rather submit than be alone, even if he took me to the O'Driscolls or the MacNeils. Just keep your neb out of trouble and keep quiet.

Moira shifted on her knees as she slowly exhaled. She resolved to make peace. Even if she didn't trust Kyle with all of her secrets, her belligerence was getting her nowhere. Waging war with Kyle on his ship was foolish and pointless, and Moira accepted it as the uneven wood bit into her knees.

"She'll be the death of you," Tomas chuckled as he handed Kyle a jug of whisky. The brisk air called for a nip or two to keep the blood pumping after hours in the bracing wind.

"But what a sweet way to go," Kyle grinned. He thought back to when they returned to the cabin after her debut in only a leine. He considered Moira's earnestness when she asked how she could convince him to return to his term of endearment. He hadn't noticed that he'd called her "sweet one" the first couple of times, but once he did, he decided it fit—at least until her little stunt the morning she came above deck in just a leine. He scowled as he thought about the sight his men had received. He trusted most of them to have the sense to look but not touch, but there were a few men on his crew that he barely trusted not to knife him, never mind leave Moira alone.

Since leaving her kneeling in the corner, Kyle had tiptoed along the passageway thrice already that day to put his ear to his door. He heard no movement, so he suspected that Moira was still kneeling in the corner, asleep on the floor or his bed, or had found amusement looking at his maps and books. Until he returned, he could accept any of them, since it kept her out of trouble.

"You haven't suggested setting her ashore," Tomas pointed out. "You've mentioned nothing about ransoming her. And I'm certain you won't set her adrift."

"Keith and I don't attack women."

"True enough. But I think you might have considered tossing her over before she called you out. It was over then."

"It was over before that," Kyle confided to his first mate. He told Tomas almost as much as he did Keith, but never everything. But this he would confess. "I recognized her the moment I saw her. She didn't have to say anything."

"So you wouldn't have let Snake Eye throw her overboard?"

"No. I wouldn't have."

"Did you plan to make her your mistress from the start?" Tomas cocked an eyebrow.

"It hasn't gone well enough for her to agree, as she well reminded me. She's an interesting set of contradictions," Kyle pointed out.

"Maybe so. But when have you ever cared enough about a woman to figure them out?"

"I'm more intrigued than anything else." Kyle had already confessed as much as he was willing, at least to Tomas. He would remain in control of the conversation, his feelings, his ship and, with a prayer, maybe even Moira. "She's a puzzle to solve."

"Och, aye. A puzzle. How much is there to figure out to get her to open her legs to you? She enjoyed what you were doing on the deck the other day." At Kyle's threatening glare, Tomas grinned and threw up his hands. "I'm not asking for a turn. Just making an observation, Capt'n."

"Are the men saying anything about having a woman aboard?" Kyle wondered.

"Not yet. But I'm certain they will. If the rough seas continue, they'll blame her. They didn't blame her when it chucked it down. They claimed that was Ireland's fault. But if an attack goes sour, they'll blame her for that," Tomas reasoned.

"Aye. And Keith has no idea she's aboard. I haven't talked to him about her yet."

"He won't step foot aboard!"

"He was the daft sod to fall in love with his captain's mistress," Kyle said with a shake of his head.

"Don't let Caragh or Rowan hear you call her that. They prefer to forget those days. She's Rowan's wife now," Tomas reminded.

"Don't we all know it? And in all fairness, he wasn't in love—or even in lust—but he liked Caragh. Who doesn't?"

"I can think of someone," Tomas grunted.

"But Alane brought her own death upon herself. The crazy bitch got what she deserved. She's lucky Rowan didn't do worse."

"From what Keith's told, I'd say we were lucky not to see Caragh in that condition. I can't imagine how such a wee thing survived that beating." Tomas shook his head before looking back at the ladder well, then at the sky. "She's been down there quite some time. Do you think she's still kneeling?"

"Probably not. But neither is she causing mischief. Likely sitting on her bum or sleeping. She'll be the way I left her as soon as she hears the key in the lock," Kyle assured.

"You never know. Your cabin could be in shambles for all you know. For a woman who appeared so meek the few times I caught sight of her at Dunluce, she's a termagant now."

"I doubt that's anything new. She just never showed it around her brother," Kyle mused.

"Then she really must trust you. A bit daft, is she?" Tomas grinned.

Kyle scowled before shoving the whisky jug against Tomas's chest. He left Tomas once more to steer the ship as he made his way down to Moira. Just as he had every time he checked on her, he put his ear to the door. He heard nothing from within, so he eased the key into the lock and slowly opened the door a crack. He peered in and found Moira sitting on her heels with her forehead against the wall. Fear that she was in pain like the first night she was aboard made him kick the door closed as he hurried across the cabin.

CHAPTER 11

Moira stirred at the sound of the door slamming shut. She lifted her head and blinked as she pushed hair out of her eyes. She turned at the sound of someone else in the cabin, her eyes rounding when she took in Kyle's horrified expression. She quickly adjusted her position to kneel without resting on her heels, her hands behind her back, and her chin tucked. She closed her eyes, waiting for the scolding she believed was inevitable.

"Are you all right?" Kyle asked as he helped her up. "Are you sick?"

"No," Moira answered, her brow furrowed. Yet again, she didn't understand Kyle. Her brother and Lizzie, even Aidan, were straightforward. She could read their thoughts and emotions as clearly as if they spoke them. Kyle kept her befuddled.

"You were leaning against the wall. Not sitting or resting against it. Your forehead was against it," Kyle stated.

"I know. I'm sorry. I didn't mean to fall asleep. I didn't realize I had," Moira apologized. "I remember leaning forward to rest for a moment, then you were coming in."

"You stayed kneeling this whole time?"

Moira looked sheepishly at him. "I sat down twice, but each time I heard you at the door, I didn't—"

"Didn't what, Moira?" Kyle demanded. Her eyebrows shot up at his tone. But he wanted to know what she'd been up to, how she thought to manipulate him.

"I didn't want to disappoint you again."

Kyle didn't know what to say. He couldn't remember the last time anyone worried about disappointing him. He supposed the only one who had was Keith. Maybe Ruairí. His men didn't. They only cared that they did what he demanded, so he paid and fed them. He hadn't believed she would really stay as he ordered. He'd even thought to find a delicious and lusty way to punish her.

"I left hours ago." Kyle wrapped his plaid around Moira before he guided her over to the chair, then pulled her onto his lap. "Are you used to that? Does Dónal punish you like that?"

Moira twisted to look at him. "No. And even if he did, I wouldn't worry about disappointing him. I would have sat or even taken a nap on purpose if he'd doled out the punishment."

"How do you know to put your hands behind your back and to lower your head? You've done it before." Kyle demanded. Once more, Moira turned bewildered eyes toward him.

"I don't know. It just seems like what I should do. I don't really think about it." Moira shrugged, growing uneasy by Kyle's shifting mood. In that moment, she would have preferred Dónal and Lizzie's predictable ones. Kyle's scared her at times.

Kyle kissed Moira's temple, sensing that he was making her uneasy in a way he didn't intend. He wanted her to wonder what he would do next, but only when she was trying to predict what arousing punishment he would demand. Now that his earlier temper had settled, he didn't want her to fear for her safety with him. Just the opposite.

"Did Aidan do anything to punish you?" Kyle prompted.

Moira's head would soon ache from how Kyle jumped from one topic to another, but she was beginning to get used to it.

"Do you mean did he hit me? No. Never. I think I relented because he was the only person who didn't make me self-conscious. He never berated me or manhandled me like Dónal did. Going out riding and fishing meant I had a reprieve from the duties I carried all day, every day."

"No, sweet one," Kyle whispered. His heart thudded when Moira sighed and nestled closer to him. Two words made her relax. He'd never imagined that such could be the case. That what he could say, something so simple as a term of endearment, could make a woman trust him, make a woman submit to him. "I didn't mean hit you. I will never do that. I will never spank you out of anger either."

"What about my first night? Or when I came up on deck in the leine? Or when I threw the book at you? You seemed furious."

"Not when I spanked you. I'm captain of this ship, and that won't change no matter what goes on between us. You were not respectful, nor were you forthcoming with what you've done or your reasons. You're aboard my ship."

"But you've been set on manipulating me. I haven't felt very trusting," Moira countered.

"That's why we're talking now." Kyle stroked back Moira's hair and kissed her temple again. "Do you understand why you've deserved them?"

"Because I've been incredibly defiant and unconscionably disrespectful several times. I know what you expect, and I did what I wanted, anyway. You're the captain aboard this ship. If I ever defy you openly, others might think they can too. The day you boarded my clan's ship, you could have killed me, but you didn't. You could have forced me, but you haven't. You could abuse me, but you won't."

"And in return?" Kyle prompted.

"And in return, I should respect your authority."

"Did Aidan decide how and where you coupled?" Kyle asked. He wasn't certain that he wanted to hear about Moira's past, but he needed to understand how much experience she had.

"Sort of. I mean, the places were rather limited. And I knew nothing that he didn't teach me, so I suppose he did decide how." Moira looked at Kyle and realized he expected her to say more, to be more specific. "I don't know what else you want to know, Kyle."

"I know you must have taken him in your mouth, and I know he returned the favor to you. But when you coupled, was he always on top?"

"Kyle!" Moira gasped.

"Did he take you from behind? Did he pull your hair or bind your hands? Did he enter your rosebud?" Kyle rattled off the questions he wanted to know before either of them lost the nerve to discuss this.

"Do you mean behind like an animal?"

"That's one way. But standing or lying down, maybe bent over something," Kyle clarified.

"Yes." Moira couldn't look at Kyle. She turned her head away and closed her eyes, but gentle fingers nudged her chin back toward him. He pressed a soft kiss to her lips.

"I'm not judging you, sweet one. I just want to know what you understand about how a man and woman can enjoy coupling."

"Enjoy? Are these things you like?" Moira murmured.

"They are. And they're things that I would like to enjoy with you."

"You wish to pull my hair?" Moira's brow wrinkled.

"You enjoy when I spank you and when I pinch your nipples. You like it rough, Moira. Don't you?" Kyle prodded.

"I didn't know I did until I met you." Moira's lips pursed and turned down as she considered how she felt about her brief time with Kyle. "Why do I like it?"

"I can't say for sure. At least, not yet. But I suspect that while I may cause you pain, you also know that I won't injure you. I may have control, and I may be bigger and more dominant, but I will never purposely hurt you. You've said you don't fear what will come next because you can predict it. Maybe you want to give up having to be in control all the time. In control of how you react; in control of your emotions lest Dónal or Lizzie, or even Aidan, see too much. In control of running a keep where no one appreciates what you do." Kyle pressed his lips gently to Moira's, offering a tenderness he didn't know he possessed. He enjoyed women, and he liked his coupling rough and fast. He was rarely gentle, but the women who took him to their bed knew that. They knew he paid well for his pleasure. But Moira was different.

"Sean often has night terrors," Moira stated. Kyle frowned, not pleased about the sudden change in conversation. When he opened his mouth, Moira held up her hand. "Please. I've slept better in your bed, and even kneeling against the wall, than I have in years. I spent most nights sleeping on a trundle bed in Sean's chamber to soothe him and to keep him from rousing the entire castle. Being aboard your ship is the first time in years that I've had no duties to worry about, no one else to tend to. I can just sleep. I don't have to be in control of anything."

Kyle nodded, understanding what she meant. He'd slept better lying beside Moira than he had since he sailed on his first ship. "I was honest the other night when I said I don't know how to care for a woman. Not really. I know how to pleasure a woman, but not to minister to your needs beyond that. But you trust me. At least with your body. If you can trust me to bring you pleasure, even if it pushes you beyond what you think you can manage, then I also wish to ensure you have everything else you need."

"You wish to take care of me?" Moira blinked owlishly.

"I do."

"What does that mean?"

"I'm not entirely sure, but I'd like you to know you can come to me for anything. Whether you need a new bar of soap, or you need to confess how you feel." Kyle held his breath, expecting Moira to rebuke him, to throw his offer back at him. She slid her hands up his chest and around his neck as she attempted to inch closer to him. Her hip already pressed against his hardened rod.

"Kyle, I believe you can show me pleasure I never imagined possible. I admit I'm curious, even excited at the prospect. But I need you to accept that it will take me time to trust you with the rest of me. I've been played a fool too many times. It's not that I never will. It's not that you're untrustworthy. I'm..."

"Scared?" Kyle provided. Moira nodded.

"I want to trust you. But I'm not ready to trust myself in making that decision. Do you trust me?"

"That's a fair question, sweet one," Kyle replied. "Perhaps a wee more than you trust me. But not entirely. Trust will come with time, as we get to know one another better and rely upon one another."

"What could you rely on me for? I must rely on you for everything," Moira noted.

"Aye. But can I rely on you not to pull any more stunts like the last few days? Can I rely on you not to stab me in my sleep? Can I rely on you to keep any confidences I share with you? You will be privy to meetings I have with Tomas. You will see maps and ledgers. Can I rely on you not to tell anyone what you see or hear?"

"Yes. Speaking out of turn could get you killed. I'm not interested in that happening. I'd rather it not," Moira grinned.

"Because I haven't bedded you enough? Because you know

you'll crave more and wish to have me at your disposal to satisfy your needs?" Kyle tickled her ribs.

"There is that. But I'd rather be here with you than with Dónal or Dermot," Moira scowled until she realized what she'd said.

"Dermot? Dermot O'Malley? Why would you be with him? The MacDonnells and O'Malleys can't stand one another."

Moira sighed as her lips twisted. She'd said too much now to avoid explaining everything. It would be a test in trust to reveal to Kyle why she'd run away. But she wouldn't tell him where she was headed. Not yet, at least.

"Dónal has never been willing to pay a reasonable dowry for me. For all he complains, he didn't want me to leave. I'm the best servant he has ever had. But he believed Dermot would make a better ally than an enemy. I don't know who else he's plotting against, or how he might intend to cross Dermot, but he signed a betrothal agreement between the O'Malley and me. I learned of it three days before you attacked my clan's ship."

"And that's why you were on it? Were you being delivered to O'Malley or trying to escape?"

"Escape. The alliance went against what the clan council wanted. None of the men stopped Dónal from intimidating me. The councilmen smuggled me out. That's why there weren't many men on board."

"Where were you headed?"

"I don't know all the details." Which was true, just not the entire truth. "South."

Moira said nothing Kyle hadn't already suspected, but the confirmation was useful. And he appreciated that they'd crossed a major hurdle far faster than he expected after their fractious last few days. He was certain there was more to her story, but he wouldn't press. Yet.

"I'm glad you're safe now," Kyle said.

"Am I, though? Will you turn me over to Dónal or Dermot if they find me?"

"And how would they do that when I don't know where you are?" Kyle asked with a straight face. Moira shivered for a moment as she witnessed what an accomplished liar he was. Always perceptive, Kyle added, "I lie better than most. I've had to in order to stay alive. But unless it can't be helped, unless it's for your well-being, I won't lie to you."

Moira nodded. She wanted to believe him, wanted the trust that Kyle spoke the truth. But she wasn't fool enough to trust the man just because he was handsome and made her body sing. She hadn't lied either. It would take her time to trust him. Sensing they'd spent enough time in serious conversation, Kyle nudged her off his lap and stood.

CHAPTER 12

Wrapped in his plaid and a leine she swam in, Moira watched Kyle dig in one of his chests before sticking his head into the passageway and bellowing to someone named Braedon. It was only moments later that an adolescent boy bounded toward Kyle but was sent off to find a pair of his leggings and a smaller leine for Moira. When Kyle had warm clothes to offer Moira, he swapped the larger leine for one that fit her better.

"Put your boots on. It's time you came above deck and met my crew properly. They know you're here. They know you're mine. But I would introduce you on my terms." Kyle crossed his arms and set his jaw as he looked down at Moira. Once more captain and commander. "It's the only way I can keep you safe, Moira. I may not always be a barbarian with you, but I must keep you safe among my crew. They must know they can't touch you without losing their life."

"I understand, Kyle. I don't know if you're possessive by nature. Maybe you are because you didn't have much as a child or because you've always shared with Keith. But I do realize who I'm on board with. I may have avoided men like your crew when Dónal hosted, but I wasn't blind or deaf. I'd rather you make it abundantly clear that I'm to be left alone than for you to neglect that."

Kyle's arms unfolded before he wrapped them around Moira's waist. He lifted her off the floor and gave her a smacking kiss before spanking, then squeezing, her backside. She squealed and kissed him back. She was ready to make her first dignified appearance on deck.

Moira stood beside Kyle on deck, any traces of her earlier submission gone as she looked the crew in the eye, meeting their suspicious assessment with her own. She'd felt Kyle's body shift, so they stood side-by-side rather than with his body angled in front of hers. She appreciated the small sign of respect. She knew he wouldn't hesitate to defend her if any man made a move, but she didn't appear to cower behind him. She didn't intend to present herself as his equal, but neither did she intend to stand in his shadow. She hoped he would allow her freedom to move about the ship, and she railed against any pirate thinking she was still the meek woman some had met before. She was certain word had already spread about her; it was inevitable. But she could present herself in the way she wanted to be seen for once: brave.

The moments of fear she'd experienced as she slipped from the keep in the dark down to the pier, then into the dinghy that rowed her out to the ship with Grady and Malone had paled compared to the terror of realizing pirates attacked her ship. Since then, her emotions were in constant turmoil with Kyle. They vacillated from exquisite pleasure to doubt to worry, but as she stood beside him and listened to him introduce her with a certainty in his tone that defied anyone questioning him—or her—she found the remnants of the wild girl she'd once been.

The one who threw caution to the wind, riding too fast, climbing too high in trees, swimming out too far. The one her mother swore could never be tamed before she had put her wants and dreams aside to care first for her dying mother, then a clan who overlooked her.

"Lady Moira is my guest, so you will accord her the respect that demands. Any slight to her is a slight to me. Pray that all I do is set you adrift," Kyle finished as he wrapped his hand around Moira's and gave it a gentle squeeze. She longed to shift her focus to him, but she wouldn't take her eyes off the crew. She wouldn't look away, lest they think for even a moment that she depended upon Kyle as much as she did.

"Thank you, Capt'n," Moira stated.

"Welcome aboard, my lady," Tomas spoke up, nudging Snake Eye, who grunted and nodded.

"Begging your pardon for manhandling you that first day," Snake Eye apologized, and Moira suspected he meant it. The man didn't appear able to look sincere about anything but wishing death upon someone, but his voice held a note of authenticity. Moira nodded and offered a brief smile in return.

"My lady, I'm Braedon, the capt'n's barrel man." The adolescent boy who'd lent Moira the clothes she wore stepped forward. "If you'd care for a tour of the ship, I'd be pleased to lead you." His gaze darted to Kyle. "Assuming the capt'n approves."

"I think that would be nice," Moira responded, turning her face toward Kyle. "Assuming the capt'n approves."

"He does," Kyle nodded before leaning to whisper to Moira. "I suspect you've already taken yourself on a tour, but there is still plenty that I shall show you that young Braedon can't." Kyle grinned as Moira's cheeks turned a light shade of pink while she cocked an eyebrow, accepting his challenge.

Moira stepped forward, but Kyle squeezed her hand and tugged her back. Once more he leaned down to whisper to her.

"I trust Braedon, Snake Eye, and Tomas with your life, but I don't trust any of the others. Senga trained Braedon well, but he's still no match for some of the larger men. Don't go into any space where you and Braedon could be cornered. Promise me."

Moira took in the gravity of Kyle's warning, knowing Braedon would die and she would be assaulted if Kyle's fears came true. She nodded and squeezed his hand.

"And lass," Kyle purred, accentuating his burr. "Dinna think ye can get away with murder. If I discover you've disobeyed me, yer other set of cheeks will be as pink as the ones on yer face before the day is through."

Moira nodded once more before turning back to Braedon. She struggled not to look back at Kyle to acknowledge how much she looked forward to her next spanking. Her core tightened as a tingle took root, making her want to squirm.

"Lady Moira, other than the ship we found you on, have you sailed before?" Braedon's question drew her attention back to her tour guide. They stood below the mainsail, and Moira tilted her head back to watch the billowing canvas. She knew Kyle could order the crew to man the oars, but the breeze carried them along as they cut through the waves. They hadn't been underway long, and they moved slowly.

Moira had spent time on Aidan's ship, almost solely in his cabin, but she hadn't sailed often. The most she'd done was a few trips to Rathlin Island, another MacDonnell keep. She'd also traveled overland to the clan's keeps at Dunaneeny and Ballycastle, and to Kinbane, the MacAlisters' stronghold. The MacDonnells and MacAlisters were allied, and she suddenly realized that she and the men helping her flee could have encountered a MacAlister ship near their coast.

"No. Only a few trips to Rathlin Castle on Rathlin, and that's not very far at all," Moira answered, coming back to herself.

"You have good sea legs on you for a landlubber," Braedon grinned then quickly added, "My lady."

"I shall take it as a compliment that you don't think I'm a completely clumsy oaf meant only for dry land," Moira snickered, making the boy relax.

"I didn't mean offense, my lady."

"I know you didn't, Braedon, so I took none. How long have you been aboard the *Lady Charity*?" Moira asked.

"Nigh on three years. Two with the Dark Heart, and one with the Red Drifter."

Moira heard the hero worship in the boy's voice, and part of her wished she could disabuse him of his notion that the life of a pirate captain was glamorous, but he knew better than she did what the reality was. He still looked wistfully in Kyle's direction.

"You must have learned a great deal sailing with two such feared captains," Moira observed, keeping her head tilted back as though she was more interested in the mast and sail.

"I have. But it was Lady Senga who taught me to fight," Braedon nodded as Moira glanced down. "Och, aye, she did."

Braedon looked around and lowered his voice before he began his tale. "She saw me training with Snake Eye one morning, and she knew he was about to skewer me. I didn't know what I was doing, and no one was going to help me. Everyone could see I didn't have the right kind of weapon for my size, but neither would I back down. She dug around until she found me a sword," Braedon paused to pat the weapon hanging from his waist. "She took on Snake Eye then the Dark Heart and talked easy as you please throughout it all. She told me where to stand, how to move, and how to read my opponent. She almost bested the Dark Heart!"

Moira couldn't help but smile as she listened to Braedon recount his experience. She recalled the time she'd slipped into the armory to investigate the swords and bows the MacDonnell warriors carried. She'd knocked over a dozen swords, sending them clattering to the ground. Her father and his men rushed in, fearing they were under attack, only to find a ten-year-old

Moira trying to hoist a sword. She'd explained that she wanted to see if they were as heavy as they looked. Her mother had despaired that Moira would always have a precocious streak.

The pride in the Braedon's tone reminded her that he was still very young, even though his voice was deepening. She wished she could have seen such a sight. Senga had impressed her from the start, and she could picture the lady pirate sparing with her mountainous, short-tempered husband. The woman was likely the only one who could have bested the Dark Heart. She slid her gaze to the helm where Kyle stood at the wheel. She felt his eyes on her time and again, but when she glanced at him, he wasn't looking at her. She waited until his eyes shifted back to hers and offered him an impish grin with a one-shoulder shrug.

Moira knew nothing about wielding a sword despite her childhood attempt. She wondered if Kyle would teach her—or maybe let Snake Eye, who apparently trained the men. She nearly laughed aloud as she pictured his reaction to such a request. She turned her attention back to Braedon as he moved toward the aft. He pointed out the mizzen and jib, which she already knew, but happily smiled as he explained the various sections of the deck. When he suggested he give her a tour of the lower deck, she shook her head.

"I don't want to keep you from your work, Braedon. And I'd like to enjoy the fresh air a little longer." Moira remembered Kyle's warning. She did not want to tempt fate nor anger Kyle. Neither were worth the possible outcomes.

"Aye. Well, I should make my way back up to the crow's nest. I'll never understand why I'm known as a barrel man when I spend my time in a nest. Birdman might suit better," Braedon mused. Moira bit her tongue so hard it stung, but it kept her from pointing out that his nest was made from a cut-down barrel. She watched as he scampered up the main mast and into his perch. She looked around once more, but jumped when

Tomas came to stand beside her. The weathered sailor wasn't as old as he looked once he stood near her. His sun-leathered face had wrinkles around his eyes and mouth from smiling. She'd initially assumed it was from squinting against the sun and scowling, but she'd seen him smile each time they'd encountered one another.

"Capt'n would like to see you," Tomas stated. Moira nodded her thanks and made her way to the wheel.

"That was short," Kyle murmured as Moira came to stand beside him.

"Braedon told me a wonderful story about Senga and Ruairí sparring on deck and how Senga taught him to fight. He pointed out the parts of the deck and sails, but I admit I already knew as much. He suggested showing me the lower deck, but I declined. I didn't think that would be wise," Moira admitted.

"Thank you."

Moira was unprepared for the simple phrase. She waited for Kyle to say more, but when he didn't, she remained quiet. Moira soon grew uncomfortable with the silence. It was as if there was far more to say, but neither knew how to voice it. She pointed over her shoulder toward the rail and looked back before raising her eyebrows in question. Kyle nodded his permission, so Moira went to watch the open sea. She couldn't see anything more than the hazy outline of land, but she knew they continued south since it was on their starboard side. She recalled Kyle saying that his brother's ship, the *Lady Grace,* was to their starboard. She leaned over the rail and looked back, spotting the other pirate ship. She'd spent many hours in Kyle's cabin, so she wondered if he'd told his brother she was aboard.

When she watched a red-headed man storm to the prow and glare at her, she was certain Kyle hadn't spoken to his brother. A whistle pierced the air from the *Lady Grace,* and Moira bit the corner of her lip as she glanced back at Kyle. Shooting one more look at the *Lady Grace*'s angry captain, she returned to Kyle's side.

"I don't think your brother is happy to have spied me. I didn't think about whether you'd told him until after he and I spotted one another. I'm sorry. Mayhap you didn't want him to know," Moira confessed. Kyle pulled her against his side and wrapped his arm around her.

"Worry not, sweet one. Keith doesn't care for women aboard ship, but that's fine since this isn't his ship. He can do as he pleases aboard his own."

"I don't want to cause problems between you two," Moira worried.

"You won't, Moira. Dinna fash."

Moira's toes curled in her boots, just as they did every time Kyle's brogue slipped through. It wrapped around her like the warmest sealskin cloak in the dead of winter and warmed her more than the finest Irish whiskey. Kyle ordered the mainsail lowered to half, slowing their ship and allowing the *Lady Grace* to pull alongside.

"Should I go below?" Moira whispered.

"Not yet. Keith will join us in my cabin," Kyle explained. Moira watched as a rope landed on the *Lady Charity*'s deck, and a crewman quickly leashed the boats together while men on each ship dropped anchor. Keith swung across the rails on another rope and landed agilely, taking his first step just as both feet touched the ground. Moira hadn't feared any of Kyle's men, but Keith's murderous glare made her want to hide behind Kyle. "Wheest, sweet one. He won't do anything. His ire is directed at me, not you. Stand tall as you did before. Make me proud again. His crew and mine are watching."

Moira swallowed, shoving her timidity to the bottom of her stomach and rallying as she watched Keith approach with feigned disinterest. She was the daughter of a chieftain, and more regrettably, the sister of one. She could pretend the haughtiness she was truly entitled to. Kyle shifted positions, so Moira stood to his left before he extended his right arm to his brother. They grasped forearms before pulling one another into a loose embrace.

Moira watched, puzzled. They acted as though they hadn't seen each other in ages, but she suspected it had been perhaps a day since they talked. She realized the twins were closer than she imagined. She feared it boded ill for her if Keith was so displeased with her presence. She prepared herself for when he would insist Kyle put her ashore, or worse, adrift. She was certain Kyle would agree, so she accepted that her time with Kyle was over before it had a chance to truly begin.

"My cabin," Kyle muttered. He signaled to Snake Eye, who came to take the wheel. Kyle kept his arm around Moira's waist as they moved to the ladder well. He swung down first, then turned back to her. He wrapped his hands around her waist and lifted her down. Sliding her hand into his, he led the trio to his cabin. When they entered, Moira looked around, unsure of where she should stand or sit. She opted to move silently toward the corner where she'd been kneeling earlier, but Kyle's single command to stop made her halt. She turned back to him, her eyes darting between the brothers. She had a momentary fear that they'd come below so they could each have a turn with her. Keith's assessing, then appreciative gaze, told her he wouldn't turn down the offer if it was made.

CHAPTER 13

Kyle watched his brother as Keith openly admired Moira. The twins had shared everything since they were in the womb, and that often included the women they bedded. He'd never been possessive about anything when it came to Keith, and his brother had always been the same. He didn't worry that Keith would begrudge him Moira's company, but he also would make it clear that they'd finally found something that they wouldn't both indulge in.

"Keith, this is Moira MacDonnell. Dónal's sister," Kyle announced with no preface. Moira startled, unprepared for Kyle to be so blunt, though she supposed it shouldn't have surprised her.

"You mean Lizzie's sister," Keith grinned. Moira's stomach roiled as she looked away. More than one man made the same assumption, but it was usually Lizzie's tart words that disabused the men of the idea. When Kyle said nothing, Moira stepped forward. She didn't understand what her role was, but Kyle had said she should stand tall, just as she had in front of his men. She decided that applied in the cabin as well. At least, for now.

"You know my sister?" Moira spoke up.

"By reputation," Keith chortled.

"And I suppose you haven't heard of mine," Moira said archly. "Because they are not the same." Her raised chin dared Keith to insinuate more.

"But your sister isn't the one aboard a pirate ship, wearing a man's clothes, or sleeping in my brother's bed," Keith pointed out.

"Who said I was sleeping there?" Moira flung back at Keith, accepting the challenge.

"Kitten's got claws, Kyle. Has she been scratching your back?" Keith turned his taunts toward his brother, but he kept his eyes locked with Moira's. They were an exact match for Kyle's emerald orbs. Keith and Kyle were absolute mirror images of one another, Moira realized. Rowan and Ruairí looked tremendously alike, but Ruairí's hair had always been a little longer and a little more sun-bleached than Rowan's. There was virtually no way to tell Keith and Kyle apart, at least not one that Moira noticed. She thought they even stood alike. If she hadn't noticed where Kyle had come to a stop, from sight alone she wouldn't be sure which man was the one she wanted to bed. But nothing about Keith's demeanor drew her as Kyle did. Just the opposite. She found him immensely unappealing.

"Enough, Keith. Sit and let's talk," Kyle barked. He waved Moira over and nodded toward the bed. He took the seat closer to the bed while Keith sat across from him. Moira stepped wide of Keith as she went to sit on the bunk. "Moira was aboard the MacDonnell ship."

"Quite the plunder," Keith snickered.

"Enough, or you can go back to the *Grace*," Kyle warned, and Keith sobered. Moira wanted to slide as far back on the bunk as she could, but instead, she sat with her legs hanging over the edge.

"Testy. She's left you with blue bollocks, has she?" Keith glared at Moira.

"Keith, I'm not jesting. Leave the lass alone," Kyle infused more steel into his voice. Keith cast an assessing look at Kyle before he nodded. Something passed between the brothers that seemed to call a truce, but Moira didn't understand what. She barely had a civil relationship with either of her siblings, let alone one where they silently communicated anything but animosity.

"What else did you find onboard?" Keith asked.

"Barrels of whiskey, all Irish," Kyle snorted, and Keith grimaced. Moira wanted to take umbrage, but she remained silent. She thought Irish whiskey was far better than the Scottish drink she'd tasted, but the two pirates clearly disagreed. "Wool, salt pork, and cheese."

"That's it?" Keith asked in disbelief. Moira struggled to keep her face impassive, knowing the cargo had barely been worth the raid. It wasn't meant to be. Her clan's council had loaded just enough to justify the voyage if anyone had stopped them before they sailed out of port. Keith narrowed his eyes at Moira. "Why?"

"The lass left home. The men were taking her south," Kyle explained with a shrug, downplaying the little truth he knew. "I was still glad for the extra cargo."

"Where were you going, lass?" Keith pressed.

"South. I don't know what was supposed to happen," Moira countered. She noticed Kyle stiffen, but he didn't refute what she said, nor did he add to his brother's questions.

"And where are you taking her now?" Keith shifted his attention back to Kyle, dismissing her.

"Wherever we sail," Kyle said indifferently.

"No."

Moira gulped as Keith's face turned red enough to match his hair.

"I don't tell you who can board your ship, Keith. You don't tell me who may sail with me aboard mine. We sail together, but we are captain of our own ships and our own crews," Kyle reminded him.

"Oh? Is she to be part of your crew now? I can imagine just how you put her to work," Keith sneered.

"Out!" Kyle bellowed as he pushed back his chair and rose. Keith grunted and rose too, the brothers leaning toward one another. Moira shot off the end of the bed and stood beside Kyle. She didn't dare touch him. She was uncertain how he might react or what Keith would read into it.

"Please, don't," Moira whispered to Kyle. "I should go before he does. Put me ashore, Kyle."

"No," Kyle hissed as he glanced down at her before locking gazes with Keith.

"Kyle, I'll set myself adrift then," Moira threatened.

"You will not. And now you have a spanking coming your way for suggesting something so daft. Sit down, Moira."

"No," Moira defied him.

"What?" Both men gawked.

"I may deserve a spanking for defying you," Moira said softly, even though she knew Keith heard her. It was the most she could do to make her conversation with Kyle feel private. "But I won't cause a rift between you two. It's obvious how close you two are. I won't be the cause of your relationship souring. I have a brother and a sister I detest. I left so I never have to lay eyes on either of them again. That doesn't mean I wish that upon you. You'll sail with Keith long after you tire of me. Set me adrift or set me ashore, but I'm just a passing distraction, Kyle. We both know that."

Kyle didn't take his eyes off Moira as he spoke to his brother, his voice calm once more. "Go back to the *Lady Grace*. I'll speak to you this evening. There is something here that can't remain unresolved."

Keith sighed before he nodded. He let himself out of the cabin without Moira or Kyle looking in his direction. Kyle's hands went to his hip as he stared at Moira. She didn't know what to make of his expression, but she sighed as she reached down and tugged at her boots' laces. She toed them off as she pulled her leine over her head and dropped it on the bed. She slipped out of her leggings and tossed them beside the shirt. She padded over to the table and pushed the stack of books aside before leaning over it. Her arms stretched out as she gripped each side of the table. With another sigh, she turned her head and rested her check on the surface before she closed her eyes. She listened to Kyle move behind her, but she gasped in shock when she felt the head of his cock slide across the seam of her entrance.

"You make a delicious sight. Maybe a spanking isn't all you wish for. Is this what you want, Moira? Do you want a man inside you again?" Kyle's voice rasped beside her cheek.

"You," she croaked.

"You want me to fill your quim and ride you?"

"Yes. Please." Moira cleared her throat. "Yes, please, Capt'n."

"Do you think you deserve my cock, sweet one?"

"I don't know, but I want it. I want you," Moira confessed as she squeezed her eyes shut, hating the neediness in her voice.

"Should I give you what you want when you haven't earned it? You've defied me twice today. You deserve two spankings. But maybe I will settle for one since you spent the morning in the corner." The tip of Kyle's cock slid past Moira's nether lips, and she trembled. He nudged it forward just enough for the bulbous head to poke inside her. "Mayhap the better punishment would be to pound your cunny then find my release across your glorious little arse and leave your cunny starving for release."

"That isn't punishment, that's torture," Moira moaned. When Kyle made no move to enter her, Moira sighed before standing up. Surprised when she turned around, Kyle took a step back. "Kyle, my temper this morning deserved your ire and my punishment. I accept that. You know I even welcome the feel of your hand on me, and you know I wish to make recompense. I spoke out of turn with your brother—more than once. But I don't regret what I said at the end. It may deserve punishment too, but I won't come between you and your brother. Deny me what you want. Make me pay restitution as you want, but I feel no guilt and no remorse for speaking up. But this," Moira moved her hand back and forth between their bodies. "If this is going to happen, please don't use it as leverage or punishment. Not like our first time."

"And if I wish to despite your pretty little speech?" Kyle asked as Moira watched him stroke himself.

"Then I can't stop you. I won't stop you. But you know my wishes now."

Kyle took a step forward, pressing Moira back against the table. He pulled his leine off as he toed off his boots. His leggings followed as he stripped down. Moira watched at first, then tentatively reached out a hand and wrapped her fingers around his rod. She stroked him as she eased onto the table. She opened her legs in clear invitation, even tilting her hips so the tip of his cock once more grazed her entrance.

"And if my wish is to drive into you over and over, even spill my seed inside you, what would you say about that?"

"Before or after my spanking?" Moira purred, stroking him and rubbing herself against him.

"You would let me spill in you?" Kyle growled.

"I don't think that would be wise. But could I stop you?" Moira cooed, but she gasped when Kyle pulled away.

"Yes, Moira. You can always stop me," Kyle stated. She sat blinking as she tried once more to follow his unpredictable moods. He ran his hand through his hair, leaving it disheveled. "My desire for you makes me act before thinking, sweet one. No one has ever made me do that."

Kyle shook his head and held out his hand to Moira. She

took it as she slid off the tabletop. He guided her to the bunk and pulled back the covers. She slipped into bed and watched as Kyle pulled the covers over her with a grimace before perching on the edge.

"If I can see your body, I won't be able to keep from touching you. There is still much we need to establish between us before you become my mistress, if that's what's to happen."

"Can we not speak about that afterward?" Moira tried not to whine, but she couldn't help it. Her body ached with unspent lust again. She felt her temper rising as she was once more thwarted.

"We will surely speak about it afterward, but we shall also agree to some things now. If we can't, then this goes no further," Kyle warned. Moira puffed another sigh; her mouth pursed and her teeth gritted as she nodded. "I suspect there are times where I will wish to be gentle and slow with you, but this was—is—not one of them. I was prepared to be very rough with you, Moira. Push you in ways that your body is likely to rebel against in the beginning. But I won't do that unless we both agree to it."

"What did you want to do?" Moira whispered, trepidation and excitement warring within.

"I told you yesterday what I enjoy. I wish to wrap your hair around my hand and to keep you head pinned in the position I want, one that would allow me to kiss your neck, your throat, your mouth. I wish to spank you even as I plow you. I wish to use my size, both my body and my cock, to dominate you until you can't decide if you're begging me to stop or to keep going."

Moira listened as her breathing became rapid and shallow, his words building the excitement that made her core burn with need. "Is it—is it domination if I've already submitted?" Moira wondered.

"Is that what you wish to do? Do you think that means you are to just lay where I put you and do nothing while I slaver over you?"

"Do you wish for me to be still?" Moira looked sheepishly at him. "If so, I fear I shall be punished too often for you to actually bed me."

Kyle lunged at Moira, pulling her beneath him with the covers separating their skin as Kyle hovered above her. Their mouths met, and she opened to him as his tongue inched forward. The kiss was as savage as each one they'd already shared. Moira's hands slid into his hair as she struggled to make space for him between her legs, the sheets pinning her in place. Kyle ripped the covers down until he exposed her small, pert breasts. His mouth opened wide, taking most of the supple flesh into his mouth. Moira's moan and restlessness earned her other nipple a painful twist. When her moan grew louder, Kyle bit the one in his mouth. A streak of pain ran from her breasts to her channel, making the burning ache to be filled excruciating.

"Kyle, please," Moira begged. "It hurts."

Kyle looked up and recognized Moira was no longer enjoying their games. "What hurts, sweet one? Am I too heavy on you? You're so tiny."

"No. I welcome the feel of you. But I—oh, God, Kyle, it hurts to not—I need—please," Moira finished on a whimper.

"And if I should like this time to last longer?" Kyle countered.

"I do, too. But I can't. Not this time. Please, Kyle. This isn't fun anymore." Moira blinked several times. "I'm on the verge of tears, Kyle. I've never felt a need like this before. I'm frustrated, and it's too much."

Kyle appreciated Moira's honesty. It was the one thing he'd intended to ask her for, but he'd grown too distracted to discuss everything he planned. He pulled away the covers between them and settled between her thighs. The tip of his cock once more brushed the scorching heat of her channel, and Kyle groaned with his own consuming need.

"Moira, you are a lot smaller than me. Before the other night, it was years since you've been with a man. If it's too much, if it's ever too much—if I push you to where you can't keep going—you need something you can say that I will know you mean stop. Something that I can never confuse your meaning. Pick a word that if you say it, I will cease that instant."

Moira struggled to follow what Kyle was saying, but the offer made her feel safe while she felt so vulnerable. "Duilesc," Moira blurted. She named a sea plant that grew along the rocks. It was an edible red algae. "I hate it. It's too salty."

"Very well. If anything we do together, or any punishment I give is more than you can manage, you need only say 'duilesc,' and I will stop. Can you remember that?" Kyle waited until she nodded. "Do you promise you'll use it? That you won't try to bear more than you can for my sake?"

Moira's eyes opened in surprise, unnerved that he knew she would most definitely try to endure anything for his sake. "Yes, Kyle."

With her acquiescence, Kyle surged into Moira. Her deep moan seemed to vibrate his cock as he settled into her sheath. He struggled not to pound into her because he wasn't certain whether Moira's moan was pleasure or pain. When she writhed beneath him, straining to move her hips, he accepted that she didn't want them to stop. With each thrust, Moira lifted her hips to take the punishing force of his. Their bodies slapped together as Kyle wrapped his arms beneath her and held her close to him.

"Kyle," Moira patted his shoulder blade. "May I? I can't wait."

"Aye. I want to watch you shatter with my cock buried in you," Kyle grunted; he thrust harder and faster as Moira screamed. Her nails clawed at his back, and her head tilted back, the cords in her neck straining as she squeezed her eyes shut.

"More," Moira panted.

Certain she'd found her release before him, Kyle wondered just how fast and hard he could piston himself into her. He welcomed the challenge; Moira's body was so receptive and pliant as her murmurs and pants encouraged him.

"Moira?" Kyle grunted. She opened her eyes and grinned before shutting them again. "Look at me. I need to see you're all right."

"I want to, but I can't. I can't keep my eyes open, Kyle. Just trust that I don't want you to stop. I haven't said that word."

"Am I not hurting you?" Kyle forced the words out as the air burned his lungs.

"But it feels better than I could have ever imagined," Moira answered. Moira's fingertips drilled into his skin as her body tightened once more, another climax ripping through her. Unable to hold back any longer, Kyle thrust again before pulling out. Without needing to stroke himself, his seed spilled across Moira's belly. He yanked the sheet up to wipe his cock before plunging back into her and holding still. He'd never done that before. Never entered a woman again after spilling. He'd always rolled off and usually gotten out of bed without looking back. But something compelled him to remain coupled with Moira, having only left her body to keep from impregnating her. She wrapped her arms around his ribs and her legs over his calves. "You won't break me."

Kyle brushed back damp hair from her forehead and kissed her temple. He eased more of his weight onto her, but he still held most of it on his forearms. He'd never felt so connected to a woman in his life. He'd lusted after plenty, bedded many, but cared about none. He wished to hold Moira every moment of every day for the rest of time. The feeling terrified him.

Moira enjoyed the silent companionship and closeness they shared in the aftermath of their passion. She wished she could drift off to sleep before Kyle moved off and away from her, wanting to slip away into perfect oblivion. But her mind was abuzz with questions she didn't dare ask but were still burning a hole in her mind. She stroked her nails along his back as her other hand rested at his waist, affection replacing desire. They turned their heads at the same time, and their mouths once more found each other. The kiss conveyed emotions neither understood. It wasn't love, or even tenderness. It wasn't impatient desire. It was deep satisfaction from sharing something so intensely intimate. It communicated their enjoyment as well as signaled their silent agreement that they both wanted this to happen again.

When Kyle finally rolled away, he pulled Moira into the cradle of his arms and stroked her hair. She nuzzled his neck before sighing. He wondered if she would fall asleep, but her fingertips ran over the bristle of his unshaven chin. With his hand on her backside, he pulled Moira's body flush with his, kissing her once more. Their bodies were too drained to recommence so soon, but they reveled in the feel of being pressed together. As the drugging effects of their coupling wore off, but fatigue set in, Kyle peered down at Moira.

"I can see about getting you some hot water. You're small enough that you will likely fit in one of the barrels if you'd like to soak in a hot bath," Kyle offered.

Moira grinned and snickered. "Are you trying to catch me in a fib, so you can add another spanking to my growing list?" At Kyle's sheepish expression, Moira giggled. "You know I snooped the first morning. That's why you warned me not to go into any small spaces even with Braedon. I'm certain you know I spied your tub in the galley. You're testing me."

"Mayhap a little." Kyle kissed the tip of her nose, then sobered. "Moira, you did earn two spankings today, but I'm setting them aside. Don't expect that to be the norm. But you've been through much in the last few days, and you have yet to learn my expectations. I also fear that your body isn't meant to be treated as roughly as I've done since you came aboard. I've pushed you too hard."

"You sound as though you regret it. Regret me being here," Moira pulled back. Her heart sank as rejection flooded her.

"No," Kyle snarled as he pulled her back against him. "I do not regret you being here. I should. I should do the right thing and take you wherever you wish. I should take you somewhere safe, so you never have to face the danger you will if you remain with me. You should make a life on land with a man who can provide for you. But I won't. I can't. I've touched you, been inside you, and I can't let you go, Moira."

Moira tucked a lock of russet hair behind Kyle's ear before she cupped his cheek. "Let me stay until we both decide this has run its course. I have nowhere to go, and I'm in no hurry to find one. I want to be on your ship, in your bed. If I didn't know better, I'd think you're drugging me. I'm still confused by why I like your heavy-handedness and desire to discipline me. I know I don't want this to be the last time we couple. And I confess, I'm curious."

"Curious? You still wish to learn more from me?" Kyle purred, more like a big cat stalking its prey than a docile barn cat.

"Will you teach me? I don't even know what there is to learn," Moira admitted.

"If you stay aboard the *Lady Charity*, your life is in danger. The English navy, the Irish, other pirates. Any could attack at any time," Kyle warned.

"And you will attack any of them when you have the chance. I understand that. I don't welcome it, but I expect it." Moira raised up on her elbow, her breasts pressed together. Kyle brushed the backs of his fingers over her nipples and trailed his finger down her deep cleavage as he listened. "I know you will keep me safe as best you can, but you're giving me the choice. And I'm telling you my answer. I want to stay with you."

"I am giving you a choice. But there is an option that you haven't told me, Moira. Where were you headed?" Kyle paused and waited for her answer. He held his breath to see if she trusted him with more than her body.

"Kyle," Moira sighed as she closed her eyes.

"Not ready to trust me," Kyle stated flatly.

"You're asking a lot of me, Kyle. I want to be here. Can that not be enough for right now? I'm already trusting you not to kill me, rape me, or abuse me. I've trusted you when you left me bound in here or kneeling for hours on end, no idea when you're coming back or the mood you'll be in. I've trusted you to spank me without trying to escape or fight you. Hell, I stripped naked and laid over your table, prepared for you to spank me without you even telling me to. You felt the need to warn me with a safe word because you knew you might push me too far, and I trusted you not to hurt me. I do trust you, Kyle. More than I should, given who you are, what you are, and how little I really know about you. I'm a fool to do so. But I do."

Moira laid down, unsure how Kyle would react. When he eased her back into his embrace and peppered soft kisses on her forehead and crown, she felt more confused than ever, but she also felt safe. Something that she'd only ever felt with Kyle. She'd never felt it at Dunluce, not even when she thought she loved Aidan.

"Will you stay with me until I fall asleep?" Moira asked before a yawn escaped. She placed her hand over his heart as her eyes drifted closed. "I need a nap." Kyle covered her hand with his and before drawing the covers over them. He considered resting his eyes, but he didn't want to miss a moment of Moira being nestled against him. Reality was outside the cabin door, and he would have to face it again soon enough. Outside their love nest was the ever-present chance that something would pull them apart. Kyle was in no rush to return to that, so he watched Moira sleep instead.

CHAPTER 14

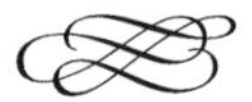

"Where do you think she was going?" Keith asked as he rocked on the rear two legs of his chair, his booted feet resting on the footboard of his bunk. Kyle had slipped out of bed with a peck on the cheek as Moira stirred, but didn't wake. He'd crossed over to the *Lady Grace* at twilight and now sat with his brother as they sorted through the unexpected events of finding Moira aboard a ship Kyle ransacked.

"She says south. She admitted that Dónal has betrothed her to Dermot O'Malley, so I know she wasn't headed there. That's why she ran—or rather sailed—away from Dunluce. According to Moira, her clan council doesn't agree with Dónal's choice of bedfellows, so they helped her escape. She hasn't told me where she was going, but I suspect to the O'Driscolls. Fionn wasn't pleased when Senga suspected that Dónal mistreats Moira, and I imagine Senga would expect Fionn to take her in. He respects Senga enough to oblige any request from one of her acquaintances. For all Fionn's sins, after what happened to Aisling, he doesn't ignore wounded women. It wouldn't surprise me if the O'Driscolls would take Moira to Senga and Caragh."

"You mean Rowan and Ruairí," Keith chuckled, and the

brothers clinked their mugs together. While Rowan and Ruairí MacNeil had once been the most terrifying duo of pirates sailing the British Isles, any who knew the men now that they were married with a child each knew it was their wives who were the most fearsome sailors between Ireland and Scotland. The couples had retired from pirating, but the MacNeils were seafaring people who depended on trade, since their island was small and had little arable land. Caragh and Senga still sailed with their husbands from time to time, and they were just as intimidating together as Rowan and Ruairí or Kyle and Keith. Both women were experts with swords and had the temerity to enter the fray whenever there were battles aboard ship. They placed family above all else, and were ruthless in defending their husbands.

Rowan was now Laird MacNeil, but Kyle and Keith visited Kisimul Castle often and knew it was Caragh–Lady MacNeil by title–who made people jump at her command. She had a charisma that made people want to do what she asked without her raising her voice or issuing threats. Senga wasn't that different, and her quiet guidance was always present. They made an indomitable team, and their husbands couldn't be prouder.

"I know I should take her to Senga myself, but I confess I don't want to," Kyle admitted.

"Having too much fun in your bed?" Keith snorted.

"Only twice," Kyle muttered.

"Only twice what? In your bed? Does she prefer the table or the wall? From what I heard, she likes the rail." Keith's boots clunked against the floor as he dove out of the reach of Kyle's fist. "What? Bluidy hell, you made me spill my whisky." Keith brushed the liquid from his leine before pouring himself more and topping off Kyle's mug.

"I've only coupled with her twice, if you must know."

"I mustn't, but now you've told me. She's been onboard more

than a sennight, and you've only had her twice? Slowing down in your auld age?"

"It's not like that. Keith, don't talk about her like she's a doxy. She's not," Kyle sighed.

"From what I heard, she came on deck in no more than a man's leine—maybe yours, maybe someone else's—and let your hand work its magic until she was moaning," Keith said with a cocked eyebrow.

"She did. And I did. But she didn't moan. And I'm certain no one actually saw what I was doing. They just made a good guess. But she's not a whore. She's like me," Kyle admitted.

"And you're trying to convince me she's not a whore?" Keith spluttered as he wiped whisky from his lips.

"I mean, she likes things the way I do," Kyle said with a pointed look at his brother.

"Ah. The way we both do. Rough."

"Yes. But not just that. She submits. Willingly. She wants to. We seem to understand what the other wants without speaking. We seem to give one another what we both need." Kyle shrugged. "I don't have a better explanation than that. But her trust has limits. I can't blame her for that. But the limit comes before she's willing to tell me where she was going."

"Then ask her where she wants to go. Maybe it's where she was headed, maybe not. But at least then you know something," Keith suggested.

"True."

"You fear she'll say she wants to go somewhere without you, or somewhere you can't follow. You don't want to ask what she wants. You'd rather know what her plans were in the past. Before you."

"You're a pain in the arse, did you know that?" Kyle scowled. "Leave reading my bluidy mind to when we're keeping each other alive in a fight."

"Blame God for making us two peas in a pod. It's not my

fault that what I would think in your place is what you're thinking too."

"So you say," Kyle grumbled. The brothers stood, both grinning. Being like-minded kept them alive while they were homeless orphans and then as young sailors. It protected them when they fought back to back, and it gave them an inexplicable way to sense when the other was in danger. Inconvenient as it might have been when Kyle wanted to keep his emotions private, neither would trade it for anything. They embraced. "I love you, brother."

"How can you not? I am the better-looking one," Keith teased, blocking Kyle's playful punch. "I love you too, brother."

While they never shared the sentiments in public, the twins always parted with the same words. They'd done so since they were children, always fearful that they wouldn't have the chance to say it again. It had stayed with them into adulthood.

"Go back to your cabin and the bonnie wench in your bed. Find out where we sail to next," Keith suggested.

"I'll let you know in the morn. But I suspect it's either south to Baltimore or east to Barra," Kyle said before passing through the doorway. He bounded up the ladder well. He paused to look around the small cove they'd sailed into before crossing the deck with quick strides and swinging across to his own ship. He entered his cabin to find a naked Moira kneeling before his chest, holding items he was certain she'd never imagined. She gasped and dropped everything to the floor.

"I was looking for warmer clothes. I swear," Moira blurted. She sighed and crawled to the nearby wall before kneeling with her hands behind her back.

"Come here, sweet one. And bring the implements with you."

CHAPTER 15

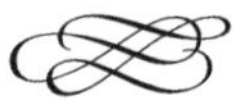

Kyle was unprepared for the sight that greeted him. Finding Moira naked and examining a marble phallus and marble anal plug was not what he expected. He'd sailed throughout the Mediterranean for years and gained various trinkets along the way. He'd discovered the implements Moira now scooped off the floor while in ports along the Grecian and Italian coasts. Women in the brothels enjoyed introducing Kyle to the various sex acts that his naïve adolescent mind hadn't imagined. It was with these women that he discovered his propensity towards being dominant. For the right amount of coin, the whores encouraged Kyle and Keith to explore fetishes, some appealing and some too shocking even for the twins. Returning to the British Isles meant finding women who would let him plunder their dark passage, but none who dared play with the wicked devices he had acquired over the years.

As Moira placed the marble items on the bed where Kyle pointed, he squatted beside the open trunk, rummaging deeper until he found what he desired. He lifted the gold chain from its pouch and fisted the cold metal. As Moira watched him, her eyes round with trepidation, he breathed warm air on the tiny metal clamps on either end of the chain. He came to stand before Moira, still surprised that she hadn't screamed in horror at her findings. He narrowed his eyes as a thought crossed his mind.

"Do you know what you've found, sweet one?" Kyle's voice was deceptively soft, and a shiver ran along Moira's spine.

"Things that don't belong to me that I shouldn't have been touching," Moira responded. "I'm—"

"I'm not angry. Just the opposite. I hadn't thought to introduce you to these so soon, but since you've found our devices."

"Devices? Ours?" Moira stammered.

"Yes to both. They are devices for us to enjoy in private. You haven't found everything; at least, you hadn't pulled out everything. And while I may have acquired them, they are ours because we will use them together."

"But what are they?" Moira whispered.

Kyle guided Moira to sit on the bed, the various accoutrement spread out between them. He picked up the phallus and wrapped his hand around it, sliding over the smooth stone. Moira's eyes widened further as her tongue darted out between her lips. "I take it you've figured out what this is."

"Y—Yes. But why would you—or I guess I—need that?"

"Because my cock can only be inside one hole at a time, and you have two others that need filling," Kyle explained. His matter of fact tone made Moira's chin fall forward in shock. "Perhaps I wish for you to suck me. I might finger your quim, but that leaves your delectable arse ignored. Or perhaps, I wish to kiss you while I fuck your arse from behind. Your cunny will ache with loneliness. This can soothe that ache. Or maybe I wish to watch you play with yourself as I stroke my cock."

Moira remained silent, swallowing over and over, nodding once. She accepted the phallus when Kyle handed it to her, running her fingers over the cool stone before timidly wrapping her hands around it. Her eyes darted to the bulge in Kyle's leggings, her attention now on the real object of her desire rather than the substitute.

"You shall have that soon enough, since I'm finding it hard to concentrate on my explanation. Do you have any idea what this is called?"

"A phallus," Moira whispered.

"It is. It's what the Romans, even the Greeks, called an erect cock. That," Kyle pointed to the marble, "is also called a dildo. It comes from the Italian *diletto*, or delight, because it can certainly delight a woman."

"Is that that where you got it? In Naples, I mean?"

"Yes. That I bought in a market in there. These," Kyle picked up the set of four different size anal plugs. "Came from a vendor in Lepanto, a village on the southwestern Greek Isles. Do you have any thoughts on what they might be for?"

Moira shook her head even as Kyle handed them to her. She looked at the smallest, then the largest, leaving the middle two on the mattress beside her.

"I pulled out today because I won't leave you with a bastard, Moira. And I won't force you to stay with me because I will neither take a child from you nor abandon one. I can spill inside you if I use your back passage."

Moira licked her lips and nodded. "I know that already, Kyle." Her cheeks flushed as Kyle sat back. She watched his jaw clench as he crossed his arms.

"Aidan?"

"Yes," Moira whispered, suddenly ashamed of her past. Kyle took the anal plugs from her hands before drawing her closer to him.

"I'm not angry. Just a little jealous. I thought to introduce something new to you," Kyle admitted.

"All of this," Moira jutted her chin at the implements, "is very new to me, Kyle. I had no idea they existed."

"Did Aidan do anything to help prepare your body for that? It can be painful otherwise." Concern filled Kyle's voice, and he prayed Aidan had been gentle with her, or he would run the smug Irish pirate through with his rustiest dirk.

"I wanted to because I understood it was less risky. It wasn't my favorite, though. It wasn't very comfortable or very satisfying," Moira admitted.

"Did he not see to your pleasure when he coupled with you like that?" Kyle asked softly.

"Not like the other way." Moira couldn't bring her eyes to meet his, embarrassed by their conversation. It was one thing to tell Kyle that she'd been intimate with Aidan or for him to deduce what she'd done. It was another thing entirely to discuss it.

"These are different sizes to help your body become acquainted with the feel of being filled back there. It will make it easier to take my cock after some training." Kyle brushed hair back off Moira's shoulder and rubbed the tension from where her neck met her shoulder. "It can also be a way to heighten your arousal when you're waiting for me."

"What's that?" Moira looked at the gold chain that now lay among the collection.

"These are nipple clamps. You know how you react when I pinch or bite your nipples." Kyle waited for Moira to acknowledge his statement. When her eyes met his, he saw the arousal that dilated her pupils. "If you wish to wear them, then you may. They will remind you of my teeth on you when you wear them beneath your clothes, Moira. Then your nipples will be puckered and ready for me to soothe when the bite from the clamp ends."

"Can you put them on me now, Kyle?" Moira murmured.

"Of course, *mo ghràidh*," Kyle replied. At Moira's look of confusion, his expression softened. "It means my dear in Scottish Gaelic."

"Ah, *mo stór* in Irish," Moira replied. She canted her head as she looked at Kyle. "May I kiss you?"

"You don't have to ask, Moira," Kyle reassured. Moira inched closer. She kneeled before him as she eased her lips against his. The fire combusted between them, and Moira wasn't sure if she climbed into his lap or if he pulled her, but she straddled Kyle's hips. Their kiss drew on until they were both breathless.

"The clamps. Put them on, please," Moira panted. Kyle leaned back and pinched Moira's nipples, rolling them between his thumbs and forefingers before breathing cool air onto them. As he continued to roll one, his teeth grazed the other, alternating until both were both tight, protruding nubs. Moira hissed as Kyle attached the first clamp but remained silent when he added the second.

"What do you wish to try next, sweet one?" Kyle purred as he trailed kisses along her neck to the sensitive spot behind her ear.

"I wish to do something for you, Kyle," Moira whispered.

"Oh?"

"Are you going to make me say it?" Moira asked. Her eyes drifted closed in resignation when he nodded. "I want to suck you."

Kyle stood from the bed and undressed. Her eyes roamed over Kyle's perfectly formed body. She noticed the various scars that stood as proof to a life of hardship and violence. His muscles rippled as they flexed before her. As she continued to peruse his physique, she sensed he was growing anxious, almost nervous.

"Do you not wish for me to look at you?" Moira asked as she stood from the bed.

"Do you like what you see?" Kyle countered.

"Are you worried that I won't?" Moira cocked a brow and waited to see if Kyle would answer truthfully.

"Of course."

Unprepared for such a blunt response, Moira stepped closer but didn't touch Kyle. "Capt'n, may I kiss you?" Kyle responded with a jerky nod. Moira sank to her knees; gathering her hair in one hand, she feathered kisses along his shaft from root to tip. When she reached the head of his cock, she whirled her tongue around the tip before licking his length. When she slid her mouth down Kyle's shaft, he thrust, his hands pressing her head toward him. Moira didn't panic, rather gripping his hips with her hands.

"Dear God, I'm ready to spill," Kyle growled. Moira drew him to the back of her throat as she worked his cock. When he tried to pull away, she looked up at him, reassuring him that she didn't want to stop. His seed shot down her throat as she forced herself not to gag. She swallowed over and over, not enjoying the taste, but enjoying the satisfaction of bringing Kyle to release so quickly. Kyle sighed as he helped Moira to her feet. He handed her a flask of whisky, and she took a long draw.

"Scottish," Moira murmured.

"Good," Kyle corrected. Moira pulled her lips in, but she couldn't hide her grin.

"Your turn, sweet one," Kyle rasped, his throaty voice sending pulses of need to Moira's nipples. His hands kneaded the mounds, making the clamps bounce, but he never touched her nipples. "They ache, don't they?"

"Yes. As does my cunny," Moira admitted.

"How do you feel, Moira? Can you play, or are the clamps becoming too much?" Kyle prepared to remove them and soothe the inevitable sting, even comfort her before easing her into release. But Moira shook her head.

"Leave them, please."

"Do they not hurt?"

"They do, but I—I like it. I want to try whatever you want, Kyle," Moira confessed.

"Perhaps one toy is enough for tonight," Kyle hedged. He

noticed the dark shadows creeping beneath Moira's eyes, and he suspected she was more exhausted than she realized. She'd slept for much of the afternoon, but he knew she didn't sleep well at Dunluce, and much had happened in the past week.

"May I decide that for right now, Capt'n?" Moira stood with her hands clasped before her, chin down.

"I will grant your request, sweet one. But I will decide," Kyle corrected. "What do you wish to try?"

Moira looked at the selection on the bed and picked up the slimmest anal plug and held it up. Kyle nodded before stepping over to the chest where Moira found the buried treasure. He pulled two vials from a pouch and held them up for Moira to see as he returned to stand before her.

"This one is a simple oil. No actual scent, but it will ease the plug into you. It's what I will use on my cock before I enter you when the time comes." Kyle shook the other tiny bottle. "This one is ginger oil. Too much will cause you serious pain, Moira. You are not to touch it. Am I understood?" He waited for Moira to nod, her eyes wide. "There may come a time when your punishment warrants me adding a small amount to a plug. We can experiment with this another night, and you may find that you enjoy a dab or two. But until I'm certain you know how potent it is, you are not to touch it. Come and lean over the table as you did earlier, sweet one."

Moira hurried to follow his directions, groaning as her sensitive nipples pressed against the hardwood. Kyle's hands slid over her backside, squeezing and massaging the flesh. As he felt her relax, he swept his thumb along the division between the two globes. After several passes, he used his thumbs to pull the flesh apart. He rested his semi-aroused sword against the sheath he wanted wrapped around it. His hands gripped Moira's hips as he rocked. She pushed back to meet him.

Easing his left hand along her pelvis, Kyle slipped his fingers into her channel. Drawing his hips away from her bottom, his other thumb tapped her rosebud several times as he watched her relax further. With one hand still working her core, he reached to the bed and snagged the smallest plug. Still working with one hand, he popped the cork from the vial and dribbled the oil along the division between Moira's buttocks. He swirled the oil around the tight hole before nudging his finger into her secret passage. Moving quickly now, he added oil to the plug and brought it to her backside.

"Easy, sweet one. You know what's happening. But it shouldn't hurt as it did before. Breathe out as I press this into you," Kyle said in soft tones. Once the tip entered Moira, he twisted as he inched it inside her. When the flange sat flush with her skin, he admired the site, his cock surging back to life. But he forced himself to ignore his intensifying need, focused on bringing Moira pleasure before they found it together. "Stand up and see how you feel."

Moira rose from the table, uncertain how the new position would feel. It was awkward, but not painful. It intrigued her as she looked back at Kyle. She nodded, and he guided her to the bunk. Once she laid back, settled against the pillows, Kyle climbed between her thighs, letting his feet dangle off the end of the bed. Without warning, he wrapped his lips around her bud and drew it into his mouth. Her moan gave him pure male satisfaction as her hand pressed his head to her sheath. He gripped both of her wrists and pinned them to the bed. She would cede complete control to him on her own, or he would cease. Her hands flexed, but it was only a moment later that she sighed. He felt her body go limp and watched as her eyes drifted closed.

As his teeth nibbled and his tongue laved, his need to thrust into her just as his tongue did became undeniable. He rocked his hips into the mattress, trying to ease his discomfort. Knowing he wouldn't last long before abandoning his current approach to pleasuring Moira, he sucked hard on her bud. Her hips sprang off the bed as she shattered. As the spasms rippled through her core, Kyle shifted up and thrust into her. Supporting himself on one forearm, he released one clamp, his mouth immediately taking its place. He licked the grooves left on Moira's silky skin. As he rocked into her over and over, he soothed the sting. When she sighed, he shifted and released the other nipple. Her moan signaled her second release as her thighs squeezed the sides of his hips. She hadn't reached for him since he'd pressed her hands away.

"Kyle," Moira moaned. "So full."

"Are you all right?" Kyle asked, praying that she didn't ask him to stop. She'd been tight the last time he buried himself within her, but the addition of the plug made her channel into a vice.

"Yes. Can we stay like this for always?"

"Would that we could, sweet one," Kyle chuckled. Moira rubbed her punished nipples against his chest, and he knew the pins and needles she felt would continue even after they finished. It would be a reminder of what they shared. As one hand continued to knead her breast, he realized that he longed to feel her hands on him. He'd never cared much in the past. As long as his bed partners did as he expected and didn't just lay beneath him, he hadn't been interested in them touching him. Now he could think of nothing else but Moira's hands exploring his body as they had the last time they joined. "Touch me."

Moira's instantaneous response and sigh told Kyle what he'd hoped for. She was desperate for more contact, to take part fully in their coupling. "Kiss," she muttered as her hands slid down his back until she grasped his backside, squeezing as she encouraged him to piston his cock into her. He captured her mouth in a wild and searing kiss that stole her breath away.

Moira's body was floating above her even as she felt Kyle pressing her into the mattress. She never imagined such a maelstrom of sensations could coexist in her body without it going up in a conflagration of flames. Her palms had itched with the need to touch him, but she gladly surrendered to him, giving all control over to Kyle. Her curiosity encouraged her to discover without hesitation each unfamiliar sensation he introduced. But his invitation to touch him set her free, a wildness surging through her that made her hips meet his with just as much force as he used.

Kyle flipped them, so he bore Moira's weight on top of him. She looked at him in surprise, but her pupils further dilated when his hand smacked her backside with a ringing echo in the cabin. He brought his hand down over and over, each spanking sparking an aggressiveness he didn't expect in Moira. She moved faster and with more determination each time he left her bottom stinging.

"You're enjoying this," Kyle said, uncertain whether he meant it as a statement or a question.

"Yes," Moira growled. She leaned back and rode him until a smothered scream tried to escape her throat. Her fingers clawed his chest as her body seized. Kyle rolled them once more, slamming into her over and over until he pulled free, his seed coating her breasts and throat. He pinched each nipple once more, making Moira shudder. He moved aside, reaching over Moira to drop the gold chain on the floor before he glided his hand over her hip until he grasped the plug. With all the gentleness he could muster, he eased the device from her rosebud before climbing over Moira and taking it to the bowl on the washstand. He wiped himself clean with a damp cloth before returning to the bed. He perched on the edge as Moira watched him. He shook his head when she tried to take the cloth from him as he pressed her legs apart.

"Let me tend to you in every way, Moira. Let me see to all of your needs, not just your pleasure," Kyle explained. When he was through and the cloth laid in the bowl too, he drew the covers over them both. "How do you feel?"

"Sleepy. My body is boneless, and my mind is clear. Everything feels warm and cheery. I ache for more while being sated at the same time. Never did I imagine coupling could be like that," Moira confessed. Kyle's arm rested beneath her neck, and his fingers and thumb glided over her skin, sending a delightful shiver down Moira's back. She sighed as her eyes drifted closed.

"I didn't know it could be like that either," Kyle admitted. Moira's eyes flew open, the look of confusion clear. "Yes, I have used those kinds of implements with women before and taken pleasure in the coupling, but never did it consume me so fully. The ship could have burned down around my ears, and I wouldn't have noticed. All I could think about was being inside you, how if felt each time you climaxed. Moira, I nearly didn't pull out. I nearly gave in to the need to finish inside you."

Moira adjusted her head to look up at him as she tried to understand what he was and wasn't telling her. "What do you mean 'those kinds of implements?' Have you not used those very ones before?"

"No, I haven't. Women in Ireland and Scotland aren't usually so adventurous with such things. Lusty and hungry, but few are prepared for that kind of unknown."

"Then why do you have them? Saving them for when someone would agree? Am I the first to?"

"Aye. Moira, you may be the only one. I can't imagine sharing with another woman what I just did with you. It was my wildest dreams come true."

"I never imagined such things, so I can't say that I've dreamed of it before." Moira's lips twitched until she offered Kyle a broad grin. "But I suspect I will every night from now on."

They laid in silence as they both luxuriated in the afterglow of their time together, but something Kyle said lingered in Moira's mind. She mulled it over, but she couldn't accept her interpretation.

What did he mean, I may be the only one? Surely, he isn't suddenly going to stop tupping women once I'm gone, and I don't think he's suddenly going to change what he enjoys. There must be another woman on the British Isles who would enjoy the devices too. I can't be the only one.

"What are you thinking about, sweet one?" Kyle's voice broke through Moira's thoughts. If he'd said anything else, they might lull her to sleep.

"I was thinking about what you said. I can't imagine how I'll be the only one you use those with," Moira stated. Kyle rolled toward her, so she laid flat on her back. He kissed her lips, but only for a moment before trailing kisses along her cheekbone to her jaw, then down her neck, to the hollow at its base. He dropped a light kiss on each nipple, the skin starting to flatten.

"I think you'll be the only one because no one and nothing can compare to what's passed between us in such a short time. Moira, you're not my captive. I won't force you to stay aboard, and I won't set you adrift. Wherever you wish to go, I will take you. But if you wish to remain here with me, I welcome you to stay. I've made clear to you my predilections, and no, you aren't the first woman to experience them. But I don't know that I can share what we just did with anyone else. I fear I would only think of you, only be disappointed."

Moira lay still as she listened to Kyle. She recognized it would be far easier for him to find a woman willing to share such sexual acts than it would be for her to find a man who would. He need only walk into a tavern and plunk down coins. But she could never ask a man, a husband, to do such things. Even Aidan wasn't a man she could imagine suggesting such things to. He might enjoy it, but she could never bring herself to mention it. Kyle understood her on an elemental level when it came to her physical needs. She had no idea if they could live together in the tiny cabin or even aboard his ship, but she was in no hurry to end their liaison. She could think of only one solution for when he tired of having her aboard.

"When you no longer wish for me to sail with you, I will find a cottage somewhere near the coast," Moira began as she trailed her fingers over a scar on his shoulder. "I shall say I'm a widow who doesn't wish to marry again. When you wish to visit me, if you do, my door will always be open, and my bed will always welcome you."

"Is that what you wish? A cottage instead of a cabin?" Kyle's chest tightened, and the ache made it painful to breathe. He feared Moira's answer, and he berated himself for being a fool for caring.

"Only once you wish for me to leave," Moira answered.

"And if I don't? If I want you to stay?" Kyle murmured.

"How about we not worry about making a plan for the future quite yet? You can find other women, Kyle, who will enjoy what you do, or at least accept what you want. I won't find a man who I can ask to do to me what you've done in a sennight. I suspect there is still plenty more for you to teach me. I would experience it all, enjoy it, create happy memories that will sustain me when we do part company."

Kyle's chest still ached. Her words did nothing to ease the pain, the fear. "But you do expect to leave me."

"I expect little, Kyle. But I anticipate there will be a time when you grow tired of me," Moira corrected.

"Why? Why do you think that?" Kyle demanded.

"Because if you wanted a woman at your side, you'd already have one," Moira retorted. Kyle rolled over Moira once again, this time straddling her hips. He grasped her wrists and pulled her arms over her head. When she didn't wince, he tightened his grip, pinning her in place.

"Did it not occur to you that I hadn't found a woman I wanted until you? Did it occur to you that I may never want to let you go? Would you stay with me?"

Moira gazed into eyes the color of Irish grass after a storm. She arched her back, pressing her body against Kyle's. She prayed he saw the willingness, the acceptance in her eyes. She felt his length pulse against her mound, and she stirred restlessly. She whispered, "Kyle, keep me as your captive. Keep me as your mistress. Just please keep me."

Kyle released a ragged breath and shifted until he slid into her sheath. Neither moved, Kyle's cock pulsing within Moira's sheath. Still clasping her wrists in one hand, he cupped her cheek with the other. Their kiss was soft and languid, their bodies at rest. This wasn't about seeking pleasure, domination and submission. It was about both of them surrendering.

"I wish I could fall asleep with us like this," Moira said wistfully.

"I won't move away if you don't want me to," Kyle assured her.

"May I embrace you, Capt'n?" Moira kept her eyes cast down. They drifted closed when Kyle kissed her forehead and released her wrists. She wrapped her arms around him as Kyle settled with his head on the pillow just above her shoulder. He still kept much of his weight off her. He would grant her wish, any wish, then sleep beside her once he was sure she slumbered.

Moira suspected Kyle's intentions stemmed from the aftereffects of such a cataclysmic coupling. She didn't expect his feelings to remain so sure, but she prayed they would. She wanted to remain with him. She had nowhere else to go, nor did she want to find anywhere else to go. The connection they shared while they lay in one another's arms was unlike anything she imagined she could share with a man. She hadn't experienced it with Aidan, and she'd believed she would remain unwed for so many years, that she'd given up hope. She certainly couldn't envision such a situation if she married Dermot O'Malley.

Moira shifted beneath Kyle, and they both groaned as the feel of their bodies still joined sparked a fresh wave of need.

Kyle looked down at Moira, and she nodded. He moved slowly within her. There was no frenzy; neither was in control. They pressed together as they gazed into one another's eyes. When Moira's release radiated from her core, it wasn't a blaze that scorched her but a toasty fire that warmed her from end to end. Kyle slipped from her, his cock resting against her mound, the friction continuing as he rocked against her until he climaxed, and she followed. Just as he had the first time they coupled for their mutual pleasure, he wiped his cock and joined them once more. They both sighed, but there was a sense of regret.

"Kyle, if we did put ashore near any open fields or even wooded areas, I should be able to gather pennyroyal," Moira said tentatively.

"What do you need that for?" Kyle's brow furrowed.

"Made into a tea, it should keep me from conceiving if you spill in me," Moira said tentatively.

"Should?" Kyle asked.

"Aye. Aidan—well, I just made sure to be careful since he—" Moira hated admitting this to Kyle. She wished there was no past to tell.

"Moira, it was before I knew you. I don't fault you for your past. I don't want you to be uncomfortable telling me things, sharing things that matter to you," Kyle reassured.

"I know. I just spent so many years never discussing it. And I know you don't like him. *I* don't particularly like him."

"How do you know that?"

"When you visited last year, and Sean came running into the Great Hall claiming Ruairí was his da, I saw the murderous look you gave Aidan. I knew you hadn't seen me before that visit because I kept out of sight during meals, but I always watched from beneath the stairs or from the kitchen door. I saw how you avoided him, giving him a wide berth," Moira explained.

"That is true, but I don't begrudge you your past," Kyle clarified.

Moira nodded. "I also know because I told Lizzie that she should use it. She was with child after Sean. More than once until I told her she should drink it before rather than after. It can prevent a woman from conceiving, but it can also rid a woman's body of a bairn."

"Is it guaranteed?"

"Nay. I suppose nothing besides not coupling is guaranteed," Moira admitted.

"But you would take the chance of me siring a bairn with you?" Kyle asked as he lay still.

"I—I might. Perhaps I have it on hand if we accept the risk," Moira hedged.

"We're anchored in a cove. There is a path that leads to a meadow on the cliffs. I will take you in the morning if you still want," Kyle offered.

"I will," Moira said decisively. They looked at one another for the space of several breaths before Kyle inched onto his side, once more pulling Moira into his embrace before they fell asleep.

CHAPTER 16

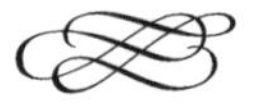

Moira awoke feeling deliciously warm, with a brawny arm slung over her waist. No light filtered into the cabin, so she knew it wasn't quite morning. She considered all that transpired the night before; she started to really take in everything that had happened since she fled Dunluce.

I get woken up in the middle of the night and told I need to run away. I do, only to spend three days at sea and have pirates attack us. What were the chances a pirate I know would raid us? A pirate I've found devastatingly handsome and dreamed of coupling with since the first time I saw him? I never imagined he'd find me attractive. I can only assume it's because I'm the only woman available. But he's said little things here and there that make me think it's more than that. But how can it be? I'm doubting how he feels, but how do I feel? What am I doing not trying to escape? Why don't I escape? Why do I have more questions than answers?

He could tire of me at any time, and then what? He dumps me ashore somewhere. I'm already supposed to be at the O'Driscolls. Do they know? Are they expecting me? Can I get Kyle to take me to Senga and Ruairí? Shite. I don't want to leave Kyle. No man has ever made me feel like Kyle does. Not even Aidan.

Moira shifted to look at Kyle.

Has he sent someone to the O'Malleys? Would he send me to Dermot for a ransom? I can't imagine why he would. He wouldn't get enough for me to make it worth it. We're close enough to them that he could have already taken me ashore. I just don't know. The only thing I understand better about Kyle at this point is how he likes to bed his women. His women? Don't fool yourself, Moira. You're his mistress, and you don't mind in the least. Why would I mind when I'm enjoying myself? Maybe one day I will end up married to a man I can't stand. At least I'll look back at my time here and remember the way Kyle made me feel. But… I need to go back to sleep. I won't figure anything out now. I'm just going to confuse myself more.

Moira yawned as she nestled closer to Kyle, but she nearly jumped out of her skin when he kissed her forehead. She hadn't realized that he was awake.

"You grew restless. What are you thinking about?" Kyle's groggy voice filled her ear.

"I didn't mean to wake you," Moira whispered.

"I'm a light sleeper. What's bothering you?" Kyle pressed. Moira remained quiet, uncertain how to tell Kyle any of her thoughts without revealing more than she was ready to tell. Kyle's hand roamed over her breasts, then tweaked her nipple. Hard. Her nipples were still sore from the clamps, so the sensitive skin reacted immediately. Need bolted from Moira's breast to her core. "You still don't trust me, Moira." Kyle murmured.

Kyle kissed along her neck as he shifted until he could suckle her breast. He was ravenous as he drew her flesh into his mouth, sucking over and over as Moira squirmed. Moira struggled to speak between gasps. "And you're still manipulating me with pleasure."

Kyle's head lifted from her breast. "No. I'm showing you that I'll tend to your needs."

"My physical needs. Will you hold my release hostage again if I don't tell you what you wish to hear?" Moira's arousal was fading as she realized Kyle's tactic. He moved across her and left the bunk in search of the candle and flint. Once it was lit, he returned to the bed and slid next to her. He realized that he'd slept on the inside more than once, and he remonstrated himself for being so careless. He should have slept closer to the edge and the door in case he needed his sword to protect Moira. He was so used to having the bunk to himself that he hadn't thought of which side he should sleep on. "Kyle? You're not even listening."

"I am, Moira. But I admit I'm distracted."

"By my breasts?"

"They are highly distracting, but no." Kyle shook his head as he glanced at where his sword rested at the foot of the bed.

"Now you won't tell me what you're thinking because I won't share my thoughts. You're still manipulating me." Moira sighed and tried to roll away from Kyle.

"I was thinking how stupid I was not to notice that I left you unguarded by sleeping on the other side of the bed. I wouldn't be able to get out of bed fast enough to protect you if we're attacked," Kyle confessed. Moira's brow furrowed as she considered what Kyle said. She glanced at him, then his sword, then the door. A shiver of fear slid down her spine. "Moira, I don't want to just take care of your physical pleasure. I know I need to learn how, but I would see to more than just bringing you to climax."

"Why?" Moira blurted.

"Because—" Kyle paused as he thought about why this seemed so urgent. "Because I want you to trust me. The only people whose trust really matters to me are Keith and Ruairí. I suppose Rowan by extension. The men trust me to provide for them, but they would do that with any captain. It's not me personally that they have confidence in. I don't know why it matters so much, but I think I want you to trust me because of what I want to do with and to you."

"You mean those implements," Moira clarified.

"Not exactly. There are things I've heard of but never tried before. I'd like to explore them with you, but for us to both enjoy it, I need you to trust me. It needs to go beyond you knowing I won't force you, or purposely harm you," Kyle explained.

Moira listened to Kyle, considering how much she did trust him. She welcomed the love play, but she'd known from the start it was more than that. She accepted his punishment because she wanted it. Moira realized she trusted Kyle more than she thought because she'd relinquished control to him and trusted him not to take advantage of that. She wanted to follow his rules; she wanted to please him in ways beyond just bringing him to climax. She'd done all of that just from her own intuition, and Kyle hadn't abused his position. He tried to wheedle information from her, and she felt manipulated at times, but he'd never denied his intentions or his methods.

"I think I already do," Moira whispered. She frowned for a moment before speaking more clearly. "When you sent me to the corner, I didn't enjoy it. I could have sat on the bed or the floor while you were gone. I could have slept in the bed. I did none of those things. Instead, I thought about how I disappointed you; how my rebelliousness made me feel worse, not better. When I call you Capt'n, it's because I want you to be in command of me. When Dónal issued orders to me and forced me to call him Chieftain, I wanted to gut him. But when you do it, I don't fear you taking advantage of me or maliciously wielding your power. I suppose it's why I haven't thought about escaping."

"Moira, you say you want to stay, but if you wish for me to take you somewhere, I won't begrudge your decision."

"The plan was for me to go to Fionn O'Driscoll, then on to

Barra," Moira stated. She waited for regret to set in now that she had revealed the information, but she felt none. Keeping the secret didn't seem so important once she shared it.

"Was it your request to go to Senga and Ruairí?" Kyle asked, fearing Moira would answer with the affirmative.

"No. I told you, the clan councilmen showed up in the middle of the night saying they had devised the plan to take me to Baltimore and then have the O'Driscolls take me to Barra. I had no part in the plan." Moira had a sudden thought. "Kyle, I didn't tell you not because I don't trust you. I didn't tell you because I don't want to go to either place. I mean, in the beginning I didn't tell you because I was too scared. But I've refused to tell you until now because I don't want you to send me away."

"Because you're having too much fun?" Kyle asked without a trace of humor.

"Kyle, I'm telling you I want to stay aboard a pirate ship and face God knows what future because I'm onboard with you. Maybe most of my reason is because I want to couple with you, because desire is overruling reason. Maybe it's something more. I haven't a bluidy clue. But nothing is making me want to run."

"What I haven't told you may," Kyle muttered. Moira's cool fingers brushed against his bristled cheek. She strained to kiss him, keeping it light and short.

"I haven't said no to anything."

"But everyone has their limits, sweet one. I may ask for what goes beyond yours," Kyle said dubiously.

"How will you know if you don't ask?" Moira pointed out.

"You've seen all but one of my devices. But I wish for you to —I wish to restrain you while I spank you," Kyle blurted.

Moira nodded as she considered what Kyle might be envisioning. She glanced at the hook in the ceiling before looking back at Kyle.

"Yes, that is one way I wish to do it. I also wish to take you from behind while you're suspended from the hook."

"Which—which way?" Moira stuttered.

"Your cunny for that."

"What else do you imagine?" Moira swallowed.

"Stretching you on the table, arms and legs bound to the table legs. I wish for you to wear the clamps while plugged." Kyle watched as Moira's brow creased before she nodded her head in understanding. "The other item I haven't shown you are a set of small marble balls. They are called *ben wa* balls, and they come from the Orient, where women carry them within their quim. I would place them inside you, punishing you if they should slip loose. I wish to watch you on the table as you wonder when I will touch you."

"What would you do?" Moira shuddered as she reached for Kyle's hand. "Capt'n, will you please touch me while you tell me?"

Kyle's fingers slid inside Moira's drenched channel. The sound of her sigh made his cock swell. His thumb rubbed slow circles over her bud as he continued to share his intimate imaginings. "I would sit between your legs and suck your nub over and over until you're breathless, pulling away just before you climax. I'd taunt you until you're ready to use your safe word. Then I would draw from you the most powerful release you've ever had before taking the balls from you and thrusting into you over and over. God, how I want to pound into you, making you scream in pain and pleasure until I spill inside you."

Moira's hands pressed Kyle's against her mound, encouraging him to add more fingers. "May I?" Moira panted.

"Aye, sweet one," Kyle growled. She strained to find just the movement against Kyle's hand that she needed. But no matter how she moved, tensed or relaxed, the pleasure remained elusive. She whimpered with frustration as her eyes pleaded with Kyle. "What do you need, *mo ghràidh*? Do you need my cock?"

"Yes," Moira wailed as she threw her head back and squeezed

her eyes shut. She writhed at Kyle's touch. She fisted the sheets as he withdrew his fingers, waiting for the feel of his cock. With her legs splayed wide, Kyle thrust into her. On a hissing breath, Moira muttered, "Fuck."

"That is exactly what I shall do to you, sweet one. Over and over until you can't see straight, until all you can think about is the next time I'll be inside you, the next time you'll feel me in command of you and your pleasure." Kyle punctuated each word with a thrust.

"Anything, Kyle. Do what you want, just stay inside me," Moira babbled, nearly insensate. They met each thrust with moans until tears streamed down Moira's cheeks. She felt them falling but couldn't understand why, when she wasn't sad or hurt. She was just overwhelmed by a need to submit to Kyle and the force he used to pound into her. His aggression only heightened her arousal. She'd never felt so needed and wanted in all her life. As Kyle whispered words of encouragement, promises of the other things he would do to her, his demands for her to submit, she wanted nothing more than to belong to Kyle. There wasn't anything she would have denied him in that moment, and she suspected that even in the calmest of times, there was little that she would refuse.

As she flew over the precipice, she gripped Kyle's arms, her fingers biting into the muscle. Her entire frame shook as the waves of euphoria crashed over her. But when he made to withdraw, she cried out, "Stay."

"Are you sure," Kyle panted. "And if you don't find the plant?"

"Stay," Moira repeated. "Just this once. I know the risk. I need you."

Kyle slid his arms beneath Moira's shoulders and brought their foreheads together. "I need you. I need to be inside you. You're mine, Moira, even if it's only for a moment. I want nothing between us." Kyle shuddered as his seed jetted from him. He knew he'd made a grave error, but he didn't regret it, at least not yet. As much as he claimed Moira by possibly planting his seed, she had claimed him. He'd never spilled inside a woman as he just had. Their father abandoned Kyle and Keith, and both men had sworn never to sire a bastard who they might unintentionally abandon. But this time, he'd given, and Moira had taken.

Moira watched Kyle as he struggled to catch his breath. She watched while he was deep in thought, but when he eased his body onto hers, he let her bear the full weight. She could tell he was hesitant until she allowed it. She felt the tension ease from him, and she suspected it was the first time Kyle ever gave himself permission to let down his guard. She stroked his back, crooning nonsense to him.

"Will you let me hold you?" Moira whispered.

"God, yes. Don't let go, Moira," Kyle shuddered before kissing Moira's shoulder. "Moira, I'm yours for as long as you want me." Kyle whispered his promise. The only time he'd given a pledge that carried more significance was when he and Keith were seven and swore they would kill before anyone separated them. He recalled the intensity of that feeling as if he were that child again. How he felt in Moira's arms mirrored it.

How the fuck can I need a woman I've known for a sennight? Why am I so vulnerable to her? What the devil is happening to me? She could knife me in the back right this very moment. She could kill me in my sleep. My heart has been dead for years, yet it suddenly feels like it will beat out of my chest just to be near her. I'm a bluidy fool. I'd do well to keep my heart guarded before I go and do something stupid like give it to her. She will leave someday. Everyone does. And she'll take my heart with her if I'm not careful. I'll give her my body, my protection, and my trust, but I draw the line at my heart.

Kyle rolled onto his back, making sure he was on the edge of the bed before he drew Moira closer, draping her arm over his ribs as her head rested on his chest.

"Don't break my heart," Moira said as she drifted to sleep. Kyle held her as he closed his eyes.

I pray the same.

CHAPTER 17

Moira sat in the dinghy beside Kyle as it drew closer to the shore. She still wanted to search for the pennyroyal, but Kyle warned her that the land where they would go looking was O'Malley land. She watched Snake Eye row while Tomas braced himself in the bow, a crossbow in his arms. Kyle had insisted that both men come ashore with them, initially suggesting he bring more of the crew. When she smiled at him as though to indulge his moodiness, he'd carried her back to the cabin and laid her over his lap. As she sat in the rowboat, she recalled what he'd said.

"Do not ever give me that patronizing smile as though my concern for you is ridiculous. I am not some child you must mollify or spoil. I will do whatever I think is needed to keep you safe. Never question me again about your protection, with your words or your mocking smile. Do you understand me?"

Moira shifted on the bench, her bottom still stinging. She'd been guilty of his accusation. She'd thought to just go along with him but hadn't taken him seriously. She realized as his hand landed against her stinging flesh over and over that he'd been right. She didn't know the dangers they might face on O'Malley land. She had treated him as a child, and her expression had been patronizing. When she went limp across his lap, Kyle had ceased the spanking. He'd leaned over and kissed her inflamed skin before massaging away some of the burn. She'd apologized throughout the spanking, but she was determined to show her contrition.

When he released her, Moira knelt between Kyle's thighs, her hands behind her back, gazed lowered. She'd asked to show her remorse by offering her thanks for his thoughtfulness. She'd relished the feel of him in her mouth, each groan a symphony to her ears. When he pulled free, she kept her mouth open, accepting the spray as it landed on her tongue, against her chin, and across her chest. She'd remained kneeling until after Kyle wiped her clean. Their passionate kiss threatened to delay them further.

"I will ease your discomfort when we return to the cabin," Kyle whispered. Moira glanced up at him and realized that he was earnest. There was no teasing or lust in his eyes.

"Thank you," Moira responded. Kyle wrapped his arm around her shoulders, buffering the wind at their backs. She leaned against him and closed her eyes against the damp air.

Would that he always looked after me. No one since Mother has worried about me.

"When we reach the sand, stay near me at all times. If you see what you need, tell me, and we go together. Snake Eye will remain with the boat and warn us if anyone approaches from the water or the beach. Tomas will follow behind us to ensure no one sneaks up on us. You walk to my left, so I can hold my sword in my right."

"Yes, Kyle," Moira mumbled as he tightened his hold, and she sighed. As her hands rested in her lap, she had a moment's temptation to cover her belly with them. She knew there was the chance that their bairn was already growing within her. She debated whether she wanted to find the pennyroyal after all. Even if Kyle tired of her, she would have something to love and remind her of their time together. But her mind flashed to Sean and the inevitable hardships he faced as a bastard. She considered the years he'd spent without a father. Even when Aidan visited, he was barely a paternal figure, teaching his son to swear and sing bawdy tunes. Could she go through life lying and saying she was a widow? More importantly, could she leave Kyle and never tell him he had a child? She knew she couldn't, and he'd already said he wouldn't abandon a child. He would never let her go if he knew.

"Second thoughts about finding the pennyroyal?" Kyle asked as though he read her mind. Moira nodded, unwilling to lie to him even if she'd just considered doing that very thing. "Wheest, sweet one. Maybe there will come a day when you will have a child, maybe even ours. Collect your flowers or leaves, and we can decide what comes next when we need to."

Moira shook her head against his chest before looking up at him. "If I wait to know whether I need the tea after last night, then I won't be able to go through with drinking it. If I'm going to, then I must do it within the next few days." Moira glanced at Snake Eye and Tomas, who studiously ignored them, even though Moira suspected their voices carried. "Can we decide once we return to the *Lady Charity*? When we can talk more?"

"Of course, sweet one," Kyle said as he kissed her crown.

"Are there any other medicinals you would have me collect? Yarrow? Willow bark? Chamomile? Angelica?"

"Maybe. I don't know what the last two do, but the first two would help with any wounds. If you find them, then I suppose so," Kyle said with a shrug. "As long as there are no threats, you can search for what you need."

"Thank you, Kyle." Moira moved to kiss his cheek when she

realized what she was doing. Her eyes darted to the other men as she shrank away in horror. Kyle's powerful hand shot out and grasped her jaw, but his touch was gentle as he turned her head toward him. He lowered his mouth to hers, pausing just before their lips met.

"In front of Tomas and Snake Eye, you need not hold back." Kyle's mouth fused with hers, his tongue sliding between her lips until it dueled with hers. All too soon for either of their tastes, the bow ran aground. Tomas hopped into the surf as Snake Eye pulled in the oars. Kyle lifted Moira onto the shore, keeping her from soaking her boots or the cloak she'd retrieved when he returned her sack.

Walking silently, Tomas led the way up the path. Moira watched Kyle, who walked beside her as his gaze swept back and forth. She suspected Tomas did the same. She glanced down at where Snake Eye stood beside the dinghy. His sword rested against his legs, crossed at the ankles, his arms folded across his chest. When they reached the meadow, Moira scanned the land in front of her. She squeezed Kyle's forearm and pointed to a patch of purple flowers and nodded. She didn't dare speak, afraid her voice would carry more than it had while they approached the beach. Kyle gestured to Tomas, who moved behind them. Moira glanced back to see Tomas walking backwards, the crossbow loaded and raised should he need it at a moment's notice.

Moira worked quickly, a prickle of fear making the hair on her nape stand on end. She pulled as much pennyroyal as she could find, bringing a smirk to Kyle's face. She returned it with a scowl of her own before searching for the yarrow. She found that and angelica, but there were no willow trees in sight. Neither could she find chamomile. She prayed the pennyroyal worked, and she wouldn't need the chamomile to settle her stomach or help her sleep.

It was midmorning by the time Moira finished. She gestured

to Kyle that she had all that she needed, lifting the full basket. He made as if to lift it from her arms, but she shook her head. She stepped close enough to keep her voice low.

"I don't want it in your way if you must swing your sword. If you carry it on your left arm, and I'm to your left, I'll trip when you drop it. If I carry it, I can throw it clear of both of us and Tomas."

"Wise, sweet one," Kyle said. The pride in his gaze warmed Moira, and she realized she desperately wanted to bring that expression to Kyle's eyes. They hurried across the meadow and wound their way down to the beach. Kyle lifted Moira back into the boat before he helped Tomas push it back into the surf. The men boarded, and Snake Eye spun it to face the *Lady Charity*.

Moira strained to listen, certain she heard voices. She looked around, but a heavy fog was gathering over the water. She had no way of knowing how far away the voices were. They might have come from land or either of the ships. She looked up at Kyle, who nodded while putting a finger to his lips. She swallowed, knowing that whoever she and Kyle heard was a foe, not a friend. She glanced at the beach again, but nothing appeared to move. She watched Snake Eye strain as he hurried to row them back to the *Lady Charity*. When she could no longer hear any voices, the sound of the oars dropping into the water screamed in her ears.

When they reached the ship, a ladder and a rope flew over the rail. Kyle made quick work of tying the basket to the rope. A deckhand pulled the basket up as Moira rushed to scale the ladder. Braedon helped her over the rail, Kyle and the other two men swinging over the rail moments after her.

"Go to our cabin, now," Kyle ordered. Moira nodded and rushed toward the ladder well. Yells and the sound of steel against steel rang from the *Lady Grace*. Moira froze and looked in the other ship's direction, but she could see nothing. The fog was like a white sheet draped over everything in sight. Kyle bellowed, "Go!"

Moira looked back as Kyle yelled to her, but it was too late. A grappling hook landed on the deck to her left, and she heard the scraping sound as someone pulled it back to the rail where it was embedded in the wood bulkhead. Men suddenly poured over the sides. She watched as Kyle sprinted toward her, but two men stepped in his path. His gaze flew to her before they forced him to concentrate on the fight in front of him.

"My lady, can you climb the mast?" Braedon appeared at her side. "They'll check the cabins and the hold if they can. But they won't think to look for you up above."

"Who are they?" Moira asked, but she already knew the answer. Her stomach flipped when Braedon confirmed her fears.

"O'Malleys. You must hurry, my lady. Now."

Moira dropped the basket and followed Braedon to the center mast. She looked up the pole and reminded herself of all the trees she'd climbed as a child. As she reached for the wooden post, a voice drifted toward her that made her blood run cold.

"There's the bitch. She'll be in my bed by tonight," Dermot O'Malley bellowed. Moira looked over her shoulder to spot a man that made her knees clap together. Pox scars riddled his face, one of his top front teeth was jaggedly broken, and blood dripped from his sword. Moira glanced at the deck beside the ogre and saw that the O'Malley had felled one of Kyle's crew members. The sound of feet running toward her snapped her out of her stupor. She searched for Kyle and found him battling an enormous mountain of a man, but he glanced at her several times. Close to him, Tomas fought, blood dripping from his thigh. She couldn't see Snake Eye.

The O'Malleys were too close for Moira to attempt climbing the mainmast. She tugged at the clasp to the cloak and let it fly away from her as she sprinted to the bow. Using her small stature to her advantage, she wove among the men, forcing her pursuers to go around or push obstacles from their path. She bound up to the forecastle deck where she'd once stood watching the sea. She continued until she could leap toward the bowsprit. Since they weren't underway, most of the sails were furled. She hoisted herself onto the beam and inched along until she passed where the forestay sail would have hung. She eased her way toward the flying jib, which positioned her over the water.

Without looking back, she dove toward the water. Landing in the sea felt like she hit a brick wall, the freezing temperature threatening to steal the breath from her lungs. Her boots filled with water as she fought to swim toward the surface. Despite the leaden feel of her shoes, she kicked and circled her arms as she moved away from the *Lady Charity*. When she couldn't remain under the water for another moment, her head broke the surface. She looked around, praying that she still pointed toward the shore. The heavy fog made the *Lady Charity* and the *Lady Grace* invisible, even as she heard the fighting continue.

"Moira!"

Kyle's voice rang across the noisy air, the desperation piercing her soul. But she knew she couldn't call back to him. If she did, her attempt at escape would be wasted. She heard smaller boats bobbing in the water, and she couldn't be certain how close they were. She longed to reassure Kyle that she was safe, but she knew she couldn't because she didn't know if she was. With the battle to her back, Moira fought the current as she made for the shore.

"The bitch jumped," Dermot's voice carried. "Find her."

Oh, bluidy hell.

Moira heard oars slap the water as she dove back under the waves, the churning sea fighting her. But she found it easier to swim under the surface than battle the waves crashing over her.

She surfaced only when she couldn't manage another stroke without gasping for air. A powerful wave pushed her toward shore. Unprepared for its strength and unable to see a foot in front of her, Moira slammed into the jagged rocks, a protruding corner slicing her forehead. The water tried to suck her back, but just as soon as it seemed to capture her it propelled her into the rocks again. Moira's head bounced off a rock, and stars danced before her eyes as she fought off the blackness at the edges of her vision.

Using her hands to guide her, Moira pictured the shore she'd seen just an hour earlier. She knew she'd found the natural jetty that formed the north wall of the cove where they had moored. She slid along the rocks to move away from the fight. She banged against the sharp wall of boulders, cutting her hands, shoulders, and arms. When her knees slammed into a submerged rock, she wanted to howl from the pain, but she pushed on. Kicking hard and caught by another wave, she sailed past the end of the jetty and into open water. She'd been asleep when they dropped anchor, so she had no idea what lay ahead now that she was free of the rocks. Rolling onto her back, Moira prayed the current would push her toward the coast and not out to sea.

Catching her breath, Moira fought the nausea that roiled through her gut, both from the painful swim and the fear that consumed her. She wasn't worried about herself, but Kyle's fate petrified her. She was confident that he could outfight Dermot or any of the O'Malleys, but there was no guarantee. She couldn't be certain that no man attacked him from behind, cutting him down. Tightness in her chest and throat threatened to strangle her.

Think, Moira. If you panic, you'll drown. If you ever want to see Kyle again, you'll get yourself to land and stay alive.

Rolling back onto her belly, Moira swam toward the shore she now saw. Outside of the natural cove, the air didn't hang heavy with pregnant clouds. She was still a fair distance from land, but at least she could make it out. Kicking and circling her arms, Moira thought about how grateful she was to wear leggings and a leine. She would be happy if she never saw another gown in her life. She would have been resting on the sea bottom by now if she'd had the heavy layers of skirts to weigh her down.

Caught in her thoughts, Moira was unprepared for a wave that pushed her sideways. She fumbled, trying to protect herself from any rocks. Instead, she passed through an opening, the sound of waves echoing against the cave walls. The turmoil of the sea ceased, and suddenly Moira found herself in a placid tidal pool. In the pitch black of the cave, Moira moved slowly, unable to predict what she might find. Using only her legs to move her forward, she held her hands out before her, protecting her battered face and chest. She let the weak tide push her along as she continued to flutter her legs.

Moira didn't know how far she swam, but her hands grazed rocks and she realized she'd found a ledge. The rocks were dry, which made her brow furrow and caused her to wince. She knew she must be bleeding from more than one place. She wondered how no fish had chased her to make her its meal. But the dry rocks signaled the tide didn't rise above the ledge. She struggled and kicked as she pulled herself from the water, the weight of her boots threatening to suck her back down. Dragging herself onto the dry land, she rolled onto her back as she gasped.

There was no light in the cave, and she could no longer see the entrance. She prayed her new haven wasn't home to anything–or anyone–who might attack. Closing her eyes, she focused on slowing her breathing. Once she was calm, she strained to hear anything that might signal danger. It was eerily calm. The water lapped against the walls rather than slapped.

She couldn't hear the waves outside or the battle upon the two ships.

I will stay here until there is enough light to see the entrance again. I pray I'm right that the tide doesn't rise higher. Please let it be high tide now. I'll wait. Kyle won't know to search for me here, and hopefully the O'Malleys assume I'm dead when I don't wash up on the beach. I'll close my eyes and rest.

CHAPTER 18

Moira came awake to the sound of something hitting the water. It was still dark in the cave, so she remained still.

"I don't think she made it in here, Dermot," a man's voice rang against the walls. A screech answered by several more filled the air. Moira realized there were bats hanging above her.

"She wasn't on the beach. The current would have carried her this way," Dermot O'Malley barked.

"Aye. But it could have just as easily pulled her under or back out to sea," a third man said.

"Row the bluidy boat," Dermot grumbled.

Moira felt along the wall and floor, trying to see if the ledge went further back. Her heart sank when she felt the wall beside her wrap around behind her head. If they rowed all the way to the end of the cave, they would find her. She recalled that when she tried to climb out, part of her struggle came from having nothing to brace her feet against. Where she lay was a ledge suspended in the water. Moving as slowly as she could, she slipped her feet into the water. Inch by inch, she eased her way back in as the voices drew closer. She sank down until the water was at her nose just as an oar cracked against the wall.

"Mind yourself," Dermot growled.

"We've come to the end," the first man announced.

"I know, you sod. Moira, do not make me wait any longer. I'm certain you are here. I will flay the skin from your arse." Moira heard a splash and a grunt, then a footstep. She assumed Dermot or one of the other men had stepped onto the ledge. She inhaled a deep breath and lowered herself until the water lapped against her lower lashes. When the footfall was near her right ear, she slipped under the water and used her hands to push herself backwards under the ledge. She remained still, conserving her energy and her air. Her heartbeat thudded in her ears. Moira blinked rapidly as it grew harder to hold her breath, her mind and her lungs urging her to surface. But as strong as those demands were, her will to remain alive and return to Kyle was stronger. The urge to gulp threatened to overpower her, but she pushed herself to wait. She felt the shift in the water and knew it was the boat moving away from her.

Once more only using her hands, she emerged from under the ledge but waited a heartbeat before she inched her head out of the water. When her nose was clear, she drew in air that made her lungs burn. But she prepared to duck down once more if she had to. The sound of oars echoed in the cavernous chamber as it moved away from her.

"Stupid bitch must be dead," the third man said. The only response was a grunt. Moira didn't care who it came from, as long as it came from a distance. She treaded water until everything went silent. Not trusting the men, she remained in the water in case they laid a trap for her. She wouldn't move until she was certain they'd given up their search. When she was confident that only she and the bats remained, she struggled to pull herself back onto the ledge. Freezing and exhausted, she lay on her side, curled into a tight ball. She knew she should stay awake, not succumb to the cold, but the fight was useless. She gave in as her eyes drifted closed.

"Where is she?" Kyle demanded as he paced the deck. He'd watched Dermot jump into a dinghy and row away from the cove. As though God or Mother Nature was acting out of spite, the fog cleared, and the sun appeared just as the battle ended. The O'Malley boats, all low-profile fustes, rowed away from the *Lady Charity* and the *Lady Grace*. Kyle breathed a sigh of relief as the sky cleared, and he realized the O'Malleys weren't sailing any of their French corvettes. Those ships carried four to eight guns each. He supposed Dermot hadn't been willing to risk losing any and saw no benefit of shooting blind. The fustes disappeared to the south end of the cove, but Dermot had rowed to the north.

"You're alive, brother?" Keith called out as he boarded the *Lady Charity*. The Lady *Grace* had maneuvered to come alongside the *Lady Charity* during the fight. The two crews worked together and forced the O'Malleys to retreat.

"Barely," Kyle said distractedly. He went to stand by the rail when he caught sight of Dermot's dinghy rounding the jetty. He strained to see, but there were still only the three heads that had moved away from the *Lady Charity*. He muttered, "Where is she?"

"You lost her?" Keith asked in disbelief. Kyle glanced at his brother as Keith turned to look around the ship. His brother's concern surprised Kyle. He was glad when Keith kept quiet, not wanting to hear anything but Moira's voice. The twins watched as Dermot's dinghy reappeared a few minutes later but remained out of reach.

"She must be dead. None of my men called out to say she's on the beach," Dermot bellowed. "And no bobbing head in the water. Your whore was worthless to begin with. Now she's worth even less," Dermot chuckled at his own jest. "I have her dowry, and Dónal is a fool. I don't have to bed the little bitch, and I have the MacDonnell's money. I'll have his fleet soon enough. Send my regards to the MacNeil bastards." Dermot nodded his head in an exaggerated act of deference. Kyle wanted to launch himself over the side and squeeze the life from the man's body as he watched Dermot's eyes bulge and his face turn blue.

"Wait," Keith muttered, his lips not moving. They watched as the dinghy inched past them until it met the last fuste. Kyle snorted as Dermot struggled up the robe ladder onto the ship. Once the dinghy was up, the O'Malleys rowed their last boat south.

"I never should have made us stop here," Kyle snapped as he looked at his brother. "This is my fault. You didn't want to, and I didn't listen. I shouldn't have taken Moira ashore. A patrol must have spotted us."

"I don't think so. At least not about the patrol. I think they've been watching us. Maybe they saw Moira on deck, or maybe as you went to the beach. But they knew who she was, and they knew she was aboard the *Charity*. They only attacked the *Grace* because they reached us first. I think they were confused and off-course in the fog. I heard Dermot's complaints when they realized it was the *Grace* they tried to board. It forced them to divide their party. Neither did they expect us to pull alongside one another to keep them from attacking on both sides of either of us."

"That has always been our best strategy," Kyle agreed, but he didn't take his eyes off the coastline.

"You wish to search for her," Keith stated. The withering glare Kyle shot him before returning his attention to the beach was all the confirmation Keith needed. "O'Malley said his men didn't find her on the beach, nor did they spot her in the water."

Keith left the obvious unsaid: there was a greater likelihood that Moira drowned than survived. But Kyle refused to give up hope. He moved to look over the other side of the ship, half expecting to find Moira clinging to the ship. When he spotted no one, he moved to the stern, then to the bow. But no one awaited rescue. Keith called to his men to look over the sides of their boat, but the twins and their crew recognized it was pointless. Moira would have called out if she'd been nearby.

"Maybe she made it around the jetty and to the coast on the other side," Kyle suggested. "Dermot might not have seen her if she was already on the shore. He said nothing about searching the beach there."

"Because there are no beaches, Kyle," Keith reminded him. "It's sheer cliff face. She'd more likely be battered among the rocks than hiding on a beach."

"Then I want her body recovered," Kyle uttered. He looked toward the jetty and pictured what lay on the other side. An image of Moira's lifeless body trapped between boulders floated before his eyes. "This is my fault."

"It's Dermot O'Malley's fault, him and her bastard of a brother," Keith corrected. "Where exactly would you have put her ashore? The land might not belong to the O'Malleys, but they make use of it as if it were. Don't you think an unattached, young woman would garner attention wherever she went? Then who would have protected her?"

"A right lot of good my protection did her," Kyle yelled. He slammed his fist on the gunwale before ordering a dinghy lowered. "You can come with me or you can stay, but I'm going to look for her."

"And you know I'm coming with you," Keith retorted. The twins climbed down the rope ladder into the rowboat with Snake Eye, Tomas, and another one of Kyle's crew members, Stephen. The last man was mammoth, with blond hair and piercing blue eyes. He resembled his Viking ancestors. He had the strength of ten men and a short temper. While Kyle didn't favor him most of the time, Stephen was strong and surprisingly agile for his size. If they encountered anyone as they searched, Stephen would be an asset.

The five men remained quiet as they rounded the jetty, the expanse of sea only widening. The distance from the end of the jetty to the cliffs was further than Kyle recalled. He remembered Moira saying she swam when she was younger, but he couldn't imagine how she could have swum the stretch of water that lay between him and land. The water was frigid even when the air temperature was warm. He knew she had boots on since they'd found none on the deck. They would have felt like leaden blocks once they filled with water, and he feared they would have acted as an anchor pulling her below.

When they neared the cliffs, Kyle called out to Moira over and over, but no one called back. They drew as close to land as they dared without being dashed upon the rocks. Nothing fluttered in the breeze or made a sound. Kyle felt the men looking at him as he strained to see in the distance anything that might signal that they'd found Moira. The men took turns rowing as they moved along the coastline until Kyle had to admit there was no chance Moira had swum as far north as they searched. During his turn at the oars, he propelled the rowboat through the water toward the jetty. He repeated her name several times, looking for any nook or cranny she might have found. But there was nothing, just the jagged rocks.

"Where do we go now?" Keith asked quietly as they came alongside the *Lady Grace*.

"We can't remain here, and if we go any further south, we'll encounter the O'Malleys again," Kyle mused. "We sail north to Wicklow. We're less than an afternoon's sail since the wind is with us. We dock and go ashore. Get horses and ride back this way. If Dermot had her hidden in the dinghy, we couldn't see. If she makes her way to the beach, then she'll take the path I showed her this morning. Either way, if she's alive, she'll be nearby."

"If she's alive, you'd better pray we find her before Dermot," Keith stated.

"Well I know it," Kyle sighed as Keith climbed up to his ship before Kyle returned to his.

CHAPTER 19

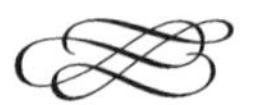

Moira's head pounded as she came awake, once again finding herself in the cave. She was still safely on the ledge above the water level, but the quiet of earlier was gone. Waves crashed beyond the entrance to the cave, and she realized that she'd entered during low tide, but for whatever reason, the cave didn't fill. She struggled past the blazing pain between her ears as she struggled to hear what woke her. She'd thought she heard a voice calling her name. But when no sound but the crashing surf reached her, she resigned herself to thinking she must have been dreaming.

With the fog lifted, Moira made out light in the distance. The sunshine filtering through the archway at the other end of the cave illuminated the space enough for Moira to gain a clearer sense of where she was. She looked up and discovered hundreds of bats hanging above her heard. Her stomach clenched as she thought about how fortunate she'd been that none bit her. She squinted to see how far the ledge ran along the wall she laid beside. It would only keep her out of the water for a few feet. As she considered what she should do next, a gust of cool air and a gush of water poured in across from her. Several bats screeched and took flight, but rather than move toward the entrance where Moira swam in, they moved toward where the air and water just passed.

Moira waited for another surge of air and water, but none came. She wondered if it was a previous one that woke her and not voices. Dreading it, she slipped back into the water and kicked across the narrow channel. With her hands outstretched once again, she propelled herself with her legs while her hands prepared to encounter more rocks. Rather than being pushed into the cave wall, Moira bobbed in the water as a crosscurrent pushed her away from the second entrance. Fighting against the tide, she found a narrow archway. She raised her hand over her head, able to touch the top of the entrance.

If the tide is in right now, then I should wait for it to go out. Maybe then the opening will be wider. I might be able to pass through it to whatever opening is on the other side. Or I might get stuck and die in a watery grave. But I could do that if I try to leave the way I came in. At least this way must lead to the other side of the jetty, the side where there's a beach I can swim to. A beach Kyle's ship could see. A beach that has a path up the cliffs.

But that's the same cove where the O'Malleys attacked. They could still be there. I have no idea what came of that fight. What if Dermot defeated Kyle, and that's why he was alive and searching for me? Or did he flee from Kyle before Kyle could run him through? I couldn't see what lay beyond the jetty because of the fog. Maybe the better choice is not to go to the beach.

Moira moved back to the ledge and hauled herself out of the water. She sat shivering, thinking it was almost warmer in the water than the damp air.

I sit here until the tide changes. Then I swim to the entrance that I came through and see what lies beyond. If there's no possibility of escape that way, then I give this narrow tunnel a try.

Moira huddled against the cold as her teeth chattered. She feared she would die of hypothermia before she had the chance to swim free of the cave that was both her sanctuary and her cage. As the sunlight faded, Moira knew she had little choice but to at least look out to where she'd swum earlier. If she waited too long, she wouldn't be able to see well enough to make a choice. Drawing in a fortifying breath, she walked along the ledge as far as she could go before she jumped back into the water. She decided it was more merciful than prolonging the agony by easing in. The swim was easier moving toward the open water since she knew there were no obstacles ahead of her. The current became rougher as she neared the archway, but the sun shone brighter as she neared the end of the narrow channel.

Treading water just inside the cave, Moira took in the sweeping vista of open water and perilous cliffs. Her heart dropped to her stomach, and in turn, her stomach dropped to her feet. There was nowhere to go but open sea. The sheer cliff-side offered no means to escape, and she dreaded trying to swim against the tide to move back around the jetty. She doubted she had the strength for that swim. She'd barely survived the first time. Turning back toward the far wall, Moira once more swam into the depths of the cave. Feeling the change of current, Moira reached out for the narrow tunnel. Raising her arm again, she found her fingers couldn't touch the top of the archway. She knew she would have room to draw a breath when she needed it.

It's now or I remain here until I die. With the way things are—no food, no fresh water, sopping wet—that won't be long. Worse comes to worst, I come back here and brave the open water. How badly do I want to live? How badly do I want to see Kyle? You know the answer to that, Moira. Move yourself.

Moira eased her way into the darkness. The tunnel echoed, making it difficult to predict where it led. Kicking with little force, Moira swam further into the recesses of the cavern wall. Every few minutes, a lapping wave pushed against her, jostling her against the wall but not impeding her progress. As the strength of the waves grew, she knew she must be nearing the opening on the far side. But her hands brushing against a wall forced Moira to stop. She looked around, but there was no light coming from in front of her. She felt the water pushing up from beneath her, and she bit back a groan. The way out was submerged. The best she could hope for was to hold her breath long enough to find the opening. The water would try to force her back into the cave. If she could just spot daylight, she would have the hope that she could find her means of escape.

Remembering what Cormac, one of the clan council elders, taught her as a child when she and his sons learned to swim, she took several slow, deep breaths, holding each one a little longer than the last. She conditioned her lungs for when she would dive into the abyss and pray that she came out the other side. Reaching below the water, she pulled off one boot then the other, instantly feeling pounds lighter. She wasn't ready to forsake the footwear, knowing she would need them on land. Fumbling in the darkness, she tied them together and slung them around her neck. On her fifth inhalation, she dove below the surface, kicking as hard and fast as she could. Eyes open but unseeing, her hands guided her as she found another opening barely wide enough for her to pass through. Never had she been so glad to be built more like a lass than a lady. Her lungs burned as she kept kicking, her hands pushing along the walls, helping her to glide through.

She desperately wanted to breathe, her body railing against her mind. But she reasoned that she was no fish; breathing water wouldn't work. Her ears rang from the pressure, and the instinct to panic and flail threatened her. She reached above her, testing to see if there was space between the water level and the ceiling of the tunnel. She knew there wasn't, but her mind demanded she try. Blinking several times to clear her mind, she continued forward. She could only keep moving forward. She'd gone too far to turn back and make it to the surface before she ran out of air. She fought the dizziness that set in as air bubbles formed around her mouth. She was slowly losing the air she held in her mouth and lungs. Her head felt as though it were in a vice, and pinpricks of light danced before her eyes.

I'm dying. This is where I will die. No one will ever know. No one will ever find me.

Moira wanted to sob, but there was no way to do it while submerged in her watery grave. As she used the dregs of her energy to keep moving forward, she realized the darts of light she saw weren't from her oxygen deprived mind. She was seeing daylight. But as she realized she'd found daylight, blackness danced at the corners of her vision. She struggled against it, the last of her air being consumed as she fought. Just as everything faded from sight, something drew her forward as though a sea god sucked on a straw.

The pressure in her head vanished, and the tightness of the confining tunnel disappeared. She broke through the surface and found herself only feet from the beach. Spluttering and with no more strength to swim, she half inched along the rock wall and half let the surf push her in. When her toes met sand, she let the surf float her onto land. Lying sprawled on the beach, Moira didn't have the energy to shield her eyes from the sun. She closed them as she wheezed, her chest more painful than anything she'd ever experienced. Her nose and throat burned, and her eyes stung. She felt like she had half the sea in her ears. But she was on land. When she no longer feared she would die if she moved, she rolled to her side and rested again before forcing herself upright.

He's not there. He left.

Moira scanned the empty cove, finding neither the *Lady Charity* nor the *Lady Grace*. There weren't any O'Malley boats either. She was completely alone.

CHAPTER 20

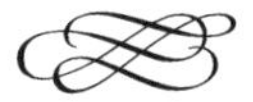

When Moira was convinced she could stand, she dragged herself across the beach, hoping to find driftwood to build a fire. To her great disappointment, there weren't even shells in the sand. With her head bobbing, she looked toward the path leading up the cliff. It felt insurmountable, even though she'd climbed it just that morning. Groaning, she sat to put her waterlogged boots back on.

What choice do you have? You have no shelter, no fresh water, no way to make a fire. You're soaking wet and just as likely to die staying on this beach as you were in that tunnel and cave. You know there's a meadow above. You know there are trees. You can seek shelter from the wind and build a fire there. There might even be a village within walking distance. But you won't know if you don't move your arse. So what's it going to be? Die on the beach after nearly killing yourself to escape that cave? Bluidy waste. Move yourself, Moira. Kyle's not here to protect you. He's not going to rescue you. For all you know he's dead, or he's given up on you. Either way, you're alone. Are you going to dissolve into a heap of tears or show a leg?

Moira trudged across the sand, instructing herself not to look up the cliff. She didn't want to see how far she had to climb. She just wanted to get to the top. But try as she might, she couldn't combat the temptation to look out to sea. The higher she climbed, the further her view. Just as she reached the summit of the path, she spotted something white on the northern horizon. Shielding her eyes and squinting, she was certain she was looking at the sails of two ships.

Kyle. But why are they sailing north? Why did he leave so soon? Did he even bother to search for me? Moira's shoulders slumped as she fought down her rising gorge and the urge to sob. *That won't get me anywhere. What I need is shelter and a way to get dry. Food would be nice.*

Moira turned off the path and stepped toward the meadow, only to ram into a man's chest.

"Just in time for supper, Moira. Then a good frigging to make our betrothal a marriage."

Moira looked into Dermot O'Malley's eyes and screamed, then vomited sea water down his leggings and boots before she turned and ran.

"Run as fast as you can," Dermot dared. "But you won't escape me like you did your idiot brother or your barbaric lover."

Moira didn't slow down. She didn't know where she headed or what she would find. She didn't know if she could escape or would die trying. But she refused to go with Dermot willingly. She bolted north, a part of her knowing her wish to catch Kyle was unrealistic, but it was also the direction away from Dermot and his men. She hadn't gotten a good look at any of them, so she didn't know if they were well-trained warriors in peak condition or heavyset slugs like Dermot. The exhaustion she'd experienced only minutes earlier as she staggered across the beach disappeared as fear once again propelled her forward. She scanned the landscape ahead of her, praying she could make it across the meadow, not caring what she might find on the other side as long as it took her away from the O'Malleys.

As the headland curved, Moira shifted directions to cut across the tall grass. She heard the labored breaths of the men chasing her, but none sounded as though they were tiring. Pumping her arms and pushing her legs as they burned, she neared the edge of the meadow. Skirting a copse of trees, but hurdling several tree trunks in her way, she caught sight of rooftops. A village lay ahead of her, but she couldn't discern its size. She prayed she could get lost among the buildings until the O'Malleys abandoned their search. Every head turned toward her as she tried to navigate the narrow dirt roads, weaving between the buildings. She knew she was a sight: a disheveled, wet stranger running through the village like a loon. But no one stood in her way, and that was all that mattered to Moira.

"Lass," an older farmer called as she neared the edge of the village. "Come inside. They won't think to look in here for you."

Moira didn't dare look back. She could only assume that she'd put enough distance between her and her pursuers that they wouldn't see her duck inside the cottage. She sprinted through the door and came to a halt as four faces turned wide eyes toward her. A woman and three children gawked at her as she stood before them, a puddle forming at her feet. The farmer's wife nodded and ushered her toward the back of the building. The older woman scrambled to find a blanket to wrap around Moira as her teeth chattered. The children continued to stare at her as Moira shivered in the back corner of their home.

The farmer closed the door and turned to Moira, an expectant look on his face. "What has you running from the O'Malleys?"

"He attacked a ship I was on and tried to take me. When I made it to shore, he was waiting," Moira said. If anyone learned her brother, a chieftain, signed a betrothal agreement giving her to Dermot, they would turn her over to him without question. The moment Dónal signed, she became Dermot's property. He need only consummate the betrothal for it to become a binding marriage. Moira would kill Dermot somehow, some way, before she allowed him to couple with her.

"Lass, the only ships that have been within spitting distance of us were the ones belonging to the Red Drifter and the Scarlet Blade," the farmer noted. Moira tried to keep her expression impassive, but it was the first time she'd heard Keith's moniker. She thought it rather fitting. "Would you have been aboard one of those vessels?"

Moira didn't know how to answer. If she told the truth, there were few plausible reasons for her to be on Kyle's ship other than being his mistress. But if she lied, then she would have to come up with a series of half-truths and complete falsehoods to explain why she wound up on the beach. There was only one thing she came up with. "I was on my brother's ship."

"Your brother?" The farmer's wife gasped and stepped around Moira to look at her face. "Your brother is a wretched crew member on a pirate ship?"

The woman squawked and flapped her hands like an irate mother goose. Moira wondered if she'd just dug herself into a hole from which she couldn't escape. She wondered if making it sound as though Kyle and Keith were her brothers would be better. She didn't want to use intimidation with the couple that welcomed her into their home and offered her sanctuary. But she wondered if it would strike enough fear in at least the woman for her to keep quiet. She would take the risk. If she erred, she would run again.

"My brothers are the captains. I was on the Red Drifter's ship when the O'Malleys attacked," Moira clarified.

"You're the Red Drifter's sister—" the farmer cocked an eyebrow. "And the Scarlet Blade's sister? And I'm bluidy King Conchobar mac Nessa come back from the dead. More likely you were his mistress."

Moira straightened to her full but unimpressive height and offered the haughtiest expression she could. She attempted to look like Lizzie. "I am—" Moira scrambled to think of a Scottish name rather than her Irish one— "Catriona MacLean." Moira realized neither Kyle nor Keith might want their clan name bandied about. But it was too late. Moira couldn't and wouldn't take it back.

"Then why do you sound like an Irishwoman?" pointed out the farmer.

"Because we fled when we were weans. I was brought to Ireland and my brothers went to sea," Moira reasoned. "Now that I'm old enough to sail with them, I do."

"You're a lady pirate?" chirped a young girl of about nine summers. "Are you a pirate queen?"

Moira gulped. She'd really backed herself into a corner. She offered a half-hearted smile before she spun yet another lie. This conversation had raced out of control, and she was now as thick in the weeds as she would have been if she'd denied being aboard the *Lady Charity* or *Lady Grace*. "I can't pick my kin. What my brothers do is their choice. I mend their stockings and darn their leines. I remain out of the way. But they are my family and all that I have."

"Are you trying to find them then?" The farmer cut in.

"That's what I wish. I fear they think I drowned at sea. Last I saw from atop the cliffs were two ships sailing north," Moira explained.

"Wicklow. If your brothers think you're alive and on land, that is the closest port they could sail into."

"How far is that?" Moira wondered.

"Half a day's sail if the wind is with them," the farmer estimated.

"And on horseback?" Moira pressed.

"A day," the farmer answered, a speculative expression settling on his visage. "Would you be thinking to go to Wicklow, lass?"

"If I had a way," Moira said, matching the man's speculative mien with a forlorn one of her own. The man only nodded before looking at his wife to communicate silently. The woman bustled forward and pulled Moira into a nook cordoned off to give the couple privacy at night. Without a word, the woman sized Moira up and tsked. She went to a chest that creaked as she opened it. She withdrew a gown but shook her head.

"You're a wee thing, much smaller than I ever was. This won't work." She dug a little deeper until she looked back at Moira, scowled, and pulled out a leine and leggings. "These were my older son's before he married and left home."

She walked over to Moira and held them up, canting her head one way then the other. Moira stood silently as she waited for the woman to offer them to her. With puckered lips, the farmwife handed them to Moira.

"You can change here, and we can hang your clothes to dry before the fire. Your boots too. Mind you, you're wiping up the puddles you're leaving."

"Thank you. Your kindness is appreciated," Moira murmured, her teeth still chattering despite the blanket taking away some of the chill. The woman grunted and stepped past the partition into the primary room of the cottage. Moira hurried to remove the sodden clothing, struggling to peel them from her arms and legs. The leine and leggings were a surprisingly good fit, so she used the already damp blanket to dry the floor beneath her feet. She hurried to gather her clothes and boots before peeking her head into the family living space. When neither the farmer nor his wife said anything, Moira crossed the room and spread out her shirt and leggings. She put her boots as close to the fire as she dared. As she stood up, a grimy little hand tugged on hers. Moira looked down to find the youngest child, a boy of about five summers.

"Tell me what it's like to be a pi-wat," the boy pleaded. Moira sucked in a breath, about to offer the only truth she could.

"I've never actually been on a pirate ship when it's attacked another boat. I only know what it is to sail on the open sea," Moira confessed.

"You've never seen your brothers set a ship ablaze, skewer the other crew? You've never seen your brother set a man adrift?" The oldest girl said with disbelief.

"They've attacked no one while I've been aboard," Moira stated. "Only the O'Malleys have attacked us."

"And why would they do that?" The farmer joined the conversation. He maintained the speculative look in his eyes, and it made Moira uneasy. The man might have offered her shelter, but the hairs on the back of her neck and forearms told her not to trust him.

"I don't know why my brothers haven't attacked with me onboard. I don't sail with them for long stretches, so I suppose they don't so as to keep me safe," Moira suggested.

"And where are you when you're not with your brothers?" The farmer inquired.

"The Hebrides," Moira answered. She was certain Kyle and Keith returned to the isles from time to time, likely to hide the booties they gained. Besides, the Isle of Barra lay in the Hebrides, and that's where she'd intended to go. Not that much of a stretch.

"Hmm. I meant, why did the O'Malleys attack?" The farmer clarified.

"Because I've heard they're pirates too," Moira said with a shrug as the middle child led her to the table and the older woman set a bowl of steaming pottage before Moira. She risked scalding her mouth because she was freezing, hungry, and unwilling to say more until she could gather her thoughts. Begrudgingly, the wife brought Moira a second bowl. By the time she finished, Moira could barely keep her eyes open.

"You can sleep over there," the wife pointed to one child's bedroll. As she opened her mouth to thank the woman, she realized she had heard none of their names. Even though she'd offered a pretend one, she'd at least introduced herself. When she glanced at the couple, she caught them staring at her as they whispered. Moira decided in that moment that she would sleep as long as she dared and slip away when it was dark. The couple was still standing together when Moira drifted off.

CHAPTER 21

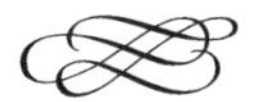

Moira awoke to the sound of the door closing. She peered around the dimly lit cottage, finding the three children sleeping within arm's reach. Silently, she crawled to the end of her bedroll and peered around the partition to find the farmwife still sleeping, light snores drifting from her. Moira also noticed that the woman slept alone. Glancing at the only window opening in the cottage, she saw the moon and a handful of stars. It was still the middle of the night. Moira could think of a singular reason the farmer would slink out under the cover of darkness. He was going to betray her.

Years of padding around Sean's chamber without waking him after soothing his night terrors taught Moira to dress and undress in the dark and without making a sound. She watched the children in the firelight, ensuring none were watching her as she changed back into the clothes Braedon lent her. Her mind flashed a brief image of him, and Moira prayed the boy survived the battle. She looked around the small area set aside for preparing food. She didn't want to steal from the family who'd already generously fed and clothed her, but she felt little remorse when she reminded herself the O'Malleys were likely on their way to the cottage now.

Finding a sack filled with potatoes, she rolled the root vegetables from the bag, then grabbed the heels of bread remaining from the night before. They were already going stale and were intended to be the next day's trenchers, but they were still edible. She nabbed a wheel of cheese, three apples, two plums, and a handful of cherries. She dumped everything into the sack and moved toward the door, but suddenly realized it wouldn't be wise to use the portal for her escape. She darted across the cottage and looked through the open hole that served as a window. There was no animal skin hanging since the weather was warm. She stuck her head out as she looked in all directions.

Moira climbed through the window, yet again grateful for her small size. She'd resented being short and wiry for years, thinking herself unfeminine and undesirable. Kyle's insatiable appetite for her cured her of those sentiments, and now she appreciated being petite since it would likely save her life twice in a day. She pressed her body flat against the wall, expecting someone to raise the hue and cry once they spotted her. When no alarm sounded and no racing feet pounded toward her, she eased away from the wall. Moira realized the light breeze carried men's voices. They did nothing to keep their conversation private.

She'd gotten herself turned around when she raced among the buildings, looking for somewhere to hide. Not knowing which direction was north, having no idea how to read the constellations, she moved in the opposite direction from the voices until she could weave her way past the blacksmith's workshop. Next door stood what she assumed was a farrier since a corral lay beside the building. Biting her lip, Moira considered her options.

If I steal a horse, I'm likely to put distance between Dermot's men and me. But stealing is a sin; God's Commandments say as much. What if the horse I steal is some family's only means to work their fields? What if they punish the farrier for my theft? What if I'm caught? Don't be a ninny, Moira. These people left me to protect myself. I owe them nothing. Maybe I could even convince Kyle to return here and leave them some coin one day. Kyle.

Moira's heart pinched as she slipped into the corral. There were only three horses tethered to a wall. Two were mares and one was a gelding. The mares looked to be finely bred, but they could never outrun the gelding. She was certain the O'Malley men who rode all rode stallions or geldings. Growing anxious as time grew short, Moira looked around for a saddle. She couldn't find one, but at least she found a bridle. Her mother and father had bemoaned her wildness and affinity for riding bareback when she was younger. She wished she could point out to them that the skill would likely save her from a man neither would have ever countenanced her marrying.

Moira slipped out of the corral once she'd bridled the horse. The animal made no sounds as Moira led it away from the other two. She glanced back at the mares, but they were disinterested in her or the gelding.

Where to now? I should go the direction the men are coming from. They'll think I'd go the opposite way, and it will take them time to double back. I need to be clear of the village and the meadow. I wonder if the O'Malleys camp under the stars or if there's a tavern or alehouse in this village.

Moira kept ruminating as she walked parallel to the path the voices came from. She jerked the horse to a stop and covered its nose with her palm when she was certain the men were even with her. She remained hidden until the voices shifted to be behind her. As she crept toward the edge of the village, she heard bawdy tunes coming from what she assumed was the tavern. The volume told her the establishment was full. The village was too small to boast such a crowd, so she deduced at least some O'Malleys were within. Between the drunken men in the tavern and the ones going to the farmer's cottage, she opted to test her luck and assume none camped in the meadow or the copse of trees she'd avoided.

Moira used a chopping block she found to help her mount the horse. It had been years since she'd ridden such a large steed, but she had ridden her father's stallion far too often, earning herself a spanked bottom. But the freedom and wildness she'd felt had been worth the consequences. She had a fleeting thought that she'd resented being punished as a child, but she'd barely questioned Kyle's discipline. Now she controlled the beast with ease despite being without a saddle. She walked the horse past the last few buildings, but her mouth dropped open as she caught sight of Dermot O'Malley relieving himself outside the tavern.

"The bluidy bitch has my horse," Dermot screamed as he struggled to pull up his leggings from around his knees. Moira snickered as the man fumbled and swore. She knew the O'Malleys moored their fustes somewhere near the cove, and she doubted any of Dermot's men rode the two mares or camped outdoors, so she safely assumed that none would follow her on horseback. Unknowing which direction she headed, Moira spurred the horse forward. As she left the village, she realized she left from the same part where she entered. Leaning low over the horse's withers, she clung to the reins and the animal's mane as the steed barreled forward. She steered the animal toward the meadow she'd run across the day before.

Kyle paced the deck of the *Lady Charity*, cracking his knuckles over and over. His crew gave him a wide berth, none wanting to be caught in the crosshairs of his temper. Keith sat on a crate and leaned back against the mainmast, watching his brother.

They'd sailed all afternoon once they left the bay and arrived in the Wicklow port just after dusk, but they'd anchored away from the docks. The fading sunlight made it impossible for anyone on land to distinguish their ship from any other merchants. They flew the marque of the Earl of Argyll, just as Rowan and Ruairí had. They had the same arrangement as the previous two pirate captains. They paid a hefty tax to the earl, and he gave them his marque to sail under, lending them legitimacy when they needed it.

Braedon inched toward Kyle with two pieces of hardtack and a strip of dried beef in his hands. Kyle glared at him, and the boy jumped back, his eyes wide. Kyle knew his expression was menacing. It was the same one he wore when he boarded ships he plundered, the same one he wore when he set people adrift. He grimaced and shook his head, not intending to scare the boy when Kyle knew Braedon was attempting to be thoughtful.

"Thank you," Kyle mumbled. He accepted the food with a nod, but once Braedon disappeared toward the galley, Kyle gave the food to Keith.

"What do I want this for? I have food aboard my own ship, or I can raid your galley if I wish," Keith mused.

"Because I'm not hungry," Kyle spat. He knew neither his brother nor Braedon deserved his temper. But the O'Malleys were nowhere in sight to be on the receiving end.

"You haven't eaten all day or night," Keith pointed out.

"Do you think Moira has?" Kyle hissed. "Do you think she's warm and dry somewhere?"

"She might be," Keith shrugged. He returned Kyle's menacing glower with one of his own. Kyle sighed and shook his head.

"I keep wondering if we missed a cave or inlet when we searched. We were gone longer than Dermot when he went looking for her. Maybe he gave up because he couldn't find her. And maybe he couldn't find her because she found a place to hide. But she couldn't hear me calling to her, so she didn't know to come out. Or worse, she's injured with no way to get out. And I left her there."

Kyle knew he rambled, but he'd always thought aloud with Keith as his silent audience. They both processed events and information that way, so Keith returned to sitting silently while his twin spoke. Kyle tried to work through scenarios where Moira survived and escaped the cursed cove where they never should have lingered. When he could think of no more, Keith nodded and stood, clapping a hand on Kyle's shoulder.

"Before sunup, we go ashore. We look around, get the lay of the land, ask some discreet questions. Once we know where things stand, we either find horses and ride south, or we sail back and scour the coastline for caves," Keith reasoned. Kyle nodded, but images of Moira stranded in a cave, freezing to death because he didn't get to her soon enough still distracted him. Keith interrupted his thoughts with a shake of his shoulders. "This wasn't your fault."

Kyle rounded on his brother and grabbed the front of the doublet Keith donned against the chill air. Kyle and Keith argued from time to time, but they'd never come to blows—even as children and adolescents. However, Kyle was ready to plow his fist into Keith's jaw. With the barest of restraint, he released Keith and shoved him away.

"Of course, it's my bluidy fault!" Kyle kicked over a nearby barrel. "I raided her ship. I brought her aboard mine. I insisted upon keeping her. And I took her out where any O'Malley could see her. Then I didn't even protect her."

"And I would have killed her," Keith said practically. "You told me she dressed like a lad, and I'd never seen her before. I would have left her to burn, run her through, or tossed her over. I'd say her fate would have been a far sight worse if I'd spotted her ship instead of you."

Kyle offered Keith a jerky nod, knowing his brother spoke the truth. Neither purposely made women their victim, but

Moira's clothing and build had made her look like a lad. Keith might have ended her life before she could have pulled off her cap to show she was a woman.

"I can't ignore that blame still rests with me," Kyle muttered.

He looked toward the shore, the docks bustling as fishing boats returned for the evening. He looked south, toward where he'd last seen Moira. The pain in his chest threatened to bring him to his knees. No one other than Keith had ever connected with Kyle so intuitively as Moira. Despite the tension between them when he kept her under virtual house arrest, they understood and accepted one another's emotional and physical needs. The happiest point of his day had been when he crawled into bed and held Moira before falling asleep. It was contentment he'd never experienced before. He could readily admit to his brother that the physical fulfillment with Moira was unparalleled. But it was the deep emotional tie, the implicit understanding of what they each needed, that he didn't know how to express. He couldn't bear losing that now that he'd found it. He'd never imagined it existed before Moira, but now he would do all that he could to have the opportunity for their relationship to develop. But if Moira wished never to see him again after what he'd put her through, he wouldn't blame her. He just wanted to know she was safe.

"Go back to your cabin, brother. Get some sleep," Kyle suggested. "Tomorrow, we start fresh." Kyle and Keith exchanged their customary embrace, whispering their pledge of undying love, before retiring to their respective cabins. Kyle sat on his bunk as he considered what he needed to do the next day. When his stomach's growling echoed in the cabin, he realized he needed to eat and to sleep. Despite not wanting to do either, he knew he wouldn't have the strength to fight Dermot again if he didn't tend to himself. And he suspected there was an almighty battle ahead of him.

CHAPTER 22

"She's not here," Kyle murmured, defeated in a way he hadn't felt since he was a young boy learning to survive among pirates. "Or maybe she doesn't want me to find her."

Kyle, Keith, Tomas, Snake Eye, and Stephen sat in a booth at one of the Wicklow taverns, The Leg of Mutton. They'd spent the early morning searching the docks in hopes Moira reached Wicklow and looked for Kyle. When nothing came of that, they made their way through the town, drawing more attention than any liked, but Kyle insisted that their presence would circulate on the wind. He reasoned that Moira might hear they were there and come looking for him. He would be just as relieved if she found him as he would be if he found her. But the sun was sinking on another day, and Kyle still had no idea where Moira was, or if she was even alive. He refused to accept that she perished at sea. He'd seen her stubborn side enough times in their brief acquaintance to know she wouldn't give in so easily. He also wanted to believe that she returned his feelings—whatever they were—and would fight as hard to reunite with him as he would do for her.

"Then we return to the ships and sail back to Arklow. O'Malley will still be there. Either he has Moira, or knows where she is, or you kill him because he laid eyes on her," Keith reasoned with a shrug.

"I'm killing him regardless," Kyle growled.

"Aye, then. Eat up and let's be on our way," Keith said as he shifted in his seat once more. Neither Kyle nor Keith were comfortable being in port in an Irish town that didn't welcome pirates. None of the men sat with their backs to the door, so the bench was cramped.

"We weigh anchor tonight. I want to be in Arklow by morning," Kyle stated. He didn't care if it meant he put his men to the oars. If the wind wouldn't get him to Arklow, his crew would.

"And do we just go ashore in our dinghies?" Tomas spoke up. "What if the O'Malleys attack the ships while we're ashore?"

"That's why I want to be there by morning. We arrive so early they can't prepare for our attack," Kyle explained. "They used the fog to their advantage. We use the early morning to ours."

The men sat in silence as they ate. Kyle left a handful of coins on the table before he made his way to the tavern owner. Whispering to the man, he promised the barkeep a pouch of silver if he kept an ear open about any young woman arriving in town alone. He would give him a second pouch if he sheltered the woman until Kyle returned. The man eagerly agreed, and Kyle prayed he hadn't just signaled the sharks to circle Moira if she appeared.

"We find O'Malley's hiding place and burn his ships," Kyle plotted as Stephen rowed them back to the *Lady Charity*. "If we find him, we bring him back to the *Charity*. I'll deal with him alone. If we don't find him or can't burn his ships, we attack on land."

The men nodded but remained silent. None of the sailors enjoyed going on land for anything more than a night with a woman, but they could fight just as well on land as they could on a ship. With sturdy legs that kept them upright even on a listing ship, they rarely had trouble defeating opponents on land when nothing moved below them. When they arrived at the *Lady Charity*, the twins retired to Kyle's cabin, where they stood over maps of the Irish coastline.

"There," Kyle said as he moved his finger from the cove where they'd spied Moira's clansmen's ship, then waited out the storm. He dragged his finger down the coast until he came to a bay. "This is where the O'Malleys lay in wait. It's where they attacked us when Senga was onboard. Moira's clansmen stopped north of there because they believed they could drop anchor and go unnoticed. It's why I thought we could remain in the area. They appeared out of nowhere when they attacked us last year, but I saw where they retreated to. I saw the cave they entered."

"If they use fustes and corvettes, the bay must not be that deep. Our dinghies won't serve us well if we're attacking. We risk running aground if we approach too closely," Keith pointed out.

"Aye. That's why my crew goes on land to find their camp or cottages. While we do away with the O'Malleys, your crew does away with their ships. If we decimate their fleet, it will be a long time before they're a scourge of these waters again. Any who survive will retreat to County Mayo with their tails between their spindly legs." Kyle straightened and crossed his arms, waiting for his brother's assessment of his plans. Keith remained bent over the map for another minute before nodding his head and standing upright.

"If we are there in time, go ashore before it's light," Keith suggested. "We row out together, and on the way, you show me the cave. My men and I burn their fleet. If you don't find them on land, or you don't kill them all, they still won't be able to follow us or sail home. They'll have no means to raid any merchants or pirates until they can rebuild. And they won't have the funds to do that without raiding."

"And if they outnumber my crew on land? Or they lay in wait with their ships and outnumber yours? What is our contingency plan then? My idea only works if we can evenly divide the task," Kyle wondered aloud.

"Send Tomas to scout," Keith stated. "The man is a bluidy wraith. I've never met someone who can be bluidy invisible like he can."

Kyle nodded before going to the door of his cabin and summoning Tomas. The captains explained their plan and showed Tomas the map. When they were in agreement, Keith returned to his ship, swinging through the air from one deck to the other, laughing merrily since both ships were underway and not tethered. Kyle heard his brother and shook his head, knowing he was just as much a daredevil as his twin.

I'm coming for you, Moira. I swear. Tomorrow eve. I will have you back with me by tomorrow's eve. I'll kill that bastard in the morn and sail for you by noon. Then I shall bring you to our cabin and worship every inch of you.

As Kyle lay on his bunk planning every kiss and touch he intended to bestow upon Moira, he didn't notice that in his mind, the cabin now belonged to the two of them.

CHAPTER 23

Kyle dozed, but fear of oversleeping kept him from relaxing into a deep slumber. They'd sailed to Wicklow only to have a disappointing morning before sailing south to where they'd fought the O'Malleys just the day before. When the hour drew near for Tomas to go ashore to scout, Kyle met with his first mate and Snake Eye. Tomas and Kyle trusted no one else to watch the dinghy while Tomas moved about the cliffs. Snake Eye had a defect in his right pupil, making it more oblong than round. He swore it was why he had better-than-average vision. He could notice movement before anyone else, which made him the perfect scout's scout. With a piercing whistle of warning to Tomas, he would have the dinghy back in the water with the oars out before Tomas hit the sand. The two men worked well as a team, so Kyle trusted them with this mission.

"If you find Moira with them, do what you can to get her separated from the O'Malleys. I don't want her in the middle of the fighting. That's what got us in this mess to begin with."

"And if she's not there?" Snake Eye asked.

"Then I don't have to worry that someone will injure her

while we slay each and every bastard who claims O'Malley as his name," Kyle said matter-of-factly. There was no rancor in his tone. It was deadpan and blunt. Tomas and Snake Eye recognized it as the lethal voice that Kyle reserved for attacking slavers. He never thought twice about punishing the slave traders before prolonging their agony by setting them adrift. This attack wasn't about looting a ship. It was revenge.

Kyle watched the amorphous outline of the men and dinghy in the moonlight as Tomas and Snake Eye reached the shore. From such a distance, he could barely make out Tomas moving across the sand, and he disappeared as he ascended the cliff. Kyle's heart thudded as the minutes passed with no hint of when Tomas would return. His mind filled with one idea after another of how his plan could go awry. He glanced down to see he clutched the rail so tightly that his knuckles glowed an unearthly white. He forced himself to relax before he looked out at the water again.

To Kyle's surprise, the dinghy was cutting through the surf, making its way back to the *Lady Charity*. He hadn't noticed Tomas crossing the beach or getting in the rowboat. He held his breath as the men approached, then climbed aboard in silence. The three men crossed the deck and went to stand where they could speak to Keith and his first mate.

"I don't ken how they are still alive," Tomas spat in disgust. "Two men posted on watch, and they're both sleeping!"

"They assume no one dares to take them on," Kyle muttered before looking at the coast again. "We make our move now. How many are there?"

"I counted two dozen," Tomas stated.

"That's it?" Keith asked in disbelief.

"Aye. We killed at least fifty of their crew during the last battle," Tomas pointed out.

"I suppose that's true," Keith agreed. "Then this should be over and done with before it's time to break our fast."

Kyle nodded with a grin. He was glad to hear Dermot didn't have hidden reinforcements that would force both crews on land. This would allow Kyle to go after Dermot, and Keith could destroy the O'Malleys' fleet. Moving in silence, the crews of both ships lowered their dinghies into the water, with five from the *Lady Charity* going to the beach, and five from the *Lady Grace* going to the cave Kyle pointed out to Keith. Kyle and his men hadn't reached the beach before an alarm went up from the O'Malleys on watch with the boats. Kyle prayed there weren't more O'Malleys with the ships than on land. By the time he reached the sand, the sound of Keith's battle had faded. As his men crept along the beach and up the cliffs, not even a breeze stirred.

With hand and arm signals, the crew of the *Lady Charity* encircled the O'Malley camp. When Kyle found Dermot reeking of whisky, he gave the signal. Honor among thieves meant Kyle's crew didn't skewer the men in their sleep. Instead, the *Lady Charity*'s crew woke them at knifepoint, dragged them to their feet, scoffed at them for having such poor guards, hurled several insults, allowed the O'Malleys a chance to fight, then ran them through.

"You come with me," Kyle barked before the hilt of his sword bashed into Dermot's temple. The rotund man dropped like a sack of potatoes. "Get him in the boat."

Kyle swept his eyes over the fallen men, and not an ounce of remorse pecked at him. These men were cut from the same cloth as he and his crew. They sealed their fate the moment they joined Dermot for the attack against the MacLean twins, and when Dermot set his sights on taking Moira.

The contracts may say he can marry her, but she's mine. Men toasting their arses in Hell don't marry.

Men from the *Lady Charity* maneuvered the unconscious

Dermot onto the ship, nearly dropping him thrice. Kyle ordered men to lift him and follow Kyle. As he approached his cabin door, he considered the hook in his ceiling. He'd tortured more than one man in that very place. But as he pictured the inside of his cabin, a resolve swept over him. Never again would he use that hook to torture a captive. The hook had become Moira's, and only she would be restrained there for her pleasure—if she agreed. He would never bring another prisoner into his cabin. Full stop. The space would be Moira's haven if she agreed to return to him. He motioned for the men to follow him to the hold.

Carrying a lit candle Braedon handed him, Kyle led the way down the ladder into the underbelly of the ship. When Dermot's awkward frame was uncooperative and slipped, none of the men made a move to prevent his fall. He landed against the hull with two thuds, first his body then his head. Now that Kyle had him confined to the hold and his men outnumbered his foe, there was no reason for him to remain unconscious. Kyle drove his booted foot into Dermot's ribs. The man groaned and tried to roll away, but that only put him next to Tomas's toes. The first mate kicked him in the belly.

"You're awake. Be a man and stand up," Kyle growled, this time only nudging him with his boot.

Dermot let loose a stream of curses in Irish Gaelic that the men could guess the meaning of. Unfazed, Kyle crossed his arms and tapped his toes until Dermot lumbered to his feet. As soon as he was upright, Tomas and Snake Eye captured an arm each and dragged Dermot to the center of the hold where there were several hooks screwed into the ceiling. With ample rope available, Tomas and Snake Eye soon had Dermot secured. Kyle added his strength as the three men pulled Dermot's arms over his head until he dangled from the rope.

Dermot watched Kyle through bleary eyes. He'd drunk himself to sleep that night, angered that he'd lost most of his men to Kyle and Keith, lost his horse to Moira, and lost her as well. He opened his mouth to spit at Kyle, but Kyle drove his fist into Dermot's face, shattering his nose.

"Where is she? She wasn't at your camp," Kyle demanded.

"Who?" Dermot asked innocently.

"Where is Moira MacDonnell?"

"I don't know where my bluidy bride is. Dead, hopefully."

"I don't believe you," Kyle sneered as he brought his palm to Dermot's cheek in a ringing slap. "We found the cave she likely hid in. You went to look for her but didn't find her, did you?"

As they sailed past Arklow, Kyle ordered torches lit and a dinghy lowered. He and Keith went alone to explore the jetty. They found the narrow opening that the crashing waves of high tide hid the last time they searched for Moira. Kyle had no evidence to substantiate his belief, but he was certain Moira was still alive. His heart and mind screamed it in unison.

"She wasn't there," Dermot conceded.

"But you found her when she left. What did you do to her?" Kyle plowed his fist into Dermot's jaw. "Tell me, and the beating ends. Play games with me, and I beat you until you look forward to me setting you adrift."

Dermot smirked but said nothing. Kyle drew a dirk from his belt, easing it from its sheath. He held it so it glowed in the candles Tomas and Snake Eye now held aloft. Kyle examined both sides before he pressed the tip against his forefinger, drawing a drop of blood. He held up the knife and his finger for Dermot to see.

"You know, just as I do, that sharks come at the scent of blood in the water. You know that there are several varieties of sharks in the Irish Sea. Big sharks, little sharks. It matters not. They will all fight for a chance to eat you. So once more, you decide. Do I beat you to a bloody pulp, then set you adrift to be disemboweled and quartered by sharks? Or do you receive my mercy and don't end up as chum?"

Not waiting for Dermot's response, he slashed his blade across Dermot's protruding belly. The knife cut through the man's doublet and sliced the skin below. Blood blossomed and spread across the material. Kyle canted his head as though he was assessing his work. He canted his head back the other direction and turned the corners of his mouth down in a mocking frown.

"You shouldn't have made me ask twice," Kyle mused. "That may draw a few of the smaller fishies. The next one will draw the beasts who will swallow you whole, like Jonah. Except unlike Jonah, God doesn't give a shite about you or your life. Unlike Jonah, the beast shall chomp you into tiny bits before swallowing you only to shite you out later."

Kyle twirled his blade left and right as he waited. Dermot remained silent, his stare belligerent and daring.

"You know you're going to die, so you think to wait me out. You think there is no reason for you to tell me anything. The trouble with your thinking is that no man has survived to tell the tales of the torture I make my captives endure." Kyle turned to his men. "Mind him."

Kyle scaled the ladder and made his way to his cabin, where he flipped open the chest that held the implements he'd had little chance to share with Moira. A lump caught in his throat, and it firmed his resolve to make Dermot's remaining hours humiliating agony. Pushing aside what Moira discovered, he delved deeper, a wave of relief sweeping over him that Moira hadn't the opportunity to discover everything he kept hidden. Retrieving what he needed, he made his way back to Dermot. With his eyes narrowed, he held up the objects he'd collected. Dermot's eyes widened, and Kyle saw the trepidation and confusion. Kyle understood Dermot knew they would inflict pain, but he didn't know how.

"Let me explain, since you seem confused." Kyle held up a plug far larger than any in the set Moira found. "I've heard from more than one whore how you like to tup them. You shall now know what it feels like. Unless, of course, you've been buggered before."

Kyle nodded to Tomas, who cut away the ties to Dermot's leggings and yanked them down. With his arms extended over his head, his belly hung below his hem, obscuring his member. Kyle howled with laughter and pointed. Following their captain's lead, Tomas and Snake Eye joined in, their laughter raucous and echoing in the hold.

"Where is it?" Snake Eye snorted. "Does he even have one?"

"Bluidy good thing you found Moira when you did, Capt'n. She knows what a man can do." Tomas pointed and frowned. "Does it even do anything? It's such a wee stick. It doesn't look like it's up to the task." Kyle and his men doubled over with laughter as they continued to taunt Dermot.

"No wonder he pays so much, and the whores still look disappointed," Kyle chortled before stepping around Dermot to stand behind him. He poured ginger oil to coat the plug, and without warning, he inserted it, making Dermot release a high-pitched howl. "Sounds like the sheep I hear he likes to fuck."

"Aye. Only quim he can satisfy," Snake Eye mused.

"Tug on it," Kyle nodded at Dermot's groin once he stood before him. "Let's see if it can poke it's head out."

Tomas stepped forward and freed Dermot's right hand. When Dermot made no move to obey Kyle's command, Kyle cocked an eyebrow at Tomas. In turn, Tomas slammed a nearby plank against Dermot's arse, making the man scream. Four more blows had Dermot reaching down to his groin, following Kyle's order.

"What do you know? It can grow," Snake Eye snickered.

"Finally, enough for this to be of use," Kyle said as he held up a ring. "Put it on."

At Dermot's confused look, Kyle huffed and looked at him as though he were a simpleton. Kyle lifted the ring for Dermot to see before he slid his forefinger through it. He held out the ring toward Dermot's groin and cocked an eyebrow, waiting to see if Dermot would catch on or if he would have to explain it. With a grunt, Dermot snatched the device from Kyle and slid it onto his rod before stroking himself. Kyle watched with satisfaction as a moment of arousal made his enemy's cock grow and pleasure entered his eyes. But as quickly as it came, it disappeared as Dermot squirmed in pain. He knew that Dermot wouldn't know how to wear it properly. Kyle grinned maliciously and didn't instruct Dermot on what to do. Kyle stood with his arms crossed as Dermot stroked over and over. When he slowed to ease his discomfort, Kyle drove his fist into the cut on Dermot's belly.

"In agony yet?" Kyle asked.

"You know I am," Dermot whimpered.

"Not able to climax?" Kyle asked casually.

"You know it feels like my cock will explode. You did this on purpose."

Kyle shrugged. "They say it's an erotic pleasure in the Orient. Maybe it doesn't fit. All my others would be far too large though." Tomas and Snake Eye chortled. "Not enjoying yourself? Maybe you can imagine how Moira would have despised you if you'd forced her to make your tiny cock try to work."

"You made your point," Dermot whined. "Enough. I'll talk."

"Then speak," Kyle said with another shrug.

"Take it off," Dermot begged.

"I didn't say slow down," Kyle corrected. "Let me hear what you have to say. Then I'll decide whether it's worth my mercy."

Sweat poured off Dermot's brow as his hand continued to move back and forth. His entire body trembled as he wheezed with each stroke. When Kyle raised his dirk again, Dermot coughed and nodded.

"She was in the cave I searched, but I didn't find her. The woman is a selkie. She swam through a narrow tunnel that connects the cave to the cove. I don't know anyone who could do that. But the bitch did." He reared back as Kyle's blade slashed his belly again. "I watched her come out of the water and climb the path. She smacked right into me. I let her run, thinking my men weren't so worthless. She made it into Arklow and hid with a farmer's family. That bastard Dónal promised me a demure wife who would cause me no trouble. She's been no end of trouble."

Kyle waited as Dermot gasped for air between groans of pain. Kyle thought how the right size ring, coupled with Moira's touch, would have Kyle groaning in ecstasy for hours. But he wouldn't be able to enjoy anything with Moira if he didn't find her. His patience growing short, he brandished his knife before Dermot's face once again. He'd never had respect for Dermot O'Malley, but his disgust grew as Dermot conceded to his demands without trying to fight back. Kyle saw the coward he'd always known Dermot to be.

"She escaped. Ran from the farmer's cottage and stole my horse. Couldn't follow her since we don't—didn't—have any besides mine."

"Where'd she go?"

"Farmer said she wanted to go to Wicklow. Something about finding her twin brothers. Brothers," Dermot cackled, then coughed. He cast Kyle a smarmy grin. "Fucking her own brother."

"And now you're not useful anymore," Kyle said with a nod toward his men. Tomas cut down Dermot's other arm. He and Snake Eye pulled up Dermot's doublet. "I shall need my toys back."

Before Dermot understood what was about to happen, Kyle sliced his blade downward, dismembering Dermot. The O'Malley's knees crumpled, but Snake Eye and Tomas kept him on his feet. Blood gushed from his groin. With a lip curled in disgust,

Kyle picked up the severed appendage and removed the ring. "Open wide."

Dermot's eyes bulged, but he complied. Kyle removed the plug, dropping it and the ring into a pouch, before his men dragged Dermot onto the deck. The man's eyes rolled back in his head, but the plank a sailor gave Kyle brought him round when it slammed into his arse. Wrists bound, the plank tucked under his arms, Snake Eye and Tomas hefted him onto the rail. Kyle gave him a shove.

The crew of the *Lady Charity* watched as Dermot crashed into the water. A whistle from Kyle signaled the crew of the *Lady Grace* to watch the inevitable spectacle. Dermot's head popped out of the water, blood coloring the water before him. Kyle counted down from ten, and as if on his cue, Dermot was pulled beneath the surface. Shark fins circled and dipped beneath the surface until both ships' crew were certain there was nothing left to watch.

The *Lady Charity* and the *Lady Grace* had been underway since the crews returned to the ships. Kyle looked to the eastern horizon where the sun was already rising. He would be in Wicklow in four hours, and he intended to have Moira in his arms in less than five.

CHAPTER 24

Moira rubbed her eyes, trying to focus her blurry vision. Between the saltwater and being overly fatigued, she struggled to see. Trying to maneuver a galloping, then cantering, horse without her full sight was proving dangerous. The horse had enough sense to avoid tree trunks, but she nearly decapitated herself with a low-hanging branch. After what Moira approximated to be two hours of riding, there was no hint of dawn over the eastern horizon. She and the horse were winded, and the route grew more and more precarious. She feared getting lost in a forest as much as catapulting over a cliff. Praying that she hadn't underestimated Dermot, she drew the horse to a halt after turning off the narrow path she'd followed out a village she never learned the name of. She suspected they were near Arklow, but she wasn't certain. She only knew she was somewhere in County Wicklow, and she was a long way from her home in County Antrim.

Never fully recovered from the bone jarring cold that morning, Moira huddled out of the wind. She urged the horse to lie down and used the steed's enormous body to buffer her. She thought about being warm again and wrapped in Kyle's plaid, or better yet, his arms. It took little time for the physically and mentally exhausted Moira to fall into a deep sleep. When her eyes fluttered open, she realized she'd slept until close to midday. In a panic that Dermot might search for her on foot or find horses, she urged her mount to rise. She prayed to the Virgin Mary in thanksgiving that no one stumbled upon her while she slumbered and that her horse hadn't run away. Guiding the horse, Moira returned to the country lane she'd been following. As she sheltered her eyes from the bright sun, she realized the path had drawn her away from the coast. She saw nothing to the east but an open expanse of grassland. She had no idea how far from the sea she'd strayed.

Mounting the horse, Moira continued in the direction she presumed was still north, not entirely sure since the sun was at its zenith by the time she set off. She wondered if she would encounter any travelers or tinkers along the road, or even a village where she could get her bearings and ask for directions. She and her steed plodded along, no longer racing away for danger. Moira wanted to conserve her horse's energy lest she had to spur him into a gallop to avoid any threat. By midafternoon, Moira was once more struggling to stay awake. Her time in the water and the cave, along with the fear that accompanied her since the O'Malleys' attack, had sapped the hardiness she'd always possessed. When she found a stream, she decided it was time for both woman and beast to rest. She dug in the sack for a chunk of bread, disappointed to find it was already rock hard. She couldn't even feed it to the horse. She nibbled on the cheese as she gave the horse the apples. Once they'd both eaten, she wandered down to the water, her horse eager for a drink.

As Moira kneeled alongside the brook, she inhaled the perfumed scent of honeysuckles. It was a smell from her childhood. Her mother had taught her how to pick the blossoms and carefully pull the stem free to release the nectar. Her mother told her about the superstition that those who wore honeysuckle would dream of their true love. The memory collided in her mind with an image of Kyle as he sat beside her in the dinghy, how he'd sheltered her from the wind. She pictured how their bodies moved in synchronicity. Her heart ached for the freedom she felt with him, even when he asserted control. She wondered if Kyle was a man who she could grow to love. The thought brought a disquieting feeling of peace and fear. As she recalled that Kyle sailed away from the cove without her, she resigned herself to Kyle not falling in love with her.

If he won't reciprocate my feelings, why the hell am I chasing him down? Why aren't I headed in the opposite direction and trying to reach the O'Driscolls? What are you hoping to accomplish? Another tumble in his bed? Rejection? Because you're a daft fool who still has hope. You hope he'll be looking for you. You hope he'll be happy to see you. You hope he'll want you back aboard his ship.

If he doesn't want me, maybe he'll be decent enough to take me to the O'Driscolls or even Barra. At the very least, he could help me secure passage to Baltimore. And if he won't, Wicklow is still closer than riding through O'Malley territory to get to the O'Driscolls. You only got separated from him yesterday morning. Go to the town, see what there is to see, then decide.

With a plan in place and a honeysuckle tucked behind her ear, Moira rose from the stream bank just as her horse released a pained whinny. The gelding stomped its hoof twice before whinnying again, its eyes rolling around. Moira saw in an instant what happened. The horse had a bee sting. The swelling was immediate. She'd seen a horse die once from a horrible reaction to a sting, so she prayed her horse wasn't like that one. She drew the animal into the water and cupped liquid in her hands to pour over the wound. The water was brisk, but not cold enough to take down the swelling. But the steed calmed, nonetheless.

When Moira believed the horse was as ready as it was going to be, she led it back to the path. However, when she tried to mount, the horse was not in agreement. It stomped and bucked, nearly throwing her into a bramble patch. With a curse and an oath, Moira inhaled deeply, then puffed out the breath. She set off on foot, foul tempered.

With raw feet and aching legs, Moira breathed easier when she spotted plumes of white smoke over the next hill. She was certain they came from holes in cottage roofs and signaled a village lay ahead. The sun was setting, and she was growing too weary to continue. When people came into sight, Moira stepped off the road and observed. It appeared to be a normal country village with farms stretching out from the perimeter. She observed a man herding a flock of sheep into a pasture, and a gaggle of geese chased after a group of children. She could hear the angry squawks and thought of the farmwife's reaction when she learned Moira was supposedly a pirate's sister. She chuckled as she turned her attention to a pair of women standing at the village well. She expected them to be suspicious at first, but she prayed they would be generous. As she approached the village, she planned her story, not wanting to trap herself like she had before.

"Lass!"

Moira turned to find an old woman hobbling toward her, her lips wrapped around gums that no longer held teeth. The woman's gray hair was pulled back into a tight knot, but strands escaped and fluttered beside her ears. She waved a walking stick as she signaled Moira to come nearer. Hesitant and suspicious herself, Moira approached with caution.

"Good evening," Moira greeted.

"We rarely get strangers. Who are you?" The woman asked, coming straight to the point.

"I became separated from my party this morning during a

storm," Moira said. She knew Irish weather, and she knew somewhere on the island it had rained that day. She also knew no one would question that. "We were headed to Wicklow, but I've gotten lost."

"And do you normally dress like a man when you sound like a lady?" The woman asked.

"Only when I travel. It's safer for me on horseback," Moira explained, and it was true. She'd enjoyed the control she had over the animal without layers of fabric in the way.

"And do you always ride bareback?"

Moira was tiring of the questions already. She'd told the woman she wanted to go to Wicklow, but the villager skipped past that. With as much patience as she could muster, she replied, "The reason I got separated in the storm was because of trouble with the saddle. It was old, and the girth was frayed. It snapped, but the thunder was too loud for the others to hear me. I had to leave it behind. I tried to catch up to the people I rode with, but I got turned around. Am I on the road to Wicklow?"

The woman worked her lips over her toothless gums as she squinted at Moira. Moira attempted to look assured of her story without showing her impatience. The woman pursed her lips before nodding. "You are in Kilmacurragh," the woman stated, as though Moira should know precisely where she was. At Moira's blank stare, the woman tsked. "You're a few hours' ride from Wicklow. You're too far west of the coast."

Moira nodded as she looked in the direction she now suspected Wicklow lay. She glanced at the western skies as the clouds turned fiery red, orange, and yellow behind the setting sun. While dusk was beautiful, it meant another night on the open road.

"Who did you say your people are?" The old woman asked.

"Moira O Dunbghaill," Moira responded. She'd chosen a clan, the O'Doyles, that lived south of Arklow and where the

O'Malleys sailed. She hoped that naming a clan from County Wexford, the next one south from County Wicklow, would make her more acceptable. The O'Doyles were large landowners, but Moira doubted anyone would know the names of the ladies in the chieftain's family.

"And you be headed to Wicklow," The woman repeated Moira's earlier statement.

"Aye. My family was going to visit extended relatives in Wicklow."

"And they would have been?"

Moira wanted to stomp her foot just as her horse did as the animal grew anxious standing around. Moira was certain the gelding was still in pain, even if he'd grown quiet. She forced herself not to snap at the nosy old biddy.

"The O Tuathaills." The O'Tooles were a powerful clan in Wicklow and Kildare, so she knew the name held weight. She prayed the village lay just far enough from Wicklow that the residents wouldn't be familiar with the O'Toole chieftain and his family. "If you don't mind, I'd like the blacksmith or farrier to look at my horse. A bee stung it a while back."

"Looks fine to me," came the quick response.

Moira bit her tongue against asking the woman if she was blind or daft. The welt on the horse's face near its eye was noticeable and troubling. "All the same, if you have a blacksmith or a farrier, I would like them to have a look."

"And what do you think a man who makes horseshoes or a man who fits horseshoes knows about bee stings?" The woman demanded.

"They know horses," Moira responded with a shrug. She'd indulged the woman long enough and made to step around her.

"What you need is the healer," the woman responded.

"And who is that?"

"Me."

Moira tried not to wince. All she wanted to do was escape

the overly inquisitive crone, and yet now, she would have to ask her for a poultice for a horse that wasn't even hers. She'd hoped to find a man who would likely grunt and bark instructions for some medicinal that he would never help her find. She would have her solution without paying a coin. The woman would surely expect remuneration.

"I'm afraid I have no coin with which to pay you," Moira admitted, but realized her mistake the moment the words came out of her mouth. The woman's scornful look told her she assumed Moira intended to pay the blacksmith or farrier with something other than coin. She clarified, "I had hoped the blacksmith or farrier could point me in the right direction, and I could find the medicinal my horse needs."

"Of course. A God-fearing lass such as yourself would never offer herself." As the old woman observed her, Moira wanted to roar with laughter.

If only you knew how I offered myself to a pirate captain. And I haven't been remorseful since.

"Can you sew?"

Moira's brow furrowed. "Yes."

"Come with me. I have a mountain of mending to do, but my old eyes trouble me. You sew; I'll treat your horse. I might even give a scrawny lass like you some meat to chew on."

"That is most kind of you." Moira forced the words out from between her lips. She scowled at the back of the woman's head when the healer turned away from her. She smoothed her features as she drew closer to other people, aware that they would stare and judge.

CHAPTER 25

Moira sat darning stockings while the healer hummed an out of key melody that made Moira's head pound. Tuning the woman out as best she could, Moira's mind drifted to Kyle as she stitched. Years of sewing made her efficient, and the task needed little of her attention.

If Wicklow was only a half day's sail from where the O'Malleys attacked us, then Kyle would have made it to port before I fell asleep at the farmer's. Did he go ashore last night or this morning to look for me? Was he disappointed when he didn't find me? Does he know I couldn't have made it there before him even without the hours in the cave? Where would he have gone after that? Too many questions with no answers.

Maybe he's going back to fight the O'Malleys, assuming Dermot was searching for me instead of fighting. That bastard would run away from a battle. Maybe Kyle will finish what Dermot started. Searching for me this morning and sailing back to fight Dermot or even looking for me would have filled the day while I've been riding with no sense of direction. When he doesn't find me with Dermot, will he give up? Has he sailed away for good? That's assuming he cares.

Even if he isn't in Wicklow tomorrow, I still have more chances of surviving there unnoticed than I do in a tiny village like this. If Dermot is alive, he may still look for me. No matter what Dermot believes, Dónal will give him nothing unless there's proof that we married, or that Dermot at least consummated our betrothal. Is that enough incentive for Dermot to continue searching for me—if Kyle doesn't go back and kill him—or will he find another clan and another bride? God, how I hope he just finds someone else.

Enough, Moira! It doesn't matter one way or another at this point. You're alone until you figure out otherwise. You can pray all you like that Kyle is in Wicklow when you arrive tomorrow. But if he's not, or he doesn't want you, then you'd do well to sort yourself out.

I refuse to return to Dunluce. I refuse to go to Dermot. What I need to do is get my head straight and figure out how to get to Barra. By the time this woman finishes the poultice, my horse will be healed or dead. Either way, the only thing I need from her for now is shelter and food, if I'm lucky. If I have to run again in the night, I will. But I need her to tell me how to get to Wicklow first. If I don't discover that, then stopping in the village will have been truly worthless. Maybe I should have pushed on, even if I had to walk beside the bluidy beast rather than ride him. But I'm here now, so time to make the best of it.

"This seems like an ancient village," Moira mused without looking up.

"Aye. The Norsemen came many moons ago and started a settlement. Been here ever since," the healer responded.

"Does that make it older than Wicklow?" Moira inquired.

"About the same age. Same wave of invaders who started this village built the beginnings of Wicklow," the old woman explained.

"Did no one live here before them? The Irish are an ancient people."

"Some tribe passed through here often, so the legend goes, but never settled."

"I can't imagine what our people must have thought when the Norsemen arrived. Did they come by sea or by land?" Moira asked. At the healer's suspicious glare, Moira clarified. "My mother told me stories of the ancient Irish kings. I always loved hearing them. Your story reminds me of hers."

"Aye, well, the story goes that they did both. They attacked by sea first, but some traveled by land and made their home here."

"I wonder if the road to Wicklow is the very same as they used," Moira said with feigned awe.

"It is."

"I wonder where the road starts," Moira said wistfully before picking up a new stocking to mend.

"By the blacksmith's," the healer said unwittingly.

"Hmm," Moira said as she bit off the end of the thread. She'd learned what she needed. Whether she left in the morning with a full belly or ran in the night, she need only look for the smithy.

Moira continued working until the healer announced her ointment was ready for Moira's horse. Before she passed the odiferous glob to Moira, she inspected Moira's handiwork. She grunted in approval and gave Moira the bowl. Moira made her way to where she'd tethered her horse in a lean-to. The horse blinked at her but didn't shift as she applied the medicinal. The swelling had gone done, but a bump remained. She prayed the ointment helped and that the horse would be ready for a rider whenever it was time to leave.

"Come in and eat, lass," the healer said. Her tone was lighter than it had been. Moira questioned whether the crone was happy with her stitching or if there was a nefarious reason to lure her back. As she entered, she noticed the woman ladling a bowl of pottage. The older woman motioned for Moira to sit at the table and laid the steaming bowl before her. Given a chunk of bread and dried fruit, Moira blew on the boiling food twice, then pretended to wait for it to cool. She ate the bread and fruit while she watched the woman move about her cooking space. It was nearing the time for the evening meal, yet the healer poured no pottage for herself.

Moira's heart sped as she glanced at her bowl, then at the woman's back. Doubt niggled in her mind about why the woman wouldn't serve herself. Moira wondered if the healer added something to the food that would make her ill. When her hostess offered her another chunk of bread and laid butter beside Moira, she dared to add a thin layer. She ate the bread, admitting to herself that the butter was a delicious addition.

"Your bread is very hardy," Moira observed. "Very filling."

"You look like you need more than bread and butter," the healer noted.

"I eat little, I confess. Makes my stomach hurt to have large meals. Won't you join me?" Moira nodded to the stool across from her. She waited to see if the woman served herself any of the pottage, but the woman took a seat with nothing before her. Pushing the now-cooled bowl before her hostess, Moira added. "I would hate for this to go to waste."

The healer nodded but glanced down at the bowl. "We are alike. I eat little too. This will last me several days on my own."

The healer's evasiveness made Moira suspect the woman had dosed the pottage with a plant that would leave Moira sick or dead. Sending her hostess the same smile she used to placate Dónal, she nodded. She didn't have to feign the yawn that tried to escape. The woman's questionable behavior made Moira wonder if she dared close her eyes within the cottage. But pragmatism won out. She needed more sleep, or she would be ill. It was the only way her body would recuperate from her time in the sea.

"May I rest my head near your fire?" Moira asked politely.

The healer's smile was too sugary for Moira's taste. She would do well not to sleep too deeply, but she knew she had no control over that. Taking a spot before the hearth, Moira closed her eyes as the woman continued to bustle around her cottage. Forcing her mind to remain busy until the healer retired, Moira eventually fell asleep.

Coming awake to the sound of a closing door for a second time in two nights, Moira lay still. She strained to hear who entered the cottage and whether they approached. Opening her eyes just a crack, she noticed a middle-aged man shaking the healer awake. In the silent cottage, Moira heard them whispering.

"Is she the woman I told you about yesterday morning?" The man asked.

"I believe so," the healer responded. "She claims to be an O'Doyle and has said nothing about a pirate nor a chieftain."

"But do you think she could be the pirate's mistress or the chieftain's missing sister? Wicklow is abuzz with word that the Red Drifter seeks a young woman who went missing. We already ken Chieftain MacDonnell looks for his missing sister. Are they one and the same, Mother?"

Moira listened in stunned silence. She wasn't sure what pieces of information to dissect first. Kyle was looking for her. Her brother was looking for her. Somehow people in Wicklow knew of Dónal's search. Word spread that the Red Drifter wanted her back.

"Did you hear her described while you were at market? When she arrived alone yesterday afternoon, I guessed she might be," the healer whispered.

"Aye. Small, looks like a lass not a woman, dark hair, and blue eyes," the healer's son replied.

"That's her."

Moira's heart raced as she eased her arm away from her side and felt for the fire poker. She wanted to sigh when she realized it was within easy reach. She knew what would happen next. The man intended to take her and ransom her, just as the farmer attempted.

"The tavern owner at The Leg of Mutton says the Red Drifter will pay him for keeping her safe, but I say I take her to the Red Drifter myself," the man said.

"Who will pay more? The pirate or the chieftain? That's who you take her too," the healer reasoned.

"Who do you think? A man will pay more for his lover than his sister. Besides, I don't think Dónal MacDonnell has the coin with him that the Red Drifter likely has on his ship."

Moira's heart stopped racing. She feared it would stop altogether. Dónal hadn't sent someone to find her; he'd come himself. She would have to find her way to Wicklow and to The Leg of Mutton. It was undoubtable that Dónal would lodge at a tavern rather than make camp. She prayed he hadn't heard about Kyle's offer and that he wasn't awaiting her at The Leg of Mutton. Without a cloak or a cap, she couldn't disguise herself. While she knew plenty of Irish women fit the exact description the man gave his mother, she couldn't imagine there would be too many of them unaccompanied in a town like Wicklow.

Without warning, the man spun in her direction and stalked toward her. Moira snatched the poker and swung it at the man's head as he reached for her. It connected with the ringing sound of metal against something hard. He staggered back, and Moira leapt to her feet. He appeared unarmed, but Moira knew he was likely to have at least one knife strapped to him. How she wished she had a knife, but the poker's length allowed her to keep her attacker at a distance lest he wanted to be skewered.

"You think to turn me over," Moira stated without preface. "Take me to the Red Drifter, and he will reward you. Take me to my brother, and I will kill you. Try to attack me now, and I kill you while your mother watches."

"I tied my wagon out front," the man said.

"Splendid. You ride in your wagon, and I ride my horse." Moira wouldn't get within arm's reach of the man.

CHAPTER 26

Kyle woke to a knock on his cabin door. Rubbing his dry eyes and wishing he'd been able to sleep through the night rather than nap, he pulled the door open to find Tomas in the passageway.

"We and the *Lady Grace* dropped anchor out of sight, but we're near Wicklow," Tomas explained.

"Thank you for waking me," Kyle said before clearing his throat. "Only Keith and I will go ashore this time. I know you disagree, but I want to draw less attention to us. If Moira is hiding, either from me or because she can't find me, I don't need every penny-pincher within a league trying to grab her for ransom."

Tomas frowned but nodded. They'd already decided on the plan as they sailed north, but Tomas had contested it. Now he had no choice but to obey his captain. When Tomas left, Kyle hurried to dress. He strapped as many knives to his legs, belt, and wrists as he could. He slung his sword at his waist. He hadn't been this armed for his meeting with Dermot. But he prayed this was the day he would find Moira, and he would fight everyone who stood in his way if she wished to be with him. He steeled himself against the possibility that she would spit in his face for endangering her and leaving her behind. He would take her anywhere she wanted. He just needed to know she was safe, see it with his own eyes, hear it with his own ears. And if she would let him touch her, he would hold her until she pulled away.

The four-hour sail took twice as long when the wind shifted against them. Rowing against the wind and choppy seas made it slow going, so it was nearing morning. Kyle once more wanted to arrive on land with darkness to hide his presence. He and Keith would make The Leg of Mutton their first stop to learn whether the tavern keeper was sheltering Moira. He made his way above deck and looked out at the earliest hint of dawn. He nodded to Tomas, who would remain in command of the *Lady Charity* while Kyle was ashore. Snake Eye waited at the rail, and Keith bobbed in a dinghy beside the *Lady Charity*. Kyle and Snake Eye soon joined Keith, and they were on their way to the docks.

The Leg of Mutton was quiet as Kyle and Keith crept inside. Men lay asleep or unconscious, Kyle neither knew nor cared. The twins slipped through the main room and made their way to the back of the first floor, where the tavern owner and his family slept. With their ears to the door, Keith and Kyle nodded before Keith eased the door open. Positioning himself at the foot of the bed, Keith stood watch as Kyle poked the man awake.

"Is she here?" Kyle demanded. The groggy man looked between Kyle and Keith, then noticeably gulped.

"No," the man whispered. With a scowl, Kyle prepared to step back. But the tavern keeper's next words froze him. "But her brother is."

"Dónal MacDonnell is here?" Kyle hissed.

"Aye. I swear I told him nothing about you searching for her and wanting her to come here. But the town can't stop chin wagging about the pirate looking for his mistress." At Kyle's murderous glare, the man coughed. "Begging your pardon, but that's the rumor. The MacDonnell said his sister was a loose woman who ran from her marriage. He said his sister gave her husband an apoplexy, then ran away with her lover—you—and he would pay in gold for anyone who brought her back. The entire town is on the lookout."

"And how did he come to be in Wicklow?" Kyle asked.

"He's been checking ports all along the coast, but he heard your ships," he jerked his chin toward Keith, "were spotted here."

Kyle glanced back at Keith before nodding at the bar owner. "The same deal stands. Protect her, and I will pay you well. Dónal MacDonnell has neither the funds nor the honor to pay what he's promised. He's more likely to kill you, so you can never tell the tale."

"I know," the man mumbled.

Kyle and Keith slipped from the tavern as silently as they entered. Stepping into the shadows, they kept their voices lowered.

"Every fishmonger, whore, and dockhand will have their eye out for Moira," Kyle grumbled. "I've made her life go from bad to worse to bluidy wretched. Someone could already have her. Someone could turn her over to Dónal, and I would never know."

Keith remained quiet, once more allowing his brother to think aloud. He nodded, prompting Kyle to carry on as Keith stood with his arms crossed, his senses on alert as Kyle focused on his thoughts.

"We need at least three men to stand watch here and two to follow Dónal when he goes out," Kyle decided. "You and I will keep looking, but we stay out of sight and only listen. Snake Eye goes back for the other men. If he hurries, he can return with them before sunup."

With only a nod, Keith walked back to the docks with Kyle. Kyle relayed his instructions to Snake Eye. Once his trusted crewman pulled away and rowed toward the ships, Kyle and Keith turned back toward the town but stopped before they left the harbor. Finding a place to hide beside the harbormaster's station, the brothers watched as dockhands showed up for work. Within an hour, the quay was teeming with fishermen, fishmongers, and men loading and unloading freight. The twins listened for any gossip about their previous visit or anyone who might speculate on their return. As the early morning hours ticked by, the brothers heard various men share their suspicions that the Red Drifter and the Scarlet Blade would return to find the woman the Red Drifter lost. They heard nothing about Dónal's presence, but they heard various outlandish theories about themselves. Some made them grin, others made them roll their eyes.

As the sun rose higher, Kyle and Keith slipped away from the harbor and went back to The Leg of Mutton. Finding his men skulking behind the building, Kyle learned that no one had seen hide nor hair of Dónal. From what they learned, the man drank like a fish, which wasn't news to Kyle. Dónal had stumbled and fallen on the steps before reaching his second-floor chamber some time in the wee hours of the morning. They assumed he was still snoring in bed. Keith and Kyle debated the merits of splitting up, and while neither relished the other working alone, they agreed it would be more efficient and less noticeable. One redhead would catch people's attention, twin redheads guaranteed more rumors than they created their last time at port. With a plan in place to divide the town between them, and instructions given on how Kyle's men should track them if they had information, the twins embraced and parted.

Moira approached Wicklow on the gelding as the man, who remained nameless just as his mother and the farmer's family had, steered his wagon along the country lane. There was more than one fork in the road along the way, so she considered it a blessing in disguise that she came with the man. Since they'd traveled in the dark and with the wagon, the journey took several hours more than Moira bargained for. But when the rooftops came into view, Moira observed the man. She witnessed his anxiousness and excitement grow. She knew he envisioned the coin he believed Kyle would give him. But Moira feared that the man would double-cross her. After all, his mother had been prepared to drug her.

"Is that Wicklow?" Moira asked innocently.

"Aye," the man grunted.

"Do you know if the Red Drifter is in port?"

"He must be if he's looking for you," the man snapped.

Taking a deep breath to keep her patience, Moira continued to coerce information from the man. "I wonder if he is at the tavern waiting for someone to bring me to him or if he searches on his own."

"He searches with his devil brother," the man said.

Kyle and Keith. I shouldn't have expected anything less. Maybe they'll find me before Dónal does.

"The Leg of Mutton sounds like it should be a tavern by a farm," Moira mused. "I suppose it's on the other side of the town since I don't see any farms near us."

"Daft woman," the man grumbled. "No. It's near the quay. Do you think pirates seek their ale and women on a farm?"

"Oh! You must be right. I didn't think of that," Moira demurred to the man, just as she had to Dónal countless times while cursing the loathsome man. "I've never been to a town with a port. I wonder if it's very large."

Casting her an annoyed look, the man nodded his head. "It's large, and it's busy. Stay close to me."

Moira opened her eyes wide and nodded. Looking back in front of her, she scanned the buildings they approached before she glanced at her companion. She kneed her horse and took off, knowing the man couldn't hope to keep up with his wagon. She heard his curses as she raced toward the town. While he might take her to Kyle, she couldn't trust that he wouldn't take her to Dónal. She slowed her horse as she came to the edge of town, not wanting to draw too much attention to herself. She sniffed the heavy, salty scent in the air and pointed her steed in the direction from which it blew.

Looking over her shoulder periodically to ensure her nameless companion hadn't caught sight of her, Moira wound her way through the streets until she heard the noise coming from the dockside. The calls of fishmongers and the sea shanties from the various crews drew Moira closer. Vigilant about her surroundings and her location, Moira swept her eyes over the crowds. She grew uncomfortable as more gazes shifted to her. She feared people would already think they knew who she was —the dark-haired, petite, unaccompanied woman who fled hearth and home to make her life as a pirate's mistress. Atop a large gelding with no cloak, she was a beacon for attention.

Moira decided she needed to find a place to stable her horse and continue on foot. She wanted to get lost in the crowds and be less conspicuous. She found a tavern with a stable attached to it. Peering around for a stable hand, she breathed easier when no one greeted her. She had no coin to rent a stall, but she couldn't just let the horse go, so she entered the structure slowly. Looking around but finding no one, Moira led her steed to the furthest stall from the door. It was clean and empty. She worked quickly to shovel hay into the stall before slipping from the building. Remaining in the shadows, Moira tucked her hair beneath her collar, hoping to make herself look more like an adolescent lad than a woman. Her borrowed leine fit better than the one she wore when Keith attacked her clan's ship, but it was still loose enough to hide her breasts.

Moira remained hidden as she watched people come and go. She listened for any snippets of conversation she could catch, but she heard nothing of use. Frustrated but resigned to setting out on her own, Moira stepped into the streets and once more pointed in the harbor's direction. Unsettled and self-conscious, Moira fought to keep her composure as people jostled her, the road becoming more congested as she grew closer to the docks. A five-minute walk brought her close enough to hear the seagulls calling to one another, and she could see the tops of masts only yards ahead of her. Increasing her pace, Moira eased through the crowd, trying not to bump into people and muttering a quick apology when she did. With the ships now in unimpeded view, Moira once more struggled to remain patient, wanting to sprint down to the docks and demand someone tell her where Kyle was. But she stopped short as familiar voices, then two unwelcome faces stood before her.

Moira looked at her brother Dónal and his second, Orran. Both men stared at her as though she were an apparition, and she gaped at them in horror. As the two men made to come after her, Moira bolted. Just as she'd run from Dermot, she ran from the two men pursuing her. She heard Dónal calling out orders to men she couldn't see. No longer caring who she bumped and jarred, Moira turned down the nearest street and then the next, hoping to evade her brother and still draw closer to the docks.

"Moira! Stop!" Dónal called, and his voice was too close for Moira's comfort. She pushed herself to run as fast as she could, crates and barrels on the docks nearly within reach. An arm looped around her waist and lifted her off the ground. She writhed and thrashed as Dónal shook her. She recognized the feel of Dónal's hold, having been pinned by him too many times before. Orran came to stand before her, sneering and drawing too close.

Moira pushed back against Dónal and kicked her foot into Orran's groin. She dug her nails into Dónal's arm but couldn't get him to release her. When he brought his other arm in front of her, she grabbed his hand and yanked it to her mouth. She sank her teeth in as far as they would go. Dónal released her at once, and Moira took off again. She scanned the ships in the docks, looking for the *Lady Charity* or the *Lady Grace*. But none of the ships belonged to the MacLean brothers. Instead, she identified several that belonged to her clan. Her brother had sailed with a full contingency to retrieve her.

A man turned toward Moira, and relief flooded her. She recognized Snake Eye just as he recognized her. She made for the dinghy he stood near and prayed she could make it there before Dónal and Orran recovered. It was to her great misfortune that Snake Eye waited at the far end of the quay. Unprepared for anyone else to stop her, she slammed into Beagan and stumbled backward. Her eyes widened, shocked to find the man who led her escape was now part of her capture.

"Don't speak, lass," Beagan murmured. "You needn't fear. We came with Dónal not to return you to him, but to be sure you made it free this time. The council came."

Moira stared in stunned disbelief before she shook her head. She strained to peer over Beagan's shoulder, seeing Snake Eye running toward her. Before she understood what was happening, MacDonnells surrounded her, effectively hiding her from sight. She recognized every man who'd stood outside Sean's chamber now escorted her back to her brother. None looked at her, but she didn't feel endangered until she stood before Dónal. He reached out for her, but Cormac stepped in front and scowled.

"That's what made her run in the first place. The O'Malley won't want a battered bride," Cormac pointed out. Moira watched Dónal cast her such an ominous glare that she feared he would kill her before handing her over to Dermot. Swallowing and keeping her eyes forward, she continued walking with the MacDonnell men serving as a shield. The group marched back to The Leg of Mutton, and Moira fought back tears. She'd reached her destination, but she'd found the wrong man. As she approached the door, she blinked several times, positive she was seeing things. Leaning against the corner of the building with his head down, she was certain she was looking at Tomas. He glanced up and winked before casting his eyes down. Moira's eyes darted from one man to another who loitered next to the building or in its shadow. They were all from the *Lady Charity*.

Entering the building, relief washed over her to know Kyle would soon learn where she was. She peered at the faces inside, but she saw no one she recognized. Her heart dropped, fear replacing the relief. Dónal reached among the men and grabbed her arm, his grip punishing. He pulled Moira forward until she stood beside him, looking at the tavern keeper and a woman Moira assumed was his wife.

"Take her to my chamber, watch her strip bare, and take her clothes," Dónal commanded the woman. Moira shuddered unintentionally. Dónal looked down and sneered at her. "You're not going anywhere."

The bluidy hell I'm not. I walked around in front of a pirate crew in nothing but a leine. I'll be bluidy Lady Godiva before I let you keep me trapped. Kyle's here. I won't have long to wait. I can manage. But I'll run out of this tavern as naked as I came into this world if that's what I must to get away from you, you smarmy bastard.

Moira nodded demurely, none of her mutinous thoughts showing on her face. She followed the woman without objection and remained silent as she stripped. The woman looked at her with pity, but Moira wasn't interested. She'd spotted the window that hung over the street below. She also noticed the bedsheets were clean. She might not have to go naked after all. She handed her filthy leine and leggings to the woman. When the woman looked at Moira's boots, Moira gave her a mulish pout.

"He said clothes. He said nothing about my shoes. They stay," Moira asserted.

"And if he beats me?"

"Then your husband is worthless if he doesn't defend you," Moira snapped.

"Like your pirate lover? Where is he?" The tavern keeper's wife mocked.

"On his way. If your husband wants to keep the extra pouch of coin the Red Drifter offered, you'd both do well to make sure I'm safe and sound when he arrives," Moira pointed out.

The woman sucked in her cheeks and puckered her lips like she'd eaten a lemon, but she gave her head a jerky nod. She backed out of the chamber, and Moira heard the key turn in the lock. She wasted no time running across the room and stripping off the sheet. She wrapped it around her shoulders and clutched it closed before she went to the window. She tried to open it, but it was sealed shut. She pounded on the glass until Tomas looked up at her. She waved to him. She pointed to the window frame and shook her head. Tomas frowned, but she knew it was from disappointment, not misunderstanding.

Moira stayed at the window, watching people pass beneath her. Tomas remained, but he crossed the street to hide in the shadows where he could see Moira. She watched as men she recognized from the *Lady Charity* materialized from around The Leg of Mutton and set off on foot. She prayed they were going to find Kyle. But as hours passed, and neither Kyle nor Keith appeared, Moira's mind leapt from one horrible scenario to another. She'd arrived in Wicklow early in the morning, been captured before midmorning, and saw no one until that evening when the tavern keeper's wife dumped a tray on the table. She scowled at Moira but didn't seem to notice the bedding laid over the bed untucked. Moira didn't want to alert the woman that she'd covered up. She feared the woman would tell Dónal out of spite. So she stood before the woman, naked and haughty. While she didn't feel like her body was anything to make the woman jealous, her feigned diffidence gave her confidence.

Too hungry to care if she was being drugged, Moira inhaled her food. It made her stomach ache, but at least she was full. She returned to the window, but the setting sun made it difficult to see anything beyond the street below. Tomas remained on sentry, but she sensed his tension. He shifted from one foot to another more frequently, and he peered toward the dock every few minutes. When he glanced up at Moira, she could tell the man's usually jovial smile was forced. As the darkness of night settled in, Moira feared some fate worse than her own had befallen Kyle.

CHAPTER 27

Kyle sat with his legs pulled up before him, his hands dangling over his knees, and his head back against the wall. Keith sat across the cell in the same position. Neither had spoken since the harbormaster's men dragged them to gaol. They'd met behind a cobbler's building during the early afternoon to compare their observations and findings. As they stepped from the shadows to return to The Leg of Mutton, men seized them. Outnumbered and not willing to die, the twins followed the commands and wound up in prison. They'd communicated with looks only twins could interpret until the door swung shut, enclosing them in darkness. There was a small window cut at the top of the wall. Since light no longer filtered in, the brothers knew it was night and therefore well past when they were supposed to rendezvous with Kyle's men. Neither doubted word spread throughout the town that the authorities had captured the twin pirate captains. It was just a matter of time until Tomas and the others heard.

Kyle feared not for his future. He didn't expect to spend long in jail, but he feared for what was happening to Moira. He'd heard about a woman seen running along the docks, but a group of men said to be MacDonnells stopped her. Kyle knew Moira was now back with her brother. He found he'd started praying since he met Moira. He was wary to believe anyone or anything listened to him, but if there was a God and he was a merciful listener, Kyle would beg for divine intervention. His mind filled with images of Moira being battered and bruised all over, just as her arms had been when they met. The bruises had nearly healed by the time Dermot attacked. Now Kyle assumed she was suffering from her brother's vindictiveness.

The charges against Keith and Kyle interested neither of them, since the list didn't nearly encompass all that they had done over two decades. But they'd argued that they sailed under the marque of the Earl of Argyll and had the earl's protection to conduct business on his behalf. The gaoler laughed as he reminded the twins they were in Ireland, not Scotland. Despite maritime law saying officials should accept their marque, their notorious reputation superseded any legitimacy the Earl of Argyll might have lent them.

So the brothers sat in the dark waiting for morning and their arraignment. They didn't doubt the gaoler and harbor-master would be foolish enough to allow Kyle and Keith outside as they moved them to see the magistrate. Tomas and Kyle's crew would already know the route and would lie in wait. It was the same routine each time authorities captured either or both of the brothers. They'd escaped more times than they would recall. But it confirmed why they loathed coming ashore anywhere in the British Isles except for the tiny island of Canna, where they stored their bounty.

And so, the brothers waited for morning to arrive. There was nothing to say, since they didn't want anyone to overhear them. They had a cell to themselves, but they knew there was a jailer posted outside their door. Kyle and Keith had made the pretense of fighting when their captors stripped them of their weapons, but both men carried weapons in places the gaoler hadn't thought to search. If all went to plan and if history repeated itself, Tomas would slip into the jail's armory and retrieve their swords and knives while Kyle and Keith were being transported.

A key rattling in the door signaled to Keith and Kyle that the time for them to see the justice of the peace drew near. The sun had already risen, making dust motes dance in the air within the cell. The brothers looked at one another and grinned, but by the time the door opened, they'd turned their good cheer into mutinous glares that made the jailer pause. Four men stood behind the one with the key. That was half the men present when they were arrested. Not daring to look at one another lest someone think it was a signal, Kyle and Keith filed out of the cell without argument. As they always did, they appeared resigned to being caught. With heads down and eyes cast to the floor, the twins lulled their captors into a sense of overconfidence.

Kyle breathed in the fresh breeze, the tangy salt air burning his nostrils. He felt at peace knowing the sea was nearby, and he was no longer encaged. As the gaoler and his men led Kyle and his brother to the magistrate's office, Kyle kept his head down, but his eyes scanned their surroundings. He expected Snake Eye to create the usual distraction, pretending to be drunk and barreling into at least one jailer. But as they drew closer to the justice of the peace's office, and nothing happened, Kyle spared Keith a glance. The look of confusion and disquiet that met him matched his. Something was very wrong. The only reason his men wouldn't come to his aid was if they feared more for Moira than they did him. His heart pounded as he looked back at Keith, knowing his brother thought the same thing.

With a roar, the twins fought against their captors, swinging manacled fists and kicking. They'd often jested about gaolers' stupidity when they shackled the men's wrists in front of them.

It only gave prisoners a weapon. While they felled the men with them, neither pirate realized how close they'd come to the magistrate's office. More guards ran toward the fight, each armed with a club. The brothers exchanged a look of annoyance before each received a blow to the head.

Moira dozed but woke several times throughout the night. She'd heard her brother's voice coming from the floor below as he bellowed and sang. She prayed he drank himself to death, but when he'd staggered into the chamber during the middle of the night only to spew vile curses at her before passing out in a chair, she knew she hadn't been so fortunate. The sun was now well above the horizon, and Dónal continued to snore. Moira spied a knife handle protruding from Dónal's boot and wondered if she was sly enough to steal it. Noise outside the door told her that Dónal had guards posted in the passageway, so the door wasn't a means of escape. But she'd had hours alone in the chamber before she'd given up and gone to sleep. She'd broken all of her nails and rubbed her tips of her fingers raw, but she'd worn away much of the grime that kept the window from opening. She suspected she could pry the window open if she had a knife to scrape the last of the accumulated dirt out of the hinges.

Sometime while she slept, Dónal woke long enough to strip off his doublet. Loathe as she was to touch any item of his clothing, it would be something she could wear. It would come to her knees, since she was nearly a foot shorter than her brother. She intended to fold the sheet in half and wrap it around her waist several times before she donned the doublet. As long as the makeshift skirt allowed her legs enough freedom to climb and run, it would cover her enough for no one to claim she was indecent. She stood by her promise to herself that she would run through the streets of Wicklow naked if she had to, but she hoped she had an alternative.

Easing from the bed, cringing when the springs creaked, Moira watched Dónal to see if he stirred. He didn't even twitch. She made short work of folding the sheet around her and putting on his doublet. If he woke while she tried to steal his knife, she would fight with all her might if she had to. If he stirred once she had the knife, she would claim she'd covered herself in his presence. Tiptoeing closer, Moira's eyes darted between Dónal's face and his knife. He snored noisily, and she prayed it would dampen any sound she made while trying to get the window open. With deft fingers, Moira kneeled beside Dónal and eased the blade from his boot. She hurried to slide it into her sleeve before she retreated to the bed. She expected him to lunge at her, but he didn't move. His breathing remained the same, and she didn't think he woke. But she waited out several minutes, sitting on the bed before she rose again and slipped on her boots.

Licking her lips, her heart pounding in her ears—she was tired of the sound after days of living in fear—Moira walked to the window. If her brother was awake, she believed he would demand she step away. But he did nothing. She looked out the window and found Tomas where she'd last seen him as it grew dark the night before. She didn't dare bang on the window to get his attention. She looked around and found Snake Eye leaning against the next building down. She wondered why the men Kyle trusted most were watching her rather than at least one of them searching for Kyle. She assumed something had happened because she knew in her heart, he wouldn't leave her to Dónal. Even if he didn't want her anymore, he wouldn't accept her being with her brother. She'd seen the murderous intent when he learned Dónal mistreated her.

With each of Dónal's snores, she scraped around the hinges. She peered back at him with every excessive inhale, sure that he was about to awake. But he never did. When she was certain the window should open, Moira pressed outward, relief flooding her when the shutters and glass moved. She glanced around to see if there was anything she could use to the climb down. The second-story window wasn't so far above the ground that she would kill herself if she jumped, but she would surely fracture whatever she landed on. She was willing to take the risk and the pain if it meant escaping Dónal. None of the clan council members had done anything to help her throughout the night. None had sneaked to her chamber as they had the night she fled Dunluce. She knew not—cared not—who stood watch outside her chamber door. Whoever it was, hadn't come to her aid.

A wave of hatred washed over Moira as she glanced back for the last time. The temptation to kill her brother threatened to override her good sense. She despised him for all the years of mistreatment, for selling her to Dermot, for keeping her from Kyle. She feared that if she stood closer, she would have already slit his throat or driven her blade into his neck. Forcing herself to focus on what she needed to accomplish rather than what she wanted to do, she placed the hilt of the dirk in her mouth and once more peered out the window. She knew she had a corner room, so she looked at the bricks that made up the outside corner of the building. They were notched, a small piece extending out in an alternating pattern. There was a window ledge just wide enough for her toes. If she could step onto the ledge, then get her toes onto a brick, she thought she might use them to climb down. If she failed, she would pitch backward and land on her back. She prayed that she didn't break her backbone or her neck or slam her head into the ground. But all three of those outcomes were better than remaining with Dónal.

If Dermot is dead, if Kyle killed him, then what will Dónal do with me? Likely kill me before taking me back to Dunluce. Either you go now, Moira, or you stay with Dónal.

That last thought had Moira climbing onto the windowsill. She glanced out at Tomas, then Snake Eye. Snake Eye caught her movement and vigorously shook his head. He darted to Tomas and shook the man before pointing at her. Tomas shook his head in time with Snake Eye's, but Moira refused to be deterred. She stepped through the window and onto the outside ledge. Not looking anywhere but at the corner bricks, she took a deep breath and reminded herself of all the trees she'd climbed as a child. She'd scaled the side of the stables countless times to watch the ships sail away from the MacDonnell dock. She'd inched along the foot of the jib and out to the bowsprit before she jumped into the sea. She was determined to do this, too.

She slid her feet along the ledge until she reached the end. She'd closed the shutter furthest from her before she moved, but she held onto the closer one. At some point she would have to release it and grab for the bricks. It was the point in her daredevil stunt where she was most likely to fall. She wished she could push the other shutter closed, so Dónal wouldn't immediately know how she escaped, but it wasn't an option. Despite hearing Tomas's stage whisper calling her name and warning her against her plan, she ignored him.

Drawing up the courage she had mustered, she reached out her left foot until she touched one of the bricks. She drew her leg back in, knowing she could reach it. She slid the ball of her right foot side to side as she inched closer to the edge of her perch. Her fingers gripped the outside edge of the shutter as she leaned as far as she could without letting go. Her fingers wrapped around a brick. It wasn't the side that would make it easiest to start climbing, but it was her target. Clutching the brick, she stretched her left leg again until her toes landed in the center of the short protrusion.

Without another thought, Moira pushed off the ledge and swung for a moment until she reached her right arm over her left, which had a death grip on a brick. Grasping another notch,

Moira steadied herself. Ignoring the strain in her shoulders and the awkwardness of her hold, she felt beneath her for the next brick. When the ball of her right foot was steady, she moved her left leg and arm down until her hand replaced her foot and her foot found a new perch.

With sweaty palms, Moira continued to climb down until she felt hands wrap around her waist and another set around her ribs. She glanced back to find Tomas and Snake Eye both lifting her down the last several feet. With her feet on the ground, she fell against the men, wrapping her arms around the hardened pirates. With only a moment's hesitation, they returned her embrace.

"Where's Kyle?"

Moira's demand was clear even if she kept her voice low. She looked back and forth at the men who stood before her, then craned her neck to see the other crew members slinking out of the shadows. She glared at Tomas and Snake Eye as she waited for a response. Their hesitation made her panic. She looked around, then faced the docks. She strained to see into the distance, but there was no sign of a head with russet waves. She turned back to Kyle's first mate, tears welling in her eyes.

"Moira, he's not dead. He's been arrested," Tomas explained.

"And you haven't gotten him out?" Moira hissed. "I can't stay here. There are too many of my clansmen in the tavern. Dónal was snoring in that chamber when I climbed out."

"And you need clothes," Snake Eye pointed out before he lunged backward, Moira's blade under his chin.

"I don't give a damn about what I'm wearing, and you know that. Prove to me he's alive, then I'll care," Moira warned. "You didn't answer me. Why haven't you gotten him out? Is Keith with him?"

"Yes. We didn't break him out because we knew he would rather us stand watch over you than leave you unprotected," Tomas responded.

"So no one is watching Kyle or Keith?" Moira asked around the lump in her throat. Her voice cracked as she asked, "Where is he?"

"Men from the *Lady Grace* just arrived. They grew concerned when no one returned to the *Lady Charity,* so they sent a party to find us. They've gone to the gaol where the captains are held," Snake Eye answered.

Moira nodded as she continued to fight the tears that burned her eyes. Falling apart and sobbing, no matter how tempting, would serve her no good. She needed to see Kyle. She looked between Tomas and Snake Eye, and with a resigned sigh, she said, "I need clothes."

CHAPTER 28

The last thing Kyle recalled was men from the *Lady Grace* rushing toward them before everything went black from the pounding his head took from the guard's club. He and Keith sat side by side, once more in the cell where they'd spent the night. This time, their wrists were manacled behind them, and their ankles sported matching shackles. Leaning their shoulders and heads against one another, they kept their voices to whispers. They each strained to hear and knew no one outside their cell could catch what they discussed.

"Did you see your men?" Kyle asked.

"Aye. Did you see any of yours?" Keith mumbled.

"No. They must be wherever Moira is. That's the only reason they wouldn't come, unless they were caught too."

"I doubt that. We would have heard them arrive, or guards would have taunted us," Keith reasoned. "I think my men knew they couldn't get to us and will look for yours. I agree that they're with Moira."

"God, I hope so. If Dónal has her, who knows how he's treating her. He may be her brother, but I will kill him if I find another bruise on her," Kyle pledged.

"What is it that's between you two? Why does she matter when no other woman has? You fight most of the time."

"I don't know. I'm not sure how to say it. You and I share the same tastes in how we enjoy women. We learned the same things in the same places as Rowan and Ruairí. We were taught how to be dominant, and it appealed to each of us after so many years of being forced into submission by one captain after another. It gave us power we hadn't had before. The women who taught us were prostitutes and did what brought them coin, but all four of us knew what type of whorehouses we frequented in Naples and the Greek Isles," Kyle reminded Keith.

"And Moira?" Keith prompted.

"She's the opposite of us. She's been controlled and dominated by Dónal, even Lizzie, for so long that she is exhausted from having to guard herself. She'd shouldered the duties of chatelaine since she was barely more than a girl. But all she's received in return for her service is her siblings' condemnation. I can't imagine how that feels. We've never been anything but best friends." Kyle paused as he remembered Moira the first time he spanked her, and the connection neither of them understood. "She's happy to relinquish control to me. She knows I will never intentionally harm her, even when there's pain involved. She knows I'll protect her—though I've done a shite job of it."

"I told you before. This isn't your fault," Keith said adamantly.

"Whether it is or it isn't, I'm not there to protect her, and I told her I would. I told her I wanted to take care of her, not just for pleasure, but take care of all her needs. I've never imagined such a notion toward a woman, but I do. It's not that I want to control everything she does or thinks, though I've certainly given her reason to think I do. It's that I want her to know that someone values her, wants her. And in return, they care enough to support her." Kyle stunned himself by articulating what he'd kept private, even from Keith.

"Do you love her?" Keith asked.

"I'm certain I could. I think I'm falling in love with her." Kyle nudged his brother's knee with his own. "My need for her differs from the one I feel toward you, but it's just as strong."

Kyle waited for his brother's hurt or angry retort. He waited for a chasm to form between them. But his words met silence, and it tore at his heart. No one had ever come between them, and he prayed he hadn't just put Moira there. He wanted her beside him, not against Keith. He nearly fell over when he heard his twin's reply.

"I hope to find that too someday," Keith whispered.

"You don't begrudge me?"

"Never. You're my brother, my twin. I have never not wanted the best for you. If she makes you happy, if she's what you need, then I wish you my best. But do you think she returns your feelings? Or is it just physical? I've heard how women respond to you. Seen it too," Keith chuckled.

"I thought it might be the same, but now I have no way to know. She may never forgive me for what I've done to her life. Who could blame her?"

"So do you think it would only be the coupling that would bring her back?" Keith wondered.

Kyle snorted. "I'm good, but I don't know that anyone is good enough for a sound tupping to make up for what she's endured."

"Then you'll know. If she wants to come back to the *Lady Charity*, to stay with you rather than go to Ruairí and Senga, then it's because she cares about you."

"Do you think she could love me?" Kyle's apprehension made his lungs hurt as he held his breath.

"Undoubtedly," Keith chortled. "What's not to love?"

A key grinding in the lock cut the twins' conversation short.

Two matching faces turned expectantly to the door, waiting to see what would come next. They both prayed it wasn't the gallows.

Moira looked at the dressmaker who cowered in the corner, Snake Eye hovering over her. Stephen stood guard outside, and Tomas stood just within the doorway. Moira had asked if any of the men had coin on them, so she could buy a gown. The men argued this was more efficient.

"Snake Eye, you must let her come and help me. None of these were cut for me, so she'll need to pin them. I'm too thin for the ones she has. Unless, of course, you want me dressed like a girl with my calves bare."

Snake Eye's glare told her he didn't find her suggestion amusing. Moira was certain Snake Eye feared for his life if Moira showed up before Kyle with her legs bare, just as she had when she strutted across the *Lady Charity*'s top deck. Learning Kyle was imprisoned made Moira think twice about storming to wherever he was held. As she and the men hurried away from The Leg of Mutton, Moira thought about what she needed to do if they were to free Kyle and Keith. Men from the *Lady Grace* had caught up to them and relayed what they'd seen when Kyle and Keith attempted to fight their way free.

"Snake Eye," Moira warned with more authority. With a scowl etched so deeply that Moira feared it would become permanent, he allowed the seamstress past. Moira stepped behind the partition and held up a gown she thought would be the easiest for the woman to fit to her. The poor woman's hands shook so badly that Moira feared she would become a pincushion. Easing the shears from the seamstress's grip, Moira made quick work of cutting down the bodice and the skirts. When both women agreed it was the right length and size, Moira slipped out of it, and they sat together. "Snake Eye, Tomas, I'm helping the seamstress sew up the gown. It'll be faster if I work with her, but you must be patient."

Moira ignored the grumbles and offered the terrified woman an encouraging smile. Neither woman spoke, preferring to focus on their tasks. Moira wished to be dressed as soon as she could, and Moira was certain the dressmaker wanted them out of her shop as soon as she could. With the gown sewn well enough to keep it from falling apart around Moira, the dressmaker quickly shoved undergarments at Moira, then fastened the laces to the gown. Moira looked down at herself and brushed out the skirts. Her mouth twisted back and forth before she stepped from behind the screen.

"I'm not sure that I want to go back to gowns after the freedom of leggings," Moira mused before she jutted her chin at Tomas. "Pay, and pay well. Don't be stingy." Moira watched as Tomas huffed but pulled a heavy pouch of coins from his belt. He handed it to the woman who said nothing but scarpered past a curtain and into her private quarters.

"That was a pretty penny this gown cost us," Tomas complained.

"And between paying her well and terrifying her, she will keep silent. As far as she knows, I've never been to Wicklow, let alone her shop," Moira noted. "How much coin will it take to buy Kyle and Keith's freedom?"

Moira looked at the men who stood before her once they were out on the street. Stephen, Snake Eye, and Tomas shifted nervously. She waited for one to speak and narrowed one eye as her brow furrowed. When they still didn't answer, she drew the blade she'd hidden in a secret pocket she stitched.

"You may be bigger, and you may be stronger, but I promise you, you are not more determined," Moira warned.

"Lass, I mean Moira—err—Lady Moira," Stephen stammered. It was the first time Moira had heard him speak. "There will be no way to buy their freedom. The magistrate will make them hang."

"The hell he will," Moira snapped. "Every man—every man who works for the crown—has a price. We just don't know this magistrate's. Don't be surprised if it isn't coin."

"So you think you're going to free the Red Drifter and the Scarlet Blade by wandering into the gaol and bribing the guard," Snake Eye said doubtfully before crossing his arms. "We've always gotten the captains free when they're being transported from gaol to the magistrate."

"And you were playing nursemaid to me and missed your opportunity," Moira snapped before her eyes opened wide. "That is one of the most ungracious things I've ever said. I'm sorry."

"You care for the capt'n," Tomas stated.

"I do. Saints and angels preserve me, and only the Devil can tell me why, but I do," Moira admitted. "Hide me somewhere you know is safe, or take me back to the *Lady Charity*. But we need to find out who the magistrate's mistress is and how many bastards he's sired. If he has neither, find the man he's buggering. Learn whether he has gambling debts. Ask around if he cares about anyone he doesn't want to see go missing. Learn what you can. Like I said, his price might not be coin."

They'd moved behind the dressmaker's shop, and the other *Lady Charity* crew members joined them. Five men stood staring at Moira as she rattled off her expectations. She snickered at their owlish expressions and loss for words. She shook her head before canting it to the side and giving them a disbelieving look.

"My brother has dubious taste in allies and trade partners. Don't you think I've heard him negotiate with the likes of Aidan and Ruairí? Do you think I could have pirates traipsing in and out of my keep without learning a few things a lady should never hear?" Moira grinned. "If I have to choose between Kyle and the justice of the peace's children, don't doubt for a moment who I will choose. If he has a man for his lover, I don't care whose life we ruin. The man should have taken care to be more discreet. If it means Kyle is free, and we can all leave together, then I will do anything."

"We know a safe house," Tomas spoke up, but Moira watched Snake Eye's shocked expression.

"We can't take her there," Snake Eye hissed. "The Drifter will murder us."

"Do you know of anywhere else that doesn't mean taking her out on the docks to get her to the *Charity*?" Tomas argued. Snake Eye clearly disapproved, but he nodded his head. Moira watched the men and suspected where she was headed.

"What's the brothel called?" Moira asked, hoping her bluntness would ease the tension. Once more, five owlish faces turned toward her. "And by the by, is anyone watching the gaol right now?"

"The Mother Hen," Tomas answered. At Moira's look of disgust and as she mouthed "mother," the men chuckled. "And yes, one of our men and a handful of the Scarlet Blade's are watching the gaol.

"The Mother Hen," Moira choked on a laugh, "is likely where you will learn everything you need about the magistrate." The men didn't disagree, but it was with great trepidation that the hardened sea criminals took the diminutive woman to the seediest brothel in Wicklow.

CHAPTER 29

Moira looked around her as she entered the brothel. The stench of unwashed bodies and intercourse permeated the air worse than any tavern Moira had ever entered. She looked around at women in varying stages of undress, most with their breasts hanging loose. For a moment, she felt a blazing streak of jealousy course through her as she wondered which women Kyle preferred. A beautiful woman with painted lips, snug bodice, and skirts hitched on either side approached, and Moira knew with certainty that she'd just found the woman Kyle sought most often. She was also clearly the proprietress of the establishment.

"The *Lady Charity* come to dock in our harbor," the woman cooed, but her eyes assessed Moira. "Brought us a little dove?"

Tomas stepped in front of the woman and shook his head. "She's with the capt'n."

Moira saw the disappointment, then anger, flash in the woman's eyes before she masked her features. The men might not have understood, but Moira did. She'd seen the same look in Lizzie's eyes early in her affair with Aidan, when Lizzie feared Aidan would return to Moira.

Moira didn't shift her gaze, locking eyes with the prostitute, unwavering in her dare. It was the other woman who looked away first, but Moira knew she was in more danger with that woman than she had been with Dónal or Dermot. There had been a chance, however small, that the men would not kill her, but she was certain the brothel owner wouldn't think twice and call it an accident.

"And where is our fair capt'n? Either of them?" The woman shifted her attention back to Tomas. "It's so much more fun with both of them."

Moira knew the comment was for her sake, but she didn't react. The woman's eyes darted back to Moira, expecting to see shock or hurt. Once more Moira caught disappointment in the other woman's eyes. She stood silently, knowing that if she spoke, they would learn nothing.

"Daisy," Tomas addressed the woman, and it nearly killed Moira not to laugh. The woman looked nothing like the fragile flower she was named for. And standing closer, Moira realized the brothel owner was far past the blush of youth. "The capt'n would be grateful if his lady could wait here while he's being detained."

"Detained?" Daisy asked before looking speculatively at Moira. "Just how grateful?"

When Tomas paused to consider his answer, Moira decided to break her vow of silence. She pushed forward and passed an assessing look over Daisy and then swept her eyes over the various undressed women.

"Not nearly as grateful as I would be." Moira raised an eyebrow, her suggestive comment shocking everyone around her. She would sell her soul to the devil if it got Kyle free. If it meant doing whatever the woman in front of her wanted—unless it was with another man—Moira cared little. She'd heard of men bedding two women, and Daisy had already said as much about the twins sharing her.

"You might be more interesting than you look," Daisy sneered.

"And a far sight more experienced than I look," Moira retorted, making Daisy's eyebrows shoot up nearly to her hairline. Moira sensed the men shifted uncomfortably around her. She slipped past Tomas to stand before him. "Whether you wish for payment up front or after, I will compensate you in just the way you're thinking if you answer my questions."

Moira's stomach churned. She wasn't attracted to the woman in the least, and she had no desire to touch her, but she would bed the woman if she had to. She would put on a show with one of the whores if she had to. She drew the line only at being with another man. She wouldn't do that to Kyle, not unless it was his wish. As she stood watching Daisy, she realized that there were countless sexual acts and pleasures she would entertain now that she knew Kyle. Her only wish was to share them with him.

Daisy nodded and turned to walk away. She shot Moira a coy smile over her shoulder, expecting Moira to follow her. Moira didn't look anywhere but straight ahead. From the corner of her mouth, she whispered. "Don't you dare move away from whatever door she takes me through."

Following Daisy down a passageway behind the stairs, Moira noticed two large men standing outside a door that Daisy unlocked. As Moira and the *Lady Charity*'s men approached, the two men stepped out to block their way. Moira narrowed her eyes and shook her head.

"I don't play unless they stand at the door. Kyle wouldn't like it any other way," Moira said. She registered Daisy's shock, and Moira suspected the other woman had never heard Kyle's given name. The intimacy it implied clearly rankled. Daisy sniffed but nodded. Moira followed her into a chamber with an enormous bed, which Moira attempted to ignore lest she get distracted imagining how many times Kyle had been in it.

"We usually don't make it here until at least the third time," Daisy mused as she stood beside the bed. Moira didn't react, keeping her visage neutral.

"We prefer the bed. It allows for quite a lot of creativity," Moira said nonchalantly. "I told you I would be most grateful if you told me what I would like to know. I suspect you are the most well-informed woman in this town. Answer my questions truthfully, and I will indulge you."

Daisy looked at her skeptically as she draped herself across the bed in what Moira assumed was an alluring position to men. Moira sat in a chair facing the bed and raised her skirts until she was certain Daisy had a clear view of her nether lips.

"What do you wish to know?" Daisy's voice had grown husky as she stared at Moira. It made Moira suspect Daisy's enjoyment of women was sincere.

"Does the magistrate come here?" Moira asked without preamble.

"Sometimes," Daisy answered without looking up. Moira trailed her fingers along the inside of her thigh.

"I suspect your ladies offer services few other places do. What does he like?" Moira's other hand pulled at her neckline, then slid one sleeve down over her shoulder.

"He likes being spanked," Daisy mumbled, more intent upon Moira's hands as the one at her shoulder slipped beneath the neckline and massaged her own breast.

"With what?" Moira asked and licked her lips.

"A cane or a paddle," Daisy said as she sat up and slid to the edge of the bed.

"How often does he come?" Moira realized the double entendre and gave a throaty laugh. Daisy grinned before she stood from the bed.

"Uh-uh. I haven't learned enough. You may look, but you may not touch. Yet," Moira said as she lifted her hand from her thigh and shook her finger. "You didn't answer my question."

"He shows up a few times a sennight, but he rarely does more than squeal like a pig," Daisy clarified.

"Does he have any bastards?"

"Likely, but none off my girls," Daisy stepped closer as Moira's fingers brushed against her folds. Moira had touched herself enough times to know she could arouse herself, so finding dew accumulating was no surprise. She knew Daisy assumed it was because of her. Moira wasn't about to correct her.

"Do you only have lasses here?" Moira asked with a pointed look. Daisy froze, growing serious. She narrowed her eyes as she grew suspicious. "You like to have both captains. Perhaps you and the captains aren't the only ones who like to have three people together. I've heard of things, though I've never seen it. Things between men. I doubt Kyle and his brother are interested in such, but others may be. Is the magistrate?"

Once more, Moira dropped Kyle's given name, reminding the brothel owner that while he'd been with Daisy, he was with Moira now. Or at least she prayed that was the case.

"I do from time to time, depending on the customer. And yes, that includes the magistrate."

"Hmm," Moira mumbled. She offered Daisy a conspiratorial smile. "From the sounds of it, he can only watch."

"Oh, he has no problems with that. A woman canes him while he buggers a man," Daisy confessed as she returned her attention to Moira's plunging fingers working her sheath. Pounding at the door interrupted them and made both women jump.

"Moira, we must go," Tomas's voice floated through the wood. "They're moving them."

Moira's eyes shot back to Daisy. She was relieved she didn't have to do anything more than tease, but she knew the woman might keep her locked in the chamber if she didn't get something in return for the secrets she told. Moira rose and shook out her skirts before calling out, "I'm coming, Tomas."

Without a second thought, Moira stepped in front of Daisy and grasped a handful of hair, pressing the woman's face to hers. Moira slid her tongue against Daisy's lips before flicking it inside the woman's mouth and pinching her nipple. Giving the nub a twist, Moira stepped back before Daisy could return the kiss.

"The capt'n and I will be back," Moira said. She hadn't a clue if that was the truth, she prayed it wasn't, but she would appease Daisy. Moira opened the door and walked into the passageway to a group of men staring at her. She kept her voice low, "I learned what I needed to. It's time for me to talk to the magistrate."

CHAPTER 30

"A lady's come to bear witness that you rescued her from pirates," the gaoler announced to Kyle and Keith, and the brothers knew no one could tell them apart. The brothers exchanged a look, wondering who their men had scrounged up from a tavern or whorehouse to plead on their behalf. This time they were surrounded by a full contingent of men. Both captains spied men from their crews, but Kyle's heart pounded when he caught sight of the dread on Tomas and Snake Eye's faces. Even the usually disinterested Stephen looked noticeably uncomfortable.

"Moira," Kyle mouthed. Tomas and Snake Eye nodded while Stephen's gaze darted to the office doors of the justice of the peace. Kyle feared Moira had been captured too. There'd been no talk of a woman being brought to the gaol, but Kyle didn't know if women were housed separately. As Kyle and Keith were herded inside, Kyle recognized a woman's voice.

"I suggest you do listen to me, because I think you'd rather hear what I have to say before I turn into the town crier," Moira stated.

Kyle jerked to a stop, and Keith crashed into him, pushing

him a step forward. Guards dragged the twins further into the chamber, but Moira didn't look in his direction. Instead she stepped up to the magistrate and whipped out a knife when guards tried to approach.

"I will speak," Moira announced. "It's just a question of whether you would like my words to be for your ears only, or if you'd like all of County Wicklow to know your secrets."

Kyle tugged against his guards as he fought to get to Moira. Whatever game she was playing was likely to get her killed. He knew she was aware he'd entered the chamber, but she never looked at him. But her next words stopped him cold.

"I had a nice chat with Daisy," Moira spoke clearly.

What the fuck was she doing at The Mother Hen? What the fuck did Daisy tell her? What did Moira do to get Daisy to tell her anything? I will throttle Daisy. I will snap the woman in half if she said or did anything to hurt Moira. I've never killed a woman, but I will kill that conniving bitch.

Keith elbowed Kyle as men pushed them into the box for the accused. He wasn't sure if he would wet himself or vomit as he watched Moira bribe the man who held all of their fates in his hand. He watched as Moira tapped her toes and drummed her fingers on the man's desk. The magistrate rose and waved off his guards.

Moira stepped around the table and spoke rapidly to the justice of the peace. Kyle watched as the color leached from the man's face, and his jowls shook. He looked at the brothers as Moira continued to speak in a whisper. Whatever she said deeply affected the man, and Kyle could only imagine what Daisy shared that could make the justice of the peace so discomfited.

"So, as I said, these men saved me from pirates. The O'Malleys were set upon stealing me away, and it was the Captains MacLean who ensured Dermot O'Malley didn't ravage me." Moira turned a doleful expression to Kyle and Keith, ensuring that everyone in attendance saw her, before she looked back at the magistrate. She narrowed her eyes and glared at him. "I saw the marque of the Earl of Argyll. He must be a very important man if he's an earl. If you've seized the Captains MacLean, does that mean you've seized the earl's goods? I can only imagine what trouble that could cause."

Moira opened her mouth in mock shock and put her palms to her cheeks, having sheathed the knife when the justice of the peace rose from his seat. The magistrate grunted before he looked at Kyle and Keith. He scowled down at Moira but nodded his head.

"The testimony of this witness, along with the marque of the Earl of Argyll, call for dismissal of charges against the men who were remanded to the County Wicklow gaol. Release them."

Moira bobbed a rushed curtsy as she went to Kyle and Keith. She said nothing, her eyes wide as she watched the manacles drop from Kyle and Keith's wrists. She remained silent as Kyle grasped her forearm in a light grip. The trio left the building without speaking, men from both crews following behind. Moira was uncertain of Kyle's mood or where he led them because they were moving away from where Snake Eye had been waiting with a dinghy the day before. When she saw the shingle dangling over The Mother Hen's doorway, she stopped abruptly.

"We have to talk," Moira whispered to Kyle. "And not in there."

Kyle looked down at her and saw the earnestness in Moira's eyes. The hand gripping her arm felt tension that hadn't been there moments ago. He wanted nothing more than to find a chamber, any chamber, and drag Moira into it. He would have settled for The Mother Hen, but Moira's expression told him she wouldn't wait. He nodded and looked over his shoulder at Keith and the others before he led Moira between two buildings.

"Kyle, I bribed the magistrate with information I bribed from Daisy. I didn't pay Daisy with coin. I insinuated that I would bed her," Moira blurted. Her words barely registered with Kyle. She'd been in the courtroom pleading in his defense, and she hadn't bolted from him. She hadn't blamed him or shunned him. He cared not what she had to tell him until he knew where they stood. He pulled her into his arms, waiting for her to reject them. Instead, she pulled at his filthy leine and stood on her toes. Their mouth collided in a maelstrom of passion. The kiss threatened to consume them as everything around them fell away, and their awareness centered upon the giving and taking of need and comfort.

Kyle tunneled his hands into Moira's hair, cupping her scalp with the care he would give a newborn. But his mouth plundered her as only a pirate could. Her hands roamed over him as they pressed their bodies together. The kiss drew on with no end in sight, neither hearing the throats being cleared. It wasn't until Keith pulled on Kyle's shoulder that they released one another's mouth, but they remained in one another's embrace.

"This is not the place to be swallowing the lass whole," Keith pointed out.

Moira's cheeks flamed as she realized she wouldn't have cared if Kyle took her against the wall with the crew of both ships watching. She wouldn't have even noticed.

"Give us a moment. Moira needs to talk to me," Kyle stated.

"Can't you do that from the safety of the Hen?" Keith demanded.

"No." Moira and Kyle responded.

Keith threw up his hands and shook his head. "I'll wait for you, but the men are going in. We don't need the entire town seeing us skulk around any more than they have," Keith warned, and Kyle nodded before he looked back at Moira.

"Are you all right?" Kyle whispered. "I've been in a panic ever since I saw you jump. God, Moira, I..."

"I know, Kyle. I've been so scared. I'll tell you everything that has happened. I promise you. You may punish me every way you see fit for what I'm about to tell you, but I have to before you see Daisy. I hate her." Moira surprised herself by her declaration. She didn't hate Daisy, but she was in too much emotional turmoil to reason with herself about why she loathed Kyle seeing the woman he'd obviously bedded several times.

"What did she do?" Kyle barked, looking back at the street.

"Fucked you," Moira muttered. Kyle tilted her chin up, and Moira huffed. "I'm just jealous. I've seen the bed. It's enormous. I can only imagine what you've done to her there."

"*Mo ghràidh,* you know what I've shared only with you. And you know how I feel about being with you. I've told you it's not the same," Kyle reassured.

"But do I? You sailed away," Moira shook her head. "This isn't what we should talk about right now. I'm just jealous and scared."

Kyle cupped her jaw and pressed a kiss to Moira's forehead. "Moira, you fought for me, and I sailed up and down the coast, killed Dermot, and will kill Dónal for you. There is no one else. For either of us."

Moira bit her lip, the cords in her neck straining as she looked guilty. "There might be. I suggested to Daisy that I would bed her if she gave me information about the magistrate that I could use to bribe him. She took me to her chamber. She went to the bed, and I sat in the chair facing it."

Moira waited for Kyle's reaction, but when nothing came, she grew more afraid than if he'd railed against her. She trembled as she stood, blinking up at Kyle. He realized she'd grown too scared to continue, so he eased her into his embrace.

"Tell me, sweet one," Kyle encouraged. The term of affection opened the flood gates as Moira sobbed and clung to him.

"I thought I'd never hear you say that again. I didn't realize just how badly I needed to hear it until now," Moira cried. In

Kyle's embrace, rather than shunned, she continued. "I pulled up my skirts and stroked my leg, fingered myself and massaged my breasts while she watched. Each piece of information earned her something else. But I swear to you, Kyle. She didn't touch me. But—I did kiss her and pinch her nipple. I did it to tide her over and suggested I would return to give her more."

"And what she told you secured our release?" Kyle asked between kisses.

"It did, and it guarantees that as long as the magistrate lives, you and Keith will never be arrested again in any part of County Wicklow," Moira answered.

"Then Keith and I should thank you," Kyle said as he took Moira's hand in his and led her back to the street.

"But, Kyle, what about what she expects?"

"Do you wish to follow through?"

Moira's eyes opened wide, and even in the dark, Kyle could see the whites. "Do you wish to watch?" Moira whispered. "Do you wish to join us? She said you and Keith like to share her."

"She says too much," Kyle growled. "You owe her nothing, Moira. But if you wish to explore being with a woman, I won't stop you. But no, I will not join you or watch."

Moira and Kyle emerged onto the street, and Kyle could clearly see Moira's confusion. He leaned down and kissed her temple before whispering in her ear. "I told you, there is no one else but you. I will fulfill every fantasy you've ever had and any you can come up with now, but I will not watch or touch another woman."

Moira gulped and glanced at Keith. She feared she would err in her next suggestion, but she would do anything for Kyle now that he was free. She tugged on his hand until he leaned over for her to whisper in his ear.

"I don't know that I will ever get over my relief that we found each other—again. There's nothing I wouldn't do if you wanted it, Kyle." She glanced again at Keith. "I've always known you and your brother share everything. Daisy confirmed that. If that's what you wish, then—"

Moira shrieked as she found herself hefted over Kyle's shoulder, and a hard swat landed across her backside. Another and another fell in rapid succession. She fisted the back of his leine as she bounced on his shoulder with each step. Her hair cascaded down Kyle's back to his legs. She couldn't see anything but the boots of the men around them. The feel of Kyle's hand was too arousing to care who saw.

"Move," Kyle barked as he stepped through the doorway to The Mother Hen. He found Daisy leaning against the bar, but she straightened when she recognized her newest guests. He walked to her and without greeting stuck out his hand. "Key."

Moira tried to shift to see what was happening, but another powerful slap landed on her backside. She gave up with a sigh and rested across his shoulder, releasing her grip on his leine.

"Drifter," Daisy purred. "How I've—"

"Not interested. And Moira is unavailable to you. Ever," Kyle snapped. "I said, 'key.'"

"But—"

Kyle cut her off again. "Do not make me repeat myself. Whatever Moira promised is null. She didn't have my permission to make such a promise. Now give me the bluidy key before I kick the door in, Daisy."

Daisy scrambled to pull a key from the ring she wore at her waist. She handed it to Kyle but glared at Moira's backside, inelegantly hefted in the air. Kyle turned back to Keith and grinned. Keith winked before he sidled up to Daisy, and their men sought out their own entertainment. Kyle climbed the stairs with Moira, but he shifted her so he could cradle her against his broad chest. Once they were inside the chamber, Kyle eased her to her feet.

"I know I told you that you could do as you wish with Daisy, and if you want to, I won't stand in your way. But now it's on your terms, not because you're indebted," Kyle explained. Moira brushed the hair from her face as she nodded. Her sapphire eyes met Kyle's emerald orbs.

"I don't want her or anyone else, Kyle. But maybe you will in the future," Moira whispered. "If that's what you want, what you need—"

"Moira, I don't know what the future holds for us. But I can promise that as long as we're together, I will not touch another woman. The thought makes my chest burn, and no thought has ever felt so wrong."

"What about what I suggested?" Moira asked sheepishly.

"You mean what earned you a spanking? And what you just got was only to warm your arse before your real spanking."

"I don't want Keith. I don't want anyone but you. But I'm telling you that I—"

"I already know, Moira. But I don't think you understand. I don't need, nor want, anyone with us. You don't have to offer or do anything to make sure I stay. All I want is you."

Moira's face crumpled as she fell against Kyle's chest. He wrapped his arms around her, but he couldn't fathom why she was crying. He didn't know if he'd disappointed her, or if her emotions overwhelmed her. Unsure of what else to do, he held her. Moira's shoulders curled in, her hands trapped between them, resting on Kyle's chest. Neither of them was clean, but neither cared. They held each other until Moira could speak again.

"I've never been enough for anyone. At least not since my mother died. My father ignored me for most of my life. He was too busy training Dónal and grumbling about how his heir never listened. Or he was bemoaning Lizzie's promiscuous behavior. He died before Aidan and I… You know how Lizzie and Dónal treat me. You and I both can imagine what Dermot would have done. I'm short and too skinny, and my hair is a dull brown. The only thing Aidan ever complimented were my eyes.

My breasts are too small, and I have no bottom. I look more like a lad than a lass. But never have I felt inadequate with you. And now you're telling me you don't want anyone else. I've just never felt enough until now."

"Moira, we both have a past. But they were separate, before we knew each other. I want our futures to be the same," Kyle whispered.

"Are you asking me to sail with you?"

"I'm asking you to spend your life with me. If you wish to sail, then yes. If you wish for us to have a cottage somewhere, then I will build one as fast as I can. I can't give you a keep like you're used to. I'm an heir to nothing, but I can give you a home," Kyle paused as he looked into Moira's eyes. His thumb smoothed her brow. "If you wish me to marry you, I will. If you wish me to love you, I will."

Moira stared at Kyle for a long moment before her tongue flicked out twice to wet her lips. "Are you saying you love me? Do you want to marry me?"

"Yes."

They stood in stunned silence, neither expecting such a declaration, but neither shied away. They just stared at one another. Eventually, Moira found her voice. "Are you sure?"

"Yes. About all of it. Moira, I don't believe in love at first sight. I didn't even believe in love when you first boarded my ship. But there is something undeniable between us. Something I don't think exists between most couples. In fact, Ruairí and Senga, and Rowan and Caragh, are the only ones I've seen it with. Maybe Ruairí's parents. But really only between the Blond Devil and the Dark Heart and their wives. I think it exists with us."

"Do you mean that sense of understanding what you need without having to say it?" Moira wondered.

"Yes. I did try to manipulate you," Kyle admitted. "Many times I tried to get the information I wanted. I'm sorry for that,

Moira. I tried to force you to trust me in ways you weren't ready for. But you weren't wrong when you said you trusted me and not just with your body. You knew from the beginning. And I knew too. I knew I could give you what you needed, just as much as I needed what you gave me. And I don't just mean the coupling. I mean what passes between us."

"Even when I feared you didn't want me and that you left me behind, that you would reject me if I found you, somehow I still trusted that you were looking for me," Moira said. "I knew I'd be safe if I could just get to you. I lived at Dunluce for two-and-twenty years and never felt as at home as I do when I'm with you. I can't fathom how you can understand me so well. But you know when I need comforting. You know when I need to let go, to not be in control. You know when I need challenging. I can't explain it. It's just in me, Kyle."

"Will you stay with me, sweet one?" Kyle asked, holding his breath.

"Yes. Maybe tonight isn't the night to decide whether I turn pirate or you retire, and maybe tonight isn't the night to decide if we marry, but I will stay with you always." Moira had never felt calmer with any decision she'd ever made. The serenity in her expression was genuine for the first time in years. "May I have my spanking now, Capt'n?"

"Good God, yes," Kyle growled before guiding her across the chamber. She forced away the questions about whether this was his regular chamber. She supposed it was since he'd demanded a key, but Daisy never said to which room. "Stop thinking about her, sweet one, or your spanking will be harsher."

"How did you know?" Moira asked with disbelief.

"Because I know you. You admitted you were jealous, and you have a sharp mind. You want to know whether this is the chamber I always use. And you assume it is, since she didn't tell me which room the key went to," Kyle stated. "Over my knee."

Moira stretched across Kyle's legs and waited as he pulled

her skirts up to the middle of her back. She waited with building anticipation, but nothing happened.

"Kyle?"

"Hmm. Just enjoying the view, sweet one." Kyle massaged her upturned globes, reveling in the feel of Moira's silky skin beneath his rough palms. "You shall receive twenty spanks for risking your beautiful slim neck by bribing the magistrate. You shall receive another punishment for jumping into the sea and nearly killing yourself when I can think about that calmly and rationally. I am not there yet."

"Yes, Capt'n," Moira stated. The first slap rang against the walls in the quiet chamber. There was no fire in the hearth, and the noise from the floor below hadn't grown loud enough for them to hear. Moira counted each spanking, thanking Kyle in between. When he finished, he eased his fingers between her legs.

"You're wet for me, sweet one," Kyle observed.

"I have been since I saw you enter the magistrate's," Moira confessed. "Then you kissed me outside, and I confess, I wouldn't have cared who saw us if you decided to couple with me."

"Do you wish for an audience, Moira? I've asked that before," Kyle said as he worked his fingers in and out of her sheath before rubbing her pearl. Moira moaned, struggling to focus on what Kyle asked.

"No. Not particularly. But if it's the choice between you touching me or not, then I don't care who sees," Moira admitted with another moan. "Please, Kyle."

"Please what, sweet one?"

"Please may I climax, Capt'n?" Moira begged.

"Yes, sweet one." Before Moira knew what was happening, Kyle flipped her around, so she was once more cradled against him. His fingers worked her. "I won't be denied seeing you while you spend in my arms, Moira."

She clung to him as her back arched from his lap. She gasped as waves of pleasure rolled over her, making her shudder as their gazes locked. As her body calmed, Kyle held her against him, and she had no interest in moving. But as her senses returned to her, she knew what she wanted to do next. She slipped from Kyle's lap and looked expectantly at his knees, but he didn't move, didn't allow her to kneel between his thighs to make restitution.

"Not until we bathe, Moira. I've been in the gaol. It's bad enough I've kissed you and touched you at all. But I couldn't wait," Kyle clarified.

"I couldn't wait either," Moira said sheepishly, then grinned.

"Cheeky," Kyle muttered as he went to the door and called for a tub and hot water. He returned to Moira and pulled at the laces to her gown. "Where did you get this?"

"At the dressmaker's shop a few streets over. Tomas and Snake Eye are very convincing when they're in a hurry," Moira chortled.

"I know Dónal found you. Did he not give you any clothes?" Kyle's eye twitched as he watched Moira retreat. He knew she would tell him what happened, and she was trying to decide how best to do it, but it only fueled his temper. "Moira?"

"I will tell you everything. But can we wait until the bath comes? I suspect that when I tell you what happened, I will have another spanking coming. I'd rather not be interrupted or have servants see my bare arse," Moira said.

"Very well. I see you have a chemise on. Slip off the gown, and I'll send it to be cleaned," Kyle said. Moira looked up at him, gauging his mood.

"Yes, Capt'n." Moira let the dress drop to the floor and stepped out of it.

"Sweet one," Kyle said as he wrapped his arm around Moira and cupped her cheek. "Whatever you tell me may earn you another trip over my knee or worse, but right now, I'm Kyle. We are on equal footing right now."

Moira nodded. She pecked his jaw since she couldn't reach any higher, even on her toes, without Kyle leaning forward. "Thank you, *mo grá*." At Kyle's expectant face, Moira smiled softly. "It means my lover…Or my love."

"*Mo ghaol*," Kyle translated into Scottish Gaelic. "My love."

The couple stood together, neither moving nor saying anything, just gazing at one another until a knock signaled their bath's arrival. Moira hung back, out of the way, since she wore only a chemise and stockings. He grimaced when he opened the door and found Daisy on the other side. She reached out for him, but he grasped her wrist.

"I understand. You wish to bathe first. Shall I scrub your back like I usually do? Maybe wash your lady's flower. She wasn't able to do much more than move her petals earlier," Daisy asked, following Kyle when he stepped back to allow the team of servants to enter with the tub and buckets of steaming water.

"And I told you I wasn't interested, and Moira is not in a position to enjoy your ministrations," Kyle snapped.

"Testy? Has she not eased the ache, Kyle?"

"What did you call me?" Kyle snarled and took a menacing step forward.

"I—I—" Daisy stammered.

"There is only one woman allowed to call me by my given name, and you are not her," Kyle growled.

"But she—" Daisy pointed toward Moira.

"She's the only one. Don't test me, Daisy. You know I don't like you when you're not on your knees." Kyle ignored both women's gasps. He was being crude, and he realized his comment was hurtful to Moira, but it was true. He didn't trust Daisy, nor did he like her. But when her mouth was occupied, she was tolerable.

"Yes, Captain," Daisy smiled weakly as she stepped back into the passageway. Kyle turned back to Moira, so he missed the hateful glare Daisy shot the couple. It made ice run through Moira's veins.

"She's going to tell Dónal where we are," Moira whispered.

"What?" Kyle asked as he glanced back over his shoulder.

"You spurned her and humiliated her. You didn't see her face, but I did. She's going to find Dónal."

"Let us bathe and eat, then we'll return to the *Lady Charity*. Would you like that?" Kyle offered.

"Only the bath. We can eat aboard your ship," Moira countered.

"She makes you that uneasy?" Kyle asked.

"Yes. Immensely."

"Then come, sweet one. We'll bathe and be on our way," Kyle agreed with a kiss to her cheek. He helped Moira into the tub and stepped in after her. Kyle's enormous frame took up much of the tub, but Moira's tiny one fit snugly against him. She leaned her head back as her eyes drifted closed. Kyle lathered a linen square and ran it over Moira's arms and legs before washing her breasts and back. He took his time washing the folds between her thighs, making her squirm in the water. He watched her grip the edge of the tub as she tried not to moan. "Do you want your release, sweet one?"

"I want to touch you first, Kyle. I haven't, and I don't want another release before you have one," Moira said.

"But that's not what I wish," Kyle purred beside her ear. "What if I wish to feel her quim squeeze my fingers just like it's going to squeeze my cock?"

"You know I'll obey. But I wish to wash you and then be the one on my knees."

"Moira, you need not make amends to me," Kyle corrected.

"I want to. There's still so much more for me to tell you," Moira admitted.

"Then you can make your restitution when we have cleared the air of everything. Let me wash your hair, and you can help me. Then I'm going to bury myself in you, Moira. I ache for you. I don't know that I can last till we go to the *Lady Charity*," Kyle said with a guilty grin, giving him a roguish charm. Moira caught her breath, overwhelmed at the ease with which Kyle smiled despite all that had happened. He was more handsome than she remembered. "I can smile because I'm with you."

Once more it felt as though Kyle read her mind. She nodded as she turned all the way around in the tub, now able to reach him. She ran the soap over his chest, foregoing the linen. She swirled soap over him with her bare hand, relishing the feel of him under her palm and fingers. As she washed him, he scrubbed her hair. They kissed as he poured clean water over her hair and she scrubbed his. Once his hair was free of suds, Moira stroked his length under the auspices of finishing where she'd left off. With a growl, Kyle lifted her light frame, drawing her closer before impaling her with his rod. Their sounds of pleasure and relief blended into a melody as they clung to one another.

They moved together as water splashed against the sides of the tub, some spilling over onto the floor. Neither cared. Moira's fingers bit into his back as she ground herself against his thrusting pelvis. It took little to send her over the edge as she rested her forehead on Kyle's shoulder. His fingers gripped her hips as he guided her over and over again as he neared completion.

"What happened to the basket?" Moira blurted.

"What?" Kyle asked in confusion.

"The basket. The pennyroyal. What happened to it?"

"Braedon hid it once you went over the side," Kyle explained.

"So you still have it," Moira gasped between words.

"Yes."

"Don't pull out," Moira panted. Her words pushed Kyle to his release as they rocked together. They remained joined as Moira sank against Kyle's chest. His brawny arms sheltering her from everything. They remained joined until Kyle feared Moira would grow too cold. He wasn't certain that she'd recuperated from her ordeal only days ago. Fear that she would grow ill replaced the afterglow of their lovemaking.

"I need to get you warm," Kyle said. He helped Moira out of the bath and wrapped drying linens around her before he went to build a fire. When there was a cheery blaze, he called down for someone to remove the bath, and he summoned Tomas. With only a towel around his waist, he instructed Tomas to find Moira another gown. He was to either get one from a local shop or from the *Lady Charity*. He explained where he'd stored Moira's sack in his cabin. Tomas suggested a fresh change of clothes for Kyle with a grin. With a mocking scowl, Kyle pushed his first mate toward the stairs.

"Kyle, that's going to take too long," Moira worried. "I don't regret taking the bath with you, but we overly lingered. Dónal is likely on his way right now."

"You may be right, Moira. But most of the men from both ships are here now," Kyle assured her.

"Kyle, I saw five MacDonnell ships in the harbor. Dónal has brought every man he could. There's likely MacAlisters along too. We just found one another, I'm scared they'll force us apart," Moira said with a trembling lip.

"Wheest," Kyle murmured as he lifted her into his lap as they sat before the fire. "Dinna fash, sweet one."

Moira closed her eyes and relaxed against him. "Why don't you sound like an islander very often? Is it because you left as a child?"

"Most likely that's part of it. But Keith and I rarely use our clan name. In the beginning, we didn't want anyone to know who we were or where we hailed from. Eventually, it stopped mattering, but we'd learned a new way to talk. It slips out from time to time."

"I know. I like it," Moira said around a yawn. "It's comforting." Exhaustion washed over Moira, reminding her that she'd yet to recover from her prolonged ordeal before finding Kyle.

"Do you wish to sleep, Moira?"

"I do, but not here. I want to go home," she said around another yawn. The word "home" made Kyle's chest feel pinched.

"Home?" Kyle repeated.

"Yes. To the *Lady Charity*. Home," Moira explained.

"Not Dunluce?" Kyle checked.

"That is not home," Moira said emphatically. "Unless we have that cottage you mentioned, the *Lady Charity* is home. I wish to sleep in your bunk."

"Our bunk, sweet one," Kyle corrected.

Moira looked up at him and smiled sleepily. "Ours."

Unprepared for another knock on the door so soon, Kyle whispered, "Give me your knife. Tomas shouldn't be back yet."

Moira nodded and padded over to where she'd hidden the knife under a pillow while the servants brought the bath and collected her soiled gown. Handing it to Kyle in silence, he signaled for her to hide behind the door. With his finger to his lips, he reached out for the handle.

"Who is it?" Kyle demanded.

"Tomas."

Kyle eased the door open, his brow furrowed. To his surprise, his first mate stood before him with fresh clothes. Tomas grinned at Kyle, but it fell when he looked into the chamber past Kyle's shoulder and didn't see Moira. Turning a worried gaze to Kyle, the first mate relaxed when Kyle tilted his head toward the door.

"You and the men can remain here with Keith and his men. I'm taking Moira back to the *Lady Charity* tonight," Kyle explained. "We don't want to be here when Dónal gets wind of where Moira is."

"Wise." Tomas nodded, then grinned again as Kyle looked down at the clothes. "There's a haberdasher a few doors down who doesn't lock up."

Moira pulled her lips in between her teeth to keep from smiling. She knew it was wrong to accept the stolen clothes, but she couldn't keep from grinning when she imagined Tomas looking at the women's clothing and trying to figure out what to nab for her. As though he knew her thoughts, he added, "I tried to find something the right size for Lady Moira, but I didn't know what that was. I brought a cloak too."

"Thank you," Moira called out from behind the door and shrugged when Kyle leaned back to frown at her. "My mother taught me manners."

"I shall teach you something," Kyle warned.

"Promise?" Moira mouthed playfully. She saw the heat flare in Kyle's eyes, and she knew her need matched his. "We should dress now," she said pointedly.

CHAPTER 31

Kyle shut the door as Tomas moved toward the stairs. In tacit agreement, they dressed themselves, lest they give into temptation and delay their departure. But Moira had no choice but to ask for help since the gown laced in the back. When they were dressed, Kyle swished the cape around Moira's shoulders and pulled up the cowl. He dropped a butterfly-soft kiss on the tip of her nose as he fastened the frog. He pulled her hood up over her wet hair before leading her to the door. The same maid who took Moira's dirty clothes had taken his. There was little left behind but the towels and tub to show they'd been there. They made their way belowstairs, and Moira looked around for Daisy. She was in a customer's lap, but her gaze followed the couple.

"She's already sent word to him," Moira warned.

Kyle looked down at her, and she prayed he wouldn't look at Daisy. Taking her word for it, he kept his eyes on Moira as they stepped off the last step. Tomas met them there with Kyle's weapons in hand. When Kyle stepped forward, Keith rose from his chair and tapped the woman's backside that had been resting in his lap. He handed the woman a coin and shook his head.

With both captains moving toward the door, the men from both ships scowled as they turned away the women they'd thought to bed and left behind the ale they'd been sipping.

Moira stole another glance at Daisy, who didn't bother to hide how livid she was. She not only couldn't have Kyle, but obviously Keith hadn't chosen her either. Now nearly every man in the tavern was about to leave. Daisy's eyes shot daggers at Moira, who only shrugged as Kyle wrapped his arm around Moira and blocked her from Daisy's sight. Kyle led Moira out of The Mother Hen and onto the street, steering them toward the harbor. They made it three blocks before a swarm of men stepped out and blocked their way. Dónal stepped forward and smirked.

"Found my wayward little sister, have you? Had a good hump at the Hen?" Dónal chuckled at his own humor. "You've had your fun; now she comes with me."

Moira instinctively stepped behind Kyle, whose hand rested on the hilt of his sword. He wouldn't be the first to draw, but he would fight until the last MacDonnell lay dying. Moira peeked around his shoulder, looking for the council men who promised their protection. They stood behind Dónal, looking very ready to fight Kyle and the other pirates.

"If I tell you to run, do it. Don't look back for me. Go to the end of the docks and hide there. Don't come out unless it's me, Tomas, Snake Eye, or my brother," Kyle commanded.

"Yes, Kyle," Moira mumbled.

"I've already chased the wench along the coast and through this town. I'm done chasing," Dónal growled.

"Then go home," Kyle said with a shrug.

"Not without my sister. And she's going to the O'Malley."

"No point," Kyle said casually. Moira recalled what Kyle said earlier. He'd already told her that he'd killed Dermot, but obviously Dónal didn't know that.

"The contracts are signed. He's getting a hefty dowry. He

doesn't care that she's soiled. Any babe of yours that she carries he'll do you the favor of drowning," Dónal said.

"You keep misunderstanding me. I knew you were rather simple, but you are a fucking eejit," Kyle said, his burr slipping into his voice as he mocked Dónal. "I told you, there's no point trying to take her to the O'Malleys. Dermot's dead. I killed him." Kyle sounded bored by the time he finished speaking. He felt Moira's hand holding onto his belt, and he sensed Keith step beside him.

"O'Malley isn't the only one who wants to trade with the MacDonnells," Dónal boasted.

"Yes, he is," Kyle stated. "No one else is daft enough to bother with you. Hell, Aidan only uses you to store his stolen goods and to fuck your sister."

"Sisters," Dónal corrected. "Did she tell you that's who took her maidenhead? Your cock must have known she was no virgin."

Kyle chortled and shook his head. "I guarantee I know far more about Moira than you ever did. I'd wager you know very little about either of your sisters. You should ask Lizzie how many times she's used pennyroyal to rid herself of Aidan's or whoever's bastards. Good Catholic that she is," Kyle taunted.

Moira watched as Kyle's words registered on the faces of the men standing with Dónal. Kyle saw it too and laughed uproariously. He tilted his head to speak to Moira but kept his gaze on Dónal. "How many didn't know they were to be fathers?"

Moira gasped, unprepared for Kyle to include her in his verbal sparring with her brother. She peered at her clansmen once more and counted. "At least seven that I can see from here. Maybe more?" Moira leaned so the MacDonnells could see her shrug.

"Even if you kept my worthless sister," Dónal said, attempting to take back control of a conversation he had never led to begin with. "There's still the matter of my ship you burned and my crew you killed."

Kyle straightened and pushed his shoulders back, making Moira realize just how colossal and intimidating his build was. She also realized that he had never used his full size with her, in order not to frighten her. But now she felt the anger pouring off him in threatening waves. He took a menacing step forward and leaned toward Dónal.

"Your men were useless at defending your sister, and I couldn't give a bluidy damn about your tiny little boat. It wouldn't have survived the storm that blew through anyway. But your men were not adequately trained even if there had been more of them. Useless," Kyle muttered the last word.

"My sister didn't choose wisely. She wasn't bedding the right men to protect her."

Moira glared at the men standing around him, none stepping forward to correct Dónal's assumption that she initiated her escape. She waited for one, any one of them, to step forward and take responsibility, but none did.

"Or maybe your clan council despises you so much, brother," Moira stepped forward. "That I didn't need to bed any of them for them to help me escape."

Kyle hissed and moved his arm in front of her. Moira wasn't sure if he did it because he feared she'd barge past him or to shield her from her clan. But Moira was fed up of holding her tongue for the sake of keeping the peace. Dónal's mouth dropped open as he turned back to look at the men who surrounded him. Kyle seized the break in Dónal's concentration.

"Run, Moira," Kyle ordered. Moira pressed a kiss to his shoulder blade and eased backwards until the pirates blocked her from sight. She lifted her skirts and sprinted down the nearest alleyway. She didn't stop running, even though she didn't hear anyone call out to her or anyone chasing her. She kept running in the direction of the harbor. Her hood had blown back, and she knew trying to hold it up was pointless, but she wished she could keep any passersby from seeing her face. She didn't stop running until she reached the far end of the docks. She dove behind a stack of crates that stood beside the end of a warehouse. She would wait there and follow Kyle's directions. But if she learned Dónal harmed Kyle but had himself survived, Moira would be the one to finish off her brother.

CHAPTER 32

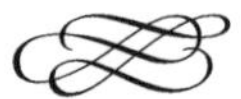

Kyle swept his gaze over the men who stood behind Dónal before shifting his eyes back to the chieftain. He'd hated many people over the years; some he'd done grave harm to, and some he'd wished to but hadn't the opportunity. But the malice he felt toward Moira's brother was unparalleled. He kept seeing flashes of Moira's arms when he met her. She'd eventually told him the tale of how she'd grazed her chin, and she'd told him more about how Dónal regularly treated her. Kyle wasn't sure where his restraint came from, but he wanted to torture Dónal in ways he'd only just thought of for him.

"If you survive this evening," Kyle called out to Dónal, "It's only because I haven't asked your sister if she wants you dead. Though I suspect I know the answer."

"The chit would likely pish herself before wishing ill on anyone. She hasn't the mettle to speak up," Dónal sneered. But his brow furrowed as the men from the *Lady Charity* laughed heartily. They'd seen Moira's mettle, and they had heard how she held a knife to the magistrate and bribed him. "What?"

"My brother is right," Keith spoke up. "You really don't know your sister. She held the magistrate at knifepoint just this very day."

"And she drew a blade on me this morning," Tomas called out. Kyle tucked that piece of information away for when Moira confessed the rest of her sins.

"From the tale Dermot told before I killed him, she not only survived most of a day in a cave, she escaped him, too. Stole his horse and rode off," Kyle added. He watched as the MacDonnells whispered amongst themselves. He observed Dónal trying to reconcile what he heard about Moira with the sister he thought he knew. Kyle saw he wasn't convinced.

"Moira may not have argued with you or spoken against you in public, but that doesn't mean she didn't have her own thoughts about you," Kyle continued. "Either you've forgotten the lass she was before your mother died, or you never knew. Moira has a deeper sense of duty and honor than you could hope for. She tolerated you for the sake of your clan. But she fucking loathes you."

"It matters not," Dónal argued. "That duty and honor demands she return with me. She owes her clan, especially since she ruined the alliance with the O'Malleys."

"You mean the one your council doesn't want," Kyle smirked. "Have you asked no one how Moira got on a ship? Didn't you wonder why your ship was missing? Someone helped her."

"Aye. Her two lovers," Dónal snarled. "Did she tell you about them, too?"

Kyle laughed.

"What's so funny?" Dónal demanded.

"I'm certain Moira hadn't been with anyone in some time," Kyle said offhandedly. "I could tell."

"You rutting bastard," Dónal snarled as he lunged forward, but the surrounding men pulled him back.

"I take exception to that," Keith cut in. "Our parents were married."

"Son of a bitch, then," Dónal hurled at the twins.

"That wasn't wise," Kyle said. "You don't speak ill of the dead. And you don't insult a man's mother." Kyle drew his sword and a dirk from his waist.

"Are you bored, brother?" Keith asked.

"Exceptionally," Kyle answered. Together, Keith and Kyle moved forward. The men from the *Lady Charity* and the *Lady Grace* drew their weapons. The hardened criminals didn't outnumber the MacDonnells, but they appeared far more intimidating.

"Enough," barked one of the MacDonnells. He stepped around Dónal, casting his own loathing glare at the chieftain. "I'm called Beagan, and I arranged for Lady Moira's escape. It was my idea that she go to Fionn O'Driscoll and from there to the Isle of Barra. I wanted her away from Dermot, and I didn't want to ally with the O'Malleys. None of the council did. We were the ones to send Lady Moira on that ship, and we were the ones who failed to man it adequately."

"Didn't you think about what might happen to Moira sailing along the coast?" Kyle asked, his sword poised for battle, but some of the tension eased.

"We thought the ship was small enough it wouldn't hold appeal to privateers," Cormac said as he stepped forward. "It shouldn't have been a long journey, and the crew was experienced."

"But you knew you would sail through waters frequented by the very man you were attempting to avoid," Kyle pointed out. "Why not sail straight for Barra?"

Cormac shifted uneasily. "Because it was more likely Ruairí and Rowan would have killed our men before they knew Lady Moira was aboard. We left things on a sour note after the battle on Lewis."

"And you didn't think the exact same thing would happen to

Moira sailing on any ship that was shorthanded? Because that's exactly what happened. I raided that ship, and your men were dead before we found Moira," Kyle explained. "Any of you who were part of this idiotic plan deserve to die for how you endangered Moira."

"What does it matter to you?" Dónal blurted. "You'll find another whore when you tire of her. And that won't be long from now. She's a mouse. You've probably already rogered ten women since coming ashore."

Kyle raised his sword and surged forward, with Keith at his side. The MacDonnells pulled Dónal into their midst and drew their weapons to shield their chieftain.

"We'll leave. We sail for Dunluce tonight," Beagan swore.

"Not good enough," Kyle snapped. "He's insulted Moira too many times. He won't live to do it again."

"You love her," Cormac stated.

"I do," Kyle answered without hesitation.

"She may loathe Dónal, but do you want to be the man who kills her own blood?" Cormac pressed.

"He may not," Keith interrupted. "But I have no such qualms. I'll do it for my brother and my sister-by-marriage."

"You're married?" Cormac asked.

"Who are you?" Kyle responded. Jutting his chin toward Beagan, "He said his name. Why haven't you said yours? I recognize you from the last time I was at Dunluce."

"I'm Cormac," the man answered. "Beagan and I have served on the council since the chieftain's father was a young man. We offer our felicitations to you and Lady Moira and wish to embark on our return to Dunluce."

"You may go," Kyle nodded, then pointed his sword toward Dónal. "But he stays."

"What?" Dónal squawked.

"I wish him dead for what he's done to Moira. She likely wishes him dead too. Your clan would be better off if he wasn't your chieftain," Kyle reasoned. "I shall do you a favor. Consider it my bride-price for Moira's hand."

Kyle watched as his suggestion tempted many of the MacDonnells. When no one responded promptly, Dónal whined and cursed, straining against the men who held him back. As a last attempt, he swore, "Aidan will avenge me."

Kyle's mouth dropped open, and he froze for a moment before a deep belly laugh rumbled out of his mouth. Keith followed suit, and it wasn't long before all the pirates laughed along with Kyle. Many elbowed one another, and they bandied about less-than-savory comments about Aidan's missing bollocks and meager endowment. Kyle watched several MacDonnells stifle their laughter, but most rolled their eyes.

"Let us leave," Beagan tried again. "Lady Moira remains with you, and you see neither hide nor hair of us again."

Kyle sucked his cheeks in and pursed his lips as though he considered the offer. He'd made up his mind before the negotiation started. He'd already known that he wouldn't kill Moira's brother without knowing her wishes. He wouldn't be the one to kill a member of her family without her approval. He merely intended to make all of them uncomfortable.

"You owe Moira a great debt of gratitude. If ever she decides to claim it, you will make good on it. You can take your sack of shite chieftain and return to Dunluce," Kyle granted them. "But you would do well to curb Dónal's power. Aidan will kill all of you in your sleep and take his son, raising Sean as a pirate. He cares not for Lizzie or any of MacDonnells. She's a convenience, just as Moira was. When he decides he no longer needs you or wants your connection, he will sever your heads to sever your ties. Mark my words. Aidan O'Flaherty will be the death of your clan if you let Dónal make the decisions."

Kyle raised the tip of his sword again as if it were an extension of a wagging finger. He noticed several nodding heads before the MacDonnells backed away from the pirates. Kyle and

Keith watched them go with arms crossed and matching smirks. Just before the MacDonnells turned toward their ships, the twins offered them mocking waves goodbye. Kyle turned to Keith.

"I need to find Moira."

CHAPTER 33

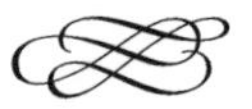

Moira watched in confusion as the MacDonnells boarded their ships. She could hear her brother's curses even from this distance. His oaths that he would get revenge on Kyle and Keith reassured her that the twins were alive. But she didn't understand how Dónal was not dead. She didn't expect Kyle to offer him any mercy. Her mind raced with explanations.

Perhaps he intends to follow and attack once we are at sea. Maybe he wishes to put Dónal adrift. How I would love to see that. When did I become so bloodthirsty? That's not a particularly Christian thought, Moira. But it is an honest one. Why couldn't he just die? Everyone would be far better off without him.

Moira observed the last of the MacDonnells as they climbed the ladders after releasing the lines that kept them secured to the docks. It wasn't long before all five ships were under sail and sliding out of the harbor. She looked around the docks, but she saw none of the men from the *Lady Charity* or the *Lady Grace*. None stood watch by a dinghy. None approached. The longer she waited, the more her apprehension grew.

Maybe something did happen to Kyle, and that's why they haven't come back. Should I check? No. Kyle was clear I'm not to leave my place unless he or Keith or Tomas or Snake Eye come for me. I have enough punishments ahead of me. I don't need to add one more, and I don't need to get lost along the way. He'll be livid if he has to search for me. Livid and frightened. I don't want to do that to him. I just want to go home. If he wishes to punish me tonight, I'll be ready and welcome it. But I would be just as happy to curl up against him in our bunk. "Our." He called the bunk ours. The Lady Charity *is home, and I want nothing more than to be there with Kyle.*

Moira peeked around the crates once more and saw a man hurrying along the dock toward her. She knew the build and the features. Relief swept over her as she stood and moved around the crates, running toward the pirate approaching her. But once she was close enough to see him clearly, she stopped.

"What is it, Moira?"

Moira shook her head as she looked over his shoulder, straining to see who else approached. She took a step back, her brow furrowed.

"Sweet one, you're safe now. We can go home. Will you not come with me?"

"You're not Kyle, Keith," Moira said as she narrowed her eyes. "Don't call me that."

"Moira, come now. I told you I would find you when it was safe. You must have seen your clansmen leave. We should, too."

"To the *Lady Charity*?" Moira asked.

"Where else?"

Moira shook her head. "Not to the *Lady Grace*? I don't know what game you're playing, Keith. But I don't find it amusing. Where's Kyle? Oh, God! Did something happen to him?" Moira tried to run around Keith, but he snagged her and drew her into his embrace. He did nothing more than keep her from running, but Moira thrashed and writhed. "Let me go!"

"Keith," a deep voice boomed from behind Moira, and she stumbled backwards when the arms suddenly released her. She spun around and dashed toward Kyle. He engulfed her in his muscular arms and held her trembling body against her, resting his cheek on her head. He shifted his gaze to send a warning glare at his brother.

"She's the only one who can tell us apart," Keith said by way of explanation.

"Why were you testing me?" Moira asked, turning her head toward Keith, but not moving from Kyle's body. "Did you think I would just go with either of you without caring who it was?"

"Because I love my brother as much as you do. I wanted to be sure you really choose him and aren't just using him to leave your family behind," Keith explained.

"It wasn't your place," Kyle snarled.

"The bluidy hell it wasn't," Keith snapped. "If she's joining our family, then I want to be sure she'd doing it for the right reasons."

"Family?" Moira whispered. She turned to look at Keith with Kyle's arms still wrapped around her middle. "I hadn't thought of that. You're to be my brother. A brother I like and want."

Keith chortled. "We shall see if you still sing the same tune in a few months or years, lass. But you're a sister I'd like to have, too. I heard once that you already claimed we're related."

Moira sucked in her lips and looked back sheepishly at Kyle, who shrugged.

"How did you know he was Keith and not me?" Kyle asked.

"Because you're nothing alike," Moira stated. Both brothers looked at her as if she weren't right in the head. Even their parents hadn't been able to tell them apart. They doubted Ruairí and Rowan could, barring when they were on their respective ships. Everything about them was identical. Moira shrugged. "You don't walk or stand the same way. Your voices are different."

"Moira, that can't be true, or other people could tell us apart," Kyle corrected.

"Maybe they don't know you like I do," Moira pointed out with a cocked eyebrow. Kyle leaned over and kissed her cheek before whispering in her ear.

"There are things about you I'm certain no one else knows. I would like to enjoy those things right now," Kyle said as he pinched her backside. Moira giggled, but Keith snorted.

"You can do that in just a moment. I really want to know how you can tell us apart," Keith insisted. Moira inhaled deeply, then blew out a dramatic sigh.

"You don't walk the same. Kyle tends to keep his right arm bent as though he's about to draw his sword. Keith, you do that with your left, but I think you intend to draw your knife first. Kyle puts more weight on his heels when he stands, as though he's prepared to fight in place. Keith leans forward on the balls of his feet as though he'll lunge. And your voices...well, you just talk to me differently. I admit I thought you were Kyle as you approached, but then you stopped. I was pretty sure you weren't Kyle. Then you called me 'sweet one,' and I knew you were Keith. It didn't sound right."

Kyle kissed Moira's temple and sent Keith a feigned glower. He eased Moira back to face him and kissed her. It was slow and soft until they broke apart, and Moira leaned her head against Kyle's chest, against the thudding, soothing rhythm of his heart. Her sigh was genuine.

"Sweet one, we can return to the *Lady Charity* now, if you wish. Or we can go to a tavern and have a hot meal before we leave," Kyle offered.

"Not The Mother Hen," Moira blurted.

"That's not a tavern," Kyle corrected with a chuckle. "I don't plan on returning there. If Keith and the others wish to, then they will. I prefer a particular fae-like woman who I think prefers me."

"I do," Moira murmured as she got lost in the intense draw Kyle's gaze held. "But I meant what—"

"Finish that thought, and I will turn you over my knee here and now, Moira," Kyle threatened. She gulped and nodded, chagrined but secretly ecstatic. "You brother is gone, and we've been given a reprieve. We can have a proper meal and sleep in a proper bed, or we can return to the ship."

"I am famished. I don't remember the last time I ate properly," Moira admitted. She glanced back at Keith, then gestured for Kyle to bend over. "Then back to our cabin. The implements and hook are there."

Kyle straightened and blinked several times before tugging Moira against him. His kiss was savage and consuming, and Moira returned it in equal measure. He lifted her off her feet and with one hand pressed against her back pinned her to him, while the other slid down to cup her buttocks. Moira's soft moan nearly did Kyle in. He wanted her with a fervor that bordered on manic, and he was certain she felt the same.

"So, shall I bring something hot back with me since you're going to your cabin after all?" Keith said with a chuckle.

"Sod off, brother," Kyle glowered. "And yes."

While Keith walked back in the direction of the harbor front taverns, Kyle helped Moira into one of the *Lady Charity*'s rowboats. He didn't want anyone to accompany them, wanting every minute alone with Moira. He hurried to reach his ship, calling up to the men who remained on watch. He tossed the rope up to them as they hung the ladder over the side. Moira had already hiked up her skirts and taken the first five rungs before Kyle realized what she was doing. He followed her over the rail, muttering his gratitude to the crewman before hurrying Moira down the ladder well. They were already pulling at their clothes before Kyle kicked the door shut and turned the key in the lock.

CHAPTER 34

Moira stood bare as she watched Kyle swing a rope over the hook in the ceiling. He'd retrieved a silk scarf from a trunk and bound Moira's wrists with it. He looped one end of the rope around where the scarf pulled taut between Moira's wrists because he was unwilling to tie the coarse material around her satiny skin ever again. Now she stood in place, raising her arms as Kyle drew the opposite end of the rope toward the hook on the wall, securing it tightly. Moira's arms stretched above her head, a tug in her shoulders reminded her that she was at Kyle's mercy. She eagerly anticipated what would come next.

"You said you had crimes you wish to confess, Moira. You've said you deserve your punishment. Admit to me what you've done, and you will earn the spanking you believe you deserve. Once that's done, all is forgiven, sweet one. Afterward, we think only of pleasure."

"Yes, Capt'n. Perhaps I can tell you my story, and you'll decide when I deserve the spankings?" Moira spoke clearly but softly.

"If that's what you wish," Kyle granted.

"You know I dove into the sea. I heard you call to me, but if I went back, it would have been a distraction to you. It would have defeated the purpose of jumping in to swim away," Moira began.

"I shall stop you there for your first spanking. You didn't trust me, Moira. Again. You didn't trust that I would protect you, so you risked your life instead."

"Yes, Capt'n," Moira agreed as she lowered her head.

"Ten spankings," Kyle announced. He stepped forward and pulled Moira against his bare body, his arousal pressed between them. His hand came down over and over as Moira counted. Her moans weren't for the pain in her backside, but for the ache in her sheath as her mons rubbed against Kyle's rod. The need for him—and the denial—was more painful than the punishment. Kyle stepped back, barely able to convince himself to finish their purpose.

"I slammed into the jetty and looked around. I could see nothing in the fog, but I didn't think the beach was where I should head. I didn't know if I could make it. I edged around the rocks and prayed I was pointed toward shore and another beach. The surf pushed me into a cave where the water was calm. I made it to the back of the cave and a dry ledge. I rested until I heard Dermot and some men approach. I slipped back into the water and hid beneath the ledge until I was sure his rowboat was gone."

"You hid from a rowboat that could've rescued you. You chose to remain alone where you might never be found instead of taking a chance of surviving with Dermot. Instead of taking a chance that I would fight for you," Kyle stated coldly.

"I didn't know if you were alive, Kyle. I didn't know if any of your men or Keith's were alive. I didn't know what Dermot might do to me before you could reach me. I would have rather perished in that cave than ever be within arms' reach of Dermot," Moira hurled at Kyle. She waited for the next spanking, but Kyle only nodded. He couldn't fault her reasons, even if he loathed the danger she was in.

"When the tide shifted," Moira continued. "I felt a change in current and tried to leave by the entrance I came through, but with a clearer sky, I knew it wasn't an option. I went back to the ledge where I'd rested. I felt a push of water and air, so I knew there was some other way in and out of the cave. I found a tunnel that was barely wide enough for me to pass through. It was longer than I feared, and I nearly didn't make it. When I got to the point where I didn't have enough air to go back into the cave, I pushed myself on. I wanted to find you more than I was willing to accept death. I saw twinkles of light and thought I was about to pass out, but I realized it was daylight. I came out on the other side of the jetty. I made it to the beach, but there was no shelter there, no means to make a fire. I took the cliff path back up and saw your sails in the distance."

"And you thought I left you," Kyle cut in. At Moira's crushed expression and hopeless nod, Kyle pulled her into his embrace. He wanted to cut her down, take her to their bunk, and make love to her. But he knew it would only leave matters unresolved for Moira, and she would remain restless until she confided everything. She sought his forgiveness and redemption because she was exhausted from relying on herself. Kyle understood she needed him to shoulder the weight of her ordeal for a while. "I was searching the cliffs for you, but the ships couldn't remain in the O'Malleys' sight. We reasoned that if you made it to land, you would try to find the next port. We sailed to Wicklow for the first time."

Moira nodded, accepting what she'd already suspected. "When I reached the top of the cliff and saw your masts, I was heartbroken. Then I slammed into Dermot. I mean, I really slammed into his chest. He tried to grab hold of me, but I broke free and ran. I ran faster than I ever have because I refused to be

Dermot's prisoner after nearly dying to avoid him. I ran across the meadow until I found a town."

"Arklow," Kyle provided. Moira shrugged.

"I ran through the town until a farmer offered me shelter in his home. I don't know who he or his family was, but they gave me dry clothes while mine were in front of the fire, and they fed me. But that night, I heard the door close behind the farmer. I knew he was going to betray me to Dermot. I changed back into my own clothes and stole some food." Moira paused, expecting her next spanking to come.

"You think I'll punish you for stealing?" Kyle chortled, his eyebrows twitching. "That's not a crime in my books. Unless it's from me."

With a shaky breath, Moira plodded along with her story. "I hid along the buildings because I heard voices well before they were near. Men were coming for me. I made it to the farrier's and found a gelding there."

"Dermot said you took his horse," Kyle chuckled.

"Aye. Rode past him while he had his leggings down to his ankles, pishing," Moira giggled, then sobered. "I rode through most of the night, but I had to stop. The horse and I needed rest, and it was too dark to be safe. It was midmorning by the time I rose. I prayed Dermot didn't have other horses or wasn't following on foot. He would surely catch up if he were." Moira waited for Kyle to admonish her for being careless, but he only encouraged her to continue.

"I made my way to another village, Kilmacurragh. An old crone spotted me and peppered me with questions before admitting she was the healer. My horse received a bee sting when we stopped for water earlier that day. She agreed to give the animal a poultice if I mended her clothes. She tried to drug me, Kyle."

Kyle's eyes widened, and Moira recognized the fear. It was the same expression that was on his face while she relayed the part about the cave. He pushed Moira's hair back and pressed a kiss to her lips. "Tell me, sweet one."

"I was suspicious about why she didn't want any of the pottage she offered. I said I was full from the bread she gave me. Once I tended to my horse—Dermot's horse—I went back inside and eventually fell asleep after the healer did. For the second time in two nights, I woke to a door closing. This time, it was a man entering. It was the healer's son. He'd heard you were looking for me, but I also learned Dónal was in Wicklow. He intended to ransom me to you, assuming you would pay more than Dónal. I whacked him with the fire poker and made sure he understood I accompanied him; he wasn't taking me. I rode the horse while he traveled alongside in his wagon. When we were near the town, I didn't trust him not to take me to Dónal instead. I rode away, knowing the horse was faster than his wagon. I stabled the horse and tried to find The Leg of Mutton. The man had said that's where you wanted me to go."

"It was. I offered the tavern keeper extra if he kept you safe. But I suppose Dónal got word of that, or chose the Leg because it was close to the docks," Kyle reasoned.

"I believe so. I was so close, Kyle. So close when I ran into Dónal. It was like running into Dermot all over again. I bolted through the streets and found the docks. I even saw Snake Eye. He tried to reach me, but Dónal and my clansmen were too close. They nabbed me and took me to The Leg of Mutton. Dónal ordered the tavern keeper's wife to take my clothes. I refused to give up my boots, arguing that he had only said clothes. I wrapped myself in a sheet and went to the window. I'd seen Tomas leaning against the building when I arrived."

"I posted men there to watch the tavern and to follow Dónal if he left," Kyle explained.

"I waited for you, Kyle. I was starting to panic when night fell, and Tomas could only shrug. I didn't know what'd happened to you. I thought I'd lost you forever. That either you were dead or didn't want me," Moira said as tears coursed down her cheeks. "I didn't want to go back to Dermot."

"At that point, Dermot was already dead. While you made your way to Wicklow, we sailed back to Arklow, found Dermot, and ambushed his camp. I brought him back to the ship. I couldn't bring him in here. Moira, this is our space. That hook," Kyle pointed with a wicked grin, "Is your hook. I took him below. Suffice it to say, there are items that you didn't find in the chest the day you found the implements. I ensured Dermot suffered humiliation and pain."

"Good," Moira blurted. "Mine isn't the only life he made miserable. I'm sure of that."

"I severed a rather important part of him," Kyle hinted. "Then gave him a plank of wood and tossed him over. I knew it was only a matter of moments before the sharks would come with the blood in the water. He is shark shite now."

Moira paused for a moment, unsure if she wanted to laugh or cry. Kyle eased her once more into his arms and soothed her as he stroked her head and back. He cooed to her and encouraged her to continue.

"When morning came, I knew I had to get away. Dónal returned in the middle of the night, drunk out of his head. I stole his dirk and his doublet before I wrapped a sheet around my waist." Moira again waited to see if her thievery angered Kyle, but he urged her on. She knew the next part would undoubtedly get her a spanking unlike any before. "Then I climbed out the window, swung over to the notched bricks, and scaled down the side of the building," Moira rushed to say.

Kyle's eyes widened larger than Moira could imagine. Fear was replaced with fury. He stepped back from her, crossing the cabin.

"Tomas and Snake Eye tried to tell me 'no.' They lifted me down the last few feet," Moira said lamely.

"Don't try to justify that, Moira," Kyle hissed. "Dónal would have dragged you out of the tavern at some point. My men would have gotten you then. I might have been able to get you then. You risked your neck for nothing!" Kyle stalked back to her, and Moira shivered. Part of her was aroused beyond reason by his predatory fierceness, his protectiveness. But part of her was wisely afraid and remained quiet. He caught her chin between his thumb and forefinger and stared into Moira's eyes. She saw fear all over again. The anger was gone. There was sadness with the fear.

"I failed you, Moira. Over and over. You did what you had to do to survive. You knew you couldn't rely on me. For that, I will be sorry until my last breath. Can you forgive me, sweet one?" Kyle was desperate, even more desperate for absolution than Moira was.

"Kyle, you didn't fail me. You tried, but you can't control everything in this world. There were too many other pieces to this story for you to have done what you wanted. I know now that you wanted me all along. I knew even if you didn't wish me to return here, you wouldn't leave me to Dónal. This isn't your fault." Moira pulled against her bindings, wishing she could wrap her arms around Kyle and for once be the one who offered solace. "Kyle, I love you."

Kyle looked into Moira's bright blue eyes, and his heart ached. "Moira, I love you. I wasn't exaggerating when I said I wish to marry you."

"Are you asking me then?" Moira said with a mischievous smile.

"Aye. I'm asking. Moira, will you marry me?"

"Aye, Capt'n."

Kyle's kiss was demanding as his hands roamed over Moira. She returned it with a need that only spurred Kyle on. His fingers delved between Moira's thighs, finding the place he wanted to bury himself and never leave. Her needy sounds drew him like a siren. His fingers worked her sheath as she rubbed her mons along his sword.

"Do you wish for your release, sweet one?"

"Good God, yes, Kyle," Moira panted.

"And if I deny you?" Kyle taunted.

"I'll do anything," Moira begged.

"And if I wish to hear the rest of your story and redden your sweet round arse for climbing down the building?" Kyle persisted, knowing his offer only drove Moira further to the edge.

"My spanking, please, Capt'n," Moira murmured, her throat dry.

Kyle spun Moira around, so she faced the porthole and away from him. He ordered her to count each of the twenty slaps, his fingers working her flesh in between each one. The desperation in her voice, but her unwavering commitment to take each blow, made them both eager. When he was finished, he turned Moira back to him. Their kiss bore the heat it always did, but there was tenderness. They both knew Moira felt better for confessing what she'd done. She'd relinquished control to Kyle, and she felt lighter despite her unspent lust.

"The men took me to a dress shop. I made Tomas pay," Moira grinned. "Then we went to The Mother Hen. You know what I did there."

"Yes. But your earlier spanking was for risking your life with the magistrate. This punishment will be for playing a game with a woman who would have forced you without a moment of contrition, then killed you." Kyle lowered himself to his knees and drew one of Moira's legs then the other over his shoulders until she was suspended by the hook and supported by him. His mouth ravaged her. He gave no quarter as he worked her swollen flesh with his fingers, tongue, and teeth. Moira released one keening cry after another as her head hung back. Kyle demanded, "Ask."

"Capt'n, please can I climax?"

"No," Kyle barked as he continued his assault on her senses. Moira was certain she would float away. The sensations coursing through her were more intense than she thought she could endure. She considered using her safe word, but she didn't want the tortuous pleasure to end. She knew anyone besides they two would have thought him cruel and savage, merciless to her. But Moira felt free. Free from the fear, free from worrying about how Kyle felt, free from doubt about her future. All she had to do was enjoy Kyle's lovemaking.

Kyle tried to keep his mind on watching Moira, ensuring she wasn't suffering rather than enjoying. But he craved every touch, every taste of her. He wanted nothing to come between them in the future. He wanted to sail away from everything they knew, so he could spend his days and nights in rapture with the woman for whom he would sacrifice everything. He saw when Moira gave up trying to fight against the conflagration of need. It was that moment when he brought her to release. His tongue lapped at her dew as she shuddered against his mouth. He eased her legs from his shoulders but kept her weight off her arms as he rose. He tugged the rope free from the wall hook and carried Moira to the bunk, where he laid her on the mattress before untying her wrists. Just as he was about to ease onto the mattress beside her, giving her time to recover, uncaring about his own raging cockstand, Moira shook her head. She pointed toward the chest that held their collection of sexual devices.

"Phallus," Moira whispered. "Or plug and ginger."

"Moira," Kyle returned her whisper, but horror filled his voice. "No. I've exhausted you. You need food and sleep, not more of this. Besides, there are no more punishments to give."

Moira's eyes twinkled as she laughed, and Kyle looked at her as though she'd lost her sense. "Not for me," she giggled. "You sailed away rather than trusting me to come back. You got yourself arrested. If I hadn't manipulated Daisy and bribed the justice of the peace, you'd be swinging from the gallows instead of making love to me. I'm most displeased."

Kyle growled playfully as he drew Moira onto her side and gave her bottom a ringing slap. "You need food and sleep. Then we'll discuss who gets the ginger. Your fine little arse may be ready sooner than I thought. Now move over, sweet one. I intend to hold you all night and all of tomorrow, and maybe well into the next moon."

Moira's grin stayed in place as she slid toward the wall, and Kyle drew the covers over them. Kyle kept his word. He held her throughout the night and most of the next three days, when Moira awoke only to eat and use the chamber pot. She assured him she was fine, but by the third day, Kyle grew anxious.

CHAPTER 35

The *Lady Charity* and the *Lady Grace* sailed north after leaving Wicklow, happy when the sun set and the town was out of sight. Kyle and Keith agreed that it was time to make a run to the Isle of Canna to store the goods they'd accumulated and recover items they were ready to trade. From there, they would continue across the Sea of the Hebrides to the Isle of Barra, which lay slightly southwest of Canna. The route would force them to either cross the Irish Sea to sail closer to the coast of England, Wales, and Scotland, or they would sail close to Dunluce and Rathlin Island before crossing the North Channel and sailing closer to Scotland. Given their druthers, the twins avoided the English coast, which meant the English navy.

During the three days Moira spent sleeping, Keith raided three ships. Kyle, through messages relayed by Tomas, told Keith to do as he wished, but Kyle wouldn't join the fight. He gave his men permission to join the *Lady Grace* during the attacks if they wished for their share of the bounty. Some did, but most remained with Kyle, secretly hovering and worrying about Moira. The attacks slowed their progress, and what should have taken a day to sail past Dublin wound up being the three Moira slumbered. They lost the wind at their backs for another four days. Moira was in a malaise for those four days. Rather than put the men to the oars, Keith and Kyle agreed to allow whatever breeze stirred to propel them. Kyle wanted Moira to have all the time she needed to rest.

But as they neared the Dublin port, Kyle was beside himself. No fever had set in, for which he was grateful, but she barely stirred in her sleep. She woke long enough to eat the three meals he insisted and to assure him she was merely tired.

Fed up of being fussed over, Moira eventually ordered Kyle from the cabin, insisting it was the only way she would get enough rest. With great reluctance, Kyle left the cabin and went above deck to speak to Keith. His haggard appearance made Keith's eyebrows shoot nearly to his hairline.

"She's that poorly?" Keith asked without a greeting.

"That's the thing. She runs no fever, has no cough, no aches and pains. She just sleeps," Kyle explained.

"Can you blame the lass? Living with you is exhausting," Keith said with a brotherly grin.

"I ken," Kyle agreed, a tinge of his Scottish burr slipping into his voice. "I ken she fled her home sennights ago, and that was likely the last time she slept well. Even there she didn't sleep much because she tended to her nephew when he had night terrors."

"And you've been quite demanding," Keith's grin broadened as he waggled his eyebrows.

"Aye," Kyle muttered with remorse.

"Kyle, she sleeps because she knows she's safe. The lass has run herself ragged for years, then everything from the last few days would have done in a weaker woman. She's with you, and she knows she no longer has to worry. She trusts you, Kyle."

"Maybe, but I still wish for her to see a healer," Kyle stated.

Keith frowned, but nodded. "I suppose it wouldn't hurt. Maybe the healer could brew something to give her some strength back," he suggested.

"That's my hope."

"Where do you wish to go ashore?" Keith asked, already certain of what Kyle would say.

"Dublin."

"You want her to see a physician, not a healer. Do you really think it's that serious?"

"I don't know. That's why I want her to see one. You know the Irish have even more myths about healing than the Hebrideans and Highlanders, but most of their clans have a physician with his own plot of land, free of rents. They are both scholars and healers. If something is wrong with Moira, then a physician is more likely to find it, more likely to make her well."

Keith realized that Kyle's desperation grew each day. They rarely went ashore in Dublin, preferring that their customers come to their ships anchored well beyond the harbormaster's reach. The threat in Wicklow was infinitesimal compared to a town as large as Dublin. Keith also knew Kyle wouldn't be dissuaded, and he secretly held his own fears for the woman he already considered his sister. He'd come aboard the *Lady Charity* three days earlier and seen Moira so deeply asleep he feared she was dead.

"I'll find one," Keith offered. Kyle nodded, relief washing over him.

"You risk much for her. For me."

"If anything happens, you need to be the one with Moira," Keith stated.

"Don't tempt fate," Kyle rushed to say.

"I'll row ashore before dawn tomorrow. I should be able to rouse someone and have him to you before sunrise," Keith promised.

"Thank you." The brothers mouthed their customary "I love

you." It was no secret to any member of their crews, but every man turned a blind eye, never speaking against their captains. It might have been a moment of softness between the twins, but they would run any man through who attempted to mock them. Kyle returned to his cabin to find Moira sitting up in bed, the chamber pot in her lap as she leaned over it.

"Moira!" Kyle exclaimed as he rushed to the bedside just as Moira vomited.

"Shh," Moira hissed. She whispered, "My head feels like I've had too much disgusting Scottish whisky."

"Our whisky isn't disgusting. If you've had a sore head, it's because you're used to that swill you Irish call whiskey." Kyle teased Moira once he saw she was well enough to cast sarcasm at him. He lifted the chamber pot from her hands and laid it on the floor beside the bed, within reach in case Moira needed it. "What else feels poorly beside your head and your belly?"

"That's it," Moira confessed. "Is there water?"

Kyle fetched the waterskin from the table and helped Moira bring it to her lips. She sipped at it until she shook her head, fearful it would all come back up. Dark circles under Moira's eyes signaled she wasn't yet recovered from her exhaustion. Her new symptoms confirmed Kyle made the right decision to call for a physician. He slipped onto the bed alongside Moira, and she curled into his warmth.

"I don't know why I'm so tired, Kyle," Moira mumbled around a yawn. "I've never slept this much. I didn't feel ill before, just sleepy. Now I feel both. I didn't care for supper, but I was hungry. My belly didn't care for it either. I cast up my accounts, and that made my head pound."

"A physician is coming in the morning, sweet one," Kyle assured her.

"No. That's not necessary. That means you have to go into some town. I don't want that," Moira disagreed.

"Keith will go and be back before sunrise."

"Mo grá —"

"No, Moira. Argue with me, and you will earn yourself a trip over my knee when you're recovered. Something is wrong," Kyle choked on the final words.

"I know. I'm scared," Moira admitted.

"Leeches," the physician announced. "She needs to remove the bad humors from her blood."

Kyle stood at the foot of the bunk as the doctor examined Moira, but he couldn't agree with the remedy. She was already weak. Kyle couldn't imagine how she would survive such a treatment.

"She's with child. She doesn't need leeches. She needs fresh air and a hearty meal."

Kyle turned toward the old woman who'd accompanied the physician. She'd introduced herself as the physician's mother and one of the town's midwives.

"Pardon?" Moira asked as she leaned forward, her eyes darting from Kyle to the old woman. She'd felt immediately at ease when the woman arrived. She was kindly, unlike the healer Moira encountered on her way to Wicklow. The physician had set her on edge the moment he lifted her hand. Now the woman's pronouncement made Moira nauseous all over again.

"I'd say it's still very early, mayhap not even a month. The lass needs some meat on her bones, then a little attention from her husband. It'll put her right as rain. A good loving always does. Granted, that's what got you in this state," the midwife said with confidence. She flapped her hand at the trio of disbelieving faces. "The lass is exhausted but now can't keep food down. She says she hasn't had her courses since she came aboard the ship, which means before she took up with him," the midwife jerked a thumb toward Kyle. "The pennyroyal in the basket on yon table is withered and old, so clearly it's not being used. And the way this man looks at his wife, I doubt he gives her a minute of peace. Not that how she looks at her husband is any more innocent."

The midwife gave her son a scolding look and brushed past him. She eased Moira onto her back and pulled back the bedcovers. She raised Kyle's leine that she wore up to her middle. The doctor turned away in scandalized disgust. The healer tsked and shook her head. "You came into the world the same as everyone else, Robby. This is why I came with you when I heard a lass needed tending." She pressed gently against Moira's middle, then grinned at her. "Are your breasts swollen and tender?"

Moira considered what the woman asked. Her breasts had ached when she rolled onto them, but she'd also assumed it had been from being near Kyle without being able to enjoy his touch. She pulled the neckline away from her chest and looked down the leine, her eyes widening. She nodded her head before she turned terrified eyes toward Kyle. She blinked back tears, but they streamed down her cheeks. Kyle pushed past the physician, and the midwife wisely stood back, having witnessed the same scene countless times.

"We're going to have a bairn," Kyle whispered with wonder. "Our own bairn."

"You're not angry?" Moira asked before dropping her voice so low Kyle strained to understand. "You're not going to leave me?"

"I love you," Kyle swore as he cupped her jaw, his fingers tunneling into her hair. He poured all of his love, wonderment, hope, and happiness into the kiss. He prayed Moira understood what he couldn't put into words. As her hands clung to his biceps, and she returned his kiss, he was certain she did.

"Told you, Robby. A little loving would put her to rights. You and your bluidy leeches," the midwife scolded as she and the physician slipped from the cabin. Neither Moira nor Kyle noticed.

CHAPTER 36

With a diagnosis in place and excitement coursing through her, Moira improved each day. While still fatigued and queasy, Moira insisted that she needed the fresh air the midwife advised. She spent more and more time above deck as the *Lady Charity* and *Lady Grace* continued their progress north along the Irish coast. She often stood beside Kyle at the helm, and he enjoyed giving her a turn at the wheel. They hadn't spoken about their future beyond the trips to Canna and Barra that the brothers planned. Moira was eager to see Senga and to meet Caragh. From stories Kyle shared, both women had given birth to sons only months before Moira and Kyle fatefully reunited.

The only wrinkle in their journey came when Moira was the one to sight a ship in the distance. She pointed it out to Kyle and eagerly asked if they would raid it. He'd looked at her with astonishment and asked if she'd lost any sense she ever had. He wouldn't raid a ship while she was aboard. He would hang back, and if Keith wished to raid, he would do so. Moira made the grave error of countermanding Kyle's decision before the crew. She'd done it on their behalf, but most of the men backed away from the arguing couple. Moira swore she would remain below deck while Kyle attacked, and Kyle cursed a blue streak about her being a bampot if she thought he was going to risk bringing the fight aboard a ship that carried the woman he loved and their unborn child. She'd narrowed her eyes and swept them over the deck, making it obvious he displeased her with how he shared the news of their good fortune with the crew.

Kyle ended the argument by hefting Moira into his arms and carrying her to their cabin. He'd been tempted to swing her over his shoulder, but he worried it would be too uncomfortable for her. But when they reached their cabin, and Moira continued to argue, he pulled her over his lap, stripped down her leggings, and spanked her soundly. She accepted the punishment, but her mutinous glare at the end, rather than her usual offer of contrition, brought them nose to nose.

"Moira, maybe it's the bairn that's making you so testy, but I am not risking your life for some bluidy cloth and who knows what else. Now you will cease," Kyle warned.

"Or what?" Moira mocked. "You're a pirate. Your men will think you weak if you keep coddling me and not providing for them." She sucked in a deep breath and tried to back away, realizing she'd gone much too far by questioning his position as captain.

"Remove every stitch of clothing on your tempting little body, Moira," Kyle commanded. He went to the chest that held the implements they'd begun to experiment with as Moira's health improved. "Bend over the table and keep your legs wide."

Kyle rummaged through the chest until he found the four items he desired. Looking at Moira's body as she stretched over the tabletop made his cock swell until he had to adjust himself. He loosened the laces and opened the waistline enough for his rod to spring free. He stood behind Moira, reveling in the sight she presented before he thrust into her. He'd seen the moisture between her thighs and knew she was as aroused as he was.

"You should not have argued with me before my crew, Moira. If you wish to disagree, I will hear you out, but only in here, where we have privacy. You know that you would have received the lash if you were one of my men," Kyle said as he leaned over Moira, thrusting over and over. He slid his hands beneath her until he cupped her fuller breasts. He squeezed until she gasped, pain and pleasure shooting through her. She pushed her hips back to meet each of his surges. "This is not your punishment, sweet one. This is your recompense to me. You will not climax, or I will deny you until we reach Canna."

"You won't," Moira disagreed. "That would only be denying yourself."

"I have no intention of denying myself anything, Moira." Kyle pulled her hips away from the table, keeping her from feeling any friction against her nub. He slammed into her over and over until she trembled with need, and he shuddered with his release. Moira cried out as he pulled free from her. "Do you wish to keep testing me, sweet one?" Kyle asked as he rubbed her nub twice, then pulled his hand away.

"No. I'm sorry. I shouldn't have said what I did. Not on deck, and not in here," Moira confessed.

"And how do I know you're not just saying that so I will ease your aching quim?" Kyle pointed out.

"I suppose you don't, but I am," Moira insisted. Kyle didn't doubt that she was, but he wouldn't offer absolution that easily. He didn't mind her disagreeing with him. But he wouldn't allow it where anyone else could hear, and he wasn't going to accept either of them throwing about insults. They'd come too far and endured too much to create hurt and resentment.

"You may have made your restitution first, but you will still have your punishment. Lean over the table again," Kyle instructed. He pressed his body over hers again but kept his weight off her, not wanting to hurt Moira by trapping her against the hardwood surface. He held out two small marble balls for her to see. "Do you remember me telling you about these?"

"Yes," Moira rasped. "I'm to hold them within my quim and not let them fall out."

"That's right, sweet one." Kyle pressed the balls into Moira's channel and felt the muscles contract around his fingers. He eased his digits out and pinched her nub. She cried out and squirmed.

"You're trying to make me drop them," Moira accused.

"You're doing very well," Kyle said, the earlier edge gone. He stroked his hand behind her shoulder blades before massaging her shoulders. "Promise me you will speak up if you think anything is harmful to you or our bairn."

"I promise, Kyle. I know what I said earlier was foolish and contrary to my promise. But I mean it. I wouldn't do anything risky," Moira assured him. Kyle massaged the globes of her backside, aroused all over again by the view. He'd yet to plunder her rosebud with his cock, but they'd been working to ready her. He withdrew the small plug that was already in place.

"You've been an apt pupil with these, Moira. I'm proud of you. But this next one will be painful. It is larger, and it will have ginger on it," Kyle warned. He'd done nothing more than dab a few drops around the rim of her rosebud the night before, so Moira could get a sense of the sting. "Your words were more than insulting, and so were your actions. Contradicting me in front of my crew does make me look weak. You knew I wouldn't do anything to correct you before the men, and you took advantage of that. By disregarding my word and as my—" Kyle stumbled over his words.

Moira wasn't lawfully his wife, even if he hadn't contradicted Keith when he implied it to Dónal. He hadn't thought of her as his mistress since the last time he'd said it, and she'd been right that she never accepted the position.

"My betrothed," Kyle continued, "you set us on the path to a mutiny. If my men think a pint-sized lass can browbeat me, then they will assume they can defeat me. You will get yourself, our bairn, Tomas, Snake Eye, Braedon, and me killed if Keith can't stop them. Those three will stand beside us, more to protect you than to side with me. I will lose any respect if my brother must come to my rescue on my own ship. You risked that, Moira. Your little spectacle is worse than you thought."

Kyle dabbed the unscented oil onto his finger and swirled it about Moira's rosebud, pressing his finger inside to prepare her, and receiving a moan in return as she pushed her hips back. A resounding slap landed against her backside. He dabbed the ginger oil onto the largest plug he dared use with Moira and cautiously eased it into her. He watched the muscles in her back tense as the plug entered her, then her legs danced around as the burn began. He'd been mindful not to place too much oil on the device, since it was her first time with that size plug and with the sensation. As the flange rested between her bottom cheeks, Kyle landed a slap on the other side from the last one.

Moira's breath caught again. The sensation of being so full wasn't entirely new after her experiences with Aidan, but it had been nearly six years. The burn from the ginger was excruciating, but the slaps eased the pain, giving her something else to focus upon. But as the sting faded from her globes, she was left with the effects of the ginger. The only benefit she saw was that every muscle between her belly and knees contracted, so she didn't fear dropping the *ben wa* balls. But as she shifted in discomfort, the balls moved within her channel, making her arousal almost as unbearable as the ginger burn. She was desperate for Kyle to ease all of her needs, and she thought for a moment he would when he helped her off the table and lowered his mouth to her breast. He swirled his tongue over her nipple before suckling one and massaging the other. She trembled with need, but Kyle pulled away just as she thought his attention to her breast would bring her to climax.

"Go to the corner, Moira," Kyle commanded. He kissed the crown of her head, her forehead, the tip of her nose, and her lips before giving her a gentle nudge.

Moira nodded and made her way to where she'd now logged numerous hours. Kyle wouldn't keep her there long that day. She'd frustrated him, even angered him as she argued, but he'd already forgiven her. He had no wish to curb her courage to speak up, and he didn't want her to resent him as she did Dónal. But he needed her to understand the danger she created by not considering where she argued, or who their audience was. They'd already disagreed strenuously about whether Kyle should continue her punishments and their play while she was with child.

Moira pointed out that farmer's wives worked alongside their husbands while carrying, and female servants in keeps still managed heavy platters while they were pregnant. She saw no difference between the physical strain she experienced with Kyle and what other women always endured. Kyle finally capitulated when Moira admitted that not having Kyle's dominance scared her. She confessed she felt adrift without him, and she pointed out that he'd promised when they met on the MacDonnell ship not to set her adrift. And Kyle agreed he enjoyed the intimacy the implements brought them when used for pure pleasure.

CHAPTER 37

Kyle slipped from the chamber and went above deck to see how close they were to the ship Moira spotted. It shocked him to recognize the captain of the ship. He groaned as he looked over to the *Lady Grace* and found Keith looking back at him with a matching grimace. Once the ships were within speaking distance, all three dropped anchor and lowered their sails. The *Lady Charity* and *Lady Grace* tethered themselves together in case the ensuing conversation didn't remain civil. The three captains walked toward the bows of their ships.

"Aidan O'Flaherty," Kyle called out. "What the fuck do you want?"

"A good day to you too, Drifter," Aidan called back.

"Not still eating the MacDonnells out of house and home, and swiving Lizzie every waking hour?" Keith asked. As the words left Keith's mouth, Kyle and Keith's expressions once more matched. These were shock, followed by disgust. Lizzie MacDonnell appeared from the hatch that led below deck. Neither brother had heard of Lizzie sailing with Aidan. Seeing their expressions, Aidan grimaced, then shrugged.

"Where is my lie-about sister?" Lizzie called as she came to stand beside Aidan, wrapping her arm around his. He fought to extract it from Lizzie's grip and leaned away from her. Keith and Kyle chortled to see Aidan was not as thrilled to have Lizzie aboard his ship as he was to drop anchor in her on land.

"What do you want with her, Lizzie?" Kyle asked. He knew he had to fetch Moira. He couldn't keep an encounter with Aidan and her sister from her, but he wanted forewarning about Lizzie's scheme.

"I wish to see my dear sister," Lizzie offered.

"You've never been an adept liar," Kyle spat. "Men ignored your lies because you're not known to refuse anyone. What do you want with Moira?"

"We have some news she needs to hear," Aidan interjected. "You really should get her." At Aidan's seriousness, Kyle nodded. The Irishman was deadly calm during negotiations, but the surety in his voice now made the hair on the back of Kyle's neck stand up.

"It'll be a moment," Kyle warned before he glanced at Keith. His brother gave Kyle an imperceptible nod before Kyle made his way below. He opened the cabin door to find Moira exactly how he expected. Her hands were behind her back to keep away the temptation. Her feet were apart, and she rested her buttocks on them, mindful of her sore cheeks. She didn't turn to greet him, instead lowering her head.

Kyle helped her to feet and pulled her into his arms. He felt the last of her tension slip away as he held her. Her deep sigh and the way her body went limp told Kyle that she felt at ease after their argument, even if it hadn't ended the way she wished. "*Mo ghràidh,* I need you to come up on deck with me."

Moira leaned back, and her brow furrowed as she noticed the wariness in his voice and his expression. She nodded and stepped back, but Kyle's hands slid down her arms until they held hers. She looked past him to the door then back at him.

"What's happened, Kyle?"

"Let me help you remove the plug and the balls, then I'll help you dress. I'll explain once you're ready," Kyle answered.

"No. You're scaring me. I want to know now," Moira insisted. "I know I sound petulant, but you never sound like this. Something is wrong, and I want to know what's happened. Oh, dear merciful God! Is it the English navy? Are they coming to take you?" Moira's face crumpled as tears threatened. Mustering her resolve, Kyle watched as she straightened her spine and narrowed her eyes.

"Easy, sweet one. You don't need to rush into battle on my behalf," Kyle chuckled. He was growing used to her shifting emotions, and rather than grow frustrated with them, he felt sorry for how Moira struggled at times. "Let me take out the plug, and you can release the balls."

"No," Moira shook her head. "You planned for me to be in that corner longer. I—I don't want to be—" Moira closed her eyes as she struggled to admit even to Kyle what she needed.

"What is it, sweet one?" Kyle asked as he encircled her in his arms once more.

"I need you, Kyle. God, how I ache and need you. At least these devices, as much as they torment me, also give me some relief. I don't know that I can think straight at this point."

"Can you hurry?" Kyle asked as he glanced back at the door, then shook his head. He stuck out his hand, palm up. "Bugger them. Give me the balls, Moira."

She nodded and reached down to retrieve the marble spheres. Kyle lunged for her, and she sent the balls rolling across the cabin floor. He backed her against the wall and lifted her until her legs wrapped around his waist. He plunged into her sheath as she clawed at his back. Their coupling was frenetic as they kissed through each thrust. Moira tunneled her hands into Kyle's hair, each tug urging him on. The plug added to the tightness they normally experienced from Kyle's stiffened rod and Moira's narrow channel.

"Kyle!" Moira cried out as her release ripped through her, and his answering cry of "Moira" blended with her voice. He reached around her and withdrew the plug, tossing it into the washstand bowl. He rested his forehead against hers as they fought to catch their breath.

"Was I too rough?" Kyle panted.

"Can we do that again?" Moira grinned.

"Cheeky," Kyle said as he playfully pinched her bottom. "Loathe as I am to let you go, you need to get dressed and come above deck with me."

"Are you going to tell me what's happening, or leave me to be shocked by whatever I find?" Moira gave him a speaking look.

He lifted the gown she'd last worn on shore in Wicklow from a peg and brought it to her. Her trepidation grew if she needed to dress as a lady. After she pulled the gown down over her hips, she twisted away from him and crossed her arms.

"Your sister and Aidan are on the ship you spotted," Kyle stated.

"Lizzie? What the devil is she doing on a ship?" Moira wondered.

"I don't know yet. It was Aidan who said you should come up," Kyle explained. Moira nodded but said no more until they stood before her sister and her former lover.

"What the fuck do you want?" Moira blurted.

CHAPTER 38

Aidan grinned, but Lizzie hissed. In turn, Aidan turned to Lizzie and glared. His mistress retreated a step before Aidan looked directly at Moira.

"You are a matched pair," Aidan said, his smile back in place. "Your lover greeted me the same way."

Moira felt Kyle's hand brush against hers before they entwined fingers.

"Husband," Kyle corrected. They hadn't legally exchanged vows, but he wouldn't risk Aidan and Lizzie having heard they were. He suspected Aidan tested them.

"You haven't answered my question, Aidan. Do it now, or I'm the one who walks away," Moira's steely tone and unwavering glare clearly referenced something in their shared past that Kyle didn't know about, but he stood beside her with resolve.

"Your brother met with an untimely end," Aidan announced.

"Dónal's dead?" Moira asked as though she wondered if it would rain. There was no emotion in her voice, no anger and no sadness.

"I was the one who demanded the alliance with the O'Malleys," Aidan explained. "Your brother failed to follow through."

"You bastard," Moira hissed. "You made him sell me. You seduced me, abandoned me, swived my sister for years, and left me to raise your bastard. Then you made my brother give me to a man who would have likely beaten me worse than my brother. You knew what Dónal did and never once, not even while you bedded me, stopped him. You are weak and pathetic."

"Moira, be reasonable," Aidan said with a smile.

"Reasonable? You were a shite lover. Little did I know at the time, but you do not know what you're doing," Moira said emphatically. "Why my sister wants you is beyond me. All I can assume is the MacDonnell men aren't any better than the O'Flaherty. Maybe it's being Irish instead of Scottish. But you took my virginity, duped me into thinking you loved me, then jumped out of my bed to go to my sister's. And you want me to be reasonable? I have been reasonable. I haven't fucking killed you."

"Moira," Lizzie gasped. "Your language."

"Sod off, Lizzie. Maybe Aidan keeps playing your games, but I won't. I haven't used a word yet I haven't thought countless times. You've mocked me, scorned me, abused me. I have hated you for most of my life, and it feels wonderful to tell you finally. That you didn't die alongside Dónal will always be Aidan's greatest error."

"You spiteful bitch," Lizzie hurled at Moira, but Moira just shrugged.

"Yes," Moira responded before turning back to Aidan. "You've told me you killed my brother. You have my sister, and she isn't trying to escape. You've done what you had to. Sail away."

"I'm not sure I care for this side of you, Moira," Aidan grumbled.

"Good thing you don't matter, O'Flaherty," Kyle cut in. "I, on the hand, do matter. And I enjoy my wife's spunk. Apparently, I enjoy quite a lot more of her, since I know what I'm doing."

Aidan scowled at Kyle but forced his attention back to Moira. "Your clan wishes you to return. I'm taking Sean with me once I return, and they need a chieftain."

"The bluidy hell you're taking Sean anywhere. I'll have him before I let you breathe long enough to touch him again. He could have just as easily been my child as Lizzie's, and I'm the one who's raised him. Touch him, and I will make sure your death is more painful and drawn out than anything the Red Drifter, the Scarlet Blade, the Dark Heart, and the Blond Devil could ever conceive of together. Sean is mine to raise." Moira snapped her mouth shut. She'd issued a demand that affected Kyle as much as her, and she hadn't paused for a breath to consider whether he would agree.

"Sean comes with us," Kyle confirmed when Aidan opened his mouth to disagree. "Neither you nor Lizzie care for the lad. Moira's the only real mother he's known. If he's Dónal's heir, then Moira will raise him until he can take his rightful place as chieftain."

Moira's heart thudded in her chest as she listened to Kyle affirm her declaration. But even though she'd heard Kyle say "us," he'd said Moira would raise the boy. She glanced up at Keith. His firm mouth and set jaw made his expression difficult to read, but she saw the encouragement in his eyes. He would defend her decision, and he would help her gain custody of Sean.

"I told you, the MacDonnells want you to return." Aidan didn't put up a fight for Sean, and Lizzie said nothing. Moira would never understand how a mother could be so ambivalent to her own child, only interested in using him to manipulate men. "They don't want a child for a chieftain, and since you're Dónal's sister and married, your children would be legitimate."

"Are you saying they wish for me to be chieftain?" Moira asked in disbelief. When Aidan and Lizzie nodded, Moira snorted. "That's rich. They wish for me to come back now, so they can continue to use me. The council thinks to control me and use me as a puppet. No."

"But Moira," Lizzie whined.

"You have no say," Moira snapped at her sister. "You're older than me. They could have chosen you, but they don't want you. From Aidan's expression every time you open your mouth or touch him, he doesn't want you either."

"What?" Lizzie gasped and spun toward Aidan, catching his expression of disgust pointed toward her, not Moira.

"If I go back, then it's as the chieftain with all the power that any man would have," Moira asserted. "If I go back, my husband comes with me. Otherwise, I sail away with him and Sean, never to look back."

"And what? Will the Red Drifter be Lady of Clan MacDonnell?" Aidan snickered.

Looking bored, Kyle shrugged. "I'm a decent cook, and I've been sewing sails and my clothes for nearly twenty years. I can manage a ship. I don't see why I can't learn to manage a keep."

Kyle gave Moira's hand three quick squeezes, and she returned them with a long one. She knew he jested about his tasks, but Kyle was serious in his support of her. She leaned past Kyle and looked at Keith, who'd remained silent throughout the exchange. If she went to Dunluce, it meant Kyle would join her. That left Keith to sail alone. He grinned at her, barely able to contain his amusement as he nodded his head. Moira realized Keith's blessing meant more to her than anything any of her clan's councilmen could say.

"The captains have other matters to see to," Moira stated. "The clan will know my decision after I see Sean. And I warn you, Aidan O'Flaherty. If you try to take that lad from me, you'd better hope you make it back to Galway and Augnanure Castle before I do. Sail along my coast again, and you will beg my husband to make me stop."

"Who are you?" Aidan asked with wonder. Neither Moira nor Kyle missed the lust that flared in Aidan's eyes.

"Kyle's wife," Moira responded as Kyle asserted, "My wife."

"Go wherever it is you're going, O'Flaherty. Moira and I will go to Dunluce when our other business is through," Kyle decided. He wrapped his arm around Moira, who welcomed the affection and leaned against him. Neither had to feign the comfort they drew from one another. Moira rested her head against Kyle's chest and looked back at her sister and Aidan. The jealousy on their faces wasn't hard to read. Moira suspected Aidan regretted giving her up now that he had Lizzie aboard. Lizzie eyed Kyle with lust. And they both envied the obvious love between Moira and Kyle. Aidan offered a clipped farewell and dragged Lizzie from the bow as he ordered his crew to hoist their sails.

"Looks like our plans have changed," Keith called out. "Canna, then Barra, then Dunluce. Moira, I expect a bed large enough to entertain." Keith offered her a roguish grin and a wink. Moira blinked several times before she burst into giggles.

"I have my own entertaining to do, brother," Kyle responded as he lifted Moira into his arms, ordering his crew to get them underway. The couple wasn't seen until the next day, but every man on the ship heard from them.

CHAPTER 39

"Moira!" Senga MacNeil called out in delighted surprise. The woman's dark braid swished at her waist as she and a strawberry blonde woman hurried to greet the guests. "I didn't think to see you again."

"Hello Senga," Moira greeted her. She turned to the other woman and smiled. "It's nice to meet you, Lady MacNeil."

"Caragh," the strawberry blonde chuckled. "Welcome to Kisimul. I didn't believe Rowan when he said he saw a woman aboard Kyle's ship. It's nice to meet you."

"Hello, Lady Moira," a deep voice came from behind her. She watched as Ruairí MacNeil approached with his cousin, Laird Rowan MacNeil, at his side. Ruairí grinned at Kyle. "MacLean."

"We need a priest," Kyle announced, and Moira choked. His concern was immediate and obvious as he reached for her. Four faces stood slack-jawed.

"He hasn't even begun to whittle in front of you," came Keith's mocking tones. "I'm surprised her feet are touching the ground."

"You need a priest to marry you," Senga surmised. Moira beamed as she nodded.

"I need to speak to Cook," Caragh said as she rattled off tasks on her fingers. "It's been ages since we've had a feast."

"Lady—Caragh," Moira caught herself before using Caragh's official title. "There's no need to go to the trouble."

"Yes, there is," Caragh corrected. "Kyle sailed for years with Ruairí and helped protect Senga. Keith nearly died protecting me. If he hadn't been with Rowan, I likely would have died from my injuries. We're happy that they're here, but we're even more excited to celebrate with you."

Moira looked up at Kyle, who'd draped his arm around her shoulders. He smiled down at her, and she was about to stand on her toes to kiss his cheek when a waft of cooking meat filled her nose. She covered her mouth and dashed behind the stables.

"Moira?" Kyle called as he ran after her. He held her hair as her morning meal revisited her in waves. She clutched Kyle's hand as she trembled from the force of her heaves. When she was certain her stomach was back where it belonged, Kyle carried her to where the others stood. Ruairí, Rowan, and Senga stood with knowing expressions, while Keith looked playfully aggrieved. Caragh hurried back across the bailey. She opened her hand to show Moira what she brought.

"The ginger should help ease your discomfort," Caragh offered. When Moira's cheeks went flame red and she struggled not to grin, five knowing faces met her eyes. Caragh and Senga shifted unconsciously, and their husbands' arms went around them. Keith was left rolling his eyes. Moira graciously accepted the sliver of ginger and chewed on it, agreeing that it eased her churning stomach.

"I'm excited that you're having a bairn," Caragh said the Scottish word with her heavy English accent. "Our children will be close in age. It'll make visits more entertaining for us all."

"I would like that. Whether we continue sailing or make our home somewhere on land, I'm happy to know we have friends to visit."

"Family," Rowan and Ruairí corrected.

"Come," Senga said. "Let's get you settled. I'll have a bath sent up while Ruairí tracks down the priest."

"And I'll settle the arrangements for the feast," Caragh confirmed.

"And I shall keep Keith out of the way," Rowan grumbled, but he couldn't contain his grin as he slapped his friend on the back. "You've been drinking that pish they call Irish whiskey. Come to my solar, and I'll give some good Scottish whisky that'll put hair on that bony chest of yours." Everyone chuckled since Keith and Kyle rivaled Rowan and Ruairí in size and strength.

Moira rested against Kyle as he carried her to a chamber that exceeded any at Dunluce. The couple remained in their chamber until just before sunset, when the MacNeils gathered to watch the Red Drifter marry a woman with the tenacity of the ancient Irish Queen Nessa. Moira was certain she'd never had a more joyous day than the one that ended with her as Kyle's bride. Kyle agreed all through the night as he made sure no one doubted they'd consummated their marriage.

Nearly a month after encountering Aidan and Lizzie, the *Lady Charity* and the *Lady Grace* sailed up to the docks at Dunluce. Moira worried about not returning sooner to make sure Aidan hadn't taken Sean, but those around her laughed and shook their heads. Kyle regaled the four MacNeils with the story of how Moira made Aidan O'Flaherty, one of the most feared pirates in Ireland, give in to her demands.

Kyle shook his head and wiped a tear from his eye as he recounted, "The bluidy eejit made the mistake of crossing Moira yet again. I swear his knees knocked louder when she threatened to go after him. She named the four most dreaded pirates in all the English Isles, and he still feared her more. The Red

Drifter, Scarlet Blade, Dark Heart, and Blond Devil could have all converged on his ship, and he would have sooner cried for his mother if Moira spat in his direction."

"He'd do well to count his blessings if it were you four he met up with," Senga said. She had no love lost for Aidan. He'd caused the worst argument she'd ever had with Ruairí. "Moira, Caragh, and I wouldn't have been so gentle as the lot of you."

Moira and Caragh had sat nodding their heads. The four pirates looked at the women in disbelief before all four conceded that the women were right.

Now, a week after that conversation, Moira climbed down the rope ladder and turned to face her former home. It was a sight she'd prayed countless times never to see again, but she and Kyle were now making their way to the keep, leaving behind the *Lady Charity*. Moira had asked Kyle several times to ensure the *Lady Charity* could sail at a moment's notice in case she wished to flee with Sean.

"I'm not going anywhere," Kyle assured her as he flexed his fingers. Moira hadn't realized her nails bit into the back of his hand. She eased her grip and offered a half-hearted smile.

"I really don't want to be here," Moira murmured. "If it weren't for Sean." As though summoned by her thoughts, a mop of ebony curls raced toward her.

"Aunty Moira!" Sean ran along the path as fast as his young legs could carry him. His excitement was what Moira needed for her homecoming. She released Kyle's hand and lifted her skirts as she flew toward her nephew. She lifted him into her arms and swung him side to side as they embraced. She nearly smothered him in kisses. Remorse flooded her as she thought about how she'd walked away from Sean, how she'd been willing to never see him again. She realized in the depths of her heart, she wouldn't have been able to stay away for good.

"I'm so happy to see you," Moira mumbled against his baby-soft cheeks.

"You brought the Red Drifter!" Sean exclaimed and squirmed away from Moira. She placed him back on the ground, and Sean took off toward Kyle. A pinch in her heart made her catch her breath as Sean so readily left her side after such a short greeting. But it reassured her that he'd been resilient during her absence. She watched Kyle bend over to be eye level with Sean, nodding his head to Sean's enthusiastic chatter. The ache in her chest released its hold as she had a glimpse into the future, seeing Kyle as a father to their unborn child. Kyle glanced up at Moira and grinned, waving her back to his side.

"Can you not give your aunty a better welcome than that?" Kyle asked Sean. "She's been so worried about you. I think she's been lonely without you."

Moira realized there was truth in Kyle's statement. She hadn't thought of Sean as often as she'd imagined when she first left Dunluce, but she had still thought of him frequently, especially as various things triggered memories.

Sean bounced on his toes as he smiled up at Moira, then launched himself against her for another hug. "I'm sorry, Aunty Moira. I just couldn't believe the Red Drifter is here! But I'm so happy to see you again. I've missed you so much. Will you sleep in my chamber tonight?"

Moira glanced at Kyle, who shrugged and nodded. She glanced back down at Sean's eager face. She and Kyle had discussed what they would do if Sean still suffered night terrors. Neither wanted to sleep apart, and Kyle was concerned for what would happen as her pregnancy advanced. They'd come to a resolution about two things.

"Sean, when we're with our family, it's not the Red Drifter. It's Uncle Kyle. We're married now. And I won't be sleeping in your chamber." When Sean's face fell, she lifted him again and peppered his face with kisses while she tickled him. "You'll sleep in our chamber tonight. We can move the trundle where I slept in into my old chamber, where Kyle and I will stay."

"I thought you were moving into Uncle Dónal's chamber," Sean said with bewilderment. Moira inhaled and sighed, knowing this was a confusing time for Sean. Even more so than any other in his brief life.

"That hasn't been decided yet. I would like to talk to you about several things before I make any choices," Moira hedged. "Shall we go inside?" Moira made to lower Sean to the ground, but he clung to her neck. She was loathe to let him go, but she knew she couldn't manage to carry him up the steep path without tripping over her skirts.

"Do you know what a barrel man does?" Kyle intervened. When Sean shook his head, he reached out his arms to the boy. Without hesitation, Sean leaned toward Kyle, who swung him onto his shoulders. "A barrel man is actually a lad who sits in the crow's nest and has the most important job. He's the captain's scout. He can see all the way to the ends of the earth. He must warn the captain of any danger, whether it's another ship or the weather."

"Am I your barrel man right now, Uncle Kyle?" Sean asked with all the exuberance of a normal six-year-old boy. The sight of Moira's grin filled Kyle with such happiness that he tugged her hand and drew her back to his side. He leaned down and kissed her.

"You do that too? Just like Mama and Aidan."

Moira sighed, knowing that was one more topic to add to the list of things she and Kyle needed to discuss with Sean. It wasn't anything like Lizzie and Aidan, and she wanted to be sure he understood that he was, and always would be, a priority in their lives.

"Lady Moira," Beagan greeted. He stood at the top of the path as they approached. Just as they were the fateful night that led Moira to Kyle, the clan councilmen stood behind Beagan. She looked at each man in turn, her eyes narrowing. The two older brothers, Curran and Cormac, looked like they'd aged decades in the time she'd been away. She hadn't noticed it to such a degree in Wicklow. The men were close to the age her father would have been, but they appeared weathered and worn down. Devlin, Finnian, and Hogan glared at Kyle, holding him responsible for Grady's death. Devlin and Finnian were Cormac's sons, and cousins to Hogan and Grady. Kyle bore as apologetic an expression as Moira had ever seen. Loman stood to the side, leaving a space for where his cousin Malone would have once stood.

Moira observed the unease with which the men watched her. It tempted her to yell "boo" to see if they jumped. She'd held no disregard for them when Kyle attacked the ship they hadn't adequately manned. But their role in her capture in Wicklow wasn't so easily forgiven. She nodded her head once to the men and continued to walk toward the keep, forcing the men to step apart. Kyle followed one step behind her, already offering deference in case she should accept the position as chieftain. They'd agreed that if they made their lives at Dunluce, their arrangement on land would be the same as at sea. On the *Lady Charity,* Kyle's word was law, with differences of opinion only aired in their cabin. At Dunluce, Moira's word would be law, with their chamber and her solar as the safe places to speak freely.

Moira brushed her fingers against Kyle's hand until their fingers entwined as they stepped into the bailey. Regardless of what the future held, they entered Dunluce as partners. Moira felt Kyle's strength in his steady presence beside her. Members of her clan watched in stunned silence as Moira and Kyle walked toward the keep holding hands, with Sean bouncing on Kyle's shoulders. They looked like a happy family.

"Lady Moira," Beagan tried again after they entered the

Great Hall, and Moira took a seat beside Kyle on the dais. Sean disappeared to play with his friends. They avoided the chieftain and lady's chairs, settling for the one Moira once occupied and the seat beside it.

"Hello, Beagan." Moira wouldn't say more until she could sense their reception to her arrival.

"Welcome home, Lady Moira," Loman smiled. She was close in age to the man, and they'd been friendly since they were children. But she trusted none of the men seated around her.

"Lady Moira," Curran began, but his eyes darted to Kyle, and a hardness entered them. Moira's lips thinned, and she turned a piercing glare at Curran.

"Before the servants even bring food out and they prepare a chamber for my husband and me," Moira stressed the last four words, "you will all accept and acknowledge that Kyle and I are married. If you are unwilling to accept him into our clan, then we leave now." Moira rose, and Kyle followed. He remained quiet, but his towering frame next to Moira's petite one only served to make him look fiercer and more protective.

"You wish for us to accept such a man into Clan MacDonell," Curran spat. "Never."

"Very well. Sean need not pack anything. We can provide for him. We shall be on our way," Moira said as Kyle pulled back her chair further for her to step around.

"Lady Moira, wait," Hogan spoke up. "My father and I bear ill will toward your husband. I won't lie and say that we don't. But that doesn't mean how we feel about my brother's death should decide the future of our clan."

Moira looked unmoved.

"Lady Moira," Hogan continued. "We were all in Wicklow. We knew you and the Re— knew you were married. We asked Aidan to fetch you after we returned, knowing your husband would come with you."

Moira looked around the table and nodded, but she didn't

take her seat. She stood and waited until she was asked to remain. Understanding her negotiating tactic, expecting the council to say aloud their desire for her to stay, Beagan spoke up.

"Lady Moira, please stay. At least until after you've eaten and heard us out," Beagan reasoned. Moira nodded and took her seat once again. When she said nothing, Beagan frowned but continued on. "We assume Aidan explained what happened."

"He said he demanded the alliance with the O'Malleys, and he killed Dónal because it didn't work out." Moira watched the men as they grimaced and frowned.

"Aidan planned to sell a supply of weapons to the O'Malleys that he was supposed to sell to us. He demanded a far higher price from the O'Malleys, knowing they had the means to pay," Beagan explained. "Originally Dónal planned take up arms against the O'Malleys once you were married in order to gain sailing rights along the coast. Aidan assured Dónal that the O'Malleys could be fooled by marrying you to their chieftain. Dónal was certain defeating the O'Malleys with the weapons we got from Aidan would intimidate other privateers from attacking our ships. What he refused to believe, and what Lizzie never learned from him, was that Aidan had already alerted the O'Malleys to Dónal's plan. That's how he negotiated the higher price."

"Aidan convinced the O'Malleys that he was doing them a favor by informing them of Dónal's—really his own—plan and selling them the weapons instead," Cormac picked up the story. "In exchange for the O'Malleys staying away from Ballycastle and Rathlin Island, Aidan could continue to use our clan as a place to store his stolen and smuggled goods. But when the O'Malleys never received your dowry, Aidan's deal fell through."

"We gave that bastard a roof over his head, a woman under him in bed, and plenty of food," Beagan grumbled. "He controls all the northern waters on both sides of Ireland. And he thought he could rid his conscience of the guilt he felt about you by no longer seeing you here."

"Aidan has no conscience," Moira said. "I was an inconvenient reminder of a failed attempt to manipulate Dónal, a waste of his time and efforts. Do not confuse the two."

"Aye, well, when Dónal learned that Dermot was dead and you were with the—your husband," Beagan stumbled. "He made the error of trying to coerce Aidan into attacking your husband and the—your brother-by-marriage. Dónal was too heavy handed and threatened to cease our arrangement with Aidan, which has protected our waters from other privateers. It pushed Aidan around the bend because his deal with the O'Malleys had already fallen through. Aidan remedied the trouble with Dónal the same way the Dark Heart handled Padraig MacAlister. He ran him through without warning."

"And now you need someone to fill the position of chieftain to make the council look legitimate. Ironically, the only choice was an illegitimate child. You wish for me to return, mind the castle, keep quiet as I used to, and let you go on about your business as you wish," Moira surmised. "I'm not interested in such an arrangement."

"Do you wish your husband to become chieftain?" Finnian asked, aghast.

"Oh, no," Kyle spoke up for the first time. "I have no interest in taking command of this clan."

"Then what?" Finnian asked before his head pulled back in disbelief. "You, Moira?"

"It's Lady Moira, and then Lady MacDonnell if I accept," Moira corrected. "Who maintained the clan's accounts? Who kept track of everything Aidan brought and took from here? Who ensured there was enough to eat, that the servants and craftsmen were paid, that crofts were repaired in time for winter? Who the bluidy hell do you think suggested that Aidan protect us in exchange for having a place to hide? You know it was none of you, and you know Dónal wasn't smart enough to think of it, and you know Lizzie never cared enough to. You may think you managed Dónal and this clan. You may think you had control. But you're a daft lot to never have seen it was me. Why do you think Dónal didn't want to marry me off for so long?"

Moira looked around the Great Hall, seeing all the things that had been neglected since she left. She leaned back in her chair and crossed her arms as she waited. The men shifted uneasily but remained quiet. Moira cast them a condescending smirk.

"How have your meals been since I left? I see no one has brought anything out for us. The rushes are filthy, and I can see where the dogs have slobbered and smeared grease into the floor. The hearth is full of soot. That's just inside. Don't think I didn't notice how the laundresses were milling about with nearly no laundry on the lines. I caught sight of the crofts with thatch that needs replacing. You must have had an almighty storm for them to be in such condition, and winter approaches. I noticed the ships bobbing high in the water with nothing in their holds but men cleaning the hulls. That tells me they have been nowhere recently. No trade? All dried up like a witch's tits." Moira tossed in the final comment for good measure. She wasn't keeping her thoughts to herself anymore, unless it benefited her or Kyle. She wasn't pretending to be meek or ignorant of how men spoke and negotiated.

The council members looked at one another, then at Moira. Eventually, they shifted their gaze to Kyle, suspicion hardening their eyes. He raised his right hand and shook his head while grinning. He was casually leaning back in his chair, but Moira knew the position was deceptive. He was ready to draw his knives and sword the moment he perceived a threat.

"Don't look at me," Kyle smirked. "I'm not interested in

running this clan. Though for what it's worth, you'd be eejits to turn my wife away. She'd kept the peace for years, and you were all too arrogant to notice. Now you reap what you sowed. You need her far more than she needs you. She has a home wherever she wishes to go. She has men who will defend her till their last breath. She has family who appreciate and want her. She's more capable of leading this clan than the lot of us put together."

"But do you intend to make your home here too?" Hogan asked.

The amusement dropped from Kyle's face, and every man at the table leaned away. Kyle's voice had a steeliness that reminded the men of how he earned his moniker. "Why wouldn't I?"

"I just wondered if you prefer the sea over land," Hogan clarified.

"What I prefer is my wife," Kyle stated.

"But you're a…" Finnian didn't finish.

"I was," Kyle corrected. "I go wherever my wife wishes. If she wants to remain here, then she has a respectable merchant for a husband. If she wishes adventure upon the seas, then a pirate I remain. It's Moira's decision."

"Never would I have thought the Red Drifter would take orders from a bitch in heat," Curran sneered. There was a collective gasp from everyone in earshot. Moira shook her head and sat back. Kyle laid a dirk on the table. His hand rested beside it, but he did not touch it.

"I love my wife." Kyle watched Curran, but everyone knew he addressed the clan. "If you think I will sail off and leave her, you can put that notion aside. If you think I will come and go to leave you to do as you please, which apparently includes bullying and ignoring my wife, I will disabuse you of that notion. If you ever speak to or about my wife like that again, I will take you aboard my ship. I will cut off your bollocks and shove them down your throat, cut off your cock and shove it up your arse, just before I cast you adrift. Do not confuse my respect and affection for my wife for weakness. And do not think I will *ever* turn a blind eye or a deaf ear to someone who threatens my wife and family. I will kill you and curl up beside Moira that night without a worry in the world."

"And before any of you think my husband will suffer an unfortunate accident to make your lives easier, there is a reason my husband and I get along so well. We are cast in the same mold," Moira said as her hand covered the handle of Kyle's knife. "And if you still think to leave me a widow, you'd do well to remember several things." Moira held up her other hand, putting up a finger for each point. "Where the Red Drifter sails, so does the Scarlet Blade. The Dark Heart and the Blond Devil may no longer be pirates, but they're ever loyal to their former first mates. You should fear Senga MacNeil and Caragh MacNeil more than you do their husbands. And they are my friends."

"If we accept your terms, you'll stay?" Beagan asked, eager to end the conversation.

"No," Moira said. "I will speak to my nephew, and I will inspect this keep and our clan. Then I will decide." The decisiveness in her voice, the command that rang clear finally permeated the last of the councilmen's minds.

"Aunty Moira?" Sean said, the child's timing as impeccable as ever. "Did Beagan and the others tell you what happened to Mama?"

Moira cast an alarmed look at the council members before she shook her head. She dreaded hearing what the others must have said to explain Lizzie's disappearance.

"They told me that Mama made many bad decisions for many years. Do you remember how she used to say Ruairí was my da? She also made some women angry because she used to ask their husbands to play with her." Despite her earlier bravado, Sean's words made Moira's face flame red. "I know she did things that hurt you, Aunty Moira. I know Aidan loves you, but Mama says she knows things that make Aidan like her better. I don't think he does."

Moira shot Kyle an uneasy look. He leaned over and whispered, "I knew as soon as you came up on deck. I suspected as much when he asked me to fetch you." Moira shook her head, unable to come to terms with what Sean said and Kyle confirmed. It was the antithesis of how Aidan had treated her since he walked away from her all those years ago.

"But Aunty Moira," Sean placed his sweaty palms on her cheeks. "Aidan took Mama to the O'Malleys. Mama is going to marry the new O'Malley chieftain. He's the brother of the man you were supposed to marry. Mama cried a lot when Aidan told her that she was going."

Moira nodded, too stunned to say anything as Sean continued. She lost track of what he said until the end. She'd gotten lost in her own thoughts about Lizzie's future, her own past with Aidan, and how much she preferred her life with Kyle. "Aunty Moira?"

"Yes, *m'fhear beag*?" Moira had missed the term of affection for Sean, whose serious expressions made him look like the little man she called him.

"I know my mama is my mama, but I've always wished that was you. I know I still have to call you Aunty Moira, but can you be my real mama?" Sean glanced at Kyle. "And can Uncle Kyle be my real da? Aidan doesn't want to be."

Moira nodded as she wrapped her arms around the little boy who had held her heart since the day he was born. She didn't love him any less now that she was married with her own child on the way. Her heart had only grown larger. She looked over Sean's head at Kyle. They both knew they'd made their decision. They would remain at Dunluce and face the future together with Moira as chieftain and Kyle by her side.

"I'm glad you're home, Mama. And I'm glad you brought me

Da," Sean whispered as he returned Moira's embrace and smiled at Kyle. Kyle pulled Moira into his lap and wrapped his arms around his wife and nephew.

"I'm glad we're home, too," Moira said as she leaned back against Kyle and kissed Sean's temple.

EPILOGUE

Moira nestled closer to Kyle, their bodies still damp from their coupling. Two decades after they said farewell to their lives at sea, the couple remained as devoted to one another as the day Moira came aboard the *Lady Charity*. Kyle ran his fingers along Moira's back as he closed his eyes.

"I'm getting on in years, Moira. You shall make my heart stop one of these days with all your demands. Needy wench," Kyle teased as he squeezed Moira's backside. Moira rolled back over onto Kyle's chest, his large body still dwarfing hers. She straddled him and kissed his neck, working her way behind his ear. Kyle groaned as his body stirred again. "I don't know how you can do that. I can barely catch my breath, yet my body is clamoring for another go."

"You shouldn't have taught me so much," Moira teased. She propped herself on her forearms, careful not to dig her elbows into Kyle's ribs. "Can you believe Tadhg is getting married today?"

"Not really. It seems like it was mere moments ago that the midwife said you just needed fresh air and more loving because you were with child," Kyle said before giving Moira a peck on the lips.

"With five children, I think you've given me quite a lot of good loving," Moira grinned and wriggled her hips. A stinging slap landed across her backside. Kyle saw the fire in Moira's eyes. It was the same one that entranced him more than two decades ago. They'd made a happy life at Dunluce, both settling into their roles among the clan. While Moira led their people, Kyle took over the training of the clan's warriors and captaining the clan's fleet of merchant ships. Some of his men stayed on and became paid warriors, but many found other ships to sail with. They'd weathered storms that challenged them individually and as a couple, but nothing ever broke their bond.

"And I shall continue," Kyle said as he rolled them over, pinning Moira's arms over her head. "When we retire tonight, *mo ghràidh,* you had better not be too tired. I have plans for us that involve your favorite marble phallus, silk scarves, and me. But until then, we must go belowstairs and be the proud parents of the over-eager groom."

"I thought Ruairí was going to slice Tadhg's head off yesterday when we found Tina and him kissing in the orchard," Moira laughed.

"Aye, well, he and Senga haven't set any better example of restraint than you and I have. None of us have."

"I was worried Keith and his family wouldn't arrive in time. It was so late when they arrived last night," Moira stated.

"All four of our families are rather large. Thank heavens Kisimul has so many chambers. Rowan and Caragh have their five children, and Ruairí and Senga have six. We have five, and Keith—good God, my brother has too many children. Eight. I can't believe they've just had another."

"I know. Sean is lucky he's Rowan's captain of the guard. He already has his own chamber, or he'd be doubling and tripling up like the rest of the children."

"They're not really children anymore, or so they remind us," Kyle snickered.

"Well, until they're all married, they're still my wee ones."

"Tadhg and Tina will be married by tonight, and the MacLeans and MacNeils will truly be family after all these years. Are you ready for a daughter after giving birth to five sons?" Kyle wondered.

"I like our lads. I love Tina, but I've never felt like I was missing anything by not having a daughter," Moira mused.

"I never imagined I could love anyone as much as I do you and our children. I wasn't sure whether I could be the father Sean needed when we adopted him, but I have never looked back. I love you, Moira. I have since the start, and I will until the very end."

"I love you, Kyle. I would have been adrift without you," Moira smiled as their bodies joined once again.

THANK YOU FOR READING THE RED DRIFTER OF THE SEA

Celeste Barclay, a nom de plume, lives near the Southern California coast with her husband and sons. Growing up in the Midwest, Celeste enjoyed spending as much time in and on the water as she could. Now she lives near the beach. She's an avid swimmer, a hopeful future surfer, and a former rower. When she's not writing, she's working or being a mom.

Subscribe to Celeste's bimonthly newsletter to receive exclusive insider perks.
Subscribe Now

www.celestebarclay.com

Join the fun and get exclusive insider giveaways, sneak peeks, and new release announcements in

Celeste Barclay's Facebook Ladies of Yore Group

PIRATES OF THE ISLES

The Blond Devil of the Sea **BOOK 1 SNEAK PEEK**

Caragh lifted her torch into the air as she made her way down the precarious Cornish cliffside. She made out the hulking shape of a ship, but the dead of night made it impossible to see who was there. She and the fishermen of Bedruthan Steps weren't expecting any shipments that night. But her younger brother Eddie, who stood watch at the entrance to their hiding place, had spotted the ship and signaled up to the village watchman, who alerted Caragh.

As her boot slid along the dirt and sand, she cursed having to carry the torch and wished she could have sunlight to guide her. She knew these cliffs well, and it was for that reason it was better that she moved slowly than stop moving once and for all. Caragh feared the light from her torch would carry out to the boat. Despite her efforts to keep the flame small, the solitary light would be a beacon.

When Caragh came to the final twist in the path before the sand, she snuffed out her torch and started to run to the cave where the main source of the village's income lay in hiding. She heard movement along the trail above her head and knew the local fishermen would soon join her on the beach. These men, both young and old, were strong from days spent pulling in the full trawling nets and hoisting the larger catches onto their boats. However, these men weren't well-trained swordsmen, and the fear of pirate raids was ever-present. Caragh feared that was who the villagers would face that night.

The Dark Heart of the Sea **BOOK 2**

The Red Drifter of the Sea **BOOK3**

The Scarlet Blade of the Sea **BOOK 4**

THE HIGHLAND LADIES

A Spinster at the Highland Court

BOOK 1 SNEAK PEEK

Elizabeth Fraser looked around the royal chapel within Stirling Castle. The ornate candlestick holders on the altar glistened and reflected the light from the ones in the wall sconces as the priest intoned the holy prayers of the Advent season. Elizabeth kept her head bowed as though in prayer, but her green eyes swept the congregation. She watched the other ladies-in-waiting, many of whom were doing the same thing. She caught the eye of Allyson Elliott. Elizabeth raised one eyebrow as Allyson's lips twitched. Both women had been there enough times to accept they'd be kneeling for at least the next hour as the Latin service carried on. Elizabeth understood the Mass thanks to her cousin Deirdre Fraser, or rather now Deirdre Sinclair. Elizabeth's mind flashed to the recent struggle her cousin faced as she reunited with her husband Magnus after a seven-year separation. Her aunt and uncle's choice to keep Deirdre hidden from her husband simply because they didn't think the Sinclairs were an advantageous enough match, and the resulting scandal, still humiliated the other Fraser clan members at court. She admired Deirdre's husband Magnus's pledge to remain faithful despite not knowing if he'd ever see Deirdre again.

Elizabeth suddenly snapped her attention; while everyone else intoned the twelfth—or was it thirteenth—amen of the Mass, the hairs on the back of her neck stood up. She had the strongest feeling that someone was watching her. Her eyes scanned to her right, where her parents sat further down the pew. Her mother and father had their heads bowed and eyes closed. While she was convinced her mother was in devout prayer, she wondered if her father had fallen asleep during the Mass. Again. With nothing seeming out of the ordinary and no one visibly paying attention to her, her eyes swung to the left. She took in the king and queen as they kneeled together at their prie-dieu. The queen's lips moved as she recited the liturgy in silence. The king was as still as a statue. Years of leading warriors showed, both in his stature and his ability to control his body into absolute stillness. Elizabeth peered past the royal couple and found herself looking into the astute hazel eyes of Edward Bruce, Lord of Badenoch and Lochaber. His gaze gave her the sense that he peered into her thoughts, as though he were assessing her. She tried to keep her face neutral as heat surged up her neck. She prayed her face didn't redden as much as her neck must have, but at a twenty-one, she still hadn't mastered how to control her blushing. Her nape burned like it was on fire. She canted her head slightly before looking up at the crucifix hanging over the altar. She closed her eyes and tried to invoke the image of the Lord that usually centered her when her mind wandered during Mass.

Elizabeth sensed Edward's gaze remained on her. She didn't understand how she was so sure that he was looking at her. She didn't have any special gifts of perception or sight, but her intuition screamed that he was still looking.

A Spy at the Highland Court **BOOK 2**

A Wallflower at the Highland Court **BOOK 3**

A Rogue at the Highland Court **BOOK 4**

A Rake at the Highland Court **BOOK 5**

An Enemy at the Highland Court **BOOK 6**

A Saint at the Highland Court **BOOK 7**

A Beauty at the Highland Court **BOOK 8**

A Sinner at the Highland Court **BOOK 9**

A Hellion at the Highland Court **BOOK 10**

An Angel at the Highland Court **BOOK 11**

A Harlot at the Highland Court **BOOK 12**

A Friend at the Highland Court **BOOK 13**

An Outsider at the Highland Court **BOOK 14**

A Devil at the Highland Court **BOOK 15**

THE CLAN SINCLAIR

His Highland Lass **BOOK 1 SNEAK PEEK**

She entered the great hall like a strong spring storm in the northern most Highlands. Tristan Mackay felt like he had been blown hither and yon. As the storm settled, she left him with the sweet scents of heather and lavender wafting towards him as she approached. She was not a classic beauty, tall and willowy like the women at court. Her face and form were not what legends were made of. But she held a unique appeal unlike any he had seen before. He could not take his eyes off of her long chestnut hair that had strands of fire and burnt copper running through them. Unlike the waves or curls he was used to, her hair was unusually straight and fine. It looked like a waterfall cascading down her back. While she was not tall, neither was she short. She had a figure that was meant for a man to grasp and hold onto, whether from the front or from behind. She had an aura of confidence and charm, but not arrogance or conceit like many good looking women he had met. She did not seem to know her own appeal. He could tell that she was many things, but one thing she was not was his.

His Bonnie Highland Temptation **BOOK 2**

His Highland Prize **BOOK 3**

His Highland Pledge **BOOK 4**

His Highland Surprise **BOOK 5**

Their Highland Beginning **BOOK 6**

VIKING GLORY

Leif BOOK 1 SNEAK PEEK

Leif looked around his chambers within his father's longhouse and breathed a sigh of relief. He noticed the large fur rugs spread throughout the chamber. His two favorites placed strategically before the fire and the bedside he preferred. He looked at his shield that hung on the wall near the door in a symbolic position but waiting at the ready. The chests that held his clothes and some of his finer acquisitions from voyages near and far sat beside his bed and along the far wall. And in the center was his most favorite possession. His oversized bed was one of the few that could accommodate his long and broad frame. He shook his head at his longing to climb under the pile of furs and on the stuffed mattress that beckoned him. He took in the chair placed before the fire where he longed to sit now with a cup of warm mead. It had been two months since he slept in his own bed, and he looked forward to nothing more than pulling the furs over his head and sleeping until he could no longer ignore his hunger. Alas, he would not be crawling into his bed again for several more hours. A feast awaited him to celebrate his and his crew's return from their latest expedition to explore the isle of Britannia. He bathed and wore fresh clothes, so he had no excuse for lingering other than a bone weariness that set in during the last storm at sea. He was eager to spend time at home no matter how much he loved sailing. Their last expedition had been profitable with several raids of monasteries that yielded jewels and both silver and gold, but he was ready for respite.

Leif left his chambers and knocked on the door next to his. He heard movement on the other side, but it was only moments before his sister, Freya, opened her door. She, too, looked tired but clean. A few pieces of jewelry she confiscated from the holy houses that allegedly swore to a life of poverty and deprivation adorned her trim frame.

"That armband suits you well. It compliments your muscles," Leif smirked and dodged a strike from one of those muscular arms.

Only a year younger than he, his sister was a well-known and feared shield maiden. Her lithe form was strong and agile making her a ferocious and competent opponent to any man. Freya's beauty was stunning, but Leif had taken every opportunity since they were children to tease her about her unusual strength even among the female warriors.

"At least one of us inherited our father's prowess. Such a shame it wasn't you."

Freya **BOOK 2**

Tyra & Bjorn **BOOK 3**

Strian **VIKING GLORY BOOK 4**

Lena & Ivar **VIKING GLORY BOOK 5**

Made in United States
Orlando, FL
24 March 2022